MR. PEANUT

MR. PEANUT
Adam Ross
Alfred A. Knopf · New York · 2010

THIS IS A BORZOI BOOK
PUBLISHED BY ALFRED A. KNOPF

 Published in the United States by Alfred A. Knopf,
a division of Random House, Inc., New York.
www.aaknopf.com

Knopf, Borzoi Books, and the colophon
are registered trademarks of Random House, Inc.

Originally published in Great Britain by Jonathan Cape,
the Random House Group Ltd., London.

Library of Congress Cataloging-in-Publication Data
Ross, Adam, 1967–
Mr. Peanut / by Adam Ross.—1st ed.
p. cm.
ISBN 978-0-307-27070-2
1. Married people—Fiction. 2. Marriage—Fiction. 3. Marital conflict—Fiction.
4. Spouses—Crimes against—Fiction. I. Title.
PS3618.O84515M7 2010
813'.6—dc22 2009041693

Manufactured in the United States of America
Published June 25, 2010
Second Printing Before Publication

For Beth

Where am I in the web of jealousy that trembles at every human movement?

What detectives we have to be.

—Harold Brodkey

I went back upstairs and looked at my wife and felt and checked her pulse on her neck and determined or thought that she was gone. I became or thought that I was disoriented and the victim of a bizarre dream.

—Statement from Dr. Sam Sheppard taken at the Cuyahoga County Sheriff's Office, Cleveland, OH, July 10, 1954, after consultation with his attorneys

MR. PEANUT

When David Pepin first dreamed of killing his wife, he didn't kill her himself. He dreamed convenient acts of God. At a picnic on the beach, a storm front moved in. David and Alice collected their chairs, blankets, and booze, and when the lightning flashed, David imagined his wife lit up, her skeleton distinctly visible as in a children's cartoon, Alice then collapsing into a smoking pile of ash. He watched her walk quickly across the sand, the tallest object in the wide-open space. She even stopped to observe the piling clouds. "Some storm," she said. He tempted fate by hubris. In his mind he declared: I, David Pepin, am wiser and more knowing than God, and I, David Pepin, know that God shall not, at this very moment, on this very beach, *Jones Beach,* strike my wife down. God did not. David knew more. And in their van, when the rain came so densely it seemed they were in a car wash, he boasted of his godliness to Alice, asked rhetorically if a penis this large and this erect (thus exposed) could be anything but divine, and he made love to his wife angrily and passionately right in the front seat, hidden by the heavy weather.

He dreamed unconsciously and he dreamed sporadically. His fantasies simply welled up. If she called from work, he asked, "Did something happen?" If she was late coming home, he began to worry too soon. He began to dream according to her schedule. "Taking the train today?" David asked in the morning. "Taking the train," Alice said. It was a block west to Lexington, where she'd pick up the subway down to 42nd Street. At Grand Central, she'd take Metro-North thirty minutes to Hawthorne, where she taught emotionally disturbed and occasionally dangerous children. Anything could happen between here and there. On the edge of the platform, two boys were roughhousing. The train came barreling into the station. An accidental push. Alice, spun round, did a crazy backstroke before she fell. And it was over. David winced. The things that went through his mind! From their window, he watched Alice walk up the street. A helicopter passed overhead. On Lexington, at the building under construction, a single girder was winched into the sky. And David imagined this was the last time he would ever see his wife—that this was the last image he'd have of her—and he felt the sadness well up and had the smallest taste of his loss, like the wish when you're young that your parents would die.

There could be no violence. It was a strange ethics attending his fantasy. He dreamed the crane tumbling, the helicopter spiraling out of control, but he edited out all the terror and pain. There was Alice, underneath the wreckage, killed instantly, or sometimes David was there, by her side, inserted just before the fatal moment. He held her hand, they exchanged last words, and he eased her into death.

"David," Alice said, "I love you."

"Alice," David said, "I love you too."

Her eyes glassed over. There could be no violence. But occasionally David became a Walter Mitty of murder. He dreamed his own agency. *He* did it. He shot Alice, he bludgeoned her, he suffocated her with a pillow. But these fantasies were truncated; they flashed in his mind, then he cut them off before the terminal moment because he never surprised her in time. He saw her recognize him as he came round the corner with knife, bat, or gun, felt her hand grip the arm that held the pillow over her face—and it was all too terrible to contemplate.

"Whale!" he screamed at her, because she was enormous. "Goddamn blue whale!" (She'd struggled mightily with depression but was now back on meds.)

When they argued, they were ferocious. They'd been married to each other for thirteen years and still went for jugulars and balls.

"Genius," she said. *That* drove him nuts. He was a lead designer and president of Spellbound, a small, extremely successful video game company. People in the industry called him a genius all the time, but during moments of doubt David confessed to her that the games they produced were inane at best, mind-killing—to his and to the kids who played them—at worst.

"I wish you were dead!" David screamed.

"I wish you were dead too!"

But this was a relief. The desire was mutual. He wasn't alone.

Later, after the quiet time, he apologized. "I'm sorry," he said. "I shouldn't talk to you like that."

"I'm sorry," Alice said. "I hate fighting with you."

They held each other in the living room. It was evening now and there were no lights on in the apartment. For hours they'd been sitting separately in the dark.

His love for his wife was renewed. How could he think the things he'd thought? They took a shower together; it was one of their favorite things to do. He put his arms against the walls and she lathered his back, cleaned the cheeks of his ass and behind his ears. When she shaved his face, she unknowingly mimicked his expression. Afterward, she ran a bath.

"You know who I was thinking about today?" David said. Things between them still felt delicate, bruised, and he wanted to make conversation.

"Who?"

"Dr. Otto."

She glanced at him and smiled sadly. Whether it was the associations his name conjured up or how long ago it was that they'd sat in his class—it was where they'd first met—he couldn't be sure. At the moment, David was sitting on the edge of the tub, Alice's ankle in hand. He had soaped down her calf and was shaving it carefully. Hair grew in different directions in different spots.

"Have you spoken to him?"

"Not for years. I read in the quarterly that his wife passed away."

"I'm sorry to hear that."

"I'm sure he's had a hard time."

"And who hasn't?" Alice said.

She completely filled up the bath. Her triceps swelled out separately, like a pair of dolphin fins; her breasts floated like twin islands. And she had the most beautiful face, the longest, finest chestnut-colored hair, and fabulous hazel-colored eyes. But she'd grown huge, and David didn't pity her, though he knew it was difficult for her to carry the weight. At her maximum this year she'd reached 288 pounds. She'd bought a digital scale (doctor's orders) that flashed bright red numbers. She'd weigh herself in the morning as soon as she woke up, her hair hanging over her face as she stared between her feet.

"I wish I were dead," Alice said.

And he wished her thin for her own happiness, but for himself he wished she remained fat. He loved the giganticness of her, loved to hold on to her mountain of ass. If he made love to her from behind, he imagined himself an X-rated Gulliver among the Brobdingnags. It was the difference in proportion that turned him on. Closing his eyes, he exaggerated her size, made himself extra small, David holding on, his arms outstretched, smashing into her rear for *life, life, life.* She was not his wife but a giant she-creature, an overlarge sex pet: his to screw, groom, and maintain. After they made love, she lay facedown on the bed, palms turned up toward the ceiling, eyes glazed open and body motionless (the weight had not deformed her, only intensified her curves, widened her like the Venus of Willendorf), Alice shot dead by David's potent love.

There were no children. In the end, it had been her choice.

"I was talking with Marnie the other day," Alice said.

David, working in his study, minimized the screen. "And?"

"She's pregnant."

Alice waited. David waited too. He put his elbow on the desk and rested his chin in his hand.

"And they just found out that their second child is going to be a girl," Alice said.

"And?"

"They only have a two-bedroom apartment."

"Go on."

"And the son, he can't share a bedroom with the daughter. But they can't afford a bigger place."

"So?"

"So they're going to have to move out of the city."

David took off his glasses, gently placed them on the table, then got up, walked to their bedroom, and leaned on the jamb.

"Can you imagine?" Alice said. She was focused on the TV; *The Man Who Knew Too Much* was on A&E. They looked at each other, smiled knowingly, then she turned back to the screen. She was deep into her second sleeve of low-fat Ritz crackers, halfway through her second bottle of wine. Crumbs lay across her chest and stomach like snow. At the edge of her lips were two upturned, grape-colored tusks.

David walked over and hugged her. When he squeezed, the crumbs on her shirt crunched.

"I'm glad it's only us," David said.

"Oh, David," she whispered, and pulled him to her. "Sometimes I don't know why you love me."

It didn't help everything, but it helped.

There was nothing left unaccounted for in David's mind. He kept a running tab of his beneficent deeds, his good husbandry. Yet what occurred to him after he'd made her happy was: Why can't I always be this good? Why can't I be here with her completely now?

It was because of the book, he realized as he sat down at his desk again and brought it up on-screen. The book preoccupied him, gnawed at him. This book, unfinished, was always there. He'd started it just over a year ago, as an idea for a video game, but it had grown into something more. It was his top secret and he worked on it like a double agent, when she was out, when she was doing the dishes or surfing the Web—marriage's half-blind times. David kept the manuscript in a large box under the desk in his study. The writing had been a process of fitful stops and starts, of bursts and binges, of terrible dead ends. He was stuck now, stuck badly, but he refused to give up. The structure was complex, perhaps overly so, but the story was impossible to tell straight. Stymied, he had to step away from it for long periods at a time. He ignored it for weeks and weeks on end. He often worried there was nothing there; then he came around, sure that there was. And after Alice fell asleep, he sometimes wandered back to his study and took it out of the box to have a look. There's something about hard copy that a screen could never convey. He had a test he liked to take. It was the mark of a strong narrative that any page plucked by chance should be gripping, should pull the reader along like a current. David read one. It *was* gripping! It *did* pull! A new idea occurred to him, a new direction to follow, possibly a way around this impasse. He thought for a moment, then found the chapter and wrote down several notes.

"David," Alice said. "What are you doing?"

"Nothing," he said, and stood still.

"Then come to bed."

He put the box back under the desk. He'd write tomorrow morning, first thing. In bed, sentences flashed like meteors in his mind.

But the next day their brightness had dimmed. While it wasn't clear to him why one night should make such a difference when it came to inspiration, it did.

It was also not clear to him how Alice had put on the weight. She began their marriage at a ripe 165, a big woman to begin with, large-boned, tall, five foot nine in bare feet; by their thirteenth year, 288. It wasn't clear to David how this had happened because her diet was so strictly limited. She was allergic to shrimp, mussels, oysters, escargot—anything with a shell. At a dinner party once, she accidentally ate a dropperful of clam sauce, and the hives she broke out in, white at their tops and pink at the base, swelled her eyes closed and turned her arms into a crazy moonscape. Her breathing was shallow. There was a doctor in the house. He happened to be allergic to bees (Alice was too) and he hit her with a shot of adrenaline (she'd forgotten her EpiPen), and she quickly deflated and lost her spots. Cashews were out, almonds, macadamias, all out of the question. Peter Pan peanut butter might as well have featured the skull and crossbones on the label. Alice rationed her poisons every day. She had a checklist on the refrigerator door, with a small table at the bottom of the sheet for her numerical conversions:

a little of this, divided by that, times a little of this. Substitute mushrooms, subtract the difference for the grapefruit. It was an allergic person's algebra, David thought, watching her tabulate before her meal, a subdiscipline of alchemy.

His love for his wife was renewed. When Alice ate, she leaned over her plate and chewed dreamily, staring into blankness, a void that hovered just off to the side of David's left breast. Every few bites, she tucked her hair neatly behind her ear—her mind running through fields, eating always relaxed her—and youthfulness was restored to her features. She was the young woman he had married. With a bit of imagination—Alice was now thirty-five—he could make out the girl she was before they'd met. He didn't disturb her. She was very hungry. How could he have dreamed of losing her?

In one fantasy, he saw himself at her funeral. Mourners surrounded him, besieging him with condolences. During the service, people spoke about her beautifully, though she was such a loner, David thought, he wasn't sure who they'd be. Later, Alice was interred, the oversized casket lowered into the ground. Then all he saw was himself, sitting there bereft. He couldn't imagine what he would do afterward. He might as well be like that little dog, Greyfriars Bobby, and sleep by her grave. Pepin shuddered. He was here to support her. His love for his wife was renewed. And then one day, Alice began to lose weight.

Before any undertaking, Detective Sheppard thought, we have our rituals. Like deep knee bends before a run or a hitter's crotch grab as he steps up to the plate. Efforts to prime the pump. The mind, body, and soul's preshot routine. Habit's comfort, Sheppard thought, loading his pipe, and habit's effect. The carpet worn down from our usual route through the house. Gums brushed away from the teeth over time. Tastes we've sampled so often we can't detect them anymore. At the police station, Sheppard spied an old whore putting on makeup, fascinated by the delicacy with which she painted on her lipstick, how she held the mirror out before her as if she were aiming a precision instrument, turning her head from side to side in the small reflection, checking her work, then snapping the compact closed and dropping it in her bag, ready to hear charges.

Murder, Sheppard reflected further, is an interruption of habit, or its culmination.

But before any undertaking, Sheppard thought, even an interrogation, the same motions apply. We orbit, we repeat. Already Detective Hastroll would be sitting before the one-way glass, staring down the suspect, thrilling, Sheppard imagined, to his own invisibility. It was always remarkable to Sheppard that you could feel Hastroll feeling you when you entered a room. Hastroll kept his back to him, staring down the suspect all the while, analyzing and focusing. And yet there was that subtle reaction Sheppard noticed as soon as he stepped inside, not a move on Hastroll's part so much as a transmission of energy. Like something electrical. It was almost as if he could feel Hastroll blink in slow disgust at his arrival.

"Ward."

"Sam."

"What do you think?"

"Guilty," Hastroll said flatly. "Guilty as sin."

Sheppard stood next to his partner. Behind the glass, the suspect, David Pepin, sat weeping.

"You could at least go either way on this one, Ward—a shadow of a doubt, at least. The man's in an authentic state of distress."

"Guilty," Hastroll said, his huge humped shoulders hunched. "Guilty distress."

"How about aggrieved distress?"

"Guilty, guilty, guilty."

The two men gazed at the suspect for a time.

"Good cop first or bad cop?"

"You go," Hastroll said.

There is the same thrill of one-way glass, Hastroll thought, as in hearing the sound of your voice recorded. Or catching sight of yourself in the background of a photograph. Or passing yourself on a television screen in an electronics storefront—a peep of a view as your image walks toward you. For you are always a secret to yourself, Hastroll thought. But there are glimpses and hints and clues.

Sheppard entered the interrogation room and sat directly across from Pepin.

"Don't even ask me," Pepin cried. "I didn't kill my wife!"

Admittedly, Alice's diet was different this time.

In the past they required various kinds of equipment, ranging from the usual to the late-night television commercial—Visa, Amex, MasterCard accepted. The nonsense approach, David called it. There were pills and special sponges, protein shakes and magic reducing belts: the usual hokum, which he purchased for her willingly. "I feel good about this one, David," she said. "I think this will do the trick." Then she handed him the 800-number and left the room to avoid his expression. A package arrived in seven to ten business days.

With the machines, assembly was often required. And ultimately, David was called into the living room to Alice's rescue, where she'd be sitting in the middle of a pile of locking screws, bolts, boards, wheels, and wrapped pieces of metal, the parts numbered and lettered (5Q, F9) spread in a circle around her as if she were ground zero, all of which David spent the next few hours collecting and recombining.

From this chaos there emerged a contraption, a Frankensteinian engine, oddly insectlike, exoskeletal, that always included a seat of some kind and to which Alice attached her hands, hips, or bound her feet; hung upside down from or spun around in; the machine, as she pumped, pressed, or pedaled, threatening to evolve from exercise station to transportation and inevitably shaking itself apart, the whole process reminding David of old films of crazy planes and whirlybirds—the ones before the Wright brothers—that fell from cliffs, ramps, or towers, or simply exploded with the effort to fly.

The cardiovascular eliminated, Alice paid meticulous attention to her diet. She cut out snacks, carbs, and empty calories and was generally miserable, but she lost weight quickly. Because of her size, she shed her first ten pounds within two weeks. She became preoccupied, obsessed, and gave David regular reports. She knew the time, to the minute, of her bowel movements. Assessing their curly and oblong heft, she could guess their approximate weight. At work, she walked the stairs instead of riding the elevator, took soy milk instead of cream in her coffee. She ate the apples, after checking them for razors, that her delinquent and schizophrenic students left on her desk. Her sex drive disappeared; she refused to be touched, and when she asked David what he thought of her progress—two months in, twenty-three pounds lost—he answered her encouragingly, because the change in her body was before-and-after dramatic. With glee, she pulled her pants away from her waist and punched extra holes in her belts. She felt thin, she said. But David was secretly pessimistic; in fact, he was certain she would fail. In one of their closets were boxes of her winter clothes, and around the same time every fall she had David bring them down from the top shelves.

"All of them?" he asked from the stepladder.

"Of course all of them," she answered from below. The dresses were from thinner days, outdated—Alice's fashions were cyclical—and in the mornings, she modeled for him while he ate his breakfast, doing quick little turns on the tile.

"Isn't this dress funny?" she said, pinching the cloth in her fingers, pulling the skirt out wide and triangular, spreading the fabric like a pair of wings. David couldn't help but laugh, a chuckle Alice thought was of joy, and she came over to him, took his head in her hands, clutching his hair and pressing his face into her chest. "This is it," she whispered. "This is the one." He looked up. She pulled his face toward hers and kissed him, then walked out the door, chin up and shoulders back—Alice gaining altitude, he thought, as she dropped ballast, a confidence in her stride that gave him a shiver of fear.

Is this it? David wondered. Is this the one?

Maybe, he thought, but most likely no. On certain afternoons, she was low. It was December, she was three months in, nearly thirty pounds gone, and the whole project seemed endless to her—impossible. She questioned her resolve. She would never drop the weight. The past week and a half, she'd lost only three pounds. Once—all right, twice—she'd cheated. (Going to work, she'd caved and stopped in McDonald's for two Egg McMuffin meals. Yesterday, when David surprised her in the kitchen, she whirled round with her face covered in powdered sugar, an uneaten donut in each hand.) She called David at the office, pulling him from the daily playtest of their new game Escher X—short for Escher Exit. It was a work of programming and conceptual brilliance. The environments were based on famous Escher prints—*Relativity, Belvedere, Ascending and Descending,* to name a few—and the challenge of the game was to guide your avatar (the white humanoid from *Encounter*) through each inescapable level, each round-and-round realm, until you found the secret means of escape, the button or tile that uncoiled the environments' Mobius strip. Though perhaps its best effect (this was on especially wonderful display in the *Relativ-*

ity level) was its replication, while you played, of the experience of looking at one of the prints themselves, of ascending a set of stairs to suddenly find yourself going down, to enter a room where someone was sitting on the ceiling, the ceiling becoming the floor, the waterfall falling up. And there were battles, of course, with all sorts of Escher monsters: the human-headed bird from *Another World II,* the alligators from *Reptiles,* the dragon from *Dragon,* the predator fish from *Predestination.* These exchanges upped your skill level with each victory and conferred more weapons on your avatar until you were strong enough for the final confrontation with your double—the stooped black humanoid who ruled the entire realm. His name, appropriately, was Mobius.

The game was beautiful. But it was also full of bugs, and they'd blown their projected release date. When David answered the phone, he was curt at first, but Alice sounded desperate.

"David," she said, "do you love me?"

"Of course I love you."

"Even if I'm like this?"

He closed his eyes and rested his head against the window. "Even if you're like what?"

"You're sweet," Alice said.

David was silent.

"Because I don't think I can do it," she said.

"Don't think you can do what?"

"It. *Die*-it. What do you *think*?"

"Alice . . ."

"I'm sorry."

"Why don't you think you can do it?"

"Because it takes so long."

"That's right."

"Because it goes so slowly."

"Because you're in the middle."

"Am I in the middle?" she said.

"We've talked about the middle."

"Tell me again about the middle."

"The middle is long and hard."

"I'm stuck in the middle of trying to lose my middle." She laughed, then began to weep.

"I'm in the middle too," he said.

"Are you?"

"Of my game." Of my book, he thought. "But that's the thing about the middle. It's like holding your breath longer than you think you can. It's the point before you black out, right before you surface. The last stretch uphill—the highest part—right before going down. Don't you see?"

"No."

"You're not stuck. You're moving. But you can't see it. *I* can see it."

"Oh, David, I want a burrito. I want a chimichanga with extra cheese."

"But you're going to hold out."

"I am?"

"You're going to resist."

"I *am.*"

"You can do this."

These conversations bolstered her. Her determination was renewed. Home from school, she went on long walks uptown, to Central Park, up to the reservoir and around the cinder track and back. This gave David precious time alone. He returned to his book, retrieving the box from underneath his desk and pulling out the new pages he'd written. He needed a change of scenery, so he moved to the kitchen table, set out his laptop, and sat down. He felt clear-minded. Focused. Everything was in order. It had seemed like years since he'd had enough peace to write.

This is what it would be like, David thought, if Alice were gone.

"Hello?" She came into the kitchen and kissed him. Her face was flushed, her cheeks cold and slightly wet. Winter seemed to trail behind her. "I'm going to do it this time. I really am. And it's because of you."

She stood there, smiling. Saw the makeshift desk.

"Were you working?"

David twirled his pen in his fingers. "I was just finishing up."

She packed her own bag lunch in the evenings, creasing the foil of her sandwich as neatly as a present and taping it closed. She stapled the paper bag and wrote MY LUNCH in black felt pen on the front, then placed it lovingly in the fridge. The whole pantry was marked in this fashion: MY CRACKERS, MY PEACHES, MY TUNA. She set out her breakfast the night before as well, her spoon, knife, and napkin arranged and ready for use, the cereal bowl turned upside down and her banana curved below it like a wide smile. It was a lonely little scene, David thought, staring at the place setting in the refrigerator's light and secretly drinking her vanilla soy milk (MY SOY MILK she wrote on masking tape), her box of cereal (MY CEREAL) next to the measuring cup, its pictured athlete—receiver, hurdler, basketball player—frozen in leaps or bounds.

"I'm ready for sleep," Alice told him.

She'd crawled under the covers and then she reached beneath her, strapped the sleep apnea mask to her face, and lay on her back staring blankly, eyes fixed on the image of her next meal. Look at how it comforts her, David thought, the calories counted like so many sheep.

She dropped off the moment he turned out the light.

While she slept, she exhaled musically, a cheerful, childlike hum. The machine whirred pleasantly. Not ready for the darkness or sleep, David lay there thinking about Escher X, his novel, and her accidental death. But then he listened to Alice breathe. And as he listened he experienced the most intense feeling of sympathy for her, a compassion that seemed to require her inertness, her unconsciousness. There was a whole world of torture she had to live through every day. He remembered a fat girl he'd gone to grade school with, how mercilessly he and all the other children had teased her—*Bobbie Jo's a hippo, Bobbie Jo's a cow, Bobbie Jo's a bullfrog, Bobbie Jo's a sow.* He still knew the song. Of course, Alice's own students tormented her as well, David imagined. They were delinquents, criminals, loonies; they had no sense. He boiled with rage against them, though she'd never mentioned a single instance of abuse. He'd heard a young couple talking about Alice once in Central Park. "Look at her," the man said to his girlfriend as David, having gone off to get Alice a Dove bar, came up behind them. "I mean, how do let yourself *get* like that?" The woman was wearing a spandex suit and Rollerblades. With her bright helmet, protective pads, and athletic body, she looked like a superhero. "I think you'd have to kill me," she said. "Promise me you will?" He'd kill her, he promised, with his elephant gun. "You're terrible," the girl said, laughing and gliding off. You *are* terrible, David thought. *I'm* terrible—because he'd laughed too. He remembered the wakes of silence he and Alice trailed behind them as they walked across Sheep Meadow, conversations interrupted, looks both he and she knew were for her. She'd walk straight ahead, tucking her hair quickly behind her ear. At parties, when they were introduced to strangers, he watched them pretend she was unexceptional. Whenever possible, he stood next to her—he was a large man himself, stocky, over six feet tall—to dampen her effect.

In bed, he slid close to her under the covers and put his ear to her back. He listened to her heart, its determined little *pah pah pah* like a hand smacking a pillow, as proportional in size, David figured, as brain to brontosaurus. And then he imagined her soul—all souls, and what they might look like. They were stalkish, spirit-forms, he imagined, that resembled the renderings of those slanty-eyed extraterrestrials, and their job, among other things, was to operate the body—their mortal vehicles! But Alice's body required special on-the-job training. It had additional levers that required exceptional soul-strength to pull, manual gears with a tricky clutch, no power steering, of course, and signs like those on the backs of eighteen-wheelers—HOW'S MY DRIVING? or THIS VEHICLE MAKES WIDE RIGHT TURNS—but enjoying none of the respect you gave a truck on the road.

In the dark, Alice hummed her single slumberous note. Surreptitiously, David fondled her. Her breasts were soft as feathers, her body (with its busy driver-soul checking dials, adjusting gauges!) bed-warmed. When she didn't respond he rolled over to stare at the ceiling and, now that he was still, his mind drifted, recalling these past five years, her transformation and where it *really* began, and he felt the same creeping sense of complicity, as if he were the cause of her disease. He must do *something* to cure her.

We tell stories of other people's marriages, Detective Hastroll thought. We are experts in their parables and parabolas. But can we tell the story of our own? If we could, Hastroll thought, there might be no murders. If we could, we might avoid our own cruelties and crimes.

He thought of his own wife, Hannah, home in bed. Was it obvious to Sheppard when he asked after her? Could he tell that he was near the breaking point? That he was in despair?

Through the one-way glass, Hastroll watched as Sheppard turned on his bedside manner for the suspect, his tone at once authoritative and warm, a bond established between the two men almost immediately. Pepin even let him reach across the table to clasp his wrist and arm—a former doctor's strategy of empathy, of gentle words and most of all *attention,* so that it was as if Pepin's choked sobs were failed attempts to describe the location and nature of his pain.

"I hate this good-cop routine," Hastroll said to himself, sitting so close to the glass that his breath fogged the pane.

Detective Sheppard did these things to relax the suspect. He thought he might take Pepin's mind off his grief for a moment and then they could talk. Though truth be told, Sheppard couldn't get his own mind off the victim, couldn't forget how he'd stepped into the kitchen and come upon Alice Pepin, thirty-five, Caucasian female, maybe 130 pounds, a gorgeous woman, really, with long, fine brown hair, hazel eyes that no one had closed, the poor thing stone-cold dead. She was lying beside the kitchen table, having fallen straight back, still seated in her chair, a broken plate and peanuts scattered next to her face, her hands clasped at her neck as if she were choking herself. Her skin was discolored—a violet hue of thundercloud, of fresh bruise—and her lips were grossly swollen, pink as intestine and distended as slugs. At the corners of her mouth and covering her teeth, blood and flecks of nutmeat.

Sheppard had walked over to the medical examiner. "Say there, Harry, what have we got?"

"Victim appears to have died of anaphylactic shock."

Sheppard turned to the woman again. Where she'd clutched her neck, her fingernails had broken the skin. "What was the allergen?"

Harry looked at him over his bifocals, stopped scribbling on his pad, and pointed his pen at the table. On it was an open can of Planters peanuts. "Her esophagus swelled shut."

Sheppard walked over. On the label, Mr. Peanut tipped his top hat and smiled, his monocle as opaque as when Hastroll's glasses caught the light. He had his black cane propped on his shoulder, his pinky pointed skyward as he grabbed his hat's brim, so he looked to Sheppard like a man about to introduce himself—a chipper fellow about to say hello.

The husband, David Pepin, sat on the couch in the living room with his face in his hands—the index and middle fingers on his left hand wrapped in gauze. He was thick-built like Hastroll, tall too, with a shock of black hair. Sheppard questioned him for several minutes, made a quick phone call, then approached Hastroll, who appeared from another room.

"Husband says he came home," Sheppard said, "and found his wife sitting at the table with a plate of peanuts."

"And?" Hastroll said.

"She ate them."

Hastroll grunted.

"He said they'd been in a fight," Sheppard said.

"Did she know they could kill her?"

"He says she knew she was allergic."

"Does she carry an EpiPen?" Hastroll asked.

"Several," Sheppard said. "He claims she hid them."

Hastroll glanced at Pepin, then whispered, "*He* did it."

"Easy, Ward."

"What happened to his fingers?"

"He said he was trying to clear her airway." Sheppard loaded his pipe and lit it. "Apparently she bit him in the process."

"You buy suicide?"

"She had a history of depression. She was on a combination of Wellbutrin and Prozac. Husband says she'd been going through a bad patch. Plus she'd also lost a lot of weight."

"What's a lot?" Hastroll asked.

"More than one hundred and fifty pounds."

"Seems to me that would make her happy," Hastroll said.

Sheppard shook his head. "She had hyperthyroidism. It can cause deliriums. Extreme agitation. He thinks she might have just snapped."

"Did you speak to her doctor?"

"Psychiatrist corroborates about the medication. Not the ideation."

Sheppard and Hastroll turned to look briefly at Pepin, who stared squarely back.

"What's your feeling here, Sam? What's the golden gut say?"

"I'd like to sniff around for a while."

"Roger that," Hastroll said.

"Try to track down those EpiPens. See whose fingerprints are on them."

"I got plainclothes on it already."

"Check his hands for traces of nutmeat or salt."

"Already did it," Hastroll said. "They're clean."

"Check the sinks. He might've washed his hands. Bag the bars of soap and the towels."

Hastroll held up a plastic bag. The towels inside were bloody.

"What about samples from under his nails?" Sheppard said.

Hastroll snapped open an enormous switchblade. "Good thinking."

"Then take him in for questioning," Sheppard said.

In the Pepins' kitchen, a CSI unit was dusting pieces of the broken plate for prints and swabbing blood samples from Alice's mouth and teeth. Two men from the coroner's office had arrived with a gurney and were waiting outside while the crime scene photographer took pictures. When he finished, the coroner's men traced chalk around the body. While they slid the bag underneath it, Sheppard studied the woman's face. Her lips had stretched away from her gums, her teeth were bared and gnashed in refusal, her hands clasped around her neck as if she could squeeze the obstruction from her windpipe as you would a splinter from your finger. So different from the expressions of suicides, Sheppard thought. Those were often sleepy or glum. Tired. Wiped out. As if they'd suddenly nodded off, like a narcoleptic. Sheppard remembered one he'd investigated, a beautiful girl who'd been jilted and had leapt from the Empire State Building observatory and landed on a cab, its roof crumpling like a soft mattress. Her left fist lay clenched over her heart, the other hand held just above her head, relaxed and open slightly. It seemed to Sheppard that if he'd jostled her shoulder she would've stirred, rolled off the taxi roof, and wandered off to bed. Or the CEO who'd blown his brains out in his office, gun to left temple, the right wall splattered with gray matter and blood as if a brush heavy with paint had been whipped across a canvas. He had only half a face, true, the one side of his head nuked outward, but there was no sign in what remained of terror or pain.

"Pretty lady," one of the coroner's men said. He was young, in his early twenties. He squatted by her feet. "Husband whack her?"

"She ate a peanut," Sheppard said.

"Get out," the kid said. He took the woman's stiff leg and tucked it in the bag.

"A peanut can kill you," his partner said. "Ain't that right, Detective?"

But Sheppard wasn't listening

The kid tucked in her other leg, followed by both her elbows; the other coroner slipped her shoulders under the flaps, then zipped up the bag. All three men stared at its black formless shape.

Then the coroners reached down. "On three," the older one said, and then they had the bag safely onto the gurney and were wheeling her out.

For a few moments, Sheppard gazed at the chalk figure. He couldn't shake the expression on her face. As he moved through the apartment, it replaced the faces on all the pictures of her like some terrible special effect, superimposing itself on the framed snapshots that hung on the walls and sat on end tables, on the Polaroids—these he stared at for a long time—that covered the refrigerator door, all of them of Alice Pepin standing next to it, with the weeks and her diminishing weight written below each shot, the series arranged in horizontal rows, a pictorial record of before and after. She looked more confident as time passed, trying new things with her appearance the lighter she became: different colored lipstick on lips that appeared fuller as she sloughed weight, lashes brushed lush on eyes that seemed larger with each passing month, hair cut shorter on a face no longer so round. Yet there was an odd sadness to the photos, a sense, even in those with the happiest expressions, of some withering effect in this ritual, of unwillingness in the eye behind the lens. Studying them, Sheppard felt his imagination—all his empathetic powers—reaching out, only to be repelled. What did his wife, Marilyn, used to say? *You never know what goes on behind closed doors.* He could see her when she'd said it, the image floating across his mind's eye. He tried to hold it still. She was standing in their kitchen, in her robe, her back to him, looking out the window—the one that faced the road—and she meant what she said not as an observation but an accusation, directed at him, of course. And that utterance, her disappointment and the regret it imparted, was something he knew he'd remember until the day he died, just as he would always remember the first time he saw her.

In the living room, high windows faced north, and outside it was that moment at the end of twilight when the lights of Manhattan were silvery and golden and occupied their own dimension, so the buildings seemed to contain them like snow globes, and the avenues, laden with headlights, looked like channels poured with molten steel. The Pepins' new hardwood floors were the color of cognac. Twin Italian sofas, long and low to the ground and appearing as delicate as Calder sculptures, faced each other across an Oriental rug, its patterns as complex as the city outside. Built-in bookshelves climbed to the ceiling, the spines a brand of wallpaper that bespoke luxuries: education, quiet, time to read. The kitchen was updated: double oven, granite countertops, so much stainless steel and stone it looked like it could withstand an artillery shell. Adjoining it was a small dining room. The long hallway to the bedroom was lined with framed posters, screen shots of video games with the titles splashed across the top (Bang, You're Dead! Escher X, Lamb to the Slaughter), and Escher prints—not reproductions but the real things, signed and numbered. Sheppard had to stop and admire them. Was there ever an artist who made the eye move as much as that Dutch master? Who invited and then thwarted your efforts to grasp the whole, at the same time making you feel trapped? White and black swans migrating on a Möbius strip. Angels tracing the shapes of demons and vice versa, shrinking from a circle's center in infinite tessellation. A man of pure white interlocked with a black gnome, the two-dimensional figures becoming three-dimensional as they split off from each other in the background, circling on separate paths toward a terminal encounter. Sheppard continued on. The hallway led past a small study to the bedroom, the space dominated by a king-size bed and a flat-screen television on the wall across from it. Bookshelves framed the headboard and climbed above it, filled with knickknacks, sculptures, photographs: she swimming with a dolphin, he in a sea kayak, the two of them arm in arm, backpacking in Hawaii or waving on a bridge in Paris. In this one Alice Pepin had grown extraordinarily fat.

Who says people can't change?

In the interrogation room, Sheppard waited while Pepin collected himself. The suspect had been leaning forward with his elbows on the table, staring at his folded hands, but then sat up and rubbed the back of his wrist across his runny nose and sniffed, pressing his forearms across his wet eyes. He cleared his throat, crossed his arms, and seemed strong suddenly, focused and ready. "All right," he said, "ask away." He was a large man, heavy-boned and sausage-fingered with coarse black hair bristling on his arms, so thickly, Sheppard thought, that you could rest a pencil on it. He grew his black mustache down to his beard and had combed his thick black hair straight back. He looked like a biker, a Hells Angel, so if you weren't careful you might underestimate his intelligence. And there was an undeniable handsomeness about him, a startling confidence in his barrel-chested physicality and sloe-eyed gaze—a surprisingly regal charisma, Sheppard observed. He looked like a Jewish Henry VIII.

"Let's backtrack a little," Sheppard said. "Where were you today? Take me through it."

He had the basic story but now wanted Pepin to expand it, to tell it again so he could watch for the telltale signs: details dropped or added, narrative inconsistencies, lies and their microgestures—split-second tells—with the body giving you away as blatantly as a kid waving behind a TV reporter. There were too many of these to count: liars often turned their shoulders away from the questioner, increased their blinking, or fiddled with the nearest thing they could find. Like actors, they needed props. They breathed shallowly. Their eyes darted. They swallowed excessively when the mouth went dry. Their pupils dilated, widening visibly, like a camera shutter expanding. They had a whole array of facial tics, whether crinkling the nose, tightening the lips, or narrowing their eyes, miniexertions that carved lines in the face over time, grooves you could learn to read like hieroglyphics. Of course, Sheppard thought, a lie didn't become untruth until another person was present. After that—especially during an interrogation—it was like an invisible, physical thing between two people, push and push back, something Sheppard felt in his very core. Yet truth tellers had their own tics: they stared off to the left, their gaze drifting inward, memory taking over. They went still when they spoke and weren't necessarily articulate. In fact, verbosity or fluency—seamless storytelling—was to be trusted least of all. But when they told the truth, ironically, the innocent often appeared utterly arrested.

"Did you go to work this morning?" Sheppard asked.

"I was going to, but then I didn't."

"Why?"

"I wanted to see my wife. I had a surprise for her."

"And what was that?"

"A present for her birthday," Pepin said. "I'd bought us a trip."

"To where?"

"Australia."

Sheppard raised his eyebrows. "How long were you going away for?"

"Indefinitely."

"You mean weeks? Months?"

Pepin shrugged. "I mean we didn't have a return date."

It took all of Sheppard's willpower at this revelation not to turn around and stare at the one-way glass. "And had you been planning this for a while?"

"No," Pepin said, "not exactly."

"Well, yes or no?"

"We'd talked about it last year. Alice mentioned that she'd always wanted to see the Great Barrier Reef. But I hadn't planned it or anything. *We* hadn't."

"So it was a spur of the moment sort of thing."

"Yes."

"That's quite a trip for the spur of the moment."

Pepin shrugged.

"It's not even really a trip," Sheppard said. "It's more like a permanent vacation."

"We didn't talk about it like that."

"When did you buy the tickets?"

Pepin sat back, looking away sheepishly. "This morning."

For the first time since they'd talked, Sheppard's gut tingled. "And when was Alice's birthday?"

"Next week."

"But you had to give her the gift today?"

"Yes."

"Couldn't contain yourself? Couldn't wait until she got home?"

"No."

Sheppard considered this. "When were you leaving?"

"Tonight."

Sheppard nodded. He picked up his pencil and tapped it against the table. He could feel his pipe in his jacket pocket and desperately wanted to smoke. "You'll admit that's a little strange."

"You wouldn't understand."

"People don't just walk away from everything like that."

"No, not usually."

"They have jobs," Sheppard said. "Family."

Pepin shrugged. "We don't really have an extended family. And I've got plenty of money. But like I said, you wouldn't understand."

"Try me."

Pepin indicated the ring on Sheppard's finger. "Have you been married long?"

Before Sheppard spoke, he considered the question, as if it were anything but straightforward. His entire life, his whole psyche, seemed collapsed into the state of being married. Even though Marilyn was dead his marriage remained an eternal present, as necessary as a shark's need to keep swimming, so quantifying it seemed impossible—let alone with a word like *long*. "Yes," he said.

"Alice and I had talked about just . . . leaving. Walking away from everything." Pepin raised his hands. "From our lives."

Sheppard squinted.

"There was nothing holding us here," Pepin continued. "Nothing holding us anywhere. No kids. It's just been us. For thirteen years."

"So?"

"So we'd come to the end of us. Does that make sense?"

In his mind, Sheppard saw Marilyn again. It was fall and she was wearing her old school sweater and leaning against the patio's screen, her back to the lake, a cigarette in her hand. He said something to her—he was rocking in his chair when he spoke—and her face darkened, and she threw her ashtray at his head, the glass shattering against the chair back and spraying his cheek. By the time he looked up from his bloody fingers she was already out the door, Sheppard hearing her car start and then the tires peeling, and yet he remained right where he was, listening in the silence that followed to the waves lapping below and feeling his wound dry.

"Go on."

"We needed to do something *new*. Something radical."

"Why?"

"To save us."

"From what?"

"From ourselves," Pepin said. "So she'd proposed we just leave."

"*She* did?"

"Yes."

"When?"

"Last year."

"So why didn't you leave then?"

"I guess I didn't think we needed saving."

"But you did today?"

"Yes."

"Why?" Sheppard could tell the man was relaxing, that something had shifted. He was swiveling back and forth in his chair confidently, riding a gentle current of truth. If earlier in the interrogation Sheppard thought he'd had the upper hand, he'd lost it now.

"Because I realized she was right."

"What changed your mind?"

"I don't have to tell you that," Pepin said.

"You might want to if we charge you with murder."

"I might," he said, "but I think I'll wait until you do."

Sheppard sat back and rested his elbows on the arms of his chair and folded his hands over his stomach. "What did you do after you bought these tickets?"

"I drove to Alice's school to see her."

"What time did you get there?"

"Around a quarter to nine."

"Anyone see you? People Alice worked with, can they put you there?"

"Sure."

"So what happened?"

"I found her in her classroom and told her about the trip, that we had to leave immediately."

"What was her reaction?"

"She said no."

"She give you a reason?"

"She didn't believe I really wanted to go, that I was doing it out of pity for her. Maybe, I don't know, because I'd missed my chance."

"So?"

"We fought about it."

"You were angry with her."

"No, but I was desperate."

"And why was that?"

"Because we were in danger," Pepin said.

"Of what?"

"*Ending.* We'd been . . . going through a bad time. Alice had been very depressed and losing a lot of weight. It affected her behavior."

"How?"

"It made her short-tempered. Delusional. She was . . . impossible to live with."

"Had you talked about separation? Divorce?"

Pepin shook his head. "But I was at my wit's end."

"But you couldn't convince her to run off."

"No."

"So what did you do?"

"She was leaving with her class for a field trip to the Museum of Natural History, so I waited in the car for her . . ."

"And?"

Pepin took a deep breath.

It was amazing, listening to him walk the plank of his own story. To someone untrained, it might seem like pure fabrication because it was so suspicious, so odd, yet he could've said anything, that he had an appointment on Pluto, and Sheppard would have believed him, because every fiber of his being sensed that Pepin was telling the truth.

"I followed her."

"Why?"

"Because I didn't want to lose sight of her."

"But you knew where she was going."

"It's strange, I know, but it seemed like the thing to do at the time."

"You tailed her all the way to the museum?"

"Not quite." Pepin began to pump his leg. "I got into a wreck."

"Where?"

"On the West Side Highway."

Once again, Sheppard's gut tingled. "Go on."

Pepin indicated direction with his left hand. "I was in the center lane following the bus, moving into the left, when someone came up behind me in my blind spot." He shrugged. "And I hit him."

"Where was this, *exactly*?"

"Just above Ninety-sixth Street."

"Were any other cars involved?"

"Not directly, no."

"What was his name?"

"Who?"

"The other driver."

"I don't know."

"You didn't get a name? A number or insurance?"

"He didn't stop."

"Then how do you know it was a man?"

Pepin blinked several times.

Sheppard felt the small fillips in his belly. "Answer the question."

"Because I . . . saw him."

"When?"

Raising his voice, Pepin said, "When I hit him, all right? I hit him, I saw him through the window, and then he kept driving. Maybe *he* didn't have insurance, maybe he was a fucking criminal. Who knows? It happens every day."

"Nothing you've described happens every day," Sheppard said.

"I'm telling the truth."

"Keep going, then."

"The car was in bad shape, so I got off at Ninety-sixth and parked at a garage between West End and Riverside. Empire Parking, I think it was. The car's still there. You can check."

Hastroll would be out the door right now.

"Then I took a cab to the museum and found Alice inside."

"Did you talk to her?"

"No. I just . . . followed her."

"Why?"

"I didn't want to bother her."

"And she never noticed you?"

"No."

"What time was this?"

"Maybe close to ten."

"How long did you follow her?"

"The whole time she was there."

"And you never revealed yourself to her?"

Pepin shook his head.

"Why?"

"I told you: I didn't want to make a scene." Then he propped his elbow on the table and pressed his hand to his forehead, rubbing it. He smiled sadly. "And it was kind of pleasant."

"How's that?"

"Haven't you ever wondered about your wife during the day? What she does when you're not around? What she looks like doing it?"

Only married men, Sheppard thought, should be detectives. They'd been to places in their hearts that single men hadn't. They could imagine following their wives without them knowing—and in fact could imagine even the most terrible things. "How long were you there for?"

"Until lunch."

"Let me get this straight. You were dying to talk with your wife, you'd driven up to the school and back, yet the whole time you were at the museum you didn't say a thing to her?"

"If I'd tried, my only chance to talk later would've been lost."

Sheppard sat back again. "What about after lunch?"

Pepin closed his eyes, exhaling sharply, then opened them. "We got separated. I lost her."

"How?"

"I went to the bathroom, but when I came back to the dining hall she and the class were gone."

"Did you manage to find her again?"

Pepin shook his head. "I looked for her, but then there was the accident."

"What accident?"

Pepin held his hands up as if it were obvious. "The blue whale," he said.

Sheppard remembered now. He'd caught the headline on CNN, the frantic interviews and eyewitness accounts, the fears of a terrorist attack. Still, he didn't make the connection. The blue whale model had broken away from the ceiling and fallen into the crowd. Amazingly no one was injured, but the museum was immediately evacuated as a precaution. "Were you there when it happened?"

"I was just coming into the Hall of Ocean Life," Pepin said, "when there was this huge crash and then white dust everywhere, fiberglass or plaster just billowing all over the place. People were panicked and running everywhere, so I ran out too and looked for Alice outside. But it was madness. The firemen and rescue crews were pushing people back. No one could give me any information, so after a while I decided to go home."

"Why would you leave?"

"It was total chaos. Home seemed like the place to wait."

"What time was this?"

"I don't remember. I could've been there a couple hours. It was three, maybe four."

"And once you got to your apartment?" Watching carefully, Sheppard could see him remembering the scene.

"She was . . . just sitting at the kitchen table with that plate." Pepin's eyes welled up. "She'd gotten there before me somehow and was just sitting there, and then she . . ." He shook his head.

"She didn't say anything to you?"

Pepin covered his mouth.

Sheppard couldn't help it; he was furious.

"She just decided—out of the blue, with nothing between the two of you but a disagreement, in fact nothing but an invitation to run away together—to kill herself?"

But now Pepin was crying. "I can't talk about this anymore."

This deep into the diet—ten weeks in and over thirty pounds lost—Alice's behavior began to change. It was the same as the onset of her depression, those weeks when she'd decide, without consulting him, to go off her medications, David missing the signs every time. She could be just as erratic, as maddeningly touchy and forgetful, as given to sudden, inexplicable crying jags.

Now her temper was short.

"Tell me what you *see*?" Alice said. She demanded he get up from his desk and follow her. She led him to the living room and pointed to a candlestick in a holder. In the evenings, Alice liked to light candles in the apartment.

"I see a candle," David said. Seized by sympathy for his wife, he'd gone out and bought her new spiral beeswax candles. Vowing not to mention this gift but wanting to wait for her to notice, he went home, fitted them neatly into their holders and, when it turned dark, lit them all.

"I see a *crooked* candle," Alice said. "I see wax all over my table."

David looked. Wax spread like a smooth scab over the cherrywood.

"Did it even *occur* to you," she said, "that at this sharp an angle the candle might drip?"

It had, but for some reason he'd ignored it. "I'll clean it up," David said.

"I don't want you to clean it up. I want you to tell me why you left it crooked."

"I wasn't thinking."

"Then I want to know why you didn't think."

Her eyes flashed, her stomach rumbled as audibly as distant thunder. It occurred to David to count Mississippis. Was the storm coming or going? "It was careless," he conceded, then went for a razor blade to scrape up the mess.

"You bet it was careless," she said.

She followed him, railing. And while walking to the front hall closet, where he kept his tools, David wondered what the neighbors must think of their marriage, though he knew that all of Alice's yelling was really about food; and when all he could find in his tool box was a box cutter, he went to the bathroom for his straight razor; and when he closed the medicine cabinet to see her face right there, wild-eyed, he pushed her out into the hall until there was space between them, then swung both his arms like an umpire calling a runner *safe.*

"I wish you'd stay fat!" he shouted.

Alice froze.

"Did you hear me?"

He took a step toward her, and she took a step back and then stopped, petrified.

"Every few months we go through this," David said. "Every time with the diet. It takes over *everything.* You call me at work, it's all you talk about at home. It takes over your moods, it kills our sex. Every time I get a *minute* to myself, every time I get some momentum going, like *clockwork* you start up with it again." He waved a finger in her face. "Do you have any idea what I could have accomplished by now? *Do* you? So I wish you'd just stay fat."

Alice stood there, feeling for the wall. Only then did David realize he was holding the straight razor in his other hand.

He left the apartment and walked downtown without a clue as to where he'd end up. It was snowing heavily, cars whispering along, hissing into a quieter distance, disappearing in a blaze of floating brake lights behind curtains of snow. Here, outside, David could no longer hold his anger together; it dispersed, flying off into the night toward the hidden towers above. He stuffed the straight razor in his pocket and scolded himself for his lack of fierceness. Perhaps he should rekindle his anger indoors. He passed a pub lit by Christmas lights, the bar crowded; but he knew that to sit and drink in a strange place among strange people would make him self-conscious, would only send him home faster. He turned up the collar of his coat. Flakes of snow landed softly on his neck and melted on his black hair. He turned west now on 57th Street and caught sight of his reflection in a black storefront; he could stand to lose weight himself. He stopped at Tiffany's, his breath fogging the small display window, the whole building seemingly built to encase these few visible jewels. Then he turned up Fifth Avenue and looked over at the gold and emerald Plaza, refurbished and gleaming, Sherman and winged victory demanding he halt. He stood before the Pulitzer fountain, mesmerized by it, the pool ruffling, illuminated from below and resembling a cascade of diamonds. He was suddenly cold, a bone-cold he imagined people stranded in the mountains or who slept on the streets in winter might feel. Alice would stop with her diet, he knew, and in a matter of weeks would gain the weight back. Things would return to how they were before; she would return to being his wife. Because this was how it always went, David thought, the way it always happened.

And sometimes it felt like too high a cost, though he now believed he had reserves of patience he hadn't tapped. He considered what she'd been through, what their marriage had cost her, how she'd changed. And he suffered such a terrible sense of self-loathing that for a moment he felt he might fall to his knees and rend his clothing, act out some biblical display of regret, or dive into the fountain to freeze away the pain.

He hurried home.

When David opened the door to their apartment, he heard the sound of retching. There was garbage on the floor, open to-go boxes that formed a Hansel and Gretel trail to the kitchen. The candles he'd bought had burned down to their wicks. He called his wife's name. Nothing. The kitchen table was a disaster of enchiladas, chiles rellenos, tacos—all partially consumed. Terrible, he thought, a feeding frenzy. She'd finally broken down and ordered in for twelve. The burritos had gash marks that leaked meat, salsa was splattered across the counter and stove, and that's where the vomit trail started.

"Alice?" he called, and heard a groan from the bathroom.

He found her semiconscious, collapsed between the sink and toilet, one arm draped over the rim, the other laced through the sink's plumbing. The room smelled of stomach acid and shit—her legs were covered in it—and her breathing was like an animal's, the shallow breaths of a bird. The walls and floors were streaked and spotted with puke, the ends of her hair matted with it so that they appeared as brittle as coral.

"Alice!" David screamed. He grabbed the phone, dialed 911, and rushed back to her. "Alice, what did you do?"

He pulled her up by the shoulders and tried to lay her down. Her eyes rolled back. Her head slumped, then struck the tile.

"What did you do?"

She whispered something incomprehensible. Spittle bubbled at her lips, then popped.

David leaned in closer.

"Mi Corazon," she said weakly. It was their favorite Mexican restaurant.

Please, sir, stay calm. Please, I need you to stay right here on the line with me, sir, and just tell me the state she's in.

Sour cream, salsa, and mole, cayenne, cumin, and chipotle: they rolled off the tongue as smoothly as her stretcher did along the hospital floor. Alice opened her eyes to look at him, his head flying upside down above her own. They hurried Alice into the OR, but before they took her away David leaned down to kiss her cheek. He let go of her hand, said her name once more, and then watched as the double doors down the hall swallowed her up.

In the hospital room, David sat across from Alice's bed and watched her for hours.

At times he dozed in his chair and occasionally slept fitfully and when he woke she was still unconscious. Once he got up to listen to her heart, and after that he went to the window; in the coned beams from streetlights below, he saw that it was still snowing; then he turned and watched Alice some more. With no change in her condition he sat in his chair and slipped off to sleep himself, a sleep of no dreams. There was snow on the ground when he woke up that morning, snow on the windowsill, snow across all the buildings and water towers of Manhattan. The wind was high and strong and gusts beat the pane, punting the glass. Gulls banked toward the Hudson. Pigeons searched for places to land. The sun rose into a clear blue sky, a white sun without warmth that reflected off the snow, and the whole world brightened with the glare. Then Alice awoke. She'd been propped upright in case she vomited again, and when she opened her eyes she opened them wide, looking calmly around at the light-flooded room, blinking once at her husband, recognizing him, then looked away.

"I'm going to change my life," she said.

David didn't know what she meant by this or how to react. But at the same time unutterably relieved to see her alive, he simply said, "Yes." She'd been unconscious for hours but seemed to have spent this time reflecting, having made this decision somewhere in the back of her mind. She was so unwilling to talk to him that morning and for the rest of the day that by evening David gave up trying. She'd been so sick he couldn't begrudge her anything, yet the longer this went on the more anxious he became. She was angry with him, angry, he knew, for the things he'd said, and every time he recalled their fight, he felt more and more ashamed.

"Alice," he said the next morning, "I'm so sorry."

She was watching the television above his head. She lay with her arms crossed, and every time she jabbed the remote at the screen he felt sure the set would fall down on him.

"Sorry for what?"

"For the things I said. For upsetting you so much."

"Is that what you think?" Alice said.

It *was* what he thought, but the look of disgust and amazement on her face was so intense that he strongly considered lying.

"You think this happened to me because of our fight? Because of something you might have *said*?"

"Well," David answered, "yes."

She jabbed the remote one, two, three times. "Then you'd be wrong."

He waited for an explanation, but none came.

"Then why does it seem like you're angry with me?" he asked.

"Because I'm *trapped* here, David. And because I am trapped here, I can't get on with changing my life. Does that make sense to you? Does it make things clear?"

"No," he said, "it doesn't."

"Well," Alice said, "that's just the way it's going to be for now."

Her doctor came by on rounds later that evening. When he entered the room, Alice was cordial and talkative, and that she seemed capable of treating this stranger with more decency and kindness than her own husband left David feeling more hurt and confused than before. The doctor checked her heart rate and blood pressure, shined a light in her eyes and examined her tongue. He was Indian, and with his long, delicate fingers—his palms were as pink as smoked chicken—he thumped Alice's back. And though it was completely irrational, the fact that he was touching her made David horribly jealous.

"Your blood tests came in," the doctor said. "You're anemic. You also have acute hyperthyroidism. Were you aware of this condition?"

Alice shook her head.

"When you diet in the future, you must monitor your nutrition more carefully."

"I will," she said. "Doctor, may we speak privately for a moment?"

"Certainly."

Both the doctor and Alice looked over at David and waited. David pointed to himself, then got up and left the room, closed the door behind him, and stood tapping his foot in the hallway.

Within a few minutes, the door opened.

"Thank you so much," Alice told the doctor.

"Of course," he said at the door. "You don't have to suffer like you do."

They both glanced at David.

"You'll be discharged tomorrow."

"That's wonderful," Alice said.

"Rest is the best thing for you now," the doctor said, and after David stepped past him he gently closed the door.

As soon as David took his seat, Alice turned over onto her side and faced away from him.

"Are you going to sleep now?" he asked.

"Yes," Alice said.

"Is there anything I can do?"

"Can you make tomorrow come faster?"

"I don't think so."

"Then the answer is no."

He sat in the dark for a few minutes, feeling another terrible wave of anxiety come over him. In the next room, a man coughed violently. "Alice?" he said.

She refused to answer.

"I thought I'd lost you. And now that you're back, it's like you're gone." He could see his wife breathing evenly, calmly, listening to him. "Say something," he said.

But she'd already fallen asleep.

She slept late the next morning, and when she woke she still wouldn't engage him. After breakfast, she took a nap. The moment she woke, a nurse came in to check her vitals, and everyone else in the hospital seemed to have an unspoken agreement with Alice that David was to be completely ignored. When the nurse left, another doctor trailed by a group of residents examined her; he explained how Alice had essentially starved herself for so many weeks that her system had gone haywire, her binge coupled with an allergic reaction to certain proteins, the combination having a toxic effect. "What we have here," the doctor said, "is something akin to kwashiorkor—essentially protein malnutrition—followed by angioedema. A bad combo, to be sure." The residents nodded, and Alice, happy to help, smiled at them and nodded back. "He's right," she said. "I barely ate." Afterward, a food allergist paid an extended visit. Midday, David went back to the apartment to get her some clean clothes, took a few hours to clean the place spotless, and when he returned, Alice was surrounded by doctors and nurses again. So it wasn't until late afternoon that she was discharged, she and David sitting in back of the cab, alone together finally, Alice pressed so close to her window and he to his that even a fat person could've shared the seat between them, and David picked up the conversation where she'd left off by asking, "How?"

"How what?" she said.

"How are you going to change your life?"

"That's my business."

"Oh," David said. On the street, he watched a man turn the corner onto Lexington Avenue. When the wind hit him, it sent his cap sailing straight into the air. He watched it fly away as hopelessly as a child would a lost balloon. "Are you leaving me?" he asked after awhile.

She closed her eyes, disgusted. "Not everything's about you, David."

She continued in this fashion at home. Though the floor was mopped, the bed made with fresh sheets, the seat of the toilet as clean as new china, and you could see your reflection in the fixtures of the sinks, Alice bustled about restraightening everything, shaking her head in frustration as she ran her finger along the baseboards. "This place is filthy," she said, flashing David her blackened finger. "I can't live like this." When he tried to stop her from bleaching the grout in the bathroom, she said, "Can I get myself situated without you following me around?" And so he retreated to sit in front of the television's blank screen, which he turned on guiltily after a few minutes, sound off. Football wasn't the same without commentary, the game a set of pointless collisions between enormous men. Commercials were like antic silent movies, the snippets from children's video games like scenes from some hellish nightmare, even though one of them was David's own. When Alice entered carrying a bucket and sponge, he couldn't take it anymore and left for the office. Though in truth there was nothing there for him to do.

So he came back to his book. He brought it up on-screen and read, standing, palms against his desk; then he sat down and fiddled with a sentence or two, reading back to where he'd gotten stuck. And staring at the screen he once again waited, which, as with many things, was often the only thing you could manage to do.

"How are you feeling?" he asked Alice in bed that night.

"I'm fine," she said, staring at the ceiling with her hands crossed over her chest.

"Are you sure?"

"Yes," she said, "I'm sure."

"Nothing you want to talk about?"

"No."

"Nothing you want to tell me?"

"No."

There was no give in her whatsoever, and this in and of itself was a new thing. "Well, good night then," David said. He sat there and waited.

"Good night," she said, then turned out the light and rolled over.

David lay watching her, wondering if her eyes were open or closed, hoping she might roll over and look at him, and when she didn't, he lay down himself, staring at the ceiling. I must be patient, David thought. I must be faithful. That would be the right thing to do. Be faithfully patient.

He woke the next morning to an empty bed.

Usually he was up first, and for a moment he suffered the same sense of disorientation and abandonment he'd had as a child when he slept over at a friend's house, forgetting where he was for a terrifying second. He smelled coffee and went to the kitchen to find Alice sitting at the table. She had her laptop open and a legal pad full of notes and presently was peeling the shell off a hard-boiled egg. As soon as he poured himself coffee and came over to her chair, she stopped what she was doing, closed the computer, and covered the pad—which David couldn't believe.

He indicated everything with a sweep of his mug, and though he'd promised himself to be patient and faithful, he couldn't help but ask, "Is this part of changing your life?"

Alice waited, and he did too.

"Are you mocking me?" she said.

He was and he wasn't, and certainly couldn't admit the former. "Of course not," David said.

Silence.

"But I think I deserve to know something about all of this."

"You do," Alice said, "but not right now."

"Oh," he said. "Any idea when?"

"No," she said.

"How about any idea of when you might have an idea?"

"Can't help you," she said.

They stared at each other, deadlocked.

He was suddenly determined not to back down. He would show her by force of will that he could wait her out in this emotional standoff, that he would draw the line here, in their own kitchen, in his T-shirt and boxers. If this is the game she wants to play, David thought, let's play! He stood stock-still until the silence between them became something absurd and useless, a pointless exertion of stamina, like a kissing marathon. He could feel his petrified facial expression; his upper lip adhered to his dry front teeth. He needed desperately to blink—his eyes were watering—but Alice hadn't. He had to swallow so badly he thought he might choke.

And he balked. He wasn't able to match her mysterious inner resolve. He slumped at the shoulders. A splash of coffee landed between his feet.

"Fine," David said, "When you're ready to talk just let me know."

He showered and dressed, then left the apartment without saying good-bye.

At work he decided that all of this was simply a phase in his wife's recovery, some sort of post-traumatic effect he had to endure. For a time, he must simply expect nothing from her. This mental approach was a tremendous relief, and he had a terrifically productive day. He felt confident, focused, and because he deserved it, he asked Georgine Darcy, the gorgeous programmer they'd just hired, to lunch.

"Took you long enough to ask," she said.

Georgine, David thought. Could she be any more different from his wife? She was lithe and athletic, hard-nosed and independent, a Brooklyn girl born and bred, leggy and blonde, exponentially less curvaceous than Alice but curvaceous nonetheless, a former professional dancer until she blew out her ACL at age eighteen. Two months ago, she'd sent David and his partner, Frank Cady, the first game she'd designed—a marvelous, all-out-fun piece of work. It was based on the great board game Labyrinth, the simple wooden box with a maze inset, its attitude and pitch controlled by a pair of knobs that you manipulated to move a small black marble through the labyrinth while avoiding the holes. Georgine's game took the marble's point of view. Your avatar, a tiny black humanoid figure, was inside the marble itself, the mazes growing in complexity with each completed level and now adjusted by the controller's thumbsticks, your avatar slamming into walls, resting against the right angles and panting, screaming horribly when it plunged down one of the holes.

He'd decided to take her to New York Noodle, his favorite hole in the wall in Chinatown, not only because the food was great but also because it was the last place on earth his wife might walk into unexpectedly. "We'll get some duck," David said, "if that's okay with you." He nodded toward the birds hung in a row before the window, hooked, headless, and baked bronze. "The tripe soup's great, by the way."

"You order." Georgine closed her menu, put her elbows on the table, and leaned forward, resting her chin on the backs of her folded fingers. Her blond hair hung lushly around her face, and her lipstick was red as an apple. "I eat anything."

He ordered two Tsingtaos. It wasn't like him to drink at lunch but he was feeling game, relaxed, it seemed, for the first time in ages.

When Georgine put the bottle to her mouth, the tip barely touched her upper lip. "I have a confession to make," she said.

"I'm officially nervous."

"I came to Spellbound because of you. Don't laugh! It's *true.* It was because of Bang, You're Dead! I remember playing that game and thinking how perfect it was. My friends and I used to name the characters after people we went to school with. There's Miss Girgus! Mr. Romano! Shoot 'em! Look out! They're trying to zap you from behind. After playing that, I thought, 'This is what I want to do with my life.' I even dreamed up Labyrinth in its spirit. It's a paean to your work."

"I'm flattered."

"You know, I saw you speak at the Electronic Entertainment Expo in Vegas last year. The seminar on omniscience in multiplayer shooters."

"You should've introduced yourself."

"I was too intimidated. I'm like, what, he's a genius and he's hot."

"Please."

"Can I tell you about a game idea I have?"

"Of course."

"It's big, though it isn't fully realized, but I can't shake it."

"I'm all ears."

"All right," she said. She sat forward, laying her arms over each other on the table and bunching her breasts together.

Oh, David thought, the tyranny of tits, the bug eyes at boobs. Her T-shirt said, WHY DID THE CHICKEN CROSS THE MÖBIUS STRIP? Staring at her apple-hard ass as they walked to their table, he'd looked up to see the answer: TO GET TO THE OTHER SIDE?

"It's called Playworld," she said. "It's loosely based on this Piers Anthony book I read as kid called *Split Infinity.* In this world, all anybody does all day long is play games. They've taken care of all their material needs, I guess, so the only currency is gaming prowess. It's like the coolest communist state in the universe. People are ranked by record and enjoy status accordingly. Strangers or friends can issue challenges in a whole range of games and skill sets, from the physical to the mental, obstacle courses to board games to hand-to-hand combat. It's how you interact socially, how you meet lovers, how you live life. Oh, and everybody walks around naked. And when they screw they put on clothes."

"I like it."

"Screwing with clothes?"

"Walking around naked."

"Ditto. So Playworld takes this idea and combines two kinds of interface. The way I conceive it, it's like World of Warcraft—a massive multiuser, the whole wide world can play, subscription-based for a revenue stream. But it's also like Facebook, where you have a profile—though in this case that also includes your skill level. Your world rank. And it's not your own picture, mind, not your identity, but a highly detailed avatar—think Second Life—that's your own Warhol of yourself or your bent or ideal version, your cartoon equivalent but as buff or thin or hot or warped as you want to make yourself. *It's you and it's not you.* We make that part super art-driven interactive. It takes the same degree of forethought to generate your avatar as Spore. So you go online with a headset like Halo. And now you're in the gaming realm, this vast space, like a carnival or a giant nightclub or Bourbon Street a hundred years from now but as brilliantly colored as a pinball machine, avatars everywhere, at different stations or fields, having competitions you can watch and cheer, everything you say and do part of the ambient noise. You can communicate with your opponents in real time, introduce yourself and make chitchat or challenge anyone there to these games. And you could play, say, Scrabble or Battleship or chess or have a race in an Escher X obstacle course or play Bang, You're Dead! . . . whatever. We could fold *all* of Spellbound's games into this world—an Aegis concept, Disney without end, new competitions and games in perpetuity. And when you play—and this is the thing—you see both the other player *and* yourself. Split screen. We're third-person omniscient *and* limited. Which is part of the draw, you see. Because you *want* to see yourself in the world—right?—but also with others. You *always* want that view. And even better, after you play this stranger, you can get to know this other him-not-him or her-not-her in this virtual space. He or she becomes your Playworld friend. Which is the draw; the most basic beauty of online anonymity. You can say *anything* you want to *anyone.* Be somebody else or yourself. It's the ultimate form of directness."

She was leaning so far forward it was like she was telling a secret. He leaned forward too.

"I don't know about you," she said, "but I feel like we walk around all the time with this other self who wants to say things and do things but can't. So let's *play,* you know? Like if I said to you now, 'I like you, David. I like the way you look. I like the operations of your mind, how talented you are. I like your hands and mouth.' But I can't say that."

"Why not?"

"Because if I did, we wouldn't be playing a game."

After David returned to the office, he called the apartment immediately, but Alice didn't answer. He tried her again half an hour later, and when she still didn't answer he slammed down the phone. He stayed late, frustrated, but by evening he had softened. Heading home from work, he bought her flowers, fresh pasta, and some low-fat ice cream. At the apartment, he rang the doorbell even though he had his key. As her footsteps grew louder, he dreamed of a warm hug of welcome, a reconciliation, perhaps. He held the bouquet out before him but rather than open the door Alice simply pulled it ajar, so to keep it from closing David had to stick his foot in the jamb. When he went inside, Alice was walking down the hall away from him. He stood in the foyer, speechless, and for the first time since she'd come home from the hospital he was angry with her. He went into the kitchen, put down his bag, and it was then that he noticed all the lights were off in the apartment. "Is energy conservation part of changing your life too?" he called out. He took off his coat and threw it on the chair and walked around turning on the lights switch by switch and lamp by lamp until he came upon Alice in the bedroom, sitting on the bed, laptop on her lap, her face lit corpse white by the screen.

David waited.

"I'm working," she said.

He looked around the dark room, at the reflection of her torso in the window, floating on the glimmering city. "Is that all?" he asked.

"What do you mean?" she said.

"No, 'How was your day?' 'How are you?' 'What's going on?' "

"How was your day?" Alice said. "How are you? What's going on?"

He flipped on the bedside light. "You'll go blind," he said, and forced a smile.

"Hardly." She went back to work.

He stood there for a long time, until it was clear she'd just continue to work uninterruptedly with him standing there, and then, without realizing what had come over him, he dropped to his knees and gathered her skirt in both his fists. "Please," he said. "Alice, please forgive me, whatever I did. Whatever I've done. Just tell me what it is. Tell me what I can do. I'll do anything, Alice, I promise. Anything at all."

He inhaled her smell and felt the fabric of her skirt, and his whole body shook. Then he heard her tapping away at the keyboard. He stood slowly, shuddering like a man squatting a tremendous amount of weight, and staggered out of the room. "Whatever," he said. "Take your time. Take as much time as you need."

He went to the kitchen to make himself some dinner. He was hungry, though the idea of cooking—the effort required—seemed so involved as to be nearly impossible. He put water on, shook some salt into the pot, poured olive oil into the water, and stared at the circular globules that slicked on the surface. He got down a can of white clam sauce—he kept a secret stash of Alice-lethal foods—and opened it, inhaling its briny smell. And when the water finally boiled he found himself mesmerized by the roiling. And now, in his solitude, he found himself thinking very clearly once again. He thought of Georgine's idea and what she'd said about directness. He thought of calling her to make love right now. He thought of his and Alice's last five years together and then what he thought was this:

We have arrived at some new phase. That, or we are about to enter one. We have been in the same place for so long we can either stay here forever—which is impossible—or not. And not is an unknown, and might not include each other, because at some point it requires both of us to hold on.

"David," Alice said.

Startled, he looked up. She stood a few paces out of the kitchen, just out of range of the smell of the sauce. She was nicely dressed, not for work so much as a date. He took a step toward her, and she pointed at the door.

"I'm going out," she said.

"Out where?"

"I have an appointment."

"What time is it?"

"It's almost seven," she said. "I'll be back before ten." She turned to leave.

"But where are you going?"

She stopped in the foyer but wouldn't look at him. "I'm going to change my life." And as if to emphasize her determination, she let the door swing closed with a slam.

One evening, Detective Hastroll came home—it was late spring and unseasonably warm—and found his wife, Hannah, in bed. It was a Friday. He asked what was wrong, and she said she didn't feel good, that she'd come home from work early to lie down. Her throat was scratchy, she said, she thought she was coming down with something. She just needed some rest. She lay there in her slip, the sheets thrown off her legs, the windows open onto the courtyard. There was no breeze and the room was stifling. Hastroll could see the beads of sweat on her upper lip and chest. She refused to look at him.

"Can I bring you anything?" he said.

"No, thank you," she said.

"Are you hungry?" he said.

"No," she said.

"Are you sure?" he said.

"I'm sure," she said.

"Is there anything I can do for you?" he asked.

She looked at him and began to cry. "There is *nothing*," she said, "absolutely *nothing*"—and here she sat up and pointed a finger at him—"that you can do for me. Except get out of my sight!"

She waited, and Hastroll waited too.

"All right," he said finally, then went into the living room, poured himself a tall drink, and sat down in his favorite chair.

That was five months ago.

Hannah was still in bed.

Hastroll was getting desperate.

Murder brings out the basics in people, Hastroll thought. It reduces their character to the simplest forms of desire.

Women, for instance, almost always kill their spouses in self-defense. It's a proven fact. There are exceptions, of course, but nine times out of ten, when a wife has shot, poisoned, or stabbed her husband, you'll find a man who somehow deserved it.

Men, meanwhile, usually kill their wives for one of four reasons: money, sex, revenge, or freedom. The first three need almost no explanation and are so common that detectives use them as a kind of checklist when they find a married woman lying dead in her apartment. Was the suspect fucking someone else? Was the wife, and did the husband know about it? Did the wife have a large insurance policy or trust fund of which the husband was a beneficiary; and if so, was the man's alibi airtight, et cetera, et cetera?

But freedom, this was the least common and most complicated reason to murder a spouse, though nearly every man who has been married understands it. And although one might argue that freedom was somehow the underlying impetus of the previous three, the shared factor, as it were, Hastroll knew from experience that murder for freedom qua freedom was something else entirely.

Men dream of starting over. Not even necessarily with another woman. They dream of a clean slate, of disappearing, of walking off a plane on a layover and making a new life for themselves in a strange city—Grand Rapids, say, or Nashville. They dream of an apartment all their own, of silence, of joining Delta Force and fighting in Iraq, of introducing themselves by the nickname they'd always wished they had. Of a time and place where they can use everything they know now that they hadn't known then—that is, before they were married. And then they might be happy.

Sitting in the living room, in his favorite chair, with his wife sobbing in her bed for hours on end, Hastroll understood this dream. Sit alone in the dark long enough, he thought, and it seems worth killing for.

"They had a couple of knock-down-drag-outs," said Rand Harper, Pepin's next-door neighbor. "But so have Havis and me." His wife, Havis Davenport, sat with him on the couch. They were in their late twenties, just married, Havis newly knocked up but already really showing. Pictures from their wedding hung all over the apartment. In the bathroom, when Hastroll had excused himself to take a leak, he'd noticed a framed page from *Town & Country;* the announcement read like a genealogy of superachievement and prime real estate, their photograph taken in the limousine that would whisk them off to their fabulous honeymoon, the two kids looking so poised, posed, and pretty, he thought, that there was nowhere to go but down.

"I think we get along very well," Havis said.

"I'm not saying we don't, sweetie, I'm just saying we've had a fight or two, and just because we have doesn't mean we're on the verge of killing each other."

"I certainly hope not," Havis said.

Hastroll looked up from his notes.

"Rand worked for Lehman," she said.

"What's that got to do with anything?"

"It's caused some *stress,*" she said.

"I don't think the detective cares about my job situation."

"Well," she said, "somebody has to."

Hastroll flipped a page in his pad. "So you never heard anything out of the ordinary?" he said.

"No," Rand said.

"Did you see either of them on the day of Alice's death?"

"To be honest," Havis said, "I rarely saw them together at all."

"Can you clarify that?"

"For several months I never even saw her. I think they were separated for most of this year. I think she was gone."

"There's an ugly duckling story for you," Rand said.

His wife smacked his arm.

"Well, it's true. She used to be this obese . . ." He turned to Hastroll. "She was fat, all right, and then—"

"What?" Havis said.

He looked at her and back at Hastroll.

"She got . . . attractive."

His wife crossed her arms, then stood up and gathered the cups from the coffee table. "Do you need to ask me any more questions, Detective?"

"No," Hastroll said.

"Excuse me then." She went to the kitchen, dropped the cups in the sink, and slammed the bedroom door behind her.

Rand sighed. He checked over his shoulder and then leaned forward, lowering his voice. "It's like she's got a demon in her belly."

"I wouldn't know."

Rand checked again to see that her door was closed. "Look, Detective, I saw a couple of things I thought were strange. I didn't want to say anything in front of Havis because if she thinks our next-door neighbor, you know, offed his wife, she'll be even more of a basket case than she already is."

"Go on."

"There *were* several months there when we never saw Alice. I can't tell you what was going on. They kept to themselves. But there was one time I came home late—it was while Alice was gone—and I saw this blonde I'd never seen before leaving their apartment."

"When was this?"

"Months ago. Three, maybe. Four. I can't be sure."

"What else?"

"The night before Alice died, I saw David on the street, talking on his cell phone."

"Why was that strange?"

"Because he was pacing in circles and really going berserk."

"Did you hear what he said?"

"He said something like, 'What do I need to do to end this?' I couldn't make everything out. But he sounded like he was at the end of his rope."

The most highly anticipated moment of Hastroll's day came right before he put the key into his front door, wondering what Hannah would say to him when he entered their apartment. He was as sensitive to her voice as a dog to a high-pitched whistle.

"I'm home," Hastroll would say, and Hannah might say nothing. And his spirit, soaring with hope, would come crashing down. Perhaps the television was on. He'd walk into their bedroom and she'd look away from the screen for a moment and say, "Oh, I didn't hear you come in," and then go back to watching. He would wait to see if she had anything else to say—she never did—and then he would go into the living room to fix himself a drink.

"I'm home," Hastroll would say, and Hannah might say, "I'm in here," which meant come in if you want to, but nothing has changed.

"I'm home," Hastroll would say, and Hannah might say, "Ward, is that *you*?" And in that emphasis was a scintilla of enthusiasm. Of love. His soul quickened every time. "It's *me*," he'd say, and hurry in to see her. Perhaps she might get up now and embrace him. Perhaps she might let him kiss her lips. Perhaps she might say, "Darling, I feel so much better today!" and stand up and stretch, then lasso his neck with her arms. If she did, Hastroll honestly believed he'd weep. He would rush into the bedroom and say, "Of course it's me." And Hannah, disappointed, might say, "Oh. I thought so." And that was all.

"I'm home," Hastroll would say, and every so often—this evening, in fact—Hannah might reply, "Could you come in here, please?" There was a distinct vulnerability in her voice. There was desire. She was on the edge of something; she had something more to tell him. Carefully, gingerly, he entered her room. She wore the same slip she was wearing the day she first lay down. He wondered how it stayed clean. Did she secretly wash it? Soak it in Woolite in the sink? But how did it dry in time? During the day, while he was gone, did she go out to the Laundromat? She did her hair and makeup, that much was clear, ate the food he left her—she wasn't starving, after all—but whenever he came home, there she was in bed, not a dirty dish to be found, the milk the same level in the fridge, wearing the same damn thing every time.

"Yes, love," he said, and stood by her bed.

"Ward," she said. She held out her hand to him.

He took it. Her palm was clammy.

She rocked his hand from side to side, then closed her eyes and put it to her lips, teeth and wet gums rubbing against his skin as if she were a cat.

He kneeled down, never letting go of her hand, taking it in both of his. She looked at him carefully, her own hazel eyes darting back and forth across his own.

"What is it, Hannah? Tell me. Please."

"No," she said, and covered her mouth. "No, just go away."

Pepin's other neighbor was an elderly man whose doorbell read BAGDASARIAN. He greeted Hastroll distractedly, wearing nothing but a pair of briefs. "If you don't mind," Hastroll said, showing him his badge, "I'd like to ask you some questions." But Bagdasarian had already turned to leave him standing in the hallway. Hastroll stuck his foot in the jamb and followed him inside. The living room was taken up by a large piano, the instrument so ship-in-a-bottle big that Hastroll was tempted to ask how he got it in here. Bagdasarian stood with his back to him, facing a mirror and a mantel lined with pictures. When Hastroll tapped him on the shoulder, Bagdasarian turned and looked at him like he'd never seen him before. Then he pointed at a photograph of a woman thirty years his junior. She wore a green dress and a small black toque. She had candy-apple red hair. The picture, Hastroll could tell by the cars in the street and the skyline behind her, was decades old.

"Das Judif," he said, his speech mauled, the syllables blunted and deformed.

"Judith?"

The man gave him a crooked smile. "Das my wife." He looked at the picture and pointed again, then touched the same finger to his lips. "Das Judif?" he asked.

Hastroll left, closing the door behind him quietly, reminding himself that no matter how much pain he felt, he must be careful what he wished for.

. . .

Hannah let Hastroll feed her. It wasn't like she was on a hunger strike. In fact, when he brought her dinner in on a tray she became as chatty as she ever was. "How are things at the station?" she'd say, or "It sure looks hot out there," or "You've seemed pretty busy lately." In fact, it was almost galling, because for those brief moments before she tucked her napkin in her slip, she was acting like a woman who hadn't been in bed for five months but instead was on the upswing after an illness, the flu, say, was a lot better, thanks, just a day away from feeling strong enough to go back to work.

Hastroll stood there, amazed and obliterated. But he said nothing. He asked if she needed anything else—"I'm great," she said—and went back into the kitchen, since eating in bed was one of his pet peeves; and then he cleaned up, since another bugbear was waking up to a mess. Though now, standing over the full sink, Hastroll thought about how what he'd cooked her tonight—butterflied chicken over couscous with lemon butter sauce and Italian parsley—had become his favorite dish to make of late; and as he thought over their years together, he realized their relationship could be described as an ever-changing menu, or a sort of *bistro à deux,* Hastroll the chef and Hannah his only customer. And if he were asked to make a final tasting menu, one that charted significant dates in their history course by course, from the beginning to now, they'd end with that dish after working through Tuscan ribollita with kale, carrots, and cannellini beans, filling and blessedly cheap; cold sesame noodles with grilled pork belly (this during Hastroll's Chinese phase) and delicious morning, noon, or night, but especially after sex; shrimp and black bean enchiladas, a Friday evening tradition ever since traditions had suddenly started to occupy Hastroll; salmon steaks poached with lemon and black peppercorns finished with a cucumber yogurt sauce (they began eating more fish once they had some dough); and finally his fettuccine with spinach in a cream sauce with mascarpone and a dash of nutmeg, a fistful of parmesan added at the end, because it was easy to make and stuffed his empty belly, and since it was just him and Hannah, after all, did it really matter anymore if either of them got fat?

He returned to their bedroom to collect her plate.

"Do we have anything sweet?" she asked.

Hastroll blinked twice. "You're kidding," he said.

"Kidding how?"

"You mean like blueberry pie?"

"That's right."

"Pineapple upside-down cake?"

"That sounds delicious, though just some ice cream will do."

Hastroll pointed at his chest and jabbed himself. "I don't *do* dessert!" Then he pointed at her. "*You* do dessert!"

Hannah smoothed the blankets over her legs and sighed. "You still haven't figured it out."

"David and I are business partners," said Frank Cady. "We started this company together. What's all this about?"

"Do you know if he and his wife had any marital problems?" Hastroll asked.

"We didn't have the kind of relationship where he'd tell me."

Hastroll looked around his office. The walls were covered with posters of Marvel Comics superheroes, some of which even he recognized (though he imagined he'd know them all if he and Hannah had any kids): Spider-Man, Silver Surfer, the Hulk. Action figurines lined shelves along with Dungeons & Dragons books, the Dune series and *Lord of the Rings,* a Wolverine phone in a glass case. A light saber, framed with an autographed photo of Cady and George Lucas; a road sign reading YOU SHALL NOT PASS, with a symbol that looked like a wizard. The credenza had four computer screens mounted on a bracket, YouTube and a video game running on two, one filled with lines of code like an endless blank-verse poem, the other a screen-saver slide show of children—Cady's, he guessed; the boy who'd just faded in and out looked exactly like him. A flat-screen television on the far wall showed five commentators above a ticker silently streaming news, everyone in the world living life through avatars, in simulacra, in worlds within worlds . . .

"For what it's worth," Cady said, "they didn't seem like they had problems. At least none beyond Alice's health."

"Why do you say that?"

"Alice struggled with her weight for years. And then she finally got it under control. But none of this matters," Cady said. "There's no way David killed his wife."

"Was there anyone here Pepin was close with?"

"Look, Detective, a guy's wife kills herself. He sees the whole thing. Why drag him through the mud?"

"I can ask around if you prefer."

Cady shook his head. His e-mail pinged. "There's Georgine," he said, "Georgine Darcy. She's a junior designer. She and David were working on some major projects together."

Hastroll could tell at first glance that Darcy had been a ballet dancer simply by how she walked with her feet turned out. She was blond, full-lipped, a poor man's Scarlett Johansson, although there was a bubble of loneliness around her, a remoteness that preceded her as she approached. He made a mental to note to get the neighbor, Rand Harper, to ID her.

"Miss Darcy?"

When Hastroll showed her his badge, all the color left her face.

"Let me see if there's a conference room available," she said, then led him down the hallway with her eyes to the ground. "We'll be private here." She turned on the light and closed the door behind her, sat down, crossed her arms over her chest, and watched as Hastroll pulled up a chair. He placed his notepad on the table and stared at her until she lowered her eyes.

"This is about David, isn't it?"

"Mr. Cady tells me that you and Mr. Pepin worked together regularly."

"We were developing several games together."

"Would you say that the two of you were close?"

Georgine put a fist to her mouth and cleared her throat. "We were."

Hastroll waited. "Did the relationship—"

"Yes."

"How long did you and Pepin have an affair?"

"About a year," she said. "We broke it off a couple of months ago."

"You both agreed to?"

She looked at Hastroll impassively. "He broke it off."

"Why?"

"He said it confused him."

"How?"

Darcy had to blink once. It was the shock, Hastroll always noticed, of pure honesty. "He was trying to get clear on his feelings for his wife. She left him for a while and then came back, but right before she did he said that so long as the two of us were spending time together, he wouldn't know if it was because of his problems with Alice or because there was really something between us."

"And you agreed with that?"

At this, two discrete tears formed at Georgine's eyes and fell. "I never seem to have a choice in these matters." She pressed her index fingers to the bridge of her nose and wiped her eyes. Then she cleared her throat, the crying over with.

"Did he talk about Alice much?"

"No."

"But he talked about her?"

"Very rarely."

"You said he mentioned 'problems.' How would you characterize their relationship?"

"Honestly?" she asked.

"A woman is dead."

"I think he felt abandoned. It wasn't hard to understand. She changed on him. She'd lost weight, something they'd gone through a million times. She'd lose weight, gain it back, and then feel like shit about herself. And he was always there for her, every time, over and over, but this time she does something radical. She loses weight for good, becomes this completely different person, and what? I think he was worried she was dispensing with him in the process."

"Did he tell you his wife was leaving him?"

"No."

"Did he tell you he *thought* his wife was going to leave him?"

"No. But I knew she was."

"How's that?"

"You'd have to be a woman to understand."

"Educate me."

"We decide things long before we know we've decided. She'd decided, all right, she just hadn't acted."

"That sounds like something all people do."

"Women need to feel safe before they make a move. She sounded to me like someone looking for a place to jump off."

"I must not understand women very well."

"I could've told you that just by looking at you."

Hastroll nodded. On the pad, he wrote, *Hannah.* "Did you tell Pepin this?"

"Did I tell him what?"

"That you thought his wife was leaving him."

"Yes."

"And what did he say?"

"He said I didn't know what I was talking about."

"Did he ever indicate that you two might have a future?"

"He never talked about divorcing Alice, no."

"Did you talk about a future with him?"

"Sometimes."

"Was he receptive?"

She shrugged.

"When Pepin broke things off, how did you take it?"

"I didn't take it well at first."

"Did you try to keep the relationship going?"

"For a short time. But I got the message pretty quick."

"You never harassed him? Never threatened him professionally or personally?"

"No."

"Do you remember the last time you made a private call to Mr. Pepin?"

"I haven't called David in months."

Hastroll got up. "Here's my card. Call me if you think of anything else." He turned to leave.

"Detective," she said.

"Yes?"

"I don't believe he killed her."

"Why is that?"

"Because he loved her," she said. "At least, he loved her more than me."

Hastroll decided he'd been too passive with Hannah. He had to force her hand. He needed a new strategy. He decided to stop feeding her.

"Ward," she said from the bedroom, "what's for dinner?"

"I don't know," he said, his face hidden behind the paper. "I already ate."

"Oh," she said. "Well, that's all right. I'm not really hungry."

Hastroll snapped the paper away from his face, chuckled to himself, and went back to reading.

Later that night, when he got into his bed, he could hear Hannah's stomach rumbling. "You *sound* hungry," he said.

But she didn't answer.

He made her no breakfast the next morning. He poured the milk down the drain, bagged up the eggs, bread, the canned soups and beans and vegetables from the pantry, the crackers, pasta, tomato sauce, and chicken broth—in short, everything they had—and left the garbage bags by the front door to take with him when he left for work. To make sure she couldn't order in, he took all the credit cards and cash from her purse—even her checkbook—and stuffed them in his jacket pocket. When he came to their bedroom to kiss Hannah good-bye, she was frowning, a little perturbed, like someone who couldn't place where she'd left her keys.

"Not a bite?" she said.

His resolve weakened slightly. "I'm sorry," he said, "I'm late. I have to get to the station."

"Oh," she said. "Okay."

He took a final peek in the refrigerator—nothing!—and felt his confidence rise. He was sure this would work! He grabbed the two enormous garbage bags (he felt like the Santa Claus of purloined goods) and left, though all day he wondered what she'd do for sustenance.

"I'm home," he said that night and then stood for a moment in the foyer. When she didn't respond he went straight to her bedroom.

Hannah was watching television. "Have you ever noticed," she said, "how many commercials there are for food? It's amazing: Milk: It does a body good. Cuckoo for Cocoa Puffs. Two whole-beef patties, special sauce, lettuce, cheese, pickles, onions on a sesame seed bun."

"How about that?"

"A1, it's how steak is done."

"Strictly speaking, that's a condiment."

"The incredible, edible egg. Beef: It's what's for dinner. *Yo quiero* Taco Bell."

"There's one right down the street."

"There are even commercials for other things with food in them. Fruit of the Loom. Banana Boat sunscreen. Have you noticed?"

"No," he said.

"Maybe you're not hungry."

"I am now," Hastroll said. His wife's list had weakened him. "You?"

She shrugged.

Hastroll thought her shoulder blades appeared prominent.

"Say," she said.

"What?"

"What's for dinner?"

Hastroll stood up straight and stared out the window. "You're on your own."

"Oh," she said. "Well, how about some water?"

"I'm busy," he said. "Why don't you get up and get it yourself?"

"Oh, well," she said and slumped against the headboard.

Hastroll took himself out for Chinese.

Four days into this new strategy, Hannah's face looked gaunt. Hastroll could see the ribs above her breasts. Seven days, and Hastroll was suffering for her, though he remained determined. He kept close tabs on their garbage for signs of takeout. Zero. She hadn't eaten a thing. He asked the doorman if he'd seen Hannah leave the building. "To be honest," Alan said, "I haven't seen Mrs. Hastroll in so long, I've been wondering if she died." When Hannah said goodnight that night, Hastroll noticed white spittle at the edges of her mouth.

He turned off the bedside lamp and snuck a glance at her in the light from the TV. "What are you watching?" he asked.

"*I Shouldn't Be Alive,*" she said.

On the ninth day, she reached for a book on the bedside table, fainted, and landed on the floor.

Hastroll, terrified, revived her with a few slaps, then put her back into bed. "Hannah?" he said. "Hannah, please say something!"

"Water," she said.

He brought her a glass that she emptied in huge gulps. "Pizza," she said four glasses later.

He ordered a large pie with pepperoni and extra cheese. She ate six slices without pausing, then sat back, wiped the red stain of sauce from the corners of her mouth and, sleepy with so many carbohydrates, lay back and turned on the TV.

"You still don't get it," she said and almost immediately passed out asleep.

"Why, Alice was wonderful with the students," said Jesslyn Fax, fifty-four, an art teacher at Hawthorne Cedar Knolls School for emotionally disturbed and sexually abused teens. "The kids adored her." A small, dumpy woman, Fax wore a brown dress with a white sweater draped over her shoulders. She had hearing aids in both ears and spoke loudly and cheerily—the permanent optimism, Hastroll thought, of the moderately talented. On her classroom walls were prints of Van Gogh's *Starry Night,* Picasso's *Guernica,* some Monet and Manet, Rothko and Rembrandt, Munch and Mondrian, an Escher or two, all the posters sharing space with charcoals by students, still lifes of fruit and self-portraits, all of them mediocre to bad, the interspersed classics grim reminders of everything the children's works were not and never would be. There were rows of easels stacked in a corner and barnacled with oil paint, and a large, abstract clay sculpture in the corner of the classroom. "We had a memorial service for her in the gymnasium to help the kids cope with the loss, and Benny Bartlett—you see that dark-haired boy out there?"

Hastroll looked. Bartlett, a heavy-set kid no more than fourteen, was playing basketball with another kid on the court outside. The net on the hoop was made of chain link.

"Why, he spoke about her just beautifully at the service," she said. "He told everyone the story of how Ms. Pepin taught him how to tell time on a regular clock."

Hastroll watched the boy for a moment. His own father, a fat, unathletic man, had never played sports with him, and he'd always vowed that when he had a child, he'd be sure to. "Why's Benny at school here?" Hastroll asked.

"Oh, he's terribly sick. He's been badly abused all his life. His uncle molested him for years. His mother's a crack addict. His father got addicted to meth and flew the coop when he was three. The boy has a third-grader's IQ. And he raped his sister."

"I see."

"But he's very sweet. That other young man out there, the handsome one, Ralph Smiley?"

He turned to look again. Smiley stole the ball from Bartlett, then stepped to the top of the key, turned around, and shot a basket.

"He was very close to Alice too. She helped him do a very ambitious social studies project on Australia's Great Barrier Reef. You should ask him about that."

"Why's Ralph at the school?"

"Since he was a little boy he's demonstrated sociopathic tendencies. He's killed a number of cats and dogs in his neighborhood, cut them up into little pieces, and buried the body parts everywhere. Plus he's a self-flagellator. At any opportunity he takes a razor to his arms and genitals, the poor dear. He's got stacked rows of keloid scars from his biceps to his wrists. That's why he's wearing long sleeves. And his poor little penis looks like the Michelin Man."

"What subjects did Alice teach here?"

"She taught GED, mostly, and social studies, though her main area of expertise was math."

"Did you ever meet her husband?"

"David? Such a nice man."

"Did she ever talk about any marital problems they might've had?"

"Not at all."

"Did she seem depressed in the weeks leading up to her death?"

"Depressed?"

"Withdrawn," Hastroll said. "Antisocial."

"She seemed quite exuberant. She'd lost over a hundred and fifty pounds this past year."

"Thank you, Ms. Fax." Hastroll stopped at the door. "If you don't mind my asking, who did that sculpture in the corner?"

Fax turned to look at it. It was three small spheres contained within the gaping hole of a larger one. It loomed. It gave off a hum. It was the only piece in the room that showed any talent.

"Why, Alice did," Fax said. She covered her mouth and began to cry. "It's called *Hunger*."

He went to Alice's former classroom. Her weight chart was pinned to the wall, off to the left of the blackboard, a week-to-week bar graph chronicling the whole year, the red construction paper bars marking her progress and climbing steadily like stairs (YOU CAN ACCOMPLISH ANYTHING! it read at the top), one pound lost one week, nine the next, then five, then four. Remarkable. In the drawer of her desk was a picture of the Pepins hugging on a park bench, Alice obese, the couple obviously in love, but the glass shattered in the center as if by a fist. Hastroll picked it up and looked at it, then rummaged around a little.

"Trouble," someone said.

He looked up. A woman in a nurse's uniform stood at the classroom door.

"I got a nose for it. I can smell it right here in this room."

"Who are you?" Hastroll said.

"Who are *you*?"

He flashed his badge.

"Nurse Ritter," she said. "I care for the kids here at the school. That is, of course, if you think medicating monsters is care."

"Did you know Ms. Pepin?"

"Not well," she said. "But well enough to tell you that girl didn't commit suicide." Ritter closed the door and sat down.

Hastroll had to get Hannah out of that room. There had to be a way. If he could lure her out, he decided, he'd rush past her, and lock the door. He tossed ideas around. He thought of releasing a bottle of moths into the room—she hated flapping things, pigeons, moths, bats—but where did you get such a swarm?

He decided to get rid of all their furniture. Not sell it. Literally give it away. Year after year, Hannah had carefully picked each new piece they'd bought. "Better to spend extra and buy something you keep for life," she'd always said, "than spend a little less and see it out on the street in five years." (Oh, his practical little wife!) They had many pieces that were of great sentimental value to her. She'd be forced to get out of bed and stop him! He called the Salvation Army. "I have an offer you can't refuse," he said. They refused. Or, more accurately, they couldn't get by his apartment for over a week, and another week of Hannah in bed seemed to him like an eternity. "Fine," he said. "I'll give it to someone else then!" He called the Association for Retarded Citizens. A person who *sounded* retarded answered the phone. "I want to get rid of all my furniture," Hastroll said.

"Okay," the person said. "Where do you live?"

"Greenwich Village," Hastroll said.

"I'm sorry," he said, "but we don't go to Connecticut," then hung up.

"Who are you on the phone with?" Hannah said from the bedroom.

"No one!" Hastroll yelled.

"Jeez Louise," Hannah said, "somebody's in a bad mood."

He called Finders Keepers, a consignment store, but when he listed everything he had—a sofa, an easy chair, a television set, a stereo, silverware, stemware, flatware, pots and pans, four lamps, a coffeemaker, a chandelier, a desk, a dining room set, a buffet, books, a machete and a saw, not a single piece in poor condition "and all of it," Hastroll explained loudly, "of exceptional quality"—they said they were sorry, they were stocked up on all those items. He called the homeless shelters and the Boys & Girls Club of America, but they didn't need his stuff. He called Goodwill, but they didn't do pickups. Finally, out of desperation, he drove to Alphabet City, went up to the first two suspicious-looking thugs he could find, arrested them, and hustled them into his car, gently pressing their heads down as they got in. He explained the situation—"You will take all of my furniture, and I'll pay for the transportation"—and brought them back to his apartment.

The men, Roscoe and Lee Browne, stepped inside and looked around. "Shoo," Roscoe said.

"Shoo what?"

"This is a setup is what this is," the man said.

"This is way too good to be true," said Browne.

"This isn't a setup," Hastroll said. "It isn't too good to be true. This is charity."

"Maybe we don't need no charity," said Roscoe.

"This is charity for me."

The two men looked at each other, shook their heads pityingly, and both went, "Tssss."

"Maybe we don't like your shit," Browne finally said.

"Please," Hastroll said, "take it. I'm begging you. Or you're under arrest."

They began to carry the furniture out the door.

"What's going on out there?" Hannah said.

"Nothing," Hastroll said. "I'm just giving our furniture away."

"Oh," Hannah said.

"That's right," Hastroll said. "It's out of here!"

"All of it?"

"Yes."

"Come on, Ward," she said. "You're kidding."

"See for yourself."

In the pause that followed, he rushed to the bedroom door, ready to pounce.

"No," she said. "I believe you."

Roscoe dropped her favorite lamp, and it shattered. Browne took down the picture she'd painted of Hastroll's rose garden and dropped that too, the frame falling apart.

"It sounds like they're really working hard," she said.

"You can't believe it," Hastroll said. "They're like a pair of thieves."

"I can hear all that space," she said. "It almost sounds like a cave in there."

"It's like being in an empty stadium."

"It must be like when we were a young couple."

"Back when we were broke."

"Like when we had nothing," she said.

"Right, when we first got married."

"You had a futon," Hannah said. "And you drank out of empty yogurt containers."

Hastroll smiled, pressing his palm to the door. "That's right."

"But you kept your bathroom so *clean*."

"Come on out and feast your eyes. It's a trip down memory lane!"

The bed creaked, and Hastroll's heart jumped. Then silence.

"Did they take the love seat?" Hannah said finally.

"They did."

"What about the dining room table?"

Hastroll winced as the men dinged the jamb with one of the legs.

"It's gone."

"Does the place seem roomier now?"

"You've got to see it to believe it."

Hastroll, thinking he heard her move, rushed to the door again.

"No," she said. "I think I'll stay where I am."

Hastroll rested his forehead against the door.

After a minute, she said, "Ward?"

"What?"

"Thanks," she said.

"For what?"

"For getting rid of all that stuff."

"Why are you thanking me?"

"Because now I won't have to clean it."

He gave the men forty bucks each and made them bring everything back upstairs.

"Something suspicious happened," Nurse Ritter had told Hastroll, "on the day Alice died."

Ritter was a tough little cookie, a Brooklyn girl like Georgine Darcy and proud of it. Her father was a fullback for the New York Giants, she'd told him, and though she was diminutive she possessed the same bluntness necessary to knock things out of her path.

"David, her husband," she said, "he shows up here at school, out of the blue, all sweaty and stressed. Agitated. Says he's got to talk with her. As in right now. You're wondering why I know this. Well," she said, "my office, it's right next door to Alice's classroom. Anyway, they have this big fight—like a pair of pit bulls ripping each other's throats out in some tenement basement in the Bronx."

"You're saying things turned violent?"

"No, it's just a figure of speech. But he grabbed her arm."

"Could you hear what were they saying?"

"So far as I could tell, they were fighting about a vacation."

"Do you remember what they said?"

"I remember it like I remember the first thing my husband said to me on our wedding night after we made love for the very first time."

"Go on," Hastroll said.

"He said, 'Christ, Thelma, I thought you was a virgin.' "

"I meant the Pepins."

"Oh," she said. "Something about leaving for Australia that night, dropping everything else. They didn't even need to pack, he says, which is crazy, she says. But then while they're arguing, I start thinking to myself. Why does a husband all of a sudden show up and demand his wife go somewhere with him? Because he's up to no *good*, I says. *Running* from something."

Hastroll paused to clean his glasses. "What happened after their argument?"

"Alice just stormed outside. David, he went and sat in his car like he was staking her out. But then he got a call on his phone and was all upset again."

"Upset how?"

"Jumpy. Fidgety. Like one of those towel-head kiosk owners when you look at their magazines."

"And then?"

"The kids, they was loading up the buses for a school trip Alice was taking them on. She boards the bus, and then he follows right behind in their car. And the next day, what do I hear"—her voice cracked—"but that she's dead."

She shook her head. "Trouble," she said, blowing into a tissue. "I got a nose for it."

Hastroll hadn't had sex with his wife in five months.

True, there had been periods when he and Hannah had lived together like a pair of monks, but this current streak broke all records. A powerful horniness had come over him. For a while he sustained himself on a steady diet of masturbation, shocking himself by how proficient and stealthy he'd become. He beat off in the shower, using Hannah's expensive conditioner for lubrication. He ejaculated into the toilet, after which he took a long, constricted, slightly sore pee. He jerked off in bed, within seconds after Hannah fell asleep, shorts down and knees up, legs forming what he liked to call his little tent of pleasure. Oddly, his panopticon of playthings never included Hollywood stars—who were they to an unglamorous detective?—but were always centered on women he knew. Recently, he'd spent much of his fantasy life screwing Georgine Darcy to tears. His questioning of her had formed the concrete basis of his fantasies and in his favorite one he came home to find her in his apartment. The bitch was robbing them, stealing Hannah's jewelry, and he discovered her as she was trying to beat a retreat.

"What are you doing here?" he said.

"Why, Detective Hastroll," she said. "I was in the neighborhood and thought I'd stop by to tell you something suspicious I'd rememered about David, and the door was open, so I came in and saw your wife's jewelry and just had to try it on, but I guess I'll be going."

He grabbed her by her wrist and threw her down on the couch. "You're not going anywhere!"

She tried to get up and they wrestled, but he threw her down on the couch again, immediately growing an erection Georgine noticed, putting the back of her hand to her forehead and staring at Hastroll's prodigious lump. "Help!" she whispered, and kicked off her shoes. "Help, police!" He lifted up the skirt of her dress and saw—my god!—that she had garters on but no underwear. Her bush was narrow and perfectly trimmed, a strip of yellow mink as blond as a towheaded child's hair.

"Police!" she screamed as he entered her. "Police!"

"Ward?" Hannah said from the bedroom. "Are you all right?"

The sound of his wife's voice was magic. It could arouse him to steel-stiffness or wilt him like a dog told to play dead.

"I'm fine!" he called, fumbling with his drawers, knocking the Kleenex box to the floor while flushing.

He'd assumed, given Hannah's current situation, that she couldn't have cared less about what he did with Mr. Penis. But one night, five months into her self-imposed sentence, she rolled over and said, "Ward, are you awake?"

"Yes," he said. He'd been thinking about the Pepin case.

They both waited. Her bed was by the window, but even with the blinds down he could make out the outline of her form. She lay on her back and moaned invitingly. Then she ran her hands over the silk of her slip, her nipples rising visibly, and she pressed a finger down into the place Hastroll had nearly forgotten. In the darkness, her form was like a silhouette of a gorgeous woman's body from the title credits of a Bond flick.

"Love me!" she moaned lustily. "Oh, Ward! Love me now!"

He jumped out of his pajama pants so acrobatically it was like a stunt from Cirque du Soleil. But when he went to remove her slip, she said, "Leave it!" which turned him on even more. He buried his face into Hannah's cunt like a wanderer who'd found water in the desert. She tasted like a hot biscuit flavored with pee. She grabbed his scruff and pulled his face to hers. They kissed, and she took his cock—it felt as thick as a Louisville Slugger—and guided him in. When he exploded—and he exploded quickly—he felt as if his heart had liquefied and then been shot out of him up through her vagina and uterus and her ovaries and up over her diaphragm and somehow down the vena cavity to her heart, his own now coating hers.

"Hannah," he moaned, "I love you. Please, I'll do anything. I'll be better. Just tell me what you want."

"Oh, Ward," she moaned softly. "You still don't get it." She waited for him to roll off her.

Detective William Stacy said, "I got something you might want to see."

Hastroll swiveled to face Stacy's desk, by which his partner, Eddie Parker, was standing.

"That Pepin character," Stacy said. "We heard you and Sheppard were investigating his wife's suicide. Little over a month ago we got a call to come to his apartment. He'd been burglarized." He tossed Hastroll the file. "Except nothing in the apartment was stolen," he said.

Hastroll read through the report.

"It had all the earmarks of a staged burglary," Stacy said. "Kind you see when a husband wants to make it look like bad guys came and robbed him before they killed his wife. A setup, but with no crime. Place was turned over—"

"But it was like was vandalism or something," Parker added.

"There were blank checks lying on the desk," Stacy said. "Wife's jewelry sitting on the dresser. Valuables. *All* there. We checked the bathroom for pharmaceuticals. Lady had a whole jar of Percocet plus loads of antidepressants. All there too."

"How did they seem?" Hastroll asked. "I mean she and her husband."

"About the break-in? Upset, of course," Parker said.

"Actually," Stacy said, "he was taking it harder than her."

"Whole thing seemed to have scared the bejesus out of him."

Hastroll considered this. "Anything else?"

"Yeah. The burglar must've been a real sicko, 'cause he jerked off in their toilet."

Hastroll looked from Stacy to Parker. "Did you get a sample?"

"Hey, we're not that dedicated."

He and Parker laughed, and Hastroll swiveled around.

"You're welcome," Stacy said.

Hastroll took off his glasses and rubbed his eyes. This Pepin character was guilty, guilty, guilty . . . but the puzzle was all in pieces. He thought for a moment, shaking his head, then he looked at his watch. It was nearly lunchtime.

He picked up the phone and called Hannah, and after ten rings realized this was his chance. He was out the door in a flash, and even put his strobe on the top of his car as he raced downtown. He imagined himself storming into the apartment and surprising her—why had this never occurred to him?—but then he had another idea.

Their apartment was on West Ninth, but he parked on Eighth and entered the building directly behind his. He jimmied the lock downstairs and walked up one flight, did a little guesstimation about which apartment was the right one, knocked, then pressed the badge to the peephole. A nurse let him into the apartment. She was Jamaican, dressed in white, and was just serving lunch to an old man in a wheelchair. He wore blue pajamas and sat with his head hung between his shoulders, tortoiselike, his bald head, wrinkled neck, and mottled skin adding to his reptilian appearance, the puffed, crescent pillows beneath his eyes pulling down his lower lids so they seemed red-rimmed, as if he'd been crying. His chair faced toward the window that looked out onto the courtyard.

Hastroll walked over to stand beside him. He could see Hannah lying in bed, eating the lunch he'd prepared for her. A songbird was singing. For a moment, he wasn't sure even of what day it was.

"Is there a problem, Detective?"

"That woman," Hastroll said, pointing across the courtyard, "she might be in danger."

"Oh, no," the nurse said. "What kind?"

"I'm not at liberty to say."

She clucked her tongue.

"Do you ever see her get up?" Hastroll asked. "Ever see her walk around?"

"Never," she said. "She's sick, I think."

"You ever see anything suspicious?"

"No. All I see is her husband occasionally."

"Notice anything strange about him?" Hastroll wondered if she might've recognized him, but it didn't seem so.

She shook her head. "He brings her meals every day."

"Do they seem like they love each other?" he asked.

This made the woman laugh.

"Oh come on, now, Detective, what kind of person could tell that from here?"

Detective Sheppard wanted a full report on the Pepin case.

Fastidious, arrogant, and hyperroutinized—put bluntly, a control freak—his partner gave Hastroll the creeps. Plus his voice was grating. It was high-pitched and nasal, incongruous for such a large, athletic-looking man. And when dealing with cases that involved the murder of a spouse, it made Hastroll doubly uncomfortable to talk specifics.

"Ward."

"Sam."

Hastroll sat across from Sheppard. Next to the man's pipe caddy was a picture of his wife, Marilyn. If it happened that Hannah died, Hastroll wondered, would he still keep pictures of her around?

"Where are we?" Sheppard asked.

He told Sheppard about Pepin's adulterous relationship with Georgine Darcy. He was looking into it further, but it now seemed the affair was over long before Alice's death and had to be ruled out as a motive. He described the lab report from forensics analyzing the samples taken from under Pepin's fingernails. There were traces of nutmeat under the nails on the ring and index fingers *only,* and the bite marks on the top and bottom of each digit matched those of his wife, either corroborating the story that he'd tried to clear her airway or confirming that he'd shoved the nuts down her throat before she'd bitten down. She'd broken a tooth on Pepin's finger, her right upper incisor, though the odontologists they'd consulted were at odds as to the cause: Dr. Wendell Corey thought the fracture was from blunt-force trauma—from a hand forced down the victim's throat—while the other, Dr. Iphigenie Castiglioni, saw the wrenching force of the husband's extricating his two fingers. Traces of salt and saliva on the palms of Alice's hands supported the suicide claim; also, her fingerprints were on the plate itself while Pepin's were absent. He told Sheppard that according to Alice's psychiatrist, Dr. Fred Graham, she had a long history of depression, but during their last session four weeks before her death, she'd been happier and more stable than he'd ever seen her, which he'd attributed to her tremendous weight loss and concomitant gain in self-esteem, though she had, Hastroll noted, refilled her prescriptions afterward. Hastroll also reported that he was going over security tapes from cameras on the Henry Hudson Parkway, the West Side Highway, and the Museum of Natural History. He told Sheppard that the couple's financials showed that in addition to their joint account, they'd secretly opened accounts in different banks, that both had rented personal PO addresses to which statements from their credit cards and checking accounts were sent, but that none of the charges on these cards seemed out of the ordinary. Alice had used hers to pay for therapy visits, medical co-pays, and prescriptions related to her diet, for workout clothes, a gym membership, and new clothing. Pepin, meanwhile, used his for costs related to his ongoing affair—hotels and gifts and the occasional sex toy. In short, the couple seemed like most married couples they'd investigated, perpetuating their relationship through games of low-grade deception, living a life of pure ambivalence, looking to all outside observers relatively happy. Pepin himself would realize no significant financial gain from his wife's death—nor did he need it, he was such a successful game designer—so money had to be ruled out as a motive. Interestingly—Hastroll had discovered this after following up with Pepin's next-door neighbors as well as the administration of Alice's school—she'd just returned from a yearlong leave of absence from her job, during which she'd embarked on what appeared to be a nine-month trip around the world; she'd flown out of La Guardia on 13 September, bound for London, returning via Melbourne, Australia, on 13 June. She'd reconciled with her husband, living with him for two months, with indications of marital strife but nothing to suggest what had ultimately occurred.

What they had before them, Hastroll said, was one of those rare and horrible cases between husband and wife—an eruption of real or emotional violence during a moment of terrible privacy—the evidence as mysterious and impenetrable as a wormhole, only the survivor knowing the truth. He didn't look at Sheppard when he said this.

Still, there were two nagging clues. The first was the staged burglary, which Hastroll couldn't make heads or tails of. Second: Pepin had received multiple calls on his cell phone over the period of weeks leading up to Alice's death that Hastroll had traced to a pay phone in the Time Warner building off Columbus Circle. Pepin's neighbor, Rand Harper, had witnessed the last call Pepin had received from this number—there was apparently a heated exchange—and the next day Alice was dead.

Sometimes, Hastroll found himself growing accustomed to this new arrangement with Hannah. It was like the perfect marriage, at least from a man's point of view. He woke up in the mornings in his bed next to hers, usually a few minutes before she did, then went to the kitchen and made them coffee. Since her self-imposed sentence, she'd started taking milk and sugar in it, and over five months Hastroll had noticed the level of the white granules sink like sands through an hourglass and imagined all that sweetness flowing through his wife's body. He'd bring her the mug and wait for her to sit up and arrange her pillows, just like she used to when she didn't live in bed, and they'd lay in their separate beds and talk for a while, and after an unspecified amount of time that depended on his day ahead, he'd excuse himself to shower. And instead of the hustle and bustle of their mornings before Hannah's domestic incarceration—vying for time on the toilet and space before the mirror to shave or pluck eyebrows—Hastroll had the shower to himself, could mess up the sink, beat off, if he felt like it, and take as long and satisfying a dump as he cared to. Before he left for the station, he'd kiss Hannah on the forehead, bring her some breakfast and a pitcher of water and a ham and cheese sandwich for later. Then he'd leave for work. And when he came home, there she'd be with the TV on, her sandwich eaten, the water pitcher half-empty, the plates on the floor, Hannah still in bed.

He grew accustomed. And in fact there were many good things about the arrangement. Even Hannah would admit she had odd rules about things, certain kinds of personal limits that for years Hastroll had unconsciously worked around. Hannah needed her sleep—eight solid hours—and she protected it fiercely, was in a bad, bad way if it was interfered with; if she stayed up too late the deprivation wrote a check that irritability cashed the next day. So he took advantage and went to late showings of first-run films; Hannah only liked weekend matinees and insisted on pictures that weren't violent.

Now Hastroll saw *everything* and felt the satisfaction of having seen *all* the films on his list and a bevy of independents and even a few remastered classics to boot, so for the first time in his life he felt culturally up to speed. And if perchance at the bar of the Soho Grand, where he made it a habit to have a cocktail after these dates with himself, a lovely young woman happened to engage him in conversation (such as Irene Winston, the cocktail waitress there, who was herself a shapelier, sexier double of Hannah from before Hannah-in-bed), he would be able to speak her language, for movies were the lingua franca of the young. And if after their talk she offered to, say, take the place of his wife, letting him ravish her at least, or after some time together suggest that he maybe kill his wife in a way that would cause him no guilt (impossible, of course) and then start life all over again, he might consider that too . . . that is, if his feelings for other women weren't so obviously entangled with his feelings for Hannah. Therefore his infidelities, imagined as opposed to real, were really a guilty brand of ménage à trois, sins of omission rather than commission, not to mention that Hastroll wouldn't start this affair unless he knew for *sure* (via a written, preaffair guarantee) that this younger, sexier, and shapelier version of Hannah would never go to bed as Hannah had (also, of course, impossible). Besides, all this was irrelevant, since every one of these fantasies was predicated on his getting up the nerve to talk with the other Hannah first—which he never did.

He grew accustomed. Hannah, usually a very finicky eater, ate whatever he made her, even broccoli, which she loathed but he loved, as it was loaded with antioxidants. Ditto wheat germ, which she'd resisted putting on her yogurt or cereal in the past, despite his pointing out that it was full of folic acid and helped prevent deformities in infants, should they ever decide to have any. "Children?" Hannah had said. "Hah!" But now, like a good girl, she ate every last bite.

He grew accustomed. He had total control of the television when he came home. So if she might say, "Ward, could I have the remote, please?" and then, when he held it out, "I can't reach it," he'd shrug and keep watching the Tennis Channel.

He grew accustomed. He didn't have to dust the baseboards or vacuum behind the sofa. If the spirit moved him, he could piss in the shower or with the toilet seat down, which he often did. He could load the dishwasher with a few plates and cups and run it anyway. He could mix colors with whites. He could buy a dog, a cat, a parrot, a parakeet, a fish. An aquarium with snakes. Gerbils, hamsters, or mice. Once he got bored with the rodents, he'd feed them to the snakes. And if he didn't like the snakes, he'd let them go free and turn into giants in New York's sewers. He could turn their apartment into Noah's ark. What the fuck was Hannah going to say? She was in bed, where what she didn't know wouldn't hurt her. But he did nothing. He reveled *only* in his freedom. In bed, she was his sick sister/mother who'd taken the place of his wife.

He grew accustomed. In fact he enjoyed how routine their sex life had become. It was sex without expectation of mutuality, sex just for him; hooker sex. He liked to get into her bed after she'd been sleeping for a while. He liked it especially after she'd been drinking. While it was perverted—sick, in fact—when she was deep into REM, drunk on dreams and wine, he began to feel her breasts. She mumbled his name or, sometimes, someone else's, and odd things rooted in memories and phantasmagoria. She moaned as he felt her up, though she might have moaned anyway. He took off his pajama bottoms and put her hand on Mr. Penis, which she stroked attentively, automatically, like an infant when a nipple's placed in its mouth. He spread her legs, put his hands on her ass, stretched her wide—she was always perfectly wet—and humped his half-asleep wife to his satisfaction. And after he came, she sometimes continued to mumble her gibberish; other times, her dreams only briefly interrupted, she went right back to sleep as if nothing had happened. Occasionally she woke demanding more, to which he'd say, "Go to sleep," and she would. Or she'd simply seem confused. "Did we have sex last night?" she asked the next morning, more than once. He'd either tell the truth and say yes or lie and say no, just to test if she'd been awake. And if he'd had a lot to drink too, he'd say he couldn't remember either, which was often the truth as well.

He did what he wanted. If he needed time out of the apartment, he went down to the courtyard and tended to his roses. He kept a bed of them long and wide enough to bury a couple of people laid head to foot. It was therapeutic to fertilize, prune, and spray them and then be rewarded for his fidelity with such vivid color, such erect beauty. Sometimes, when he brought the cuttings up, he'd place a particularly beautiful flower on Hannah's breakfast or dinner tray. But this of all things seemed to enrage her the most, and she'd throw the flower at him, cursing him with all her might—another thing he liked about the new arrangement. Because when she yelled at him her words somehow lost their sting—an invalid's complaint, since she wouldn't get up—and he'd simply turn, walk out of the room, and close the door.

He missed her when he was out in the world, true, remembering how she once took his hand or arm without asking, or slid up behind him and held him around his waist, or whispered in his ear things they might do later, but now he always knew where she was, at home and in bed. Yet after the "I'm home" and the dinner making, the eating and the "How was it?," the dishes, the trip to the freezer, and the sound of whiskey tinkling over the ice cubes, a longing sometimes came over him as he sat there in his favorite chair, a longing for Hannah that he didn't completely understand, a longing not just for the woman he'd married but also for a time when the present didn't press down on him, hunching his shoulders and tightening his back. A longing, he surmised, for youth, though it was more complex than that and involved a state of mind he could no longer remember—an Alzheimer's longing, disorienting, ephemeral, irretrievable. The feeling, as when someone bumped into you in a packed subway car, was completely new, unexpected, and uniquely terrible.

It was a longing for what it felt like when they'd first fallen in love. Is this, he wondered, what it means to grow old together?

There was only one problem he had with their arrangement now that he'd grown accustomed to it. He couldn't remember what their life was like before, no matter how hard he tried, his memory always coming up short. He could recall doing things together, but it was as if they'd happened to characters in a film watched with the sound off or to shadow-figures in someone else's dream. He *did* remember the long drive from New York to Knoxville to meet her family—a straight shot of twelve hours—but nothing about how he'd felt about her then or anything they'd said to each other during the trip; forgot how it was that watching her mouth move excited him. He *did* remember their honeymoon on Kiawah Island, how they'd walked hand in hand for hours on those beaches so wide and flat, her palm always remaining dry in his. He recalled the strange sense of romance he'd felt gazing at the wide-armed shrimp boats trolling offshore, how he and Hannah had talked of buying one and making what seemed like the perfect life together. But he could *not* remember what *she'd* felt at these moments, though he was certain she'd told him, nor what making love felt like then, when her body was so precious and new, though he knew that it once was.

He'd struggled, recently, to remember anything she'd ever said.

How did people erase themselves like this? he wondered.

There was only Hannah in bed.

Hannah in bed.

Hannah.

Say her name once, say it over and over again, say it in reverse, and the effect was always the same. At first it was her name and then it was like a heartbeat and then, like a heartbeat, it was something you couldn't hear.

Self-canceling, it was hide-in-plain-sight magic. She had managed to make their life together disappear.

Out of the blue, Hastroll got a call from Georgine Darcy.

"I'd like to talk with you in private if you don't mind."

"Meet me in the bar of the Soho Grand."

They sat together in one of the booths, which were dark, enclosed, and felt safe. Darcy ordered a martini, drank it, then ordered another. While she waited for it, she lit a cigarette with shaking hands—"Arrest me," she said—and when she tapped off the ash it was as if she were knocking fruit off a branch.

"I always pick the worst men," she said. "If I had a sense of humor about it, I'd say it was a talent. But it's not. It's something in me. Like I emit a frequency only certain breeds of boys come running to. And what's insane about it is that no matter how many times I tell myself to look for certain kinds of things in a man, the opposite things, it doesn't change anything. The ones who love me I find repulsive. The ones I can't live without don't love me back."

Hastroll continued to wait.

Finally, she said, "Can you explain that, detective? I'd think in your line of work you'd have some insight."

He looked at his large hands folded on the table, hardly considering himself an articulate witness. "The heart," he said, "is half criminal. The trick is to be vigilant. To keep your eyes open, so if you get a look at this side of yourself you can make a positive ID."

Darcy lit another cigarette. "What do you do after that?"

Hastroll shrugged. "You turn yourself in." He looked at his watch. "You have something to tell me, Miss Darcy?"

"I wanted to give you this," she said, sliding an envelope that was several inches thick across the table. "I thought you'd want to have a look."

Using his switchblade, Hastroll cut the envelope open, then pulled out a stack of pages.

"It's David's book. He gave it to me to read before he broke things off. Needless to say, it wasn't high on my priority list afterward. But last week, out of the blue, he calls me and asks for it back, so I got curious," she said. "The first lines were what grabbed me."

When David Pepin first dreamed of killing his wife, he didn't kill her himself. He dreamed convenient acts of God.

. . .

Things finally came to a head between Ward and Hannah.

Usually, he came straight home from work, but it was Friday night, it had been a long week, and he wanted to *do* something. He'd seen all the movies, so that was out. He considered going to hear some music, but he'd always preferred the idea of this to actually doing it. He thought it might be fun to have dinner with friends, but he and Hannah didn't have any; even if they did, how could he explain her absence? Frustrated, he took himself to the bar at the Soho Grand and sat there with other men without women—a whole roomful of them—and for a moment he wondered if their wives had gone to bed too.

Hastroll had four drinks and headed home.

Hannah had gone to bed in May and now it was September and he couldn't help but notice that in the fall, once the weather has changed, the lights of the city seem to shine brighter than at any other time of year, that on these cold, clear nights, everything seemed honed to a vorpal sharpness, and what in God's name was the point of them continuing like this?

He searched his heart and mind for the reason behind Hannah's self-internment but like every other time came up empty. Then suddenly something occurred to him: the way to get her out of bed. The one thing he hadn't tried was to simply ask her.

True, he'd pleaded with her a great many times, though never per se to get out of bed. This time, he promised himself, it would be different. He'd use an amazing trick he'd discovered when they fought, a unique development he guessed happened only to people who'd been together long enough to know each other's complaints by rote. One night, after several years of marriage, when an argument began to escalate, he'd said to her, "Stop. I love you, Hannah. Let's just step out of the ring!" And miraculously they did stop, and then embraced. They ventured on as if the fight was nothing more than a speed bump in an otherwise smooth evening. All was forgotten. Game over. Reset.

Love.

He was buzzed now—drunk, to be honest—but believed with total conviction that if he were to walk into Hannah's room with enough positive energy and encouragement and say, "Hannah, come on, up up up! I've got champagne and cheese and crackers. Let's have ourselves a snack, then you can get yourself ready and we'll go out!" she'd just climb out of bed. She would respond to his enthusiasm like someone suffering aphasia, not to what he said but to his happy face. She'd be out of bed before she knew it. The key here was the element of surprise. He'd barrel her over with excitement. So sure was Hastroll of this plan that he stopped at the liquor store and then the market and splurged on a bottle of Dom and a round of brie (Hannah's favorite) and a box of Carr's crackers. He would, in the words of some of the hoods he arrested, do things up right.

All the lights were off when he got home.

This threw him, to be sure, but he strode undaunted through the living room, where the blinds were drawn, Helen Kellered himself around the furniture, then came to and opened the bedroom door. Inside, he could make out his wife's form divided into stripes of glare through the venetian blinds, sitting in bed with her arms crossed.

"Hannah, come on," he said, "up up up!" and when he snapped the light switch, nothing happened. The bulb was dead.

"It doesn't work," she said.

It was like she'd punched him in the stomach.

"The TV's dead too." She pressed the remote quick, three times, in demonstration. "I thought the power might be out, but I can hear our neighbor's TV upstairs."

The paper bag in his hand felt like it weighed two hundred pounds. He put it down.

"I even changed the remote's batteries." She opened the bedside-table drawer, which she always kept full of Duracells. "I guess I watched it too much."

Hastroll slumped onto his bed.

"I watched so much TV I killed it," she said sadly.

He heaved an enormous sigh.

"What's in the bag?" she said.

"Champagne," he said. "Brie." He had to look inside to remind himself. "Crackers."

"Oh," she said.

"Want some?"

She peered into the darkness, then sat back again. "No," she said. "No, I don't think so."

"I thought . . ." he said. But then he scratched his head, which felt so heavy he let his chin drop to his chest. "I thought," he said to his legs, "if I came in here with some champagne and appetizers and enthusiasm that you might get up and go out with me."

"Out?" she said and laughed. "Out as in where?"

"Out," he said, "as in the world. But just the living room would be fine."

"Oh," she said as he watched her ghostly form smooth the sheets. "No thanks."

"Why?" he said, and looked up.

She shrugged her shoulders, held them there, then let them fall.

"That's not good enough," he said.

She did it again like a child.

Hastroll stood up and put his hands on his knees so they were eye to eye. "That's *not* good enough."

She grimaced in pantomime. "Sorry," she said.

He saw his fist hit her square in the mouth but restrained himself. "*That's not good enough!*"

She stopped looking at him and mutely stared out the window with her arms crossed.

"Did you hear me?"

She didn't move.

"Is that how it's going to be now? You're not going to talk to me either?"

She didn't speak.

"You . . . fucking . . . bitch!" he said.

He grabbed the grocery bag and walked out of the room and slammed the door so hard it seemed the whole apartment rattled. "Fucking *bitch*!" he called. "You hear me? Fucking bedridden, childish *bitch*!" He turned on all the lights and pulled up the shades. "Bitch in the *dark*!" He went to the kitchen and took down their two Waterford champagne glasses, the pair her parents had given them as a wedding present, took the flute he imagined was Hannah's and pitched it with all his might to the floor, where it disintegrated on impact. "Broken-*glass,* bedsore-*ass* bitch!" He popped the Dom, drank the overflow, poured himself a glass, and downed it. Poured another, downed that too. "Cham*pagne*-in-my-ass bitch!" He removed the Brie from its box and took a bite out of the wheel, rind and all, then laid out five Carr's crackers on the counter and smashed them in pistonlike succession, one for each month, shouting, "Bitch, bitch, bitch, bitch, bitch!"

He drank the Dom like soda, then smashed the empty bottle in the sink, and began a conversation with his wife.

Though it was at once with her and with himself, the kind of conversation you have if you've been driving alone for a very long time, a thinking aloud that strangely focused one's thinking, the monologue half an act, really, verging on melodrama, and what Hastroll said could've made sense *only* to the two of them. It was almost as if Hastroll was speaking a different language, closer to tongues, one that worked strictly by allusion to their mutual history, that had no more context than an overheard telephone conversation—and a dark, ugly language it was. "But *you* don't plunge, oh no, you say, 'Just let it dissolve.' Have you *ever* seen it dissolve?" And: "You say we need to this and you say we need to that, but *we* means *me* and me needs *we*!" And: "Swallow *my* pride? Did you say swallow? Say again? Oh. *Swallow.* Sorry, I don't know what that *is.*"

Needing a drink, he went to the buffet and poured himself a tall one and sat down in his favorite chair, drinking his drink and thinking that he'd be good and hung over tomorrow, no avoiding that now. He could drink water, take Vitamin C and aspirin, add some Vitamin G, stuff himself with pizza, a burger, or wings and fries—it wouldn't matter. There was no going back once you passed a certain point of drunkenness. Just like murder.

He picked up the phone, dialed the number they'd traced to Pepin's cell and, completely spent, let the pager ring; and when it beeped he dialed in his number and waited for what seemed like an eternity. He put his head back and stared at the ceiling, for so long that he imagined the ceiling was the floor, a perfect floor that had never once been walked on; and he imagined himself moving around the apartment like this, looking down at Hannah sleeping on the ceiling, tapping the salt shaker and letting it sprinkle onto his plate below. Then, to Hastroll's surprise, someone called him back, and he picked up before the second ring. "Who's this?"

"Who's this?" the man said. His voice was high register: evil.

They waited.

"You first," the voice said.

"This is Detective Hastroll."

"Never heard of you."

"Your turn."

"I don't give my name to strangers."

Hastroll heard a foghorn in the background, a siren wailing, a sound of distant thunder—but that was out his window. A storm was moving in.

"Is there something you want?" the voice said.

"Yes."

"What?"

"An admission."

"I'm listening."

"A confession."

"Go on."

"You killed her."

"Who?"

"Alice Pepin. He hired you, didn't he?"

The voice laughed wickedly. "She killed herself," he said finally.

"I don't believe you."

"No blame! It was perfect!"

"Tell me to my face."

"You're a drunken fool."

"I swear I'll track you down!"

"A lonely, blubbery moron."

"Meet me now! I want to see you!"

"Well, well, well," Hannah said.

To Hastroll's amazement, there was Hannah, standing across from him in her slip. The sight of her on her feet was so unbelievable that he heard his mouth drop open with a *click.* She leaned forward slightly, a little wobbly.

But before he could say anything, she laid into him. "Is that your *girl-friend?*" she said.

He gently cradled the phone.

"Someone to keep you occupied? Give you a little TLC in the meantime?"

"You're being ridiculous."

He got up and walked toward her as she walked backward, the arm's-length space between them like an invisible object with which he forced her into their room. He had that same odd feeling he'd often had whenever they fought. It was partly shame, he guessed; the neighbors must've heard them. But he also had a nagging suspicion they were being watched.

"I *knew* you wouldn't be able to hold out," she said. "I *knew* you'd break down."

"Hannah, you don't know what you're talking about."

"In sickness and in health, hah!"

"Darling, please."

"As if *I* haven't been alone, either. But *you* can't be alone, *can* you?"

"That's not true."

"Who is she? What's her name?"

"There is no she!" But he couldn't help himself. Thinking of the other Hannah, he felt himself grin.

"You're smiling!" she said.

He could play bad cop with the most hardened criminals, could poker-face a confession from the worst trash, but try to lie to his wife and his tell was as obvious as a boner in pajamas. "I'm not," he whined. He was, in fact, on the verge of laughter.

"Is she going to take care of everything I don't? Are you going to gut her too? Withhold everything, you impenetrable fuck?"

And then Hannah slumped into bed again and wept.

"Oh, enough with you," he said. He turned to leave and then turned around, watching her back shake as if she were cold, and he went to touch her shoulder. Though whether he did it to caress it or do something else entirely, he didn't remember later, but she whirled on him and smacked his hand away.

"*Don't!*" she screamed.

The blow knocked him against their bedside table. Her water glass fell to the floor and shattered. He felt a zinging up his arm: her diamond ring had sliced open his palm.

And in the dark Hastroll went blind with rage. He took the pillow and pressed it over her face. "*Enough* with you," he groaned. It was delicious to use all his strength, to push down on her face with the force of every punch she'd ever asked for that he'd pulled, to punch the center of the pillow again and again and again without the recoil of shame. (Incest wasn't a man's first taboo; it was hitting a girl.) She bucked under him, trying to bridge from her neck, and as her arms flailed at him heedlessly, Hastroll became aware—not now but in the horrendous hours later—that in murder there is a crucial midpoint, a gap one can cross only with discipline and determination, and that, like any task previously untried (like learning a sport or writing a novel), doesn't disclose the details of its unfolding or the necessities of its accomplishment or the actual *time* it requires (in seconds, minutes, or years) until the act itself is perpetrated. He had to press his knee to her chest while her nails dug into his palms where he gripped the pillow; his teeth, when she shoved her fingers up his nose and into his mouth, bit through flesh to pebble-hard bone. In a last surge of adrenaline, she managed to separate the pillow from her face and gasp, "Ward, please . . . " But he pressed the pillow down again. The storm had broken over the city, the thunder, lightning, and rain spraying their windowpanes, washing down the brick and feeding his roses, funneling through gutters and roaring through sewers in torrents—all that channeled force part of the energy he used to seal the pillow over her nose and mouth and muffle her screams. And soon her blows became drunken and soft and, as all strength left her, almost sensual. Until finally she fell motionless, like someone who'd just slipped off to sleep.

He backed off of her, off the bed, and then looked.

Her head was a pillow, the sheets around her legs. Her slip, in the dark, was impossible to distinguish from the covers. She'd become part of the bed.

Now he had to dispose of her body.

This would be the effect of shock, he realized later, the disconnect brought on by trauma, and in the bathroom, after thinking through other crime scenes and searching the apartment for the tools, after wrapping his feet in Ziploc bags and his hands in latex gloves and his head in Hannah's shower cap, he turned on the shower, deposited her corpse into the tub (why did the dead feel lighter alive?), then sawed off her arms at the shoulders, her legs at the hips, her head at the neck. The blade produced a horrid smell; it was like a dentist's drill to tooth. He ran the shower to drain the blood while he worked, her torso limbless at its sockets and perfect where still intact like some ancient Greek sculpture fashioned of meat. Her limbs landed loudly in the tub as he severed them, a thud that conveyed their weight like a neighbor dropping something heavy on the floor above. The steam from the shower misted his glasses, which he took off so as not to see. Then he packed her up, fitting her body parts into his suitcase like luggage puzzled into the trunk of a car. Next he walked Hannah in hand through darkened streets toward the river, soaked under his slicker and hat not from the cold rain sheeting Manhattan but by the sweat sopping his shirt. At the promenade he dumped the contents over the railing, watching what could no longer be called Hannah disappear into the black water, his conscience as void of guilt as her body was of blood. And now, finally home and sitting in his chair, he heard himself sobbing, because he realized he'd killed her.

He woke.

It was dark in the apartment and the telephone was in his lap.

He went to their bedroom and saw that Hannah was sleeping. She looked peaceful lying there, and while at once grateful beyond measure at the same time he felt the bitter hangover from their fight, so he wanted nothing more than to crawl into bed with her like he used to when they were young and say, "I had a nightmare." She would ask, "What did you dream?" And though he'd never been more than a detective and never would be, in *that* moment he felt himself to be the richest man alive. They would lace their arms and legs through each other's and fall asleep. But tonight, soaked in sweat, he went to the bathroom and ran the tap and splashed his face, burying it in the towel. Then he looked up at his reflection, and it horrified him.

He saw the man he'd become since Hannah had gone to bed. His suit and shirt were wrinkled, his tie pushed out from under his jacket, a dishevelment only the chronically distracted could effect. His hair, gone gray during these past five months, made him look ten years older than thirty-five. His mouth, on a face slack with extra weight, looked permanently turned down. Worse, he seemed as impassive as some of the killers he'd interrogated. That more than anything was what struck him. Men who killed serially suffered a unique lack of affect. You felt this in advance, a physical pressure before they entered a room. There was something impenetrable and thick behind their eyes, a gaze that was shark-dumb. They were people, Hastroll thought, who could not be touched by love.

He put his head on his arms and wept bitterly that their life had become this.

He wept because he was alone in a secret corner of his apartment weeping.

He wept so forcefully that it almost sounded like someone gasping with laughter.

He wept until he became nothing but this sound.

Then Hannah appeared at the door.

She appeared from out of the apartment's darkness as if emerging from a black pool. And the sight of her—the unexpectedness of her appearance—terrified him. She looked half-asleep, mishmashed, like a child gathered from bed. She stood for a moment in the light, squinting, a little wobbly in the legs. Then she reached out and rubbed his neck and leaned on him at the same time. "There," she said. "There, there." Her hand when it touched him carried a static charge, and he winced. She was the witch who'd conjured his misery, who could lift the spell to save him, and she'd now arrived to welcome him to this pit where she lived. And seeing her standing before him, limitlessly powerful because of this dual nature, Hastroll was even more afraid.

"What is it?" she said.

"I can't stand it," he whispered.

She took a step closer to him and he covered up.

"Can't stand what, baby?"

"It's like you don't exist."

Gently, she slid her arm over his shoulder and leaned down to him, pressing her forehead to his ear and then nuzzling it with her nose. She wore a sweet-smelling perfume, but her breath was rank. "Now," she said, "you finally understand."

Detectives Hastroll and Sheppard were in the Time Warner building, sitting in the coffee shop in Borders, staking out the phone booth—"Maybe the only one left in Manhattan," Sheppard had observed—by the bathrooms where the calls to Pepin had originated. "Now let me get this straight," he'd said. "First we call this guy's pager."

"That's right," Hastroll told him.

"Then we wait to see if he calls us back from that phone booth."

Hastroll dialed. "And then we arrest him."

"Things like that don't even happen in movies," Sheppard said.

Hastroll punched in his number, then put down his cell.

They sat for hours on end, taking breaks only to go to the bathroom or grab a bite.

"How's Hannah?" Sheppard finally asked.

"Good, thanks."

Hastroll and Sheppard spent the time reading Pepin's manuscript, the former passing each page he finished to the latter, though occasionally he considered sharing the news that Hannah was pregnant. But he'd no more tell a stranger on the street this than he would Sheppard—especially not him. Sooner or later, he'd find out by himself. And it was Hastroll's feeling that if you were lucky enough to keep love, to talk about it would always seem like bragging, no matter how generous the listener's spirit.

He and Sheppard ate smoked salmon and crème fraîche sandwiches and Diet Coke for lunch and waited hours without a single call. In his gut, he believed they would catch the suspect, and in his mind he pictured what he'd look like when they finally set eyes on him. Someone thin and bald, cobra-headed, like James Carville; fey, lispy, conceited, perhaps a bit of a puss, like John Malkovich. Early that evening, when a man finally did stop to make a call at the booth, Hastroll stood up, his cell phone buzzing in his pocket; and when he got a look at him finally, he was reminded of how the suspect in a composite or the person in your mind never looks like the real killer, is almost never the person in the actual world, his own surprise at this man's appearance reconfirming the enduring truth that we have our backs to the future.

He was extremely short, five feet in heels, wearing a khaki sport coat and blue jeans. His brown hair, with long straight bangs, hung very long in the back—a mullet, really. His black eyes were gerbil-like, as beady and opaque as marbles, and although he was diminutive he was stocky, built like a wrestler or a dwarf strongman. He was so low to the ground he'd be hard to knock off his base.

"Excuse me," Hastroll said, Sheppard standing behind him.

The man replaced the receiver, then looked up. "What do you want?"

Hastroll showed him his badge. "We'd like to ask you a few questions."

"About what?"

"Alice Pepin."

"Never heard of her."

"Not according to her husband," Hastroll said.

"Interesting," the man said.

When Hastroll grabbed his shoulder, the suspect spun him into the wall with an aikido move, caught Sheppard with a vicious blow to the throat, then ran out of the store, sliding down the escalator's rail and tearing through the lobby, sprinting across Columbus Circle and into Central Park. Hastroll possessed surprising pursuit speed for a large man but was confident while he huffed that Sheppard had already called in backup; he could hear sirens approaching even now. The man ran toward the ball fields but jumped a fence and ducked into a tunnel, Hastroll close behind. Here the suspect suddenly stopped, turned, and spread his legs wide in battle stance, producing from his sleeve a butterfly knife that he flipped open with so much rehearsed fanfare it gave Hastroll a chance to bend over and catch his breath. Blade locked, the man proceeded to shred the air between them, slicing and dicing with incredible whirling-dervish karate moves, chops, and roundhouse kicks so fast that the spill of air trailing his limbs sounded like a Wiffle bat swung wildly. He ended his death dance with a short bark, the knife held above his head, his other hand flipped palm up to Hastroll like a crossing guard's command to halt.

"I'll flense you like a pig!" he said.

Hastroll pulled his switchblade, then changed his mind and drew his gun, shooting the knife from the man's hand and emptying a round for good measure into each of his knees. "Stop," he said, "or I'll shoot."

Later, through the one-way glass, Hastroll watched as Sheppard sat down across from Pepin and lit his pipe. He puffed twice, then took Pepin's file out from under his arm, removed the manuscript, and slid it toward him.

"That doesn't prove anything," Pepin said.

"True," Sheppard said. "Until we traced those calls you received from this man." He slid the mug shot across the table. "We arrested him yesterday."

Pepin crossed his arms.

"We've had an interesting conversation," Sheppard said, lighting his pipe. He was sitting with his back to Hastroll, and through the glass it looked like his head was smoking.

Pepin leaned over and looked at the picture, then leaned back. "I want to see my lawyer," he said.

Admittedly, Alice's diet went differently this time.

No pills, no updates, no three easy payments, no assembly required, no thirty-day trial, no money-back guarantee. No Bowflex, no ThighMaster, no inversion boots; no Atkins, no Zone, no South Beach. No labels on her food and no microanalysis of her progress. No before-and-after snapshots—only after, David thought, and nothing like before. Just a YMCA membership and twice-a-week sessions with a trainer, which she told him next to nothing about—"It was good today," or "It was hard today," or "I really wasn't into it today"—and then only when David pressed, if he bothered to press at all.

"Alice," David called from the kitchen, where he was reading the paper. She was in the bathroom and he could hear her drying her hair. "I was going to stop at the supermarket after work. Anything in particular you'd like for dinner?"

"Whatever you want to make's fine with me," she said.

"Anything?" he said, disbelieving.

"Right," she said. "Whatever."

Yet still no change in her remoteness. He'd come to think of it like a sailor does of weather: something you endure—whether squall or dead calm—but nothing you can control. You just ride it out. This, after all, was their voyage together, wasn't it?

"I won't be home anyway," she added.

He went to the bathroom and looked through the doorway. Topless, she was combing her hair in front of the mirror, the space still hot from her dryer. Her remarkable voluptuousness—of her cheeks, shoulders, and breasts, her thighs banking inward to her comparatively dainty feet, her body so long untouched—surprised him so utterly that he went weak-kneed with desire. "Where will you be?" he said.

"I have a meeting after school."

He studied her again. Still she was enormous, but less so. She'd lost more weight than ever before. He should be happy for her. "What kind of meeting?"

She stopped brushing her hair and glanced at his reflection, he thought, like someone considering her options. "A work meeting," she said.

There'd been a lot of those recently, though for what, or with whom, she wouldn't say. Admittedly, David, grossly suspicious, had done some detective work. While she was in the shower, he fingered her purse, zippered it open, and gently plucked out her wallet. After removing strange business cards whose names—Dr. Alex Brulov, Dr. Fred Richmond—meant nothing to him, he memorized the numbers for future investigation and read what scribblings Alice had made on them. Some notes were so cryptic they made him positively paranoid: *Meet D at 3 for special* or *Resume Wish: search opps in Ill, Tex, or D.C.* Who was D, and what was so special? And by "resume" did she mean to continue? Or was it résumé for job opportunities in Illinois, Texas, or Washington, D.C.? He checked her cell phone for incoming, outgoing, and missed calls—the names and numbers most often of people Alice worked with or David knew, though when he dialed the ones he didn't recognize he reached doctors' offices he'd never heard of and whose receptionists stonewalled him—information about a patient, even a spouse, was confidential—before hanging up. Since she'd opened her own bank account, he checked her check register and flipped through the carbon imprints to get a sense of her financial doings, but nothing looked terribly suspicious. He made surreptitious calls to the school's office to cross-check her schedule against where she said she'd be, and usually that's where she was. He cracked her voice-mail password (their anniversary) and listened to several messages, all work related, before snapping the phone shut in shame. He even searched her e-mail account and found nothing there, either, although the screen name, which she hadn't changed, gave him pause: mrpeanut.

He sat back in his chair and stared at the screen. Was that another lifetime, David wondered, or just yesterday?

It was odd how marriage flattened time, compressed it, hid its passing, time past and time present looping on each other, foreground gone background and back, until the new was the same as the old and the past impossibly novel and strange. For years now, they'd existed in a state of stasis. It was like a dream, an iteration expanding from the center that seemed much longer and much shorter than that. A typical day: He got up to a kitchen he'd cleaned spotless, no matter how elaborate their dinner the night before, and made their coffee. He foamed her milk and added sugar, taking his with milk alone, and carried both cups into the bedroom, waiting while she rearranged the pillows. She looked up at him, ready now, so nearly horizontal that it was like laying a cup on a corpse, her drinking a matter of lifting her lips to the mug instead of the opposite. She thanked him and then turned on the radio, the volume always set to low. They sat together in the lightening room, David waiting until she was fully awake, then he asked her how she'd slept. If either of them dreamed, they shared, though Alice always revealed more and always relied on him for interpretation. "I have to get up," she'd finally say. She showered first, in order to get ready for school, while he went to the kitchen to get more coffee, fetch the paper from the front door, and boil himself an egg, thinking over the ruffling water that his life was only a history of such mornings, an ever-growing pile of eggs, the shells by now filling up the kitchen, spilling out into other rooms. He sat at their breakfast nook by the window, all the rooftops lit up by the rising sun, or shiny with rain, or padded with snow, went from the front page to Op Ed to Sports to the satellite's view of the nation's weather, always bypassing the first section, the long middle, all to the sound of her hair dryer. There was the quiet time while she put on her makeup. And then she appeared dressed, today's person. He never once saw her eat breakfast during the week, though every morning she opened the refrigerator for a futile look. She told him good-bye, kissed him, and left. In the quiet apartment, he finished his breakfast, showered, dressed, made the bed, did his dishes, and then left too.

Did she exist during this time? Did she wonder, "Does he?" She called him from school sometime in the morning, just to check in. Usually they discussed dinner, agreed on a menu, said they loved each other. She rarely crossed his mind for the rest of the day. He stopped at the market on the way home. When he arrived at the apartment, she was reading the paper in the kitchen, the first section folded back on itself or her laptop open, and having a snack. They didn't speak much initially. She was around children all day and needed her quiet time. He made himself whiskey in winter, vodka in summer, the sound of ice cubes hitting the bottom of the glass tracing the very contours of silence. He took a sip, heard the newspaper pages turning. At some unspoken point, he turned on the radio and started cooking. Over dinner, they talked about their respective days, though at times David became aware of his yawning ignorance about most of her life and of hers about his. He did the dishes while she washed her face and brushed her teeth. She put on her pajamas in the bedroom, the one time all day he was sure to see her naked, a sight that made him wonder when her nakedness had stopped being a miracle. And yet it still could be, the sheer R. Crumb fullness of her, the cloud-soft breasts large as throw pillows, their size and perfection demanding attention, there to press an ear against, the heart beating beneath, if he listened closely, as amazing as surf in a shell. Watching his wife approach their bed made his heart race with anticipation, Alice edging toward it like a child at a pool, her plunge requiring both an inner negotiation and a logistical plan: a knee up first and then a slight fall to her extended hand, the pose held as she timbered slowly toward him, her landing setting the springs creaking, her weight indenting her side of the mattress and rolling him ever so slightly toward her. She put her arm over his chest, the limb so heavy that it was like catching a log. They watched TV, not a fat person in a single commercial unless the advertisement was for losing weight, the same silence between them as intense for commercials with infants (diapers, detergents, toys). Their marriage, David occasionally reflected, could be measured as a sequence of late-night television shows: *Love Connection,* Letterman, *The Daily Show,* someone somewhere writing the show that would carry them through the rest of their lives. "David," she often asked before he drifted off, "are you going to sleep?" He was. She was too. Did he turn off the television? Did she?

Then it was morning again.

Naturally there were deviations from this routine—he working late, she at a meeting—but he forgot each of them as soon as the next one came. He tested her to ensure he wasn't alone in this. "I don't remember either," she said, and laughed. And of course there were significant events in their lives—that is, history—but for some time now it seemed that recalling them, or plucking a coherent narrative from this mindless flow, this endless reloop, required the mental effort of reconstruction, a focused recollection of things prior to this long tranquillity that were overwhelmed by and set apart from the here and now. But perhaps that was *exactly* the task at hand, David thought, the only way out. For underneath this there were unspoken truths, things that had happened or they were waiting for that comprised the very bedrock of their marriage, which went beyond issues and that David boiled down to three:

She was fat.

His book wasn't done.

And Mr. Peanut.

In the summer of 2004, their eighth year together, he and Alice began to talk about having children.

David remembered the year clearly because Spellbound Games, the company he and Frank Cady started, had just released their first shooter, Bang You're Dead! for play on Xbox. Within months, it was a hit worldwide. Negative press was a huge boon. CNN did a story on it, as did *60 Minutes* and the *New York Times.* He and Frank were even interviewed on *Larry King Live.* The game, rated M for Mature, took place in a sprawling public school, its rules the same as the game from childhood. When you spotted an opponent, you pointed your hand—an imaginary gun—and fired and said, "Bang, you're dead!" and he or she mimed a dramatic death. In David and Cady's version, you began by choosing your avatar's clique—the Jocks, the Goths, the Cheerleaders, the Nerds, the Geeks, or the Teachers, to name a few, each having specific defensive powers and various forms of agility and mobility. Then you chose your own appearance, from hair color to race to body type. Finally—and this was what really made it great—you chose your weapon, your gun: Laser-Pointer Hand, Spitball Hand, Static-Electricity Hand, Rubber-Band-Gun Hand, Cootie Hand, Acid Hand, Dry-Ice Hand, Bunsen-Burner Hand, Taser Hand, Mace Hand, and Dragon-Touch Hand, each appendage popping on and off like a prosthetic, as outsize as Popeye's forearms, mechanized and interchangeable and carrying, of course, limited ammunition or charges, multiple hands to be amassed and replenished over the course of the game, which took place during a single school day. The goal was to wipe out every other clique until you ruled the school. The graphics were cartoonish, pure Super Mario, the carnage spectacular, especially with the Dragon-Touch Hand (risky because you had to get close enough to touch your opponent, fabulous because his or her head exploded on contact). There were single, multiplayer, and massive multiplayer options, and soon kids all over the world were having it out online. The media response was huge and psychologists took sides. Some thought the game fomented violence and it would encourage school shootings; others thought it provided a cathartic, nonphysical release. Parents were outraged. Gamers bought it up like candy.

"Did you play Bang You're Dead! when you were a kid?" David said to an enraged caller on *Larry King*. "You didn't think anybody was dying, did you? Did you kill someone because you played it? Clearly not, because here you are, talking to me. I think kids today can tell the difference too. So bang! You're dead! Next caller, please."

Development and royalty money began to flow into Spellbound like mad, so much so that he bought their apartment outright that year. Lying in bed, each with a drink in hand, each exhausted, she buried beneath tests and lesson plans, lines of code and images from playtests burned onto his retinas, talk about children seemed to have arisen naturally, what with their successful adulthoods opening before them like a pair of wings. They'd met at a small college in Virginia, David in grad school in computer design, Alice getting her undergraduate degrees in mathematics and education. After marrying a year later, they'd agreed that what they wanted first and foremost was to get established. Now in their late twenties and early thirties (she and he respectively), they felt blessed by luck, by their jobs—Alice was teaching at the Trinity School—and by each other, but most of all by the most precious commodity in Manhattan: space.

It was a conversation that lasted for months, the first stage of conception, really, this future only one of many to make it downstream and penetrate their brains, of boy or girl and what constituted being ready, of favorite names—all of this wheat separated from the chaff of old boyfriends and girlfriends, despised classmates and beloved teachers, cousins and enemies, one-night stands and dead pets, a veritable discarded universe of bad associations and ridiculous situations. Collectively, it evoked in David a mixture of feelings. Giddiness, on the one hand. Children were marriage's magic, making it a family. To make a child was like pushing the button to trigger the obverse of nuclear war: mutually assured creation. The willful act of utterly altering your lives, it was *radical.* Even the attempt to make one potentially changed everything. For there were no guarantees, David thought now, were there? Though you started the process believing there were. Yet at the same time their talk sparked frustration, anxiety, and often struck him as pure abstraction and, to a degree, distraction. It made him defensive. Selfishly, he wondered if Alice didn't love him as much as she used to. It made him worry their sex life had fizzled somehow, that Alice was bored, and that a child, with all of its attendant busyness and business, served to replace something that was fading between them. Because a child would be the end of something, he'd thought then. It would be the end of *just them.*

He didn't tell this to his wife.

The conversation was continuous and knew no boundaries or schedule. They picked up with it at breakfast or when they called each other from work. It was never a non sequitur and always fair game. It was always there. A child spotted on the street, on the bus, peeking over the seat of an airplane at the two of them like a cuddly Kilroy, appearing at the table at a couple-with-kids dinner party, often with a gorgeous sitter in tow, as if she were a fringe benefit to the whole package, the child's hair still tubby-time wet, Johnson & Johnson clean, pj's smelling pristine, boy or girl or the whole brood well-behaved, crazy-cute, super-smart, early-to-bed-and-late-to-rise—"Easy," according to the parents. Their children were allusions to David and Alice's private discussions, to their marriage's next chapter, procreation's promise of happiness if his mood was right. And if it was wrong, a child was some sort of conspiracy by which those with children could rope the two of them into the same situation. His knee-jerk reaction was that he had to rebel.

Yet sometimes, while the two of them made love, David was tempted in his fit of passion to pluck out her diaphragm, the very idea of that thing inside her slightly suffocating to him, the annihilation of his sperm causing him physical pain—and killing all those millions of possibilities, his poor penis people! The whole exchange seemed like a microscopic game of Missile Command, and the very thought of ejaculating inside an unprotected Alice was enough to bring him to the verge.

"Oh God," he cried. "Take it out. Take it out, Alice, *please*!"

"You're ready?" she said.

He stopped. "Are you?" he asked.

She took his face in her hands. Looked at him. Shook her head.

"No," she said, "I'm not."

But afterward he felt the most terrific sense of relief. They'd nearly made a terrible mistake.

The conversation continued.

Once, while David was waiting to board an airplane, he saw a mother try to stop her inconsolable daughter from crying. But what made it unique was how loud the girl was. She wailed. She howled. She screamed, no shit, at the top of her lungs, for so long that it made the expression at once literal and surreal too, as if the squalling were a gnome standing on a ladder inside her neck, the topmost rung by her tonsils, and pulling down on the cord of uvula to hold her mouth open, using the girl's whole head as a kind of loudspeaker. At first people were embarrassed, distraught for the mother, but as the event wore on it turned into a situation. Uncalled for, security came. "We heard screaming," an officer said. And then people within banshee range began to snicker and then laugh, David among them. He even called his wife.

"There's this girl," David said. "She's screaming. She's just a kid. Listen." He held up his phone.

"I can hear her," Alice said. "Is this a joke?"

"No," David said. Then Alice laughed too, like it was cute, like it was *just kids.* Whippersnappers.

And this soon became part of their conversation as well, although he never told her what had happened afterward. The child screamed on and on, for so long now that the noise was ambient, ignorable, something you could fall asleep to, "The Star Spangled Banner" playing over hissing TV snow, and while David watched, both awed and amused, the man in a suit sitting next to him lowered the magazine from his face and said, "You have kids?"

"No," David said, and chuckled. This girl's energy was amazing. Her sheer stamina convinced him she was gifted. A siren singing her siren song.

"Don't," the man said. And then he looked at him until David looked back. "They'll ruin your fucking life."

David studied the child until his plane boarded. When he turned back, the man was gone.

The conversation continued. Much of David and Alice's talk was standard-issue, of course, and repetitive. In music, the term was augmentation: the same notes drawn out over longer periods of rhythm, chords widened over time. Even choosing not to talk about it was talking about it.

"Are we talking about this again?" David asked, and laughed. He and Alice were sitting together in the kitchen's breakfast nook. He was drunk. It was only a Tuesday. A Tuesday!

"I say we find some pot," Alice said, pouring herself more wine, "and get high."

Though what he thought she'd left unspoken was: *While we can.* It was as if choosing to act like a kid made you more of an adult. They drank and drank, then they screwed—angry, tear-your-clothes-off sex—and in the morning, he thought to himself: How long can we keep ourselves so amused?

It wasn't always amusing.

The conversation could turn toxic, metamorphose and metastasize, could turn on *them.* In fights, they'd put their unconceived child between them and make it take sides: the original preparental sin.

"You're out of your *mind,*" she said, "if you think I'd ever have a child with someone as selfish as you!"

"Then *don't,*" he said, "because I don't want a kid. *You* want the kid."

"I *knew* it," she said. "All *along* I knew!"

"Knew? Knew what? What did you *know*?"

"Nothing! I know *nothing*!"

"And why is that?" David said. "Huh?"

"Because you never say what you feel! And I'm never going to expose a kid to that—*ever*!" She turned to walk away.

"Oh, go ahead," he said. "Just walk away. That's a great fucking lesson to teach!"

"*Fucking* lesson?" she said. "Everything's fuck, fuck, fuck."

"Oh, *please,*" he said.

"Oh, *fucking* please," she said. "Oh, *fucking* Dad. *Fucking* Mom."

"No," David said, waiting to spear her with a glance: "No fucking *Mom* at all!"

But the kid they hadn't had also made them better people.

"I'm sorry," David said later.

It was evening now and no lights were on in the apartment. For hours they'd been sitting separately in the dark. Hands in pockets, he'd appeared at their bedroom door.

"You're right," he said. "I have a potty mouth."

"No," she said, "*you're* right. I threw a temper tantrum."

"I had a meltdown."

"I should take a time-out."

They laughed, and when they were silent again, he said, "Alice, I don't want you to think I don't—"

"Don't say it," she said.

It was like practice, David thought, like playing house. The child they hadn't had was watching them, refereeing, keeping them honest. He or she was already improving their characters. Their boy or girl would tell their spouse one day, "I never once saw my parents fight."

Later, David and Alice made love. They thought about you know what. But the fight had made them both doubtful, so they didn't.

What were they waiting for? David wondered. Or were they waiting for nothing? Was there something he hadn't said? Was there something Alice needed to tell him?

"I need to tell you something," she said.

They were in their bed, their California king. Days had passed, weeks, months. Summer was at an end. Their conversation had lasted a whole season. It was evening, they had drinks in hand and the television was on. Even when they were broke they'd splurged on this bed. They *had* to sleep comfortably together. Every couple had their unbreakable rules: no shared bank accounts, no going to bed angry, no eating the last X. Their rule: No sleeping in separate beds. Spatially, that was tantamount to divorce: mere coexistence. Separate beds would mean the end.

"I died once," Alice said.

The woman knew how to get your attention, he thought. It was her loner's knack, the ability to stand out when necessary. He turned off the TV and adjusted his pillows.

"When was this?"

"When I was eight," she said.

It was early spring, she said, and stormy outside. Her parents had a fire going and were watching TV—though when Alice said parents, he had to note that she meant her uncle Ladd and his wife, Karen, for they'd raised her, and in his mind he pictured their lakefront home in Bay Village, Ohio, a suburb of Cleveland. He imagined their long sitting room, pine-paneled and carpeted, with pictures of animals—a lion, a pack of wolves, a leopard—on the wall. Ladd was no nature lover, really, this simply a reflex of naturalist kitsch. Alice had come to live with them under sad circumstances. Her mother, Dorothy, pregnant with a boy six years Alice's junior, had died in labor, along with her son. Her father, Thomas, a successful inventor, went into such a tailspin that he handed Alice off in order to recover; he managed to gather himself together and remarry four years later, but never collected his daughter. And though she always spoke lovingly of Ladd and Karen, her lingering sense of abandonment was amplified, David thought, by the fact that her uncle and aunt had no children of their own, so Alice was treated from the minute of her arrival as a privileged boarder they provided for, along with the distant contributions of her father, but who was fundamentally alone.

As she'd said, they were watching television after dinner, riveted by the coverage of Prince Charles and Lady Di's visit to Australia. In the living room, her "parents" had the only pair of reclining chairs that faced the TV screen, so Alice was at the other end of the room, by the fireplace, reading an Archie comic and eating a seedless orange. The volume on the television was turned high, the rain and wind making a fusillade against the roof. Occasionally her aunt and uncle would turn and say something to each other, but she couldn't hear them over the roar of flame, of the storm, of the talk on-screen—and then she began to choke.

It was terrifically sudden and unexpected, like being dunked from behind in a pool. It was also as if her body had played a trick on her, by shocking the air from her lungs. She was unsure for a moment how to react, oddly embarrassed, like she'd farted in a crowded room. She cupped her hand and raised it to her mouth, ready to catch the mass when she spit it out, gagging as hard as she could, but there was no movement in her throat, and the sound that came from it was merely a small quack. She gagged again, her ears popping with the effort. Already she was at the bottom of the pool, every bubble blown from her lungs. She looked up. Ladd and Karen, no longer talking, were focused on the television. She could see only the tops of their heads above the chairs, their bodies hidden forms to which she reached out until her arm dropped in exhaustion. She doubled over, her fingers clutching her neck. It was like magic or being shot. Some giant bag containing all her energy had burst from inside her to spill across the floor. Little black flames licked the edges of her vision, and it was then she registered something she'd known unconsciously since coming to live with her aunt and uncle, something she'd felt since her mother had died and her father had abandoned her, something she'd seen whenever she told Ladd and Karen about her day and they'd ask questions her story had already answered or one of them left the dinner table to grab the phone when it rang, something that was part and parcel in the very room's furnishings, the knickknacks on the coffee and end tables Karen always reminded her were fragile, the gun closet left unlocked, the two chairs before the television, all of these arranged without a child in mind. It was something she hadn't been able to articulate until now.

She'd have to save herself.

She turned all of her concentration inward to this wet fist of pulp in her throat, focusing all her muscular control on her esophagus, as if she could squeeze the obstruction out. She braced the tip of her tongue against her bottom teeth and forced a gag, trying to clear the passage, but nothing happened. When she gagged again, she could feel her tongue's deepest reaches, and it made her head shake. It felt as if her temples were about to explode. Though she tried once more, it was like bench-pressing a car: dead weight. She became distinctly aware of the tightness of the mass's suction, of its perfect, globbed seal around her throat. She was now a torso, neck, and head; the rest of her limbs had been washed away like sand. Without oxygen, her sense of her own extremities was contracting, her awareness circling down a drain.

She began to float, and it seemed as if she was swimming underwater in the darkest night. Either surfacing or diving—there was no telling—she'd either taste air in a moment or feel the freezing edge of thermocline. It was quite pleasant, actually, pure anticipation. She made one last effort—as futile, really, as trying to see your hand in pitch darkness.

Then she was dead.

She knew she was, and it wasn't a completely unfamiliar experience. More of an awareness, in fact, an eternal state of now—the same, she thought, as being an embryo, the buried memory of that waiting state. She was submerged, there was nothing there, and time wasn't a concept but an environment.

She came to, but very slowly. Her limbs were utterly still; only her eyes moved. She was like a cat waking in a patch of sun.

Her mouth was full. She inhaled, sucking the pulverized meat back into her throat, then spit it out.

For a long time she lay right where she was.

Ladd and Karen were still watching television and finally Alice pushed herself up on her hands and knees and spit up the remainder, a long rope of drool that refused to detach itself from her mouth.

Between her palms, the mass lay in a formless mound, almost all of its orange pigment gone. She looked up, and through her tears the TV's light was in shards, like a child's rendering of a star. Then Ladd and Karen turned to stare at her.

"I'm alive," she said to them.

"Of course you are," Karen said. She looked at her husband, shook her head, and turned back to the screen.

"I'm alive," Alice said, and began to sob.

For a very long time, she wept in David's arms. "You've got to promise," she said to him later, "that we'll never do that to a child."

"We won't," he said. "Ever. I promise."

She cried for so long that she soaked his shirt, then fell asleep in his arms.

Perhaps, David thought, the most important parts of the conversation were the things they didn't want to repeat.

He lay there thinking. Did he have a story? He didn't, and that was his great problem. He did everything he was supposed to do. He had a job and was successful at it. He was a good husband. But on a fundamental level, it was as if his own life hadn't occurred to him.

He turned off the light.

"We could make a baby now," she whispered in the middle of the night.

Many weeks had passed. They'd reached out to each other in dreams, as they often did, fondling toward lovemaking, a sleepwalking kind of foreplay that somehow made them freer with each other. After speaking, Alice bit her lower lip and looked at him in the dark. They hadn't spoken of any of this since her story. David himself had nearly forgotten about their conversation and thought Alice might have as well. But the conversation was over, apparently. A decision had been reached. Either he'd passed some sort of test or she'd worked something out. Although now that they'd arrived at this point, it surprised him that it was so unmomentous. He couldn't bring himself to meet her eyes for very long. He could say, "No" or "Yes," but instead said, "We could."

David was holding her diaphragm, the device lathered with white spermicidal paste. It was part of their ritual for him to insert it before he entered her—*a rite of passage,* he liked to joke—but he'd never taken the time to examine the thing, which he did now. It looked like the top of a newly iced cake. He placed it gently on the bedside table, wiped his fingers on the comforter and, while they made love, couldn't take his eyes off of it. He felt like some virgin triangulating his pleasure, repeating *dead kittens dead kittens dead kittens* so as not to come too fast. He was desperately disengaged. They were procreating. Having intercourse. Twice Mr. Penis went soft, slippery, and had to be slipped like sausage back into the casing. It was the worst sex they'd ever had. And when he finally came, he thought: It doesn't matter.

His disengagement—this first thought—haunted him.

"I think I'm pregnant," Alice told him. And from the two blue lines on the home pregnancy test to her first trip to the OB confirming the same, from the odd dissociation that he felt holding her in his arms in the bathroom and at the doctor's office—"We're going to have a child," she said excitedly—David feared this thought had somehow poisoned her womb, causing a deformity in the fetus, that it had set off some karmic ripple that could only lead to disaster. He knew it wasn't rational, but the anxiety was relentless. Make her abort this thing, he thought. Wipe the slate and start clean. Then he regretted these thoughts too. He'd gone from feeling nothing to living in perpetual fear, and when he had the opportunity at the end of the month to fly to Honolulu for a week at a gamers' convention, he was thrilled. Just being near Alice exacerbated his dread, convincing him that something was wrong, perhaps because she'd been terribly uncomfortable as soon as she became pregnant, as if the condition itself was slowly killing her. She suffered a broad range of symptoms: sharp pelvic pain from uterine spasms that doubled her over or sat her down suddenly, clutching her stomach no matter what she was doing, then rendered her still. She was regularly, violently ill for most of her second month. To call it morning sickness would have left out the rest of the day: she clapped her hands to her mouth getting out of bed, into bed, and walking toward the bed, morning, noon, and night. She vomited on the train or the bus. She upchucked out the car window when David drove her to school, her drool trailing from her mouth like a comet tail. She barfed, it seemed, at the mention of certain people and places, at the smell of coffee and curry. Of course these symptoms caused Alice some alarm too, though it was more about the process, the rumors of pregnancy confirmed, something seen on television that was now happening to you. "You really do puke," Alice said. "You feel like you've got the flu, just like they say." Mostly, she took it in stride. Mostly, she seemed overjoyed. "Mr. Peanut," she said, "made me sick today. Mr. Peanut," she went on, "must not be very happy." She sometimes wondered aloud, "I wonder what Mr. Peanut will look like."

Ruminant in bed the night before her sixteen-week ultrasound as Alice was ruminating over the toilet, David found himself newly terrified, the pregnancy itself, this thing inside her as deadly as an asp. A child could bring them great joy, true, but it could also kill her. It had killed Alice's mother after all—a fact that had somehow got lost. All the medicine and technology, all the focus on the embryo, made you forget about the mother. And so it *did* matter. It mattered because there was risk.

"Come with me to Hawaii in a few weeks," he said when she finally lay down beside him. He didn't want her to come and knew she'd say no. But he wanted her to feel wanted, in which case she'd happily stay put. "You need a break," he added.

"I can't," she said, rubbing her belly. "We wouldn't make it."

It mattered because there was risk, he thought again. This occurred to him even more powerfully the next day while Alice was stretched out on the table in the ultrasound technician's darkened room, quiet and made peaceful by the fossil-colored, fun-house-mirror image on the screen, her guts gone calm for now, as if the translucent gel the tech had rubbed over her belly was an anesthetic. David held her hand and watched the screen over the nurse's shoulder, aware of the difference between their expressions—Alice's beatific, like the wand pressed to her abdomen was a joystick varying levels of bliss, his own facial muscles tensed into a squint—while they saw the fetus drip and dart into view, its bones gone liquid and then coalescing to hardness again, as delicate as a bat's now, its movements as quick and as seemingly predatory, a creature built for speed. Suddenly it curled to a stop, the whole body hunched in his wife's gut.

"It's moving a *lot,*" the tech said, then looked at them and nodded ominously.

This made him want to ask if something was wrong, but he was too scared. The technician toggled along, capturing images, taking measurements, cropping and enlarging as if she were doctoring a photograph, measuring the diameter of the brain and stomach, checking the vertebrae and spinal cord, magnifying the heart from every angle, the ventricles discretely visible and winking as they sucked amniotic fluid—*blood,* David thought—like the mouth of a giant squid.

Alice turned to him and smiled. "Look at Mr. Peanut!" she said. "Can you believe that's him?" He smiled back, and when she turned again to watch he squinted once more, aware for a moment that he was holding his breath. Then the tech amplified the volume of the fetus's heart—background noise he'd barely noticed, ambient but unrecognizable until now, a sound of *p*'s and *e*'s mixed with saliva, a lisping that filled the room, like boys make when they imitate the bang of a gun.

Don't you hurt my wife, David told it.

Her pregnancy was progressing normally, Dr. Redundi assured her after the exam, and true, the OB explained, the morning sickness she was suffering from was acute, but not uncommon. The uterine spasms might be indicating other problems, perhaps endometriosis; if they continued for another week or so, she'd want to look carefully at Alice's diet. But she was satisfied for now. The baby looked perfectly healthy. Her discomfort could abate at any time. So when Alice experienced a complete cessation of symptoms several days before David was to leave for Hawaii—it was her twenty-second week—she changed her mind and decided to go along.

She didn't like to fly. In fact, she loathed it. It was a testament to the power of movies that *Fearless,* about a group of passengers who miraculously survive a plane crash, had permanently scarred her, traumatizing her with an extended graphic sequence—they'd watched the film together—that depicted the inside of the cabin upon impact: the seats came unbolted in rows and carried people on crests of force, the energy ripping infants from mothers' arms and sending luggage down the aisles at warp speed, slicing through dangling ganglia of oxygen masks, the tangled tubing indistinguishable from flayed guts, the passengers wide-eyed when the rent fuselage revealed gashes of ground and sky. This montage, David imagined, must have played itself out over and over again in her dreams, always pressing near the surface of her consciousness the moment she got near an airport, because even at the gate her breathing became shallow and by the time they reached the walkway she was dizzy, her face seasick-green, and when the plane finally took off, after the accusation that he'd forced her on board, her palms were sweating like tidal pools in his own and her breath went rank for reasons he didn't understand.

"What was that?" she said after there'd been a rumble, as they climbed, as Queens fell away, her wedding ring pinching his finger until his skin nearly broke. She buried her face in his arm.

"Those are the wheels," David said, pressing his forehead to hers. "They're retracting."

She clung to him tightly as he waited and held her close. She seemed to relax, finally, and this relaxed him too. She'd closed her eyes, so he closed his for a time. At every sound, her fingers contracted in his. It was a night flight under a full moon, and soon they'd climbed over that impossible land on top of the clouds, that great glacial meringue as pristine as a ceiling and also never to be explored. Ever since he was a boy this particular view had thrilled him. Give him emptiness. Endless fields of snow. A city devoid of people, wide avenues empty of cars. His thoughts turned to the apocalyptic movies he'd loved growing up: *Damnation Alley. A Boy and His Dog. The Omega Man.* (*The last man on earth,* its poster read, *is not alone.*) The plots now escaped him, but they weren't important. It was the open space that he recalled. The freedom. Vastness. Speeding down Park Avenue at a hundred miles per hour, weaving through expressways littered with wreckage, the smoke and gutted skyline rising into view. Give him strange beds in the apartments of total strangers. Let him forage without guilt through other people's rooms, pull down clothes from racks in abandoned stores, spend nights in ancient buildings preserved in museums. In these places he would find his true love. She was out there. When they found each other they wouldn't be afraid; each would look at the other and understand.

It was odd to be so pleasantly haunted: to want such things. These were dreams, after all, engendered by someone else's. Had he and Alice found such an understanding? He could remember believing they had. Yet it was more often in his own dreams that he recalled this, in the dreams of somehow losing her that he became aware of his singular need. "I had the worst dream," he would say, just waking, still half asleep. "Tell me," she said. "I dreamed that you left," he told her. And at the same time it was the view out his window and those thoughts of living at the end of possibility that woke him up now, increasing altitude bringing him back to earth. We're having a child, he thought, and it *does* matter. This fear and anxiety—for Alice, about everything—carved not a path for love but a canyon, wide enough and strong enough to channel the greatest force. *We're having a child.* Could he feel it twitching inside there? He put his hand on her stomach. No. Becoming aware of their child inside of her was *his* part of the process. It was a beautiful, wonderful thing, as mysterious and remarkable as flying and life's greatest surprise, because you *knew* it was coming but still couldn't inhabit the womb; you could glimpse but not know this person any more than you could wander through this world of clouds beyond the window. You could only peer, and that only set you back to dreaming. Holding his palm to his wife's stomach, David resolved that he must be strong.

She slept through dinner and he set hers aside for later. After he ate, he dozed briefly himself. When he woke, the first movie they were showing was ending. He checked the time. The captain announced they were above the Grand Canyon, but David could see nothing but blackness. He removed the safety pamphlet and considered the different points of exit in the event they went down. In an open-water crash, the plane floated all of a piece, as if built for just that. Would he and Alice be able to survive on a desert island? Have their child there? First you must make a fire. But desert islands didn't exist, or at least the possibility of getting so lost. There were no unknown places in the world.

He ordered himself a drink and when the attendant returned with it, he discovered he had no cash in his wallet. Alice's purse sat between them, and searching through it he noticed the small box of Unisom, a sleep aid whose active ingredients were antihistamines and which the doctor had cleared her to take. He figured the length of flight and took two pills himself and ordered another drink, then settled in to watch *Dodgeball,* the movie that had already begun, but the earphones were on the fritz, the sound as garbled and static-filled as a mayday sent from the center of a storm, so he took them off and closed his eyes and then sleep came over him, fairy tale deep, the kind that arrives when everything you have to do on earth is done, that allows you to pass from one world into the next . . .

He woke to a crash.

It felt as if the plane had been broadsided, for it was knocked to the left by an impact at the tail that sent a creak down the whole fuselage. People gasped, as did David, not because he was afraid (nothing about flying ever scared him) but because Alice was gone. The seatbelt lights flashed on, their game-show gong tolling repeatedly, the captain asking people to return to their seats in a voice that sounded comically calm. They'd hit some bad chop, he explained, and were trying to climb out of it. "We're looking for some good air," he said. Out the window, no clouds now. Nothing below but the ocean. It seemed sickeningly close, molten iron in texture and streaked with chalk-white glare from the moon. David, looking up and down the aisle, saw two attendants rapping on one of the bathroom doors, knowing full well that his wife had locked herself in. Puzzled that she hadn't wakened him, he went to unbuckle his seatbelt, but the moment he touched the clasp the plane plummeted, so suddenly that in the seat in front of him the liquid in the man's drink rose in a neat stream from the cup he held, gone airborne above his tray table before landing back in place without the loss of a drop.

This fall sent another collective gasp through the passengers, and when the oxygen masks dropped down from above there were screams. They were being shaken now, the vibration landslide-loud. David's skull was trembling, his teeth rattling. The captain was speaking again, inaudibly. A woman across the aisle from David said, "What did he say?" and he shrugged. "I can't hear him either," he said, already getting up. The woman gripped the arms of her seat, pressed her head back, and began to cry. David approached the flight attendants, one of whom had already sat down in her jump seat and was clipping her four-point belt together. When she saw him, she ordered that he sit down. Then another blow, the shockwave seeming to crack the whip down the coach compartment, bending David's whole tubular view. He grabbed the headrests to steady himself and then, as if they were rungs in a ladder, pulled himself hand over hand toward the bathroom. Passengers sat staring forward, utterly blind. But there was no need to fear flying, David thought, since it was out of your hands. Nearly everything was.

"You have to sit down, sir," the attendant snapped. "You have to take your seat *right now.*"

"My wife's in there."

"It's very dangerous for you to be in the aisle."

"She's pregnant. Please, let me get her back to her seat."

The vibration seemed to intensify. A child was crying.

"I need you to hurry," she said.

He knocked on the door, interrupted by a prodigious rumble and pitch. What, exactly, made all this noise? Was it the wind? His wonder that a machine so complex could take such punishment and still function amazed any inkling of fear out of his system. He knocked on the door again and called loudly to Alice. When she didn't answer, he knocked harder and shouted her name. He could hear something inside. She was saying something back to him now.

"Alice," he said, "are you all right?"

He put his ear to the door; she was speaking.

"Alice," he said, "let me get you back to your seat."

The plane fell yet again and for a moment he was weightless, his whole mass drifting toward his head like the bubble in a tilted level, his soles rising just above the floor; then he landed. Both flight attendants had sat back, their eyes closed, each gripping the buckle of her belt's clasp like the harness in an amusement ride. One of them was exhaling, her lips pursed, pushing steady breaths out, *one, two, three.* He heard his wife cry out from behind the doors. She was beyond embarrassment, he thought, so perhaps he should be too. She'd given herself over to panic.

"Alice!" He shook the door handle. "Just let me get you to your seat."

The latch snapped and David folded open the door. And when he did, the lavatory light went out and Alice was sitting there in the dark on top of the toilet, sobbing. Her arms, skirt, and blouse were covered in blood, as if something had exploded in her lap. And splayed out in the crèche of her two hands was a newborn, though it looked more like some rendering of a starved alien. Its large eyes were barely shut, its mouth pulled open by the dangling weight of its head. It was a boy, covered in yellow paste and blood smears, trailing the umbilical cord between its spindly legs—a boy who bore a shocking resemblance to David himself.

"Please," she cried, holding the baby toward him as if in offering. "Put him back!"

. . .

Two doctors who happened to be on board set up a treatment area in the flight attendants' station, the curtains drawn closed while they worked. It was a makeshift bed of seat cushions and blankets and pillows on which they laid them, the dead boy swaddled in hand towels from first class and at rest now on Alice's chest. The young oncologist—Nina Chen—had asked David if he wanted to cut the umbilical cord, and he couldn't bring himself to say no, though immediately afterward he went lightheaded, and Chen had him sit against the wall with his head propped between his legs. The older doctor, a pathologist named Solomon Green, had removed Alice's clothes and cleaned her off. There were bloody rags everywhere, which both doctors picked up and bagged without compunction. They had managed Alice's shock, and Green was now taking her vitals. She was conscious, running a fingertip along her still baby's cheek and talking to him as if he were alive, oblivious to all else around her, speaking so softly that he couldn't hear the words over the whine of engine noise, now that they'd finally found better air. She seemed radioactive with grief. David could feel her unspeakable anguish pressing against his internal organs and beaming through the whole plane.

Chen took him outside the curtains. "Your wife is stable," she said. "She doesn't seem to have suffered excessive bleeding."

"Thank you."

"Does she have a carry-on bag?"

"Yes."

"Are there any clothes in it?"

"I don't know."

"Please check. It would be good to change her before we land."

"Yes, of course."

"I was going to give her a sedative. Is she allergic to any medication?"

"No."

"Are you?"

"No," David said. "I don't . . . I don't want to take anything." He looked at her. "Don't make me take anything."

She smiled weakly and touched his arm. "I'm going to go back in and see how she is."

"Do you know what happened?"

Chen shook her head. "No, I couldn't say."

"Not a single idea?"

"It would be irresponsible for me to guess."

As she turned, he stopped her again. "What . . . " he said. "What do we do with him?"

Chen squinted and shook her head. "You mean the child?"

"Yes."

"Let her be with him for now," she said. "Just let her hold him."

Thankfully, Alice's carry-on had a dress in it. He also took out some clean underwear, and as he put her bag back, he could feel everyone in the cabin looking at him. The old woman who'd questioned him during the storm put a hand on his elbow, and when he turned she asked if his wife was all right. And what if she wasn't, David thought. What would you have me say? She took his hand—this complete stranger, so thin she couldn't weigh more than eighty-five pounds, the frames of her glasses seeming to extend beyond the perimeter of her face—and pulled him toward her. Kneeling down, David hated her for foisting this sympathy on him.

She clasped her other hand over his. "I have two daughters," she said, "but I miscarried twice. It's God's way. It means your child was never to be of this world. It means He needed it in Heaven."

But he *was* of this world, David thought. He thanked her, then went back to sit with Alice, down the aisle every passenger staring at him with an expression of unabashed fascination. He wanted to curse them all.

Chen and Green were standing outside the curtains talking, and when David approached they gently pulled them open. Alice hadn't shifted from her position and was still holding the baby in her arms and talking to him, nodding her head and cooing, rocking the body softly. She seemed delusional, so utterly remote, so out of his reach, that it was like seeing through the wrong end of a telescope. He wanted to ask the doctors about her behavior, but his own horror was overwhelming enough and he didn't want to add to it by learning anything new. And then Alice spoke.

"I know we'd talked about Henry, but now that I see him I like the name David better."

When she stared at the small form, he felt as if he'd lost her permanently.

Then she looked up. "Do you want to hold him?"

He did not.

"He looks like you," she said, and smiled as she held him out.

The body was so small—the size of a Coke bottle—that it seemed unnecessary to use both hands. Shaking, David got to his knees at the foot of her pallet and took the child, afraid he might drop him, might press too hard on his little body and somehow defile it, and afraid that if he looked at him he might turn to stone. He crossed his legs, holding the bundle before him, and there in the circular fold, the baby's face was frozen midwhisper or midkiss, his skin pink, venous, nearly paper-thin, the body as small as a G.I. Joe. He already had a small patch of black hair. The limbs were still, yet David couldn't help reaching into the swaddling to take one of his hands between thumb and forefinger, the small specks of his nails distinct when he pinched the hand lightly. He went on to look at the feet—the bones ship-in-a-bottle miraculous, the toes curled delicately—before carefully tucking the leg back into the swaddling. It seemed he was watching himself from above as he did all of this. What was the point of all this biological work? All these cells upon cells duplicating over and over again in this act of creation? In every aspect of proportion and disproportion he could see how as yet unmade the baby was. Was there any salvation or comfort in seeing this? He examined the face once more to be sure. The resemblance was uncanny, but he couldn't connect himself to it. This was more like some remarkably strange animal at the zoo.

Out of nowhere, Alice said, "We're going to lay him to rest here." Then she waved a hand vaguely, as if to indicate the air.

Through the two squares of the ambulance window, Honolulu seemed to David no different from any other city in America, no island paradise, just another web-weave of overpass and underpass, of highways coursing past dilapidated buildings and streets without pedestrians. His face, his whole outer being, was like a shell. He rested his hand on Alice's leg but wouldn't look at her—at them. If he did, he feared he might disintegrate. From the airport they passed along a waterfront full of giant cranes and navy ships—it reminded him of Baltimore—and then onto the freeway, David realizing afterward that it was Pearl Harbor.

Fifteen minutes into their trip, however, the landscape changed and he spotted homes built into the lush mountainside around him, with bare black rock peeking out from them, the houses nestled into the trees white and rectangular, two-level, oddly plain, their wide windows seeming to catch the light of the brilliant blue sky, all of them oriented toward the Pacific sparkling off to his right. Though hardly mansions, they evoked an impossible luxury of hillside, altitude, ocean view, and a breeze that freshened the spirit just to see, all that and the owners' belief that what they deserved in life could, coupled with determination, become *real.* Something so simple: I will live in Hawaii and see the ocean every day. The people who lived here must be smarter than me, David thought. They understood themselves well enough that they'd made such a life possible.

He patted Alice's leg, glanced at her and the child, then turned away again. My God. He wanted to apologize to her. To confess a crime. She lay holding their child and was still so utterly remote. Coming over a rise, looking past the paramedic through the windshield, he saw a giant hull of rock sloped at its tip like a scimitar, humped at its peak with a nape like some breeching sea creature, and then a whole land mass came into view, extending beyond the stacked towers and white beachfront hotels of downtown Waikiki that stood in elemental chiaroscuro—the prow of Oahu. That mountain, he realized, was the iconic Diamond Head, its slopes carved with runnels like dried clay a giant cat had gouged, the rock above unscathed and uninhabitable, so ancient compared to the man-made structures along the coast that it seemed wholly new and beautiful. Again David could make out houses built around the base, glinting like piled diamonds beneath low clouds that were as tall as mountains themselves. And he thought his own imagination for life had somehow failed him. It was so beautiful here it shamed you. And then it occurred to him that given what had happened to them, his wife lying next to him on a gurney with their dead baby, even now he was thinking the wrong thing.

He wanted to say something to Alice, but after gathering the courage and then looking at the two of them he was still afraid to speak. "What hospital are you taking us to?" he asked the paramedic.

The man was a native, heavyset, with skin the color of caramel, his long ink-black hair tied back in a pony tail. "Kaiser Permanente," he said. As if it made any difference.

Upon arrival, the doctors took his wife to run some tests, and the child went with her. He wasn't told how long she'd be gone, so in a daze he took a seat in the waiting room and stared at the television, his mind adrift. The local news reporters somehow looked the same. Anchorman, weatherman, sportscaster: all shades of different races but a universal type. Suddenly sure this was a dream, struggling for several moments to breathe, he thought of Alice's story of choking. So much hope in the telling, he thought, even in a saga of such loneliness. Their conversation had been meant to exorcise misfortune such as this. It had been, he realized, a gathering before a leap of faith, kind of a long prayer. And he was sure his one bad thought—*It doesn't matter*—had broken it. He wanted to confess this to his wife. If he did, he knew she'd cast him out forever, which he deserved. But she'd be purged of him, therefore safe. Exhaustion suddenly overwhelmed him and he slept again—for how long he didn't know. He hadn't set his watch, and when he woke he had no idea what time it was; he looked for a clock, though by the brightness and angle of the sun out the windows he guessed it was morning. It struck him that their luggage was still at the airport, and that he'd forgotten Alice's carry-on bag. What was wrong with him that he couldn't think on her behalf?

And he was starving. Tired as he was, the idea of food became an obsession. How long had it been since he'd eaten? If he could fill his stomach, he might find some peace and sleep more easily. But where? And how long would he have to wait? He thought he should book a hotel room but then remembered he'd already reserved one at the Mandarin. He was here for work, after all. Work? Nothing was as it should be. And he suddenly felt certain that every single step in their traveling from New York to Oahu, every single word they'd spoken and act they'd committed leading up to now had been for the express purpose of their child dying.

"Are you Mr. Pepin?"

"Yes."

The doctor standing before him was Indian, tall and thin fingered, with a long, regal nose.

"I'm Dr. Ahmed," he said, "the attending OB. May we talk?"

"Yes."

The waiting room was empty, so the doctor sat down next to him.

"I'm very sorry for your loss," he said. "Are you holding up?"

"How is Alice?"

"She's stable. The doctors on the plane did an excellent job."

David nodded. His hands, at rest on his thighs, felt as if they might float up above his head, so he put them between his legs and used his knees to trap them.

"We got some results back," the doctor said. "Your wife's pregnancy was interrupted by a disorder called thrombophilia. It's a clotting disorder. Quite common, I'm afraid. Nearly one in five women suffer from it. Do you understand how clotting works?"

David shook his head.

"When tissue is injured, red blood cells and platelets stick together to scab over a wound. They pile on an injury and seal it." He laid the palm of one hand over the top of his other. "Unfortunately, the disorder causes what you might call incorrect clotting, or a kind of misrecognition. Your wife's body treated her pregnancy as an injury. Clots embedded in her uterus, sheared off the placenta"—he brushed his palm over the top of his hand as if lighting a match—"and this led to her miscarriage."

David had no idea what to say. He'd hoped knowing might grant him some comfort, but this was so abstract that he felt no better.

"Mr. Pepin," Dr. Ahmed went on, "I can understand your grief. It is, however, extremely fortunate your wife's condition has been discovered before you flew home. We don't let patients with this disorder take long flights without an intensive regimen of blood thinners in advance. Your legs, the veins there," he touched his own thigh, "they're aided by muscle contractions for circulation. Without medication, people with the disorder can have clots form there and then drift into the heart, lungs, or brain. Resulting in a massive stroke, or pulmonary embolism, or heart attack."

David waited.

"On your flight back, your wife could well have died," he said. "She could just as easily have died coming here. And so you might have lost your whole family."

It was so odd, David thought, to be so far from home and talking to a man you'd never see again tell you about losing everything. "Can I ask you something?" David said.

"Yes."

"Are you sure this disorder was the cause?"

"Yes."

"It couldn't have been anything else?"

"No."

David waited for a moment. "You're sure?"

"I'm positive." The doctor put a hand on David's shoulder.

"Can I see her?"

"She's sedated right now."

"What about the baby? What happens to him?"

"We'll let him stay with her for a while—with the both of you. There's no rush."

"When can I see her?"

"She's in room three eighty-two. You can go there now."

"Is he with her?"

"Yes, but she probably won't be awake for another hour."

In his mind, David pictured mother and child. "I'm very hungry," he said. "Is that wrong?"

"Of course not," Dr. Ahmed said. "The cafeteria's on this level. Go out those doors and follow the signs."

David piled his plate with so much food it was appalling.

They were serving a buffet breakfast, and in addition to the usual fare there was pineapple, of course, watermelon, cantaloupe unlike any he'd ever tasted, and coconut syrup so unusual and sweet and perfect with pancakes that he vowed to stock up on it before leaving. And while eating he again wondered what was wrong with him. How could he feel so hungry? It was as if he'd been on some sort of fast during his wife's pregnancy and now that their baby was dead it was over. And then once more an overriding sense of fatalism came over him, an uncanny sense of strangeness about this journey in which everything had happened in an unbreakable, predetermined sequence. And following this same chain further into the future, he had a terrible premonition of his own fate.

"Mr. Pepin?"

It was an older man who'd addressed him, and at first glance David thought he was a pilot. His stiff blue uniform had epaulets on the blazer and a set of wings pinned to the breast. He held his cap in his left hand—a briefcase tucked under his arm—and he held out his free hand to introduce himself, his grip firm and dry. "Dr. Ahmed told me you'd be here," he said. Though he was at least in his sixties, the man's expression was fresh, alert, with a youthful glint in his blue eyes. He was very pale, nearly albino, as if he'd meticulously avoided the sunlight his whole life. Smelling of pepperminty Barbasol shaving cream, he was thin and fit, and David could imagine him slapping his flat stomach in pride. His white crew-cut hair was still thick, without any sign of thinning, a full head's worth that he'd take with him to the grave. For the first time in many hours, in the gentle beam of this man's attention, with his groomed uprightness and grandfatherly scent, David felt safe.

"I'm Nathan Harold," he said. "I'm with United Airlines. I'm a disaster liaison, though my field of expertise is transportational psychology. May I have a few minutes of your time?"

David nodded, and the man eased a chair out and sat down. He placed his thin black briefcase on the table, snapped the locks, produced a folder with *David and Alice Pepin* on the tab, then closed the case and stood it next to his feet. There was a set of wings emblazoned on the folder's cover, over which he crossed his hands. "Let me first extend the airline's deepest regrets, and my own. I'm so very sorry."

David found himself suddenly embarrassed by all the food he'd heaped on his plate, and now, even more acutely than before, he felt a crushing sense of guilt. He was afraid his expression might give him away, or might otherwise be wrong, so in spite of the man's kindness, he struggled to look at him.

"How's your wife doing?" Harold asked.

"I haven't seen her yet," David said. "She's still sedated."

"How are you managing?"

David could focus only on Harold's hands, which were beautiful, large, and powerful. His nails, from the crescent moons of his cuticles to the neatly trimmed edges, seemed cared for not vainly but fastidiously. They looked as if they'd never once been bitten or chewed. And then the man did an amazing thing: he unfolded his clasped fingers and turned his left palm open toward David, as if he'd detected his fascination and was holding it there for his inspection—a palm more striated and densely webbed with lines than any he'd ever seen before. It caused him to briefly raise his eyes to Harold's—he was smiling warmly—and then look down at his open hand.

"I had my palm read once in Italy," Harold said, "in Palermo. I was in my twenties then. Long time ago. Anyway the woman, a gypsy, she said two things to me. First she said that I was an old soul. She could tell by all the lines. She said I'd lived many lives before and had the potential for great wisdom. I don't know about that, but then she showed me this line." With his index finger he traced the pronounced line that started at the base of his palm below the middle finger, to where it intersected the first groove that ran perpendicular to it and stopped. "She said it was my fate line and that because it stopped like this, it meant my fate wasn't predetermined. It was wide open. This was because I didn't know myself, she said."

David looked at his own hands. His palms—he'd never noticed this before—were bare of such striation. But he had the same fate line: interrupted, incomplete.

"It's amazing what we believe if we hear it at the right time," Harold said. "When she told me this, I somehow felt like a failure, as if I suffered some crippling blindness about myself. Ever since then, from the day of that reading, I felt like everything I did with my life was an attempt to complete this line. Isn't it odd that a total stranger could have an influence like that?"

David nodded.

"You don't feel like you own your feelings now, do you?"

"No," David said.

The man flicked a finger at David's plate as if knocking on a door. "Can I get this for you?"

"No, thank you," David said.

Harold put his wallet back. "I'm glad you're eating."

Something in David eased infinitesimally. The man's tone, the very sound of his voice, promised a future that was not of this event.

"I'm here for several reasons, Mr. Pepin, first of all for aid. When something tragic happens in our skies, we do our utmost to extend sympathy. But sympathy without action, that's an empty emotion. Mainly I'm here for the purposes of reentry."

“I don’t understand.”

“Adjustment,” Harold said, “to *earth.* I’m here to make sure you didn’t leave your whole life in the sky.”

Waiting, David crumpled his napkin and rested his wrists on the table, staring at his hands once again. No matter how anyone tried to help him now he felt like he was being interrogated.

“I know it sounds mysterious,” Harold said. “Let me begin practically. I have your family’s luggage. It’s in a car parked outside, along with a driver from the airline. If there’s anything you and your wife need from it, any particular article, even all of it, I’ll have it brought to you right now.”

David nodded.

“Did the doctor say how long Alice would be hospitalized?”

“He said she had to go on blood thinners to get home. He said it was dangerous for her to fly right now.”

“Will you stay at the hospital?”

David shook his head.

“Why don’t you tell me what hotel you’re staying in, and I’ll have the driver deliver your luggage immediately. If you find your stay here is extended, everything’s there. He can bring anything back to you at any time.”

“We were supposed to be at the Mandarin Oriental. But . . .”

“You don’t know where you’ll be,” he said.

“No.”

“Do you feel like you’re still moving? Like when you drive for a long time and try to sleep afterward, but it’s like your mind’s been windblown.”

“Yes.”

“That’s why I’m here.” Harold put his two index fingers up, then pressed their sides together. “It’s a condition, David, like shock. A person suffers a disaster traveling between two points in the air. It’s a unique brand of trauma. For two reasons. First, it’s the initial act of faith when you fly—the obvious thing you put out of your mind in order to board. That your reptile brain knows at thirty thousand feet you’re at risk of death. Second, because we travel at such great speeds and in such complex systems and routes, should anything interrupt the connections required for us to move between these locales, should we somehow get thrown out of that sequence of departure and arrival, then our most fundamental sense of security is blown from our possession as surely as if it had been detonated. The psychological and spiritual aftermath of such an event can be devastating.”

David was able to look up now, and the man’s eyes were blue and comforting.

"Something happens between two points," Harold said, "something in the air, and it's as if our own lives have been shot, like Phaethon's, right out of the sky. What we suffer is a kind of obliteration. Faith—all sense of trust—blasted from our souls. Wherewithal and judgment from our minds. Confidence from our spines. Happiness from our hearts. And *nerve* from the very core of our being. So many essential things cleaved from us and trailing smoke piece by piece from the far-flung point of impact that you'd think it was a permanent calamity. It makes us hole up. It makes us not want to move."

David listened.

"Remember when the space shuttle exploded?"

"Of course."

"Do you remember where you were?"

"Yes."

"You'll never see another launch now without thinking about it. You'll always think it could happen again. SLSD is a syndrome: Sudden Loss of Suspension of Disbelief. It's why certain elderly people lose their ability to drive. They can't get up the *nerve* to pass or merge. Trucks in their lane send them careening toward the shoulder. They drive fifty-five in a gesture of desperate obedience. To calm their nerves they observe the law to the letter. They've seen so much misfortune that they're paralyzed. They're convinced the road is full of imminent disaster."

David nodded.

"You said the Mandarin Oriental, correct?"

"That's right."

"Your stay there will be taken care of by the airline. If you wish, we'll upgrade your accommodations for the duration of your wife's convalescence."

"What if I want to go home? Or if my wife does?"

"Then United will fly you and your wife first-class on the first available flight to any place in the world you wish to go. Here . . . " He opened the folder and handed David a card that was paper-clipped inside the cover. He underlined the number on it with his pen. "That's my cell. If I'm unavailable for any reason, you'll be forwarded to the on-call liaison. But I'm never unavailable."

"Mr. Harold," David said. "I'm sorry to be so blunt, but this feels like I'm being rewarded for something tragic."

"No, sir. You're being attended to. Assisted. And by very experienced professionals. By the *friendly* skies. Here." He slid David a stapled packet of papers from the folder. "That's a list of doctors associated with our airline.

If you need consultation or a second opinion about anything over the next few days, consider using any one of them as a starting point."

"Thank you," David said.

"Which brings me to the most difficult part: arrangements."

"I don't understand."

"For your child."

It was amazing, David thought, how many things death foisted upon you. Even a meeting like this.

"It seems cruel to bring it up so soon," Harold said, "but we'd like to help with this as well. We'll pay for every cent of your child's burial, of course. We have numerous local undertakers with whom we're associated. We own cemetery plots on all the islands. We can also make arrangements in any state in the country. Again, we feel it's our obligation. We'd be honored if you'd let us assist."

"I don't know what to say," David said.

"There's nothing to say. We're with you until you and your wife feel your feet have touched the ground."

Harold sat silently for a time, his hands crossed in front of him.

David stared at his food—its freshness already dimmed, the colors mixing with one another, syrup with egg yolks with butter, all of it disintegrating, congealing, decomposing. "I should probably go upstairs and see Alice."

"Of course," Harold said.

David wiped his mouth. He put his napkin on top of his plate. He looked at Harold, who was staring at him patiently, and then looked down again.

"Are you all right?"

David shrugged, feeling pinned to the chair.

"If you feel the need," Harold said, "you can ask me."

David couldn't bring himself to look at him.

"Ask me," Harold said.

David's eyes brimmed full. "Was it me?" he said. "What I thought? Do you know?"

"Yes," Harold said, "I do."

"Tell me. I need to know."

"It wasn't you, David. It was neither you nor anything you thought nor any choice you made. You weren't part of the equation."

"Are you sure?"

"Yes, I am."

"How can you be sure?"

"Because it's the nature of the event."

"That doesn't explain anything."

"Now, listen to me." He reached across the table and put his hand over David's. "You think what just happened to you is some sort of culmination. Like the end of a chapter. That it *had* to happen exactly like this. But it didn't. It's no culmination at all. You have no agency here. It's the effect of travel. When people travel, and especially when they fly, they see the choice to do so as unique. That's part of its lore, its miracle and romance. Its magic. People give special status to their point of departure. 'That flight that went down,' a person says. 'I was scheduled to take it, but my cab got stuck in traffic.' As if God had intervened. They afford divine status to this means of transportation. It was, in fact, just a *flight* they were trying to catch. *That* was the end of the sequence. It was where they were *going,* so it had to be. But they're wrong. Because when they *do* catch that flight, they take travel's interstitial nature and apply it to themselves. Once they're on that plane, they see it as a break in their life's sequence, a kind of limbo or safe haven. But life travels with you. Think about it. Divorces have occurred on planes. People get engaged up there. Children have been conceived miles high. They've been delivered, healthy, up there too. And people die—of coronaries, strokes, aneurysms. They have a drink, then slip off to permanent sleep. They choke on airplane food. They're saved. People fall in love. Books are finished, both being written and read. Great discoveries and scientific breakthroughs are made. Yet in spite of all this, people think of travel, of movement, as a kind of reprieve from life. But they're wrong. Movement isn't a reprieve. There *is* no reprieve. Movement is our permanent state." In closing, he squeezed David's hand firmly.

"Tell me again that you're sure," David said.

"Of all the thoughts we think, it's only those that actually manifest themselves that seem significant. But the thoughts just before the event are like the fortune in the cookie. The fortune's as random as the thought."

"Promise me."

"Think of all the thoughts we think. Think of all the ones we don't remember."

"Please."

"It was nothing you *did,* David. I promise there was nothing you could've done."

David laid his other hand over Harold's and pressed his forehead to their clasped hands. It was like a sculpture over which his tears ran. "Why couldn't I have been a better man?" he said.

"You will be."

"Why didn't I think something else?"

"You already have."

David sobbed. More than anything, he wanted to see his wife, to hold her.

"Ease her down now," Harold said, "ease her down."

Dr. Ahmed put Alice on a program of blood thinners and kept her under observation for the evening. The next morning, she and David agreed to have their son cremated.

The boy's ashes were presented to them in a white rectangular plastic container the size of a small Thermos, along with a death certificate that specified David Pepin. The dates of birth and death were the same, of course. The remains felt somehow heavier than the child had, which David found utterly mysterious.

Alice received the urn without any noticeable reaction, having become more and more withdrawn. At the same time, David sensed within her a gathering anger, though he was strangely unafraid. He knew this was due to his conversation with Harold.

Just as David had felt that her pregnancy cleaved Alice from him, it seemed the child's death had as well. There was nothing to be done about it, however. He'd already accepted it somehow. But what came afterward was something else entirely.

While Alice was in the hospital, he made several calls to Harold, and the comfort he enjoyed from these talks was immeasurable. Of course, his first concern was Alice and how to help her down as well. When the doctor indicated she'd probably be discharged that afternoon, he called Harold immediately, unsure how to proceed. Harold's advice, albeit cryptic, made a kind of higher practical sense that David couldn't comprehend until he made use of it. "Be firm with her, but flexible. You must listen carefully for any opportunity either to take charge or to acquiesce. The more carefully you listen before taking action, the more gently she'll land."

A few hours later, when Dr. Ahmed confirmed that Alice would be discharged immediately, David asked her what she wanted to do. The question angered her.

"What do you mean?" she said.

"Would you like to go home," he said, "or would you like to stay?"

"Here?"

"Yes."

"You mean take a vacation?"

"No," David said. "I mean just be here. The two of us. I don't know what to call it. But I'm not ready to go home. I spoke with Mr. Sobel at Trinity and told him you'd had a medical emergency—that we weren't sure yet when we'd be back."

Alice smoldered visibly over this. "Did you tell him what happened?"

"Of course not," David said.

She crossed her arms and stared out the window. In the morning light, the weight she'd gained from the pregnancy was more apparent: a roundness to her arms, the hint of belly pressing out of her gown. He turned to see what she was looking at. Palm trees waved in the parking lot below. In the distance, mist snaked through the volcanic mountains.

"What would we do here?" she asked finally.

"Why don't you let me handle that."

When she didn't reply, he took her silence as a decision.

He promptly informed Harold, who sent them a car. When she saw it, Alice asked, "Why all this?"

David balked, or trusted his gut—he wasn't sure which. But he was certain she must not know they were being helped. "I just thought it would be easier," he said, though he had no idea what to do next. He would consider the hotel a kind of home base until he had a clearer plan.

In the car, Alice placed the urn in her lap and held it there. If she was waiting for David to mention it, he didn't say a thing.

The Mandarin Oriental was located at the dead end of the Kahala neighborhood, where houses were built on real estate of impossible value, and blocks and blocks of walled-off, Spanish-style stucco homes ran parallel to the ocean. The hotel's gorgeous modern design stood in stark contrast to the residences around it, with two adjacent towers of white and ocean blue, its structural lines built out with white girders from each window, so the various wings appeared to be surrounded by stacked, transparent cubes, a kind of scaffolding that somehow lightened the structures, made them seem as if they could, like a pair of gliders, ride the air. The towers backed up to the Waialae Country Club at the base of the Ko'olau Ridge, a house-speckled mountain lush with trees that climbed like a slow-building wave into the distance, all the homes facing the ocean, though it was impossible to see the water until you entered the hotel itself. The high walls of a third, perpendicular structure—a giant porte cochere—blocked all sightlines, making the strand beyond it seem even more private from the other side. David and Alice were treated like royalty upon arrival—Harold's doing, David knew. One of the managers, a Japanese man named Murahashi, gave them a personal tour after they checked in, showing them five restaurants on the premises, several shops, the pool, spa, and gym. He then walked them through the porte cochere that led to the beach. Two long jetties enclosed the reef-calmed waters, the long, private strip of sand demarcated by a dense web of palm trees. "This is a very popular place to marry," Murahashi said, and as if on cue, a handsome Japanese bride and groom appeared, walking toward a white gazebo that faced the ocean, the bride clutching her train happily, the two of them leaning into the breeze, their families seated in chairs on grass as immaculate as a fairway. Murahashi walked David and Alice through the restaurant off the beach, the Plumeria, an airy room filled with mahogany, its floors of cool slate. Alice seemed unfazed by the beauty of it all.

"Of course," Murahashi said, leading them into a gigantic courtyard, "our permanent residents are what make the hotel so famous." Before them was a giant man-made lagoon, walled off at its far end by two-story suites, the lagoon itself in two discrete pools that formed a figure eight. Here a pod of dolphins played, tended by trainers—all young women in blue bathing suits—who stood on a floating platform that bisected the main pools. The women were so uniformly beautiful, the creatures so wondrous, it was as if the dolphins were shape-shifting gods attended by nymphs. People were watching from everywhere on the lagoon's circumference: the wide terrace off the porte cochere; the gated, surrounding walkways; the swimming pool near the beach. Joy seemed to radiate from the water. A large blue mat was set up on the floating platform—four of the women kneeled around it, holding it by the edges—and when one of the trainers held her hand up over the surface, a dolphin appeared, then nosed her palm and chirped: a piercing sound that reverberated through the cove. When the woman quickly flicked her hand, the dolphin slipped from the water in a silky leap that didn't even ruffle the surface and landed on the middle of the mat, its entire body curled up into a crescent, and much larger than David had imagined. A trainer positioned near its head wrote something down on a clipboard.

"What are they doing?" Alice asked.

"They're checking her weight," Murahashi said.

"Why?"

"To make sure she's progressing well."

From the corner of his eye, David saw his wife smile.

Their suite—enormous, airy, plant-filled, with honey-colored hardwood and teak and rattan furniture—hovered over the dolphin lagoon and the Pacific. The king-size canopy bed was covered by a goose-down duvet and sheets of Egyptian cotton so soft they made David lust for sleep. Exploring, he opened the sliding plantation shutters and stood on the lanai. The palms below bent in the trade winds, the clatter of their blowing leaves mixing with the dolphins' whistles and the *whoomps*—like depth charges—they made when they landed from a flip. Applause followed from the ever-present crowd. He let the hissing breezes fill his ears. He closed his eyes, then opened them. In the water, out in the lagoon, snorkelers floated in pairs, drifting, their bodies motionless, as if they'd been shot out of the sky. The reef they hovered over—mottled blue-green—was visible from this height. Farther out—many hundreds of yards—fishermen stood on a distant sandbar before a line of breakers that roiled but never reached them. Due East was Diamond Head, as majestic and immovable as some ancient craft. And everywhere the contained, humbling feeling of being in the middle of the ocean. The place was so beautiful that for a moment he forgot.

"Alice?" he said when he came inside.

On a small end table, she'd placed the urn next to a stunning bouquet of white roses. Water was running in the bathroom.

He knocked; when she didn't answer, his heart caught in his throat, and he let himself in. She was lying in the large soaking tub, its jets on full, her mascara running down her cheeks. Was it from her bath or had she been crying? The longer they were together, the harder he found it to say anything to her.

"It was nice of you to send flowers." She looked up at him and mustered a smile, this seeming to exhaust the little energy she had.

He stood waiting, again, for what he wasn't sure.

"This is the most beautiful bathroom I've ever seen," she said.

He looked around. The room was all gray marble and teak, with vanities and closets at either end with luxurious robes neatly hung on wooden hangers. There was a large, glass-enclosed shower, its spout the size of a Frisbee. The toilet, inset between shower and bath, had a door for privacy as well as a phone. "It is," David said.

"If I had a bathroom like this, I'd feel like we'd truly made it." She looked around as if seeing the place anew.

"Maybe we will one day."

Alice said nothing.

"You never know," he said.

"No," she said, "you don't."

There was nothing more to say, so he left her alone and called Harold from the bedroom. "I can't talk to her," he said. "*We* can't. It's like a black hole."

"That's all right, David. That's fine for now."

"No, it's horrible."

"It'll pass." His voice, as always, was calm.

Dying for a drink, David opened the wet bar. "Thank you for the flowers," he said, and looked at the note. It read *Love.*

"You thought of them," Harold said, "not me."

This was true. When they'd entered the lobby, a bride was having her pictures taken, holding an enormous bouquet, and he'd thought: If I could fill the room with flowers for her, I would. "Are you saying you're a telepath?"

"I'm a good listener."

"What are you hearing now?"

"Why don't you tell me?"

In his mind, David saw his wife cradling their child in the airplane bathroom. As much as he wanted to forget that, he never would. And there was something else.

"I need to confess something."

"What?"

"It's like a crime. But it's not something I did. I don't know how to say it."

"You will when you're ready."

It was akin to love, David thought, to trust a person so immediately and completely, a feeling as real as being hungry, which of course he was.

"Have you made dinner reservations?" Harold asked.

David looked at his watch: just after six o'clock. "No."

"When would you like to go?"

"In an hour, but I might have to cancel. I want to see how she's feeling."

"All right."

"What should we do?"

"When?"

"Tomorrow."

"What would you *like* to do?"

"I don't know. When we travel, Alice usually makes all our plans."

"I understand."

"I'm not very curious."

"That's fine."

"I only travel for work."

"We'll take care of it."

"She does everything."

"Don't be so hard on yourself."

"I never do anything."

"Easy, David."

For a moment, he wasn't even sure if Harold was real.

"Go on," Harold said. "Ask me."

"It's the wrong thing to be thinking about."

"No it isn't."

"What *is* Diamond Head?"

"It's a dead volcano. Though in Hawaii, it seems that none of the volcanoes are truly dead."

Later, at dinner, Alice asked the same question. If she was impressed that he knew, she didn't let on. It was just background noise, a brief pause between their respective engorgements, the only thing they'd paused to speak about. He ate relentlessly and had never seen her eat so much either. She ordered calamari to start, a large plate meant for sharing that she consumed without coming up for air. She ordered tuna tartare and then the sea bass, the last served on a bed of risotto; finally, for dessert, a cheese plate. Throughout the meal, he listened to her breathing through her nose.

"What will we do tomorrow?" she asked once the last plate was emptied.

"It's a surprise," he said.

"What if I don't like your surprise?"

"Then we won't do it. You can just tell me what you want to do instead."

"What if I want to go home?"

"That's fine."

"I mean *now*. Tonight."

"That's fine too."

"Don't keep fucking agreeing with me, David. Stop being so goddamn compliant."

He waited. Her anger was so barely containable that he was afraid to move.

"Don't try to turn this into *fun*," she said.

"I won't."

She sighed, then folded her napkin disinterestedly.

"I think we should stay here for a while," he said. "I just want to wait."

She said nothing after that.

Later that night, he woke to her sobbing, at times wailing so loudly he was sure security would start pounding on the door. He tried to hold her, but whenever he did she flung her elbows and arms at him, so he finally gave up and left the bed, their physical distance seeming to calm her ever so slightly. She lay there, her back heaving in the dark, piled in the sheets, mumbling something into the pillow, and he stepped out onto the lanai and shut the door, her grief twisting his lungs.

After several minutes he came back inside.

"Talk to me," he said. "Please."

He waited. She went still. Then she got onto her knees, the sheets curled around her like a pedestal.

"Don't make me say it," she said.

He fled the room, went to the bar downstairs, and drank until he couldn't keep his eyes open. When he came back upstairs she was asleep.

He woke in the middle of the night to find her gone. The doors to the lanai were open and the sound of the breeze and palms filled the room, the curtains floating as gently as the tentacles of jellyfish. He called her name, but the terror he felt made breathing difficult. He was sure she'd stepped out onto the veranda and jumped, so sure that after getting up he was afraid to lean over the side and look. He could imagine her body down there, white and undiscovered under the moon. It would not, he thought, be such a bad way to die, and considered it for a moment himself. He imagined the fall. He could imagine the peace it might bring; how long would the fall take? He wondered too what it would be like to return home without her, without anything: the plane ride back, the cab to the apartment, opening the door and stepping inside. What would it be like never to hear her voice again? A kind of loneliness, he supposed, from what he was feeling now, the kind that was nearly self-canceling, a loneliness he couldn't conjure up. *In* love, you could never remember what it was like to want it. *In* love, it was impossible to conceive of the other truly being gone. As for the coming of a child, you couldn't prepare your heart for it. There was nothing to know until it happened. It was all new.

He went downstairs to look for her. The shops were closed, the gates down. In the lobby, a Japanese clerk was doing paperwork at the front desk. She looked at David, smiled too brightly for the hour—past three in the morning—and went back to her job. A Hawaiian man buffed the floors. In the lounge, a clerk was already setting up coffeemakers, restocking condiments, and pushing a cart on which there were newspapers from all over the world. David stepped out onto the large terrace, the one that overlooked the dolphin lagoon, and spotted Alice on the walkway below.

She was leaning against the fence that surrounded the two pools, her chin resting on her crossed arms. He knew she could hear him coming, and when he stood next to her she didn't speak. It was humid, but cool. Even in the dark, he could see the goose bumps on her arms. He leaned against the fence as well and waited, too afraid to try to hold her. Occasionally the dolphins surfaced, gray figures on black water, making small jet sounds as they exhaled.

"I don't think I can go back," she said.

"Back where?"

"Home."

He wondered for a moment if these animals, so long around people, shared the same curiosity that humans felt about them.

"Would you stay here?" he said.

"I don't think so."

"Where would you go?"

"I don't know. But I'm terrified of our apartment. I had a dream about us walking in there, and it woke me up."

"Why?"

"Because when we left he was inside me."

They didn't speak for a minute or two.

"Would you take me with you?" David asked.

"I don't know," she said.

He could feel the dolphins swim by: a pulse of energy that didn't even disturb the water's surface, except for a slight wake you noticed only when little waves rose suddenly up the rocks lining the shallows. They never seemed to *break* the surface, merely spreading it gently, like curtains, over their heads and backs. "What was it like?" he asked.

"What?"

"Being pregnant."

"What do you mean?"

"The feeling."

He recalled what Harold had told him about listening. There were, of course, different versions of this—or, rather, all sorts of unheard sounds: a lazing dog exhaling while waiting for you to call it; the silence of a room after a fight; the sound of a stadium where people were leaving before a loss; toys waiting in a playroom for the child; the book on the shelf that's been whispering to you. He heard Alice relax, as if whatever was roiling within her had stopped churning for a moment.

"It was like you were special," she said. "I don't know how else to describe it. But it was like the world was better. You had something inside you that made you more alive."

If he were struggling to speak with her, she was struggling to look at him.

"I want to go to bed," she said.

In the morning, they slept late. David ordered coffee and suggested they get something to eat.

"Good," she said, "I'm starving."

The front desk called to confirm their reservations to swim with the dolphins at ten thirty, and when he told her about this, she seemed pleased.

At breakfast they sat outside, facing the ocean. Alice chose the buffet: pancakes rolled into long cigars and soaked in syrup; a ham, cheese, and chive omelet made fresh at the omelet bar; another plate piled with fruit, bacon, and prosciutto, even a few pieces of sushi. David, his stomach weak from the night before, had oatmeal and coffee.

"Let's sit out here for a while," she said, turning to face the water.

The waiter came and she ordered another mimosa and then sat rubbing her belly.

"My God," she whispered, looking out at the Pacific.

He didn't ask.

Nor did he ask what the dolphin trainer had told her as they waded out to the middle of the lagoon, whatever it was that made Alice laugh so hard. He was simply glad to see her seem happy. Along with four other guests, the trainer led them through a series of close encounters and tricks—the dolphin spinning like a top, more than half its body out of water; skimming backward in similar gravity-defying fashion; fetching three rings flung in three directions, collecting all of them, it seemed, the instant they hit the surface—and then took Alice alone out into the middle of the pool. On a small island there was kiosk where people checked in for these adventures and were given life vests and masks labeled SEA QUEST, and David walked halfway up a narrow staircase overlooking the pool to take pictures. The morning sunlight bejeweled the surface of the lagoon, softening every shot, making the images too beatific, too postcard-perfect, but the joy on his wife's face redeemed them, made them more personal and completely uncontrived. Watching her applaud every trick, and listen to the trainer as they treaded water, and talk with this stranger, he had that precious glimpse of Alice in the world without him, encountering an unabashed joy that seldom if ever presented itself to her—this, moreover, an emotion she didn't really trust. He thought of her childhood stories, of her acute loneliness, of feeling unwanted, of the belief built into the very core of her character that she was somehow undeserving of love. She *guarded* herself against joy. Their child had brought these defenses down, of course, sent them tumbling like the walls of Jericho. And he admired how, so soon after what had happened, she'd found the strength to give herself over to joyousness here and *now.* "You seemed to enjoy that," he said when he met her outside the gate.

She squeezed the water from her hair, took off the life jacket. "What's not to enjoy?" she said.

Later, they took a cab into Waikiki, though the moment they got there David realized he'd made a terrible mistake. Nothing was beautiful here, nothing took your mind away. It was like a shopping district in any American city, and if you looked straight down Kalakaua Avenue you might as well be in Atlanta or St. Louis. David and Alice walked the streets aimlessly, passing Tiffany's, Banana Republic, the Gap, Niketown, Brooks Brothers, and Gucci, Bebe, and Abercrombie & Fitch interspersed with one T-shirt store after another, some of them gigantic hybrids, multipurpose shops for all tourists that sold cheap surfer shirts, macadamia nuts, coconut syrup (David bought some), sunscreen and sun hats and sunglasses, wine and beer and liquor, followed by an open-air market whose kiosks—made of fake palm leaves and real bamboo—were full of snow globes, leis, grass skirts, bathing suits, tribal kitsch and faux Hawaiian sculpture ranging from totem poles to dolphins and killer whales, signs that read Hang Ten! photo booths and food stands, square after black-velvet square of turquoise and silver rings, shark tooth and sea turtle necklaces, puka beads stacked one strand atop another on a peg as long as an African's neck, regionalized knickknacks worn only by the tasteless or infirm, produced in some factory hidden away on the mainland or by children in India or China.

It was wearing on Alice too. "I don't need any of this," she said.

"I know."

"I have zero interest in shopping. Especially this junk."

"I didn't think you did."

"I want a drink," she said. "I want to sit down."

One of the hotels facing Mamala Bay had a patio restaurant with uncomfortable, wrought-iron chairs, the servers who patrolled it barely out of their teens. A Cruzan rum card on the table said MAI TAI! David's beer came in a clear plastic cup—garbage, he thought, that would soon end up in the ocean. Small birds raided every crumb that fell to the floor and swarmed any of the plates the busboys were slow to clear. David counted an astonishing number of fat people.

"I'm starving," Alice said, looking over the menu.

From here they had a clear view of Waikiki Beach, that famous strip of sand everyone's seen somewhere, in movies or on television or postcards as ubiquitous as images of the Grand Canyon, so in person it seemed it fell far short of one's expectations, seeming instead diminished and banal. There were surfers everywhere, boys and girls and old men and teens, both close in and out far, riding sets of waves so long they seemed to stretch as far as the eye could see, the water clotted with swimmers and boogie-boarders navigating between catamarans and large pleasure craft that barreled toward shore at breakneck speed while small planes flew overheard, the sheer density of the crowds like some time warp back to Coney Island of the forties, the black-and-white photos of that beach showing it to be so choked with people there was no sand to see, no reason even to come except perhaps to hate the proximity of your fellow man; it would be like riding the rush-hour subway for fun, he thought, and for the lifeguards glassing these masses from their towers, a drowning among so many bobbing heads and arms and legs must be impossible to catch. From this vantage, Diamond Head seemed nearly overwhelmed by all these people and towers on the beach, by this disease of development, so this majestic sight now could be a sculpture symbolizing America's ugliness and failure. Terrible, he thought.

"Terrible," Alice said.

Couple telepathy, they called it. Not that her disapproval affected her appetite. She ordered a main-course chef's salad with her bacon cheeseburger, a banana daiquiri, a slice of key lime pie. When the food was placed before her, she ate without pause and left nothing for the birds.

"This can't be Hawaii," she said finally.

"I know what you mean."

"This can't be all of it."

"No."

"We can't have come here for this." She began to cry.

"We didn't," he said. "I promise."

"Then get us *out* of here," she said.

When they got back to the hotel, she arranged for a cabana at the beach. He told her he wanted to rest in the room for a while and would meet her later.

The minute he was upstairs, he called Harold.

"We need to go somewhere else," he told him. "Somewhere pure."

They went to Kauai.

Though he didn't know it at the time, this was exactly the place Alice needed, that she'd been searching for since the death of their child—though neither did she realize this until they arrived.

Only a half-hour flight from Honolulu, it's the westernmost island of the chain, circular in shape, a mere ninety miles around, composed primarily of mountainous, undevelopable land. When checking in at the airport, David was given—thanks to Harold—a brochure thick with maps and so much geographical information that he could only skim it, along with the key to a condominium on the north coast.

Alice hadn't been searching for beauty, though there was a superabundance here. Later, looking at the pictures from the trip, as he did quite often, David would reflect that Kauai's beauty was something that photos didn't really come close to capturing.

For instance, the sweeping view from their lanai, situated on a cliff hundreds of feet above the ocean. To the northeast was a lighthouse shaped like a baby's bottle and from that distance no bigger than a fingernail. The pictures didn't suggest the loneliness of the little red-and-white tower with its clamshell glass, which to David seemed like the perfect place to live out your life if you needed to disappear.

Nor did the pictures capture David's terror staring at the stars on those nights when Alice cried herself to sleep, with a dull moan like an old engine turning over endlessly, resounding through the sliding doors of the lanai even if he plugged his ears. Never had he seen a sky as wide or brilliant as this, or as terrifically violent; he saw tens of shooting stars every night, and, once, what he was sure was a comet because of its slow progress across the horizon, its head brighter than any other star, its tail flickering clearly, on a cataclysmic collision course with who knew what or when or how many light-years away. This sky wasn't star-hung but star-flung, the universe from this vantage a stage of explosions and near misses. No picture could yield his state of mind, an anxious span of minutes, of hours, spent wondering, semiparalyzed, that since nothing truly bad had ever happened to him until now, why was it impossible to think that this was only the beginning? That the rest of his life was an inescapable strip of suffering, relooping on itself for as long as he breathed. Nor did the pictures capture how golden the sunlight was in the morning or the relief those first rays gave him as he lay on the edge of their bed.

The pictures didn't capture the grandeur of Waimea Canyon either, the silence of its reddish brown mountains, a quiet augmented by the sight, miles and miles distant, of waterfalls hundreds of feet high, cascades reduced by perspective to tiny hairs, their movement still perceptible, a braided shimmer, your mind tricking you into thinking you could just barely hear their crash, or of what it was like from that lookout to spot goats in the valley two thousand feet below, or to dream of what life was like as many years previous, to have come here with the Polynesians, to have set foot on this place and thought you'd discovered paradise, to imagine yourself down there, hunting these creatures. To understand that a life based on survival as opposed to love was perhaps desirable. That after seeing this, all apocalyptic dreams seemed a pathetic longing for such simplicity. Nor did the pictures confirm Alice's seriousness when, staring out over that precipice, she flatly said that she no longer felt like a woman and that if the feeling didn't return to her, then she wanted to die.

Neither did they give you a true sense of how sheer the climb was down to Hideaway Beach in Princeville, the rusted railings wobbly on cement stairs steep as attic steps—"They should call it Fall Away," David said—built literally *off* the edge of a cliff, as if the house to which they'd been attached had fallen into the ocean, since chunks of the last step had eroded and you had to jump *down* to the path, this adding to the comedy and terror. They didn't render the slipperiness of the switchback trail you traversed, where your hands were burned by the rope lines you used to half rappel down at the risk of tumbling two hundred feet and bouncing off solid rock webbed by palms. They didn't communicate the conviction that for all Kauai's beauty there was always a concomitant anxiety about your safety: rip tides could take you; tiger sharks could ambush you from below; the nothingness of the Pacific stretched out and could carry you away.

No picture conveyed the power of the current at Ha'ena Beach, water too dangerous to swim in, where sign after yellow sign warned of lethal drop-off and shore break, the stickman figure crushed by stickwaves and washed out to sea. ("No wonder you never see stickmen," David said to Alice, "those idiots are all dead.") DANGEROUS MARINE LIFE! the signs read. DO NOT APPROACH THE MONK SEALS! NEVER TURN YOUR BACK ON THE OCEAN! David's pictures didn't communicate the invisible speed of the shallow river mouth they tried to cross that afternoon in order to reach the reef beyond, how it knocked their feet out from under them while they held hands and slid toward the giant surf—it was like being swallowed—and were finally beached in the shallowest stretch of stream, the last safe patch between tributary and ocean, as if the water itself had been trying to snatch their lives away. (Only after, calmed down, could they laugh about it.) Pictures didn't render how miraculous it was to watch three Hawaiian boys, none older than twelve, ride these same monstrous waves on boogie boards, the total control with which they banked away from the jetty, the *trust* to come so close to crushing onto rocks, immune, it seemed, to both current and tide. "It's like they're playing on explosions," Alice had said. Nor could photos seize the splendor of the rainbow that suddenly appeared, arcing from the water to sand, the light appearing as near as ceiling and as wide as highway, or how it retreated from her grasp as she tried to walk after it.

The pictures didn't hint at how peaceful the half-mile descent down to Secret Beach was on a root-tangled and rock-littered path enclosed by a canopy of trees and brush that formed a bower so dense that it insulated you completely from the sight and sound of the ocean. They caught only glimmers of how impossibly gorgeous the young couple who climbed toward them there really were. The man was tall and sandy-haired; unshaven and sharp-featured, he carried a surfboard and stepped from rock to root as surefooted as a mountain goat. His Hawaiian wife, as if to confirm she was some sort of island princess, wore a lily in her hair. Their barefoot son followed close behind, a long-haired boy wearing a Rip Curl surfer's shirt. Seeing Alice stop to watch *him* was like seeing an arrow pierce your beloved's heart or a possible future passing you by.

He never took a picture of the urn but knew where it was at all times. Alice kept it on a small table by the door to the lanai. She placed an orchid in a small pitcher next to it, its petals so blue they seemed lit from within.

The pictures *did* reveal the weight she'd gained during the two weeks they were there, over fifteen pounds that puffed her cheeks, fattened her arms and legs, and if you stacked and then flipped them in sequence, the change looked like a nickelodeon before-and-after. After every enormous meal, she would sit back, exhale, and rub her belly.

Out of hundreds of photos, only one was of the two of them together. That picture was taken during their hike along the Na Pali, near the end of their time on Kauai. The trail began at Ke'e Beach, the very end of the highway that otherwise encircled the island but for this sixteen-mile stretch of towering, eroding coastline. The trail ran hundreds of feet up into the cliffs. After consulting maps and guides Harold had given him, he told Alice they had three choices. They could hike two miles in to Hanakapi'ai Beach and turn around. They could press on for two more miles and try for the Hanakoa Valley, an all-day round trip. Or if she was interested in a really extreme challenge they could go another five miles to Kalalau Beach, a strip of sand so remote and protected that boat landings were illegal. They'd have to camp there overnight, which required permits, and would need to be fully outfitted. Stage by stage, he warned, the trail became more difficult and dangerous; in fact, some parts were so narrow that even the lightest rainfall made them impassable.

He explained this with an indifference that bordered on contempt. Exhausted, finished, he was over the nights of endless crying, not because she didn't deserve all her grief but because she always dared him to comfort her, and he was over the anger she leveled at him when he did. He was tired of going into another bedroom to sleep, of her not looking at him and not letting him touch her, of her not saying whatever it was she needed to say. He wanted to go home, and if she'd come along, he wanted that too. So when she brightened and said she'd like to go all the way to Kalalau Beach, eleven miles in and at least a two-day trip, he was taken completely by surprise—if for no other reason than on such an expedition they'd be obliged to communicate. They would have to rely on each other.

When he called this plan in, Harold advised him not to do it. Only highly experienced hikers could make it, and several people died on the trail every year. The outing to Hanakapi'ai was feasible, he said, the hike itself difficult enough that they'd have a sense of accomplishment. But otherwise, he couldn't responsibly approve.

They were also supposed to leave in three days. By now it was late morning, and they were scheduled to get outfitted for a hike that Alice was set on. "I've always wanted to do something like that," she'd told him.

David found her on the lanai after she returned from a swim. Her back was to him, and he was standing in the kitchen now, watching her through the veranda's glass door, noticing the fat handles around her waistline, the thickness at her calves, extra weight he felt whenever he held her hand to help her up the path from the beach to their condo. He slid the door open and stood beside her along the railing. "I want to talk about this trip," he said.

He made his case, having had further discussions with a local. When he concluded it was too risky, she said, "Since when do you care if it's dangerous?"

"What are you talking about?"

"You know what I mean."

"No, I don't."

She crossed her arms.

"What is it, Alice?" he said. "Just come out and say it."

"It's nothing."

David buried the heels of his hands into his eyes. "I can't take this anymore," he said. "I just—"

"Just *what*?"

He had no idea. "What do you want to do?" he asked resignedly.

"I want to *go*," she said. "This is the Everest of hikes, right? I want to do it. I need to do *something*."

"No, *please*."

"Take me or I'll go alone."

He heard her but wasn't listening, at least not as Harold had advised. Instead he imagined the narrow trail hundreds of feet up, the two of them weighed down by full packs, the rain coming suddenly—before Alice, her feet slipping out from under her, would suddenly be gone.

He'd take her, of course, if only to see her quit.

"Fine, then," he said.

Harold expedited the permits and they were fully outfitted by the end of the day. Before they left, however, David told her they should pack for home, and he made the arrangements.

They hired a cab to Ke'e Beach, where park rules stated that you weren't supposed to leave a car overnight. They rode together in silence as they drove west, around the northernmost point of the island, winding up switchbacks from which they glimpsed the ocean through the trees, the cliff faces dimpled with branches you'd be clutching for dear life headed down. They crossed single-lane bridges over inlets whose currents ran with visible force down the mountains and out to sea, where locals sat outside lean-to shacks with hand-painted signs advertising MAPS or GUIDED TOURS, rows of surfboards and kayaks lined up behind them.

"What do you mean," David finally said, "that I don't care if it's dangerous?"

Alice, sitting shoreside, was peering out the window at every sharp turn and looking down. "Are you really going to bring this up again?" she said.

"Yes," he said, "I am."

"Then you're going to be talking to yourself all day."

He closed his eyes, shook his head. If he could get her alone somewhere, somewhere completely private, he'd kill her. He would break a rock over her head and split her skull open so that he could see, just for a second, what the fuck was in her mind.

Ke'e Beach was jammed with hikers, beachgoers, and snorkelers. The entrance was shrouded in darkness, embowered by mountain foliage on their left that jailed off a clear view of the ocean to their right. Cars were parked everywhere in the makeshift lot crisscrossed by ancient roots that pythoned across everything, pitching the vehicles at crazy angles and making them appear abandoned, dented from all the wear and tear and splashed as they were with mud. Furious, David got out of the cab and walked on to the trailhead, leaving Alice to pay the driver and talk to herself while she tried to catch up. He read the advisories and, looking at the maps, felt a rush of adrenaline ahead of his fear. The trail was like a skyscraper staircase straight up, composed of what looked to be a frozen river of rocks.

He turned to look for Alice, who'd already stopped to adjust the straps on her pack and retie her boots, underestimating, he thought, what lay ahead, and when she put her arm through a shoulder loop and lifted the pack she staggered backward slightly from its weight, rolling her eyes in annoyance and cursing under her breath, as if she were here against her will. It made David sick with disgust, with husbandly portent: there was fighting and venom to come. Pack finally secured, she snapped her belt strap and caught his eye; he pointed up and began to walk.

He pressed ahead during the initial ascent, anger and anxiety making him rush, and he put a solid twenty-five yards between them. He didn't even want to speak to her. *He* didn't care if it were dangerous? *She* was the one making him take her. Livid, he pushed himself harder. When he did glance back, the distance between them had increased, but she wasn't even looking to see where he was. He knew she knew what he was doing. It was a challenge, a game of chicken. He was daring her to either storm off or keep up, the latter forcing her to realize the futility of completing *her* expedition. The harder he pushed, the sooner she'd fail—the sooner, that is, they'd be safe.

But keep up she did. He finally had to slow down himself, due not only to the difficulty of the climb but also to the overwhelming beauty of the Na Pali. During the ascent the trail was rocky, pocked with boulders he had to climb over, slide down, or hug around, the path interrupted by streams, staggered by roots that tripped him and threw his pack toward his head and sent him falling forward, only the steepness of the incline catching him, saving him from injury, a thing to remember coming down. Along the steepest section there was nothing to see but the trail in front of you. The foliage was so dense it blocked both sun and breeze and acted as a blanket that trapped the humidity. But at the top there was a clearing and the wind hit him full force, cooling him down, the sun drying the sweat from his shirt. To his right was Ke'e Beach below, the bathers the size of commas; ahead, the fluted cliffs of the coast jutted out one after the other like the toes of a giant reptile, their faces so thick with vegetation they looked covered in fur. From this vista he could see for several miles. A white tracery of surf was etched along the line where the rocks plunged into the water.

The sight calmed him, as the ascent had cleared his mind. He knew what he wanted: to get his wife back. He needed her. He now wanted them to leave. It was time for this to end. David looked down the trail and Alice was laboring toward him. She had caught up, and perhaps she too had detected the clearing where he stood waiting. When she stopped, he would apologize. He was sure the spectacle of this place would soften her heart too.

"Look at this," he said when she came up to him.

"*Fuck* you," she said, and walked on, disappearing around a turn.

David blinked, half laughed, then hurried after her.

He got to where he was right behind her. He would've liked to walk next to her, but the trail was too narrow: cliffs to the left, sheer drop-off to the right. With her pack on, he could only see her legs, and, when she gestured, her hands and arms. So he talked to the back of the pack. "Fuck *me*?" he said. "What did I do?"

"Don't even talk," she said.

"We haven't talked since we got here."

"You haven't wanted to."

"That's *all* I've wanted to."

"You don't *say* anything," she said. "You just repeat everything *I* say."

"I'm waiting for *you* to speak."

"Please."

"I'm waiting for you to look at me for once."

"Oh, of course it's me."

"Here we go."

"It's *always* me." She half turned, speed walking. She'd pinched her thumbs to her index fingers. "I am a *leper* to you."

"Oh, for Christ's sake."

"A *lep-per.*"

"Can you cut the drama? Pull yourself out of it for a change? So I don't have to be the one who has to wait and then apologize."

"You and your fucking apologies. You think they undo everything. Like a goddamn reset button. But there are things you can't undo."

"Like what? Like *I* did something?"

"Don't make me say it!"

She stopped so suddenly he nearly slid into her. She turned her back to the cliff and walked up the slope backward to let a group of hikers who were coming from the other direction pass. David couldn't tell if they'd heard their argument.

He and Alice walked silently for a time.

"I'm waiting," he finally said.

She didn't reply.

"I'm waiting for you to *say* it."

She said nothing.

"It's like the prize behind door number three. I can't fucking *wait* to hear."

She tripped.

He saw it happen before she did. He was sure when he saw it that she'd never make the whole hike. She wasn't in shape; the pack was too much. A mile and a half in and already she couldn't lift her feet even over such a small rock, her left foot catching on it, and this sent her falling to the right, toward the edge of the cliff, and when the pack slung forward she landed hard on her shoulder, her momentum throwing her feet in the air. David's heart stopped. But she came to a halt, fortunately, and lay there. Another foot and she would've gone over. He bent to help her up.

"Don't touch me," she said.

Another group of hikers approached them. When they saw Alice brushing herself off, the leader asked if she was all right. David said she'd taken a little spill and would be fine. In the presence of these strangers she collected herself quickly, her cordiality galling to him. The trail was so narrow that passing required a kind of clownish maneuvering. You faced the oncomers, got as close as you could, and shuffled in place.

The group finally passed, though Alice just stood there for a moment. A helicopter thundered overhead, the engine roar louder than the subway or a fire truck, NA PALI SKY TOURS it read on the craft. It was so noisy it almost spoiled the place.

Alice tucked her hair behind her ear, waiting.

"Let me see your shoulder," he said.

Begrudgingly, she turned to let him examine her.

Her right shoulder was scraped along the deltoid, berries of blood in full bloom. Around the edges, it was already purple. "Can you move your arm?"

"Yes," she said, refusing to demonstrate. "I'm fine." Out of the corner of her eye, she looked at him.

He wiped the sweat above his mouth with his palm. "I'm sorry," he said.

She stood there.

"Can you carry your pack?"

"It hurts a little."

He sighed. It was quiet now. He felt remorseful and wanted to kiss her. "It's beautiful here," he said.

She nodded.

"Let's just get to Hanakapi'ai," he said. "We can take care of the cut and then reassess."

She cleared her throat.

"Do you want to lead?" he said.

She stood there like a child. "You go," she said finally.

They had to face each other as they pivoted around. He smiled, but she wouldn't look up.

Their pace slowed considerably over the next half hour. Every time he looked back, Alice was struggling, limping slightly and adjusting the straps on her shoulder. When he asked intermittently how she was holding up, she said she was okay, so he stopped asking. After an hour, they came to a precipice wide enough for a dozen people to stand on. A boulder formed a natural bench, shaded by a small tree—a perfect place to rest.

She stopped and slipped out of her pack, wincing as it slid over her shoulder. Then she sat and lifted her right foot. "I have a blister," she said. She took off her shoe and sock.

"Let me take care of that," he said. The blister was on the outside of her big toe, the skin hanging there, white as cream.

With Second Skin and medical tape in his pack, he prided himself on his readiness. She let him tend to her—this gladdened him—and when she put her shoe back on, he said, "Maybe we should turn around."

"I want to keep going," she said, remaining seated.

A family appeared from around the corner, day hikers with only water bottles, headed back to Ke'e Beach. The mother and father looked to be in their late forties, the two boys in their teens. They stopped at the lookout and regarded the view. David nodded at them.

"Would you take our picture?" the mother said.

Agreeing, he took her camera. The parents stood formally, a boy before each of them. Would sights such as these, he wondered, always make them sad?

"Should we take your picture?" the woman asked.

David looked at his wife.

She flexed her ankle and then, for the first time in weeks, regarded him with something approaching warmth.

"Yes," she said.

She got up and stood next to him. He took off his pack. Before he knew what was happening, she put her arm around his waist. It almost made him jump, he was so startled by her touch. Gently, he rested his arm on her injured shoulder.

If you were to look at the picture, he thought many months later, you'd think they were happy.

They left the lookout and within the hour were making the descent to the beach. They could see it in flashes as they switchbacked down the terraced trail, though it was like looking over a terrace without railings, the sheerness of the drop scaring them back from the edge. The shape of the valley leading to the beach was like an arrowhead driven between the cliffs, treacherous work going down. David, wary from his earlier stumbles, was extra careful. But even with the utmost caution he still slipped, the rocks coming out from under him when he leaned too far back, so he had to sit down and skid to a halt. He fell three separate times but continued without pause, urged on by the promise of a break in this labor, of food, a relief from the weight of their packs. We'll never make the campsite, he thought. They stopped only once, at a wooden sign that was painted brown, the letters yellow. At the top, in white, was a skull and crossbones; at the very bottom, a stickman swimming in a red circle with a red slash through it. **WARNING.** MORE DROWNINGS OCCUR AT HANAKAPI'AI THAN AT ANY OTHER BEACH IN KAUAI. DO NOT SWIM UNDER **ANY** CIRCUMSTANCES. Beneath this warning were five sets of marks adding up to twenty-three.

But Hanakapi'ai didn't look deadly at all, in fact seemed positively benign. At the last leg of the descent the trail was broken by a river of boulders—oblong, gray, and smooth, as small as bird's eggs or as big as cars—that ran down to another terraced formation, a six-foot face they had to climb down to get to sand. Like Ke'e, the place was crowded with day hikers, more serious folks resting from the eight-mile round trip to Hanakoa Valley, and several hard-core expeditionists on their way back from Kalalau. The beach was much wider than it had seemed from above and easily three hundred yards long, with a giant cave at the far end, its mouth open to the sea. In the cliff wall beside it, people had stashed their backpacks and boots and hung their socks and damp shirts to dry, the hikers themselves lying in the cave's shade or sitting where the waves broke and cooling off in the spray. Ahead, parallel to the water, was a gigantic tidal pool as long as a football field. In spite of the warning sign, maybe twenty children were swimming in the ocean beyond it.

"How do you feel?" David said.

"I'm tired," Alice said. "My shoulder hurts." She was sitting on a nearby rock, her pack at her feet, an energy bar in her hand. She chewed as if it were a nearly impossible exertion, then took out her water container and drank. "And I'm hot."

"I'm hot too," he said.

"I didn't think it would be this hard."

"I didn't either," he lied.

But she no longer seemed angry, and this elated him. The burst of confidence reminded him that he'd swum in lagoons but hadn't yet been in open surf. If they turned around, this might be his last chance. "It doesn't look so bad," he said.

He looked at her, then back at the water, and she looked with him. From here the waves appeared no bigger than those he'd swum in before.

"I'm going to go in," he said.

"It said you shouldn't. That it's dangerous."

"I'm sure it is. But look at the kids." He could hear them laughing. "I'm going to cool off."

She gazed at the water longingly, then finished her energy bar.

"Do you want to come?" He stretched out his hand to her, emboldened that she'd touched him, that she'd relented. "Come with me," he said. "Just to the edge."

She crumpled the wrapper and stared at him.

"You can call for help if I start to drown," he said.

She took his hand and walked up to the water, where he could discern some of the threat. Only a few feet out, the shore break was intense, and the waves were much bigger than he'd thought—the biggest he'd ever seen. They rose up as suddenly as cobras and then struck, a pile-driving force he could feel in his feet, the two of them pelted by the spray flung high into the air. Undaunted, David took off his shoes, Alice too, and they walked to where the foam washed over their feet. "That feels good," she said. When the water went out, the pull made him queasy. She was still holding his hand. They watched their feet reappear, half-buried in sand.

"It doesn't look so bad," he said.

"No."

The group of kids rose on the swells, laughing.

"Get through one wave and we're there," he said.

She looked at him, and he thought of Harold: she was waiting for him to decide.

"We'll be fine," he said.

They stripped down to their bathing suits and waited, the children laughing like mad. He let several waves break, getting a feel for the timing, and when he felt ready he pulled them in.

There was a sharp drop-off hidden by all the roiling water, so they were immediately up to their chests. He felt the current's full force now, and it made him hesitate. Turn around, he thought. But then, like the moment right after you sat down on a ski lift, the undertow yanked their feet out from under them. Alice, still holding his hand, quietly spoke his name. His feet skidded along the bottom. The water was nearly up to their armpits. "We should—" he said, but then a wave rose up. He felt so scared and stupid he had to laugh out loud because he now realized it was by far the biggest wave he'd ever seen. It was too late to do anything but commit. He pulled Alice forward, trying with all his might to speed her up, the top of the wave sloshing with its own falling weight. When they dove into the wall, her hand was ripped from his. He hugged the bottom, feeling the wave suck past. Silence first, then blackness, then light. Looking up, he saw towering glaciers of foam, as if he were hovering over an arctic landscape. He surfaced, turned, and saw his wife, or her limbs, in the wave's humped back, Alice dismembered—arm, foot, leg, arm—rolling into view as she tumbled to shore, the parts carried as fast as if on a train. Then the wave broke and spray shot into the air with a concussion he could feel. And Alice was thrown out with so much force that she tumbled end over end on the sand, momentarily on her hands and knees. Then she sat up, coughing.

"Are you all right?" he called.

She sat sullenly and said nothing.

"Are you okay?"

She got up and walked toward the rock where they'd left their packs. Behind him, he heard a young girl's voice. It was as if he'd been transported. There he was, with the kids suddenly, maybe fifty yards out. He turned to look at Alice again. "Should I come in?" he yelled.

She sat on the rock, dejected.

So they were back to not speaking.

He turned and floated with the group. Why had he waited so long to brave this? He talked with a few of the kids while they rose on the swells. They were from San Francisco, on a high school trip. They'd spent the night at Kalalau Beach, an expedition they'd planned for months. The hike there was insane! One girl said it was the scariest thing she'd ever done.

No matter what they did, David thought, no matter how hard they tried, they'd always come back to this place of disappointment. That picture the woman had taken of them flashed through his mind, and how Alice had reached around his waist to hold him. If they stayed here much longer, there'd be nothing left between them.

When he turned around again, she was gone.

Her pack was gone too. Racing ashore, he looked up the river of rock that split the trail but didn't see her, though her footprints led in that direction. He found the towel in his pack and dried off, quickly got dressed, and hurried up the path. Day hikers were clambering over the giant rocks as he raced up. Alice was nowhere to be seen. How, in such a short time, could she get so far? He came to the split. One arrow directed him back to Ke'e Beach, the other further down the Na Pali to Hanakoa Valley, two miles in. He looked around again, scanned the beach once more. Nothing. Given her physical state—given everything—surely she'd head home. He looked up the switchbacks toward Ke'e but couldn't see anyone at this angle. He called out her name—some passing hikers looked at him quizzically—and when there was no answer he rested his palms on his knees and whispered curses so nonsensical it sounded as if he were speaking in tongues. He looked up, hands on his hips, panicked. This was an enormous commitment. If she'd pressed on toward Hanakoa and he went to Ke'e, it might be twenty-four hours before they saw each other again. Or worse.

He chose to head back to Ke'e.

He felt confident in his decision. She had no reason to go the other direction. Nor could she reasonably consider the hike doable, especially after the strain of these first two miles. Even now, the fatigue he felt as he labored back up the switchbacks was humbling, and the idea of hiking into Hanakoa seemed ridiculously foolish, far beyond his stamina. He found himself on the balls of his feet, taking giant steps forward, gasping for breath. In his mind he saw Alice tumbling in the wave and being thrown to shore. He felt awful. Terrible things happened when minor miscalculations like that were made. He'd nearly rescued her mood. They had nearly been *past* this. Somehow he needed to make things up to her. To show her that for as long as they'd been together, for better or worse, she'd always been foremost in his thoughts. Why did he require her absence to realize this? What was wrong with his soul that he always forgot?

Hurrying, he shifted into a state of pure, mindless movement, stride after stride. He made the summit and once more looked down at Hanakapi'ai. That was when he saw her.

Through some blessed instance of good fortune he saw her across the valley Hanakapi'ai formed, as far along the trail toward Hanakoa, and as high, as he was toward Ke'e now. She was standing there on this mirror ledge, looking in his direction, then down the trail ahead of her. It was as if they were standing in facing skyscrapers. She had her thumbs tucked under the straps of her pack and was considering something, then turned again and was looking right at him—he was sure of it! He waved but she didn't wave back. He jumped around and waved both arms. He said her name silently and screamed it but saw no acknowledgment. He suddenly lost confidence. Perhaps she couldn't see him. From this distance she was as big as his thumbnail. Something had given her pause. He waved and waved and did a worthless calculation—his watch said 1:23—and guessed that with the descent and subsequent ascent to her position plus her already substantial head start she was at least an hour beyond his reach—and that if he made haste.

He screamed her name again, waving both arms, and whether she heard him or not she turned and continued along the trail, soon disappearing.

He moved recklessly, zigzagging like a skier, sometimes slipping and then tripoding down, once falling badly enough that he had to stop and repeatedly flex his smashed knee. His blood sugar had plummeted. With everything that had gone on today, in all of his distraction and anger and relief, he'd neglected to eat. He took off his pack and took out the peanut butter and banana sandwich he'd made and ate on the move, making sure to drink water as well. Now he was too scared to be angry. This terrible silence that had come between them had brought them into what felt like dangerous territory, as if they were stuck in the middle of a tightrope over a gaping chasm and now had to find the skill to somehow maintain their balance together and cross over safely. Within half an hour, he made the river of rock and passed the sign that said HANAKOA VALLEY 2 MILES. Perhaps because of eating he caught a second wind, but his fear soon intensified. This stage of the trail was of a completely different order of difficulty than anything he'd yet encountered. The accessibility of Hanakapi'ai from Ke'e and the sheer number of tourists who hiked it made that leg comparatively smoother and well-worn, the tens of thousands of feet demarcating and softening the trail. This, however, was all loose stone and shale, the slope so steep that David felt as if he were on all fours the whole climb. Nor was there the comfort of the occasional inbound hiking party. They would've seen Alice, of course, and could tell him if she were close or far. No, this leg was for the serious, the prepared, but he climbed relentlessly. Another half an hour in and he still hadn't seen a soul.

When he reached the top of the trail where she'd been standing, his heart sank. He wondered for a moment if she too had seen what lay before them and had stopped because of it.

Ahead—and he could see a solid mile—the trail became a treacherous strip only slightly wider than a balance beam, the rock wall to the left so sheer he thought he'd have to press his hand against it and run his fingers along the stone like a child strumming a picket fence as he passed by. To the right, the drop-off was acute, the edge rounded by erosion. Absurd. He pictured Cary Grant and Eva Marie Saint scaling down Rushmore in *North by Northwest.* If your right foot came out from under you, you'd slip into the void. If you tumbled forward, your pack would knock you sideways and then you were dead. Just proceeding would require an inner negotiation with panic, arbitration between the need to keep your eyes on the path and the vertigo it brought on, the foamed edge of the ocean bursting in silence far below. Come up on the short end of that haggling and you might find yourself paralyzed with terror. You might dig your fingers in and choose not to move until someone came along. And then you might grab your rescuer and take him or her down with you. Perhaps, he thought desperately, if I wait for a few minutes Alice will appear. Ahead, the cliffs bulged in humped succession, with the trail visible at each horizontal apex. Alice might be *right there* at any moment. But after what seemed like an eternity, David gave up. He couldn't help but wonder if she'd gone over since he couldn't fathom how she'd gotten so far. And going over was like a magic trick, an act of total disappearance: no one to see you fall, your death forever destined to be only imagined by loved ones. Going over was like getting plucked from the world by God.

He believed the safest, most efficient way to proceed was to leave his pack here, before the path narrowed further. His goal would be strictly one of pursuit. He stripped it off and took his water bottle and as many energy bars as he could stuff into his pockets, then ran through a checklist. Was there anything else he needed? He had a waterproof top, but there wasn't a cloud in the sky. Sunscreen? A first-aid kit? If he didn't take these, would he regret it? The need to bring along his rain gear felt significant. He thought of Harold: *The thoughts just before the event are like the fortune in the cookie. The fortune's as random as the thought.* He wanted to laugh. It was like the wave he'd dived under earlier. Only by facing such a crossing would you consider making it. Otherwise, you could spend your whole life avoiding any such event.

He began to walk, though to call it walking was an exaggeration. He found himself leaning so hard to the left, against the cliff, that it retarded his progress and made him overcorrect each time he took what might be called a step forward—a measuring out of distance, heel to toe, as if he was sneaking out of a room—and sometimes trapped his rear foot behind the other and, stuck, took in hesitant fear a complete step backward. And several times he leaned left so hard that his feet shifted under him, a half-inch slide he could feel in his spine, his palm pointlessly smacking the rock as if for a handhold, this slight slip causing him to suddenly throw out his right arm before regaining his balance and pivoting, his hands, stomach, and cheek to the cliff now, his back to the sea, these moments so utterly terrifying he had to stop and close his eyes while he caught his breath. Then once again he started forward. After several minutes of this, the pace began wearing on him. Slowness, he realized, would be his death. Walking faster, he'd be better off. Certain actions could be destroyed by close attention, short-circuited by overawareness, like swallowing. Committed to this new method, he took three determined breaths and proceeded forward, trying with all his might to move at a normal pace, to blot out the drop-off while thinking when else he'd have such a view. But it didn't work. It was like walking along a skyscraper's ledge. For several minutes he concentrated so hard on the walking that he forgot he was here to find his wife.

But he soon began to make better time. Whether from practice or confidence, the slight widening of the path in places or perhaps his instinct for self-preservation, he somehow achieved a suspension of disbelief about the very journey he was making. Death was right there, and so, with his left-hand fingers barely skimming the rock and his right arm stuck out over the abyss, he walked at normal speed until both arms hung safely at his sides; he let his vision shift slightly inward, kept his eyes fixed on a point several feet ahead, slowing only when he outpaced his own balance like a toddler running so fast the force threw him toward a fall. If he allowed himself to think—such respites quite rare—or became self-conscious, he came to a complete stop. But he got back up to speed quickly, recapturing his inner rhythm until it was thoughtless, and until that thoughtlessness in turn aped fearlessness. This whole process—the thinking about movement you took for granted, then taking it for granted—was the beauty of the trail, he managed to reflect, was a kind of accomplishment, and when he looked up after a long time (the reward for his trial) Alice was just ahead, and he stopped.

She herself had stopped, though clearly she didn't realize he was right behind, and seeing her all at once jeopardized his own confidence. She was at the apex of the curve, struggling to press on, and now he could appreciate by dint of perspective just how narrow and dangerous the trail was. She was clearly exhausted, and when at that moment she went wobbly moving forward, the pack seemed even more precarious. It was like watching some fool carrying a stack of boxes, the gaps between them widening just before they tumbled free. She threw her right arm out to balance herself, and that was when he saw that she was carrying the urn in her hand.

"Alice!" he called.

She stopped again and gingerly turned to her left until she was nearly facing him. He could see her face peeking around the pack's frame. She was in a state long past tears and terror, even resignation. It was an expression he'd never seen, a kind of vacancy. It was a look he felt on his own face.

"Stay where you are," she said. "Don't come near me."

"What are you doing?"

"I said stay away. Do you understand? You're cursed."

He was still coming forward. He couldn't help it. "What are you talking about?"

"Everything you touch withers," she said. She was speaking as if they were walking alongside each other, her tone without affect. "Every choice you make is a trap."

"Alice, come on. Let's turn around. Let's go back."

"You take another step and I'll jump!"

He stopped.

"There *is* no back," she said, "don't you get it? Back is all up there." She pointed at the sky.

"Please, I'm begging you. I'll leave. Just promise me you'll turn around."

"It was you," she said.

He froze, leaning against the side.

"You wanted me to say it, so now I am."

He was crying.

"Admit it," she said.

She was only yards away—a stone's throw—but he couldn't move.

"You wanted this," she said. "You wanted him gone and now me too."

"Alice, please stop."

"So I'm going to finish this. Do you understand? This is *my* choice. I'm going to take care of him myself or die trying."

She was just within his grasp, but before reaching out he turned around to see where he was, and when he looked back she'd started to walk again.

"Wait," he said.

She fell.

It was a more sickening sight than he ever would've imagined, so much more terrible than he ever would've dreamed. As she turned back toward the trail to continue, she went too far, her pack clipping the cliff, acting as a brake and yanking her upper body back, her soles sliding out from underneath her, her feet sticking straight out. Miraculously, she fell straight down—back to cliff and face to sea—and landed on her ass, then stopped, the heel of her right hand (she managed somehow to hold on to the urn) pressed into the edge of the trail, both her legs and most of her buttocks hanging over the side. Only the bottom of the pack's frame, dug in like a grappling hook, kept her from going over.

She sat bolt upright, teetering.

David rushed over and when next to her was aware of the exertion required to maintain her position. Her triceps were quivering. Her chin pointed up and straight out, she was using all the strength in her neck, and her stomach muscles were trembling beneath her shirt.

"Oh God," she said.

"Don't move."

"I'm going over."

"*Don't move.*"

She was completely balanced but couldn't hold it much longer. Though he wanted to grab her he knew not to. If she slid and he grabbed her arm or her pack, he wouldn't be able to support her. Over the side there were no footholds, nothing to press up against. He looked at her whole body. It was like getting close to a priceless statue you weren't allowed to touch.

"Why did you bring me here?" she said.

He was listening to her and not. He'd turned his right side toward her and was almost kneeling, his right hand near hers; then he got an idea of what they had to do.

"Why did you make me come?" she said quietly, her tone between resignation and fury.

"You have to listen to me. I know what has to happen."

"I told you we weren't going to make it, but you made me."

It was so quiet up here in all of this open space. He quickly thought it all through once more.

"Admit that you made me!"

Searching the cliff for anything like a handhold, he found one and tested it.

"You should've protected us," she said.

He had to ignore her now.

"*You should've protected us!*"

"I need you to listen to what I'm saying. If you don't, we're going to die."

He was losing her. She was sobbing and using every iota of energy she had. She shook her head back and forth against the pack.

"Do you want us to die?" he asked.

She didn't answer. Furious, she just looked at him. "Take him," she said.

She opened her fingers slightly, and he took the urn and placed it safely behind him on the trail. "You're going to have to let go," he said.

"Goddamn you!"

"You're going to have to let go for a second and take my hand"—he held up his right—"with your right. Okay?"

"You son of a bitch."

He spoke barely above a whisper. "Okay?"

She was listening.

"Nothing sudden," he said. "I'm going to take your wrist, and the second you let go, you take mine. Wrist to wrist." He held his hand to the side of her face so she could see it. She closed her eyes. He screamed her name till she opened them, then spoke quietly again. "You might slip at first, but I can lift you. Enough that you can get a foot underneath. Do you understand? You've got to get a leg underneath you and *stand up*."

Her eyes were closed again, as if she were making her own plan. Her whole body was shaking with effort.

"Tell me you understand." He was losing her. "Tell me or I'm going with you."

She nodded.

"I need you to *see* it. I need you to think it through."

She nodded again. Her arms were trembling.

"On three," he said.

He counted aloud, pressing his left palm and left cheek to the rock, twisting the ball of his left foot into the trail, bracing his left thigh against the cliff. He flexed his knees, the other half of his weight distributed on the outside of his right foot, which he positioned just beside the edge of her pack. He slid the fingers of his right hand gently around her wrist, his fingertips touching lightly at first, and once he was sure she wasn't startled by the pressure he squeezed as hard as he could.

"Three," he said.

She grabbed his wrist. It was a choice. She could've abandoned him, could have launched herself *out* to spite him or save him, to insure that only she would die, or she could've yanked him forward and killed them both. But she didn't. She grabbed his wrist while he held hers and tried to do what he'd told her to.

Her whole weight ran up his hand, from forearm to bicep to shoulder, her life filling his whole right side. He lifted her straight up with all of the strength he had, but as she got her right foot underneath her, he felt her lean forward. She had to. Because of her pack, there was nowhere else for her body to go. His eyes were closed with the effort, with fear, and as she stood—the outside of her right foot braced on the outside of his—he felt her whole body drift out over the edge, her torso leaning forward, her head beyond her feet, like a ski jumper riding the air. She swung her left arm in circles for balance, whirling it counterclockwise again and again. She'd managed to stand, but when he opened his eyes he saw that for a split second he was the only thing suspending her weight and she was the only thing keeping him from tumbling forward. In that split second, they were each pulling with full strength from the other, making a kind of arch. Finally, she was able to lean back—these last inches were gentle—and get her feet underneath her again; and then she stood up straight.

"Have you got it?" he said.

He held her hand; she held his. Her chin was still pointed up. All she could see, he imagined, was sky. And then she sobbed once, a clear, single cry that sounded like relief.

"I've got it," she said.

She was still facing the sea, her pack leaning against the cliff. She took a deep breath, then exhaled. Their hands, still gripping each other's, were shaking. A helicopter flew toward them, the tremendous noise from its engine rending the moment. She watched it bank left and pass overhead; then she turned to face him.

That picture of his wife's face: her expression well beyond exhaustion and grief and elation, in a state of having been saved and having saved herself. The picture of her *relief.* Of having seen something terrible through. He wondered, was that what a woman looked like after she gave birth? Did she have that same expression of amazement and pain, of loss and gain? So much risk in the making, David thought. Making life could utterly break your heart. It was an expression as mysterious as the Mona Lisa's, one that disclosed everything about her he couldn't and wouldn't ever know. And it was an image he tried to keep, but it finally disappeared, and once it was gone he could never recapture all the sadness and joy of their marriage. It was the picture he kept in mind over the next several days and the day before they left the island for home. Alice said there was one more thing she had to do: scatter their child's ashes. She knew exactly where, and when she told him, he called Harold to set it up.

"Has she forgiven you?" he asked.

"I think so," David said.

"Well, be sure to forgive yourself."

David thanked him for everything, then said good-bye. Harold booked them a helicopter tour of the island out of Princeville airport, with one special stop. Alice wore a new dress she'd bought—a white dress with red lilies—and wore a red lily in her hair. She told the pilot what she wanted to do, though he'd already been told. This helicopter ride: so much force, so much lift above your head that it was like being dangled by the scruff of your neck thousands of feet in the air. Through the windows, the views were worth any amount of money. Descriptions of Kauai would always fail; it was simply a place you had to see. They headed southwest first, came around the Na Pali coast, and passed over Kalalau Beach—"It would've been nice if we'd stayed there," Alice said—before turning due east, running the gauntlet of Waimea Canyon, then climbing above Mount Waialeale. "That's nearly fifty-two hundred feet," the pilot said. "You're looking at the wettest spot on earth." The summit was cloud-covered and it was raining, as if on cue. "If we stick around for a while it might break," he said. So they circled.

David would keep this picture of his wife's face in his mind the following year, when she miscarried again. As before, and despite the blood thinners, she could only carry the child to nineteen weeks. She was riding the train to work and felt contractions, got off in Harlem, called an ambulance, and delivered another boy en route.

Two years later and seventy-five pounds heavier, her blood pressure reaching dangerous levels while on the highest dosage of medication she could take, she lost their third child in the middle of the night. She'd gone twenty weeks. This too was a boy.

"I'm done," she told him in the hospital.

She quit her job at Trinity midyear.

"Rich kids," she said. "Helicopter parents. None of these people need me."

Why should he begrudge her relief? He could take care of them—made plenty of money, more than he'd ever dreamed of—and could protect her until she was well. The gaming business was exploding.

She was hospitalized later that month with depression. She came home after several weeks of treatment, only to spend the next five months in bed.

She emerged, though when she did it was as if they'd slipped into a long dream: a Mobius strip of now.

Three years passed, or was it a millisecond?

Secretly, David began writing a book. It had started as a treatment for a video game, but the description soon became a narrative and then grew from there. Both were forms of making, of creative acts, but he needed an expression beyond games. God forbid Alice should ever read the things he'd written. It had started with his dreams. She died in airplane crashes, carjackings, in burglaries gone bad. Muggings where she resisted her assailants. She suffered shark attacks, pit bull and bear maulings. Freak accidents at zoos. Car and train wrecks. Or during her commute, while she sat reading, the clot that had formed silently in her leg drifted to her heart or lung; or, like a firework, rose to her brain and detonated—and he was free. He needed to disguise these fantasies, some aliases for himself, an art that was oblique but provided a directness of experience, veiled autobiography that let him investigate with his own eyes. He had a breakthrough after the first chapter. Leave it to a gamer. He would create avatars.

Like a magic trick, right before his eyes, Alice became fat.

"Mr. Pepin," the policeman said, "I have some terrible news about your wife."

He woke.

God forbid his wife knew what he'd written, that she knew his mind, but most of all God forbid she knew what he'd thought on that spectacular morning over Mount Waialeale. The clouds parted. At the summit was a small lake, which in that brief moment of clearing, of sunlight, winked like a shining eye.

"Are you strapped in?" the pilot said.

"Yes," Alice answered.

"Go ahead," he said. She opened the door, and the wind blew the flower from her hair. The pilot hovered, holding their position. She turned the urn over and loosed the ashes, which under the spill of the rotor blades disappeared immediately. Watching this, David suddenly saw everything that had brought them here on a continuum: from the idea of a child, to the talk of making one, to conception; from ultrasound to stillbirth to cremation; the boy's progress from idea, to being, to dust. Because at that moment David suffered the knowledge of something he'd kept hidden, from Harold, from Alice, but most of all from himself: that it was only when he saw his son's ashes poured out, saw his remains become part of that lake, mountain, and sky, that he believed the boy was real.

When Detective Sheppard's wife was being killed, he was fast asleep and dreaming. He had passed out on their daybed at the foot of the stairs, where he often napped, and what roused him was Marilyn shouting his name. Though for a dreadful moment he paused, unsure of where he was or whether she'd shouted at all—he even considered slipping back to sleep—until she cried out his name again. And later he would remember the dream as vividly as the night's events, and couldn't tell the difference between them, memory leveling images from both—a fact that tortured him to this day.

In the dream, he was holding their second child in his hands. Marilyn was four months pregnant, but in the dream their little girl had been born and he held her swaddled, staring into her face. He was kneeling on the beach of their house, the one on Lake Erie; this was back in the days before he'd fled to New York, a lifetime ago, when he lived in Ohio. Marilyn stood in the water and watched them, the waves lapping her feet. In their child's face, he could make out aspects of both of them, Marilyn's high cheekbones and hazel eyes and his own thick lips recombined into something so beautiful and new he could neither have imagined it nor been able to describe it if asked. He smiled at her, and she smiled back, and this reaction, either in imitation of his own moon features or in response to his joy, irradiated his heart with love. And then he heard his wife scream his name.

He rolled off the daybed and took the first three steps to their bedroom in a single bound. He thought Marilyn might be convulsing—she'd suffered uterine spasms during her first pregnancy—and ran through medical procedures while pulling himself up along the banister. Their room was at the top of the stairs. He felt the breeze blowing in off the lake through the open windows, his eyes adjusting to the darkness, his momentum carrying him through the doorway. He saw a form . . .

He felt a blow at the back of his neck. His knees gave out, his eyes filling with black water. And one last time before he lost consciousness, he heard Marilyn cry his name.

Mobius—for that was the only name he gave—refused to talk to Hastroll. It was Sheppard he wanted—Sheppard only. Hastroll could torture him, he said, inject him with truth serum or strip him naked and spank him until he was black and blue, but he demanded to speak with the doctor alone.

"You mean the detective," Hastroll said.

"I mean bring him now."

Hastroll, peering at Mobius through the cell's bars, shook his head. "I don't make deals."

"Fine," Mobius said. "Then I'm going to kill myself."

Hastroll stared impassively at the wee man and, in a rare moment of levity, grabbed his sides and laughed.

In response Mobius pinched his nose with his right hand and covered his mouth with his left, which was bandaged. He swung his little legs freely while sitting—his knees were bandaged also—and Hastroll watched, mesmerized, while his legs slowed with each passing second, until finally his face turned blue.

"Hmm," Hastroll grunted.

Then Mobius fell over unconscious.

Sheppard came to see him the next day.

When he stepped into view, the man beamed. "Dr. Sam Sheppard, it's a *pleasure.*"

Sheppard lit his pipe, took two puffs. "I'm not a doctor anymore," he said.

"True," Mobius said, "but you'll always be Dr. Sam to me!"

The guard brought Sheppard a chair, and he sat down across the bars from the midget.

"That's better," Mobius said. "Let me get a look at you. Why, you haven't aged a bit. Still fit as a *fiddle.* Still a *handsome* dog. Do you know that for years I've been obsessed with your case?"

Sheppard looked at his watch, then put his pipe back in his mouth and puffed, Mobius appearing for a moment to live in a world of thick, white smoke.

"You know," he said, "you may be the only man in America to be both guilty and *not* guilty of killing his wife. Convicted *and* exonerated. Did he, didn't he? He didn't, he *did*! They *still* don't know. And the fascination with your story . . . it never ends. They made *The Fugitive* television series about you and then they made that into a movie. There've been books written about you. You even *wrote* a book! Yes, of course I read *Endure and Conquer.* It was terrible! The description of your first trial entered the lexicon. A 'carnival atmosphere' is what they called the O. J. trial, but that's the exact expression Justice Tom Clark coined to describe *yours.*"

"I've tried to put all that behind me," Sheppard said.

Mobius smiled. "It's pretty to think you could."

Sheppard puffed some more on his pipe.

"So," Mobius said.

"So?"

"Quid pro quo."

"Go on."

"In exchange for the whole truth about Alice Pepin, I get two things."

"I'm listening."

"First I want to hear from your lips everything that happened on the last day of your wife's life."

For a moment Sheppard remembered Marilyn's smashed face turned toward him where she lay on the bed, her forehead covered in crescent-shaped gashes, her upper incisor ripped out, her pajama top pushed above her breasts and her panties pulled down, her pubis moist and glistening, her legs pinned under the bed's crossbar, blood whipped across the walls of the whole room as if a wet dog had shaken itself out right there, haloing outward over her bed and his, covering the walls, even flecking the ceiling. Around her whole head, like a lacquer-thick nimbus, there was blood as well. Sheppard kneeled on her mattress to check for a pulse. Nothing.

"What's number two?"

"I want to read David's novel."

"Why?"

Mobius laughed. "To see how I came out."

Sheppard tapped his pipe clean.

"All right," he said.

Mobius clapped his hands together, then rubbed them. "Shall we get started?" he said.

"Where would you like to begin?"

"At the beginning, naturally."

"There are many places to choose from."

"Start that Saturday morning," Mobius said. "July 1954."

That morning, Marilyn Sheppard woke to the sound of a bottle rocket.

Judging by the light in the room, it couldn't have been much past seven, but already kids were shooting off fireworks in anticipation of the Fourth tomorrow, as they'd been doing all over the neighborhood during the past several weeks. Marilyn didn't mind, but the noise terrified their English setter, who now sat curled in the corner of the bedroom, shivering and drooling. "Kokie?" Marilyn said, and sat up in bed, slapping the covers twice. "It's all right, Kokie. Up." The dog sighed and stayed put, staring at her mournfully. Of course, all loud sounds scared the poor girl. The noontime siren sent her scrambling under the kitchen table. When bad thunderstorms gathered over the lake, she pushed into the bathroom and huddled there next to the toilet, her thrumming rattling her collar. When Marilyn and Sam fought, it sent her cowering. And lately it had been an endless cycle of random terrors: the crackles of Silver Salutes, reports of Indian Uprisings, the occasional White Whirls or bursts of Red Chrysanthemums exploding over the water, followed by the fusillades tonight—a pre-Fourth show over Lake Erie—and the big finale tomorrow. Then what? Marilyn imagined another week of kids using up whatever fireworks they hadn't shot off. Couldn't she take the poor dog somewhere quiet? To her father's house, maybe? But he lived an hour away and she was already short of time.

Another bottle rocket flew past the window, its little jet sounding like paper tearing, followed by a small clap. Kokie whimpered.

Marilyn got out of bed and pressed her lips to the screen. "You're scaring my dog!" she yelled.

On the beach below, two boys in bathing suits burst from the bushes laughing, each with a quiver of missiles. The baby inside Marilyn kicked twice—or else those were spasms—and the pain was so sharp she had to rest her weight on the sill.

Please, God, let this one be a girl, Marilyn thought, if only for the company and another member of the beleaguered Girls' Team: someone to marvel with her at Sam's inability to do a single household chore, not simply because he didn't want to but because he didn't know how. Look at that bed, she thought, gazing at his unmade bed by the window. The man could crack a person's chest and massage his heart back to beating, but for him making up the bed was an imponderable mystery. Let this one be a girl, so on days like today that consisted of housework, cooking dinner for tonight's guests (the Aherns were coming over), errands and still more cleaning (that their son, Chip, would immediately mess up), with grocery lists to be made and then the shopping and all the things that had to get done to prepare for Sam's goddamn interns' cookout tomorrow (a party that would leave her land side while her husband water-skied with them all afternoon), she'd at least have a little bit of camaraderie with a daughter by her side, a little bit of help.

The pain stopped and Marilyn stood up straight.

Last Tuesday, over dinner, Sam had said, "I thought we'd do the intern thing again."

She was in the process of cutting Chip's hot dog into bite-size pieces. Seven years old and the boy still couldn't manage this. "What intern thing?"

"For the Fourth. Like we did last year."

She held her fork and knife crossed above her plate. "Today's Tuesday, Sam."

"Well," he said, "I already told them it was happening."

"Told who?"

"The interns," he said. "Plus my family. The Houks too. And the Aherns."

"That's more than forty people."

"We'll just cook out."

Marilyn put down her fork and knife, folded her hands on the table, and looked at her husband, who, at the moment, was concentrating on garnishing his hot dog. Along its length he ran lines of mustard and ketchup and mayo and relish as carefully as if he were laying brick. A brick, Marilyn thought, would come in handy right now.

Sam looked up. "It's not like it's a fancy meal."

A smile twitched across her face. The party was, of course, an announcement as opposed to a request, though some time ago she'd demanded, upon penalty of divorce, that such would never be made again. Which had changed nothing, obviously, and made her wonder: if the small things about her husband's behavior couldn't be changed, how could the big things?

They could fight this out now, Marilyn thought, but once they started it would spiral out of control into things that couldn't be resolved, only forgotten, and these memories would slam them back to where they'd been a few weeks ago, and she hardly wanted to go there. Which was the trick, Marilyn thought: not to go back.

"You're right," she had said.

At the window, Marilyn watched the boys run down the beach until they disappeared. Then she rubbed her eyes with the heels of her hands, tucked her hair behind her ears, crossed her arms, and looked out over the water. It was a perfect day. Not just for the breeze or absence of humidity but also for an almost painful clarity in the light—white light, she thought, as in August. She could see *everything,* it seemed. Even down at Huntington Park, several hundred yards away, she could make out a man sitting in his white van, parked at the lot that overlooked the lake, as stunned, Marilyn imagined, with the day's beauty as she was. On days like this their beach seemed tropically bright, the water impossibly blue, with scuffed clouds and a glare off the sand that made it hard to look at directly. When the wind rustled the leaves by their second-story window, it felt as if their house was a boat setting sail.

Where to start? she thought.

There was a thump in the next-door bedroom, then a long-drawn-out groan. Sam's friend, Lester Hoversten, was up. The thought of spending the morning with him was so unpleasant that she'd managed briefly to forget he was here. Hearing him moan and stretch now only compounded her frustration: he was another of Sam's announcements. "Les lost his job," Sam had said, leaving for work on Wednesday, standing at the kitchen door with his back to her. "He's going to stay with us for a few days."

It was chicken to tell her this at the last second, almost a parting shot. "You invited Lester to stay with us?" she said.

"He's a colleague, Marilyn. He needs my help."

"Jesus, Sam, you act like we had some little disagreement."

"In Les's mind, that's probably all it was." He let the screen door close and walked to his car.

Marilyn was about to follow him out when Chip came barreling into the room and threw his whole weight into her legs, clutching at her shorts and hanging off her, stopping her progress as if he and his father were a tag team. She kneeled down to face the boy. "You're too big to be doing that," she said, and shook his arms.

Then Sam's black form reappeared at the door.

"How could you be so inconsiderate?" she said.

But it was Dick Eberling, the house and window cleaner. He had her husband's height and build, balding in nearly the same way. He looked uncannily like him, in fact. He stood at the door sheepishly—Marilyn heard it rap closed—with his head cast down.

Sam's car pulled out of the driveway.

"Oh," she said. "No." She put a hand to her forehead. "I'm sorry, Dick. I thought you were Sam."

Eberling, clearly relieved, looked up at her and smiled. "I'm sorry Mrs. Sheppard, I should've knocked."

Hoversten's voice snapped her out of memory.

"Is there coffee?" he now asked through the wall.

Marilyn hurried to dress—she'd be damned if she'd let him see her in her nightclothes—and went downstairs.

Of course it was on a morning like this two years ago, Sam off to the hospital and Chip still asleep, that she and Hoversten had had their "disagreement." A good ten years older than her husband, he'd gone to medical school with Sam in California, their enduring camaraderie maddening to her not only because Lester was an obvious screwup, a philandering alcoholic who made passes at nurses so blatantly they refused to be in a room alone with him, but also a man who'd regularly invited Sam out on double dates whenever Marilyn was away.

That morning, she was doing dishes when Hoversten slid up behind her and pressed his nakedness against her gown, the ends of his open robe seeming to wrap around her legs like tentacles. "Need some help?" he whispered.

For a moment Marilyn was so shocked she froze.

Hoversten, taking this hesitation for consent, pressed himself into her harder, cupping her elbows in his hands and sliding them down to her wrists. He put his lips on her neck. "Come on, Marilyn," he said. "I saw how you looked at me last night."

She turned and slapped the soaped sponge against his chest.

"Hey," he laughed, staggering back and looking down at the bubble-wound. His erect cock listed right, like an inchworm reaching for a leaf. "Don't be so mean."

"Of course I looked at you," she said. "We were *talking.*"

"No, no," he said, and stepped closer. "I caught you staring."

He *had* caught her. At dinner the night before, she'd stared while he spoke to her husband, at the bald head splotched with eczema, at the gathering teardrop of fat beneath his chin, at the small teeth that reminded her of a child's, wondering if there was a single thing a woman could find attractive about him, amazed that he could sit across from her so comfortably after having flagrantly disrespected her, expecting her to write off all the other girls he and Sam had double-dated in California as bygones, trifles who didn't mean anything. Then his eyes had darted toward hers, pinning her, and he smiled at her smugly. She cursed in her mind, looked down at her plate. And now here he was, hot with his own misunderstanding.

"Lester," she said. "Thank you for showing me your thing." She put her hand on her side, dismissing his penis with the sponge. "Now, why don't you go play with it in private."

He snorted, shook his head. "You're a tease. You know that, Marilyn?

"Don't flatter yourself."

He tied his robe closed, then turned and stomped off. But he'd kept a respectful distance ever since.

Back down in the kitchen, Marilyn put on coffee and felt the craving, as the aroma hit her, for a cigarette, considered washing Sam's breakfast plate and skillet—he'd made himself bacon and eggs, leaving her the mess—only to change her mind and decide to go down to the boathouse. She could get the place picked up, she figured, arrange all the life jackets and towlines and skis, and steer clear for a while from the pack she'd hidden in Sam's study. By then Chip would be awake, so she could take him to breakfast *and* be out of the house and off to the grocery store without having to see Hoversten for a second longer than she had to, if at all. This new plan appealed to her sense of efficiency. It was really the only way to get everything done in time, since there'd be no free time tomorrow. But once she thought about it, tomorrow wouldn't be so bad. She could get a couple of the interns to help with the grilling and the serving; they'd do anything she asked, just to get in her good graces (and Sam's), and she could get some water-skiing in herself. And if she was lucky and things went smoothly today she might find a few minutes to herself.

After walking down the long set of stairs to the slip, though, her spirits sank. The place was a complete disaster. The boat was filled with skis and damp towels and life jackets, empty beer cans and a cooler full of what Marilyn guessed was rotten food. And the boat itself hadn't been properly tied off, its prow bumping into the pilings with every small wave. In all, it was a mess so terrible that it could have been made only out of spite.

"Goddamn you, Sam," she muttered.

She turned and walked back up the steps to the house.

She entered the kitchen through the patio, fully expecting to see Hoversten drinking coffee and reading the paper. But the house was silent. He must've gone back to sleep. Walking quietly, she slipped into Sam's study, pulled back *Cardiology,* and took out the pack of Chesterfields. There was a box of matches next to Sam's pipe caddy, and she lit up, then came around his desk and sat down on his red leather chair. Next to the radiator were three loaded shotguns. She'd asked him twenty times to put them away. On his desk was a picture of the two of them taken many years ago, both so young it was conspicuous how they'd aged. They were sitting in his car, a Plymouth Fury. The top was down and they were facing backward, Sam's arms around her. This was in California in '44, the year Sam had started medical school. He was thinner then. Had more hair. Was kinder. They were in Big Sur—the Chapmans had invited them out to their ranch—and you could make out the cliffs beyond them and a light mist rolling in off the ocean. She remembered nothing of that day except how cold she was and how Sam had resisted putting the car's top up. This picture had replaced all her memories and come to represent a time in her life when she'd thought her husband incapable of cruelty, of their future as something unfolding toward better things, as opposed to this eternal now, where every day carried with it a choice between moving forward and calling it quits.

There he is, Marilyn thought. The man I fell in love with.

She sat in Sam's chair with her feet on the desk and tilted her head back, watching the smoke she exhaled rise to the ceiling. She shouldn't be smoking when she was pregnant, she knew, but the cigarette enclosed her in just this moment, when nothing reminded her of anything else but that the house was quiet. She took a last drag, then blew a steady stream of smoke at the photograph.

What to do?

In the kitchen a few minutes later, staring at a legal pad list of errands, chores, and food so long it filled the page, Marilyn considered doing none of them, acting so cool for the next twenty-four hours that her husband would be amazed by her organizational ability; and then, right around the time his guests were set to arrive, she could pack Chip and Kokie in the car, drive to her father's house, and leave for good. She closed her eyes and took a deep breath and let her thoughts drift down this pleasant path.

Dinner, she wrote, and underlined the word: *cottage ham, green beans, rye bread.*

Dessert, she wrote next, underlining again. She put the end of the pen in her mouth, then added: *blueberry pie with ice cream.*

It was Sam's favorite.

Mobius was bleeding through his bandages, thick red circles showing on his knees and hand.

Since Marilyn's murder, Detective Sheppard had struggled with the sight of blood.

"Let's talk time line," Mobius said. "I'll play detective."

"All right," Sheppard said.

"That morning. July third."

"Yes?"

"You're up early."

"I was up at six," Sheppard said.

"Even though it's a Saturday."

"Yes."

"And you head to the hospital."

"I was there just before seven."

"Your father founded the hospital, didn't he?"

"He did. My brothers, Richard and Stephen, worked there as well."

"You run into Stephen in the parking lot and talk about your plans for the holiday weekend."

"He was going to spend the day on his sailboat, and I reminded him about the interns' party. I'd invited him and his wife, of course."

"And then you both head into surgery."

"It was a pretty routine morning."

"Until they bring in the boy."

"Yes," Sheppard said. "Around ten that morning a boy was brought into the OR who'd been hit by a utility truck."

"He's not breathing."

"He lost consciousness and stopped breathing as soon as we got him on the table."

"So you crack his chest."

"Yes."

"And massage his heart."

"That's right."

"What does a heart feel like?"

"Like a tennis ball," Sheppard said. "It's harder than you think. It springs back to shape no matter how hard you squeeze it."

"Interesting," Mobius said.

Sheppard shrugged.

"But the boy dies."

"Yes."

"And when you inform the father, he berates you."

"The father told me his boy couldn't be dead because he spoke to him right after the accident. That he was lucid and that I must've murdered him."

"What did you tell him?"

"I told him it was the nature of internal injuries. That they kill in secret. That you could be functioning normally until the moment your organs shut down. And I told him I was sorry."

"Then what?"

"After finishing up at the hospital, I stopped off to see my mother and father."

"And after your visit?"

"I went home. I did some work around the boathouse. We were having the hospital's interns over the next day and there'd be skiing, so I checked the outboards, made sure they had enough gas for the party. Got the towlines together, the skis, the life jackets. Then it was time for cocktails."

"What time was that?"

"Around a quarter till seven. Then we went over to our neighbors', Don and Nancy Ahern's, to have some drinks."

"But I thought they were coming to your house for dinner."

"It was an odd habit we'd fallen into. The girls said that if we drank at one house and ate at the other it split up the mess."

"They lived nearby."

"Right down the street."

"What did everyone drink?"

"The girls had whiskey sours. Don and I had martinis."

"What'd you talk about?"

"I told Don about my day. About the boy who'd died."

"You were troubled by it."

In the waiting room, the boy's father took two steps back from Sheppard and pointed at him, then looked around the room at the other people, his eyes wild. *You,* he said. *You must have killed him somehow. I was talking with him driving over here. He sat next to me in the car. He was fine.* He shook his finger again. *You wanted my boy dead!* He stretched out both his arms. *None of you let this man near your family! He's a killer, do you understand? He killed my child!*

"Yes," Sheppard said.

"Then what happened?"

"Marilyn left to go finish dinner."

"How much longer did you stay?"

"A few minutes, maybe. I got called in to the hospital."

"Why?"

"To look at x-rays. A boy who'd broken his leg."

"What time was it?"

"Around half past eight."

"You were back quickly?"

"I came back as soon as I was done," Sheppard said.

"Did you eat right away?"

"No, Marilyn was running behind. Don was listening to the Indians game, so I took the kids to the basement to hit a punching bag I'd installed down there while the girls finished up."

"Where did you eat?"

"On the patio."

"What about the kids?"

"In the kitchen."

"It was a nice night."

"There was a gorgeous sunset."

"Marilyn made a good dinner."

"Cottage ham, green beans. Blueberry pie."

"What about afterward?"

"After dinner we watched the fireworks. There was a big pre-Fourth show. Then Don took the children home and put them to bed."

"What time was it?"

"Around ten thirty."

"Did he come right back?"

"Yes."

"Then what?"

"The girls cleaned up the kitchen. Don finished listening to the Indians game on the radio. I sat in the living room and rested."

"And then what?"

"I helped Chip fix his model airplane."

"You let the boy stay up late."

"No. He came downstairs in his pajamas. He loved airplanes, birds, anything that could fly. He came downstairs and asked me if I would fix it before he went to sleep. So we went to the basement and glued it, though I told him it probably wouldn't fly well anymore."

"Why?"

"The wing had broken. It was balsa wood. Very delicate."

"How did Chip react?"

"He said that it was okay so long as we'd tried."

"Then what?"

"Marilyn put Chip to bed."

"What did you do next?"

"We all sat down to watch a movie."

"What was it?"

"*Strange Holiday.*"

"Starring who?"

"That little man. Like you."

"Claude Rains," Mobius said. "What was it about?"

"A man who comes back from a vacation and finds America taken over by fascists."

"Was it any good?"

"Terrible. I couldn't watch it. Plus I hate movies."

"What do you hate about them?"

"They're overdetermined."

"Meaning what?"

"In a movie, everything means something. If a man says, 'That tank's filled with compressed air. If you're not careful, it will explode,' then you know that at some point the tank will explode."

"So?"

"So life's nothing like that."

"You don't think?"

"I know."

"I know I'm going to die in this cell."

Sheppard refilled his pipe. "How's that?"

Mobius smiled. "David's novel is going to kill me."

Sheppard lit up, puffed twice.

"Then what happened?" Mobius asked.

"I was exhausted," Sheppard said. "So I snuck over to the daybed and fell asleep."

"Where was that?"

"Just off the living room, by the stairs to the second floor."

"What do you remember next?"

"I remember sitting up and seeing everyone watching the movie. Then Marilyn turned and said something to me."

"What did she say?"

Sheppard puffed on his pipe. He could see Marilyn turn toward him from her chair, a rocking chair whose back partly hid her face. Her hair was down and she waved him over to sit with her, but he didn't leave his spot. And something about not moving, about staying where he was, was so pleasant and comforting that he likened it to childhood, that moment when his parents would check in on him, saying his name once or twice while he pretended to be asleep. Marilyn was wearing white shorts and a short-sleeved shirt with little wing designs, and she waved for him to come over again. It is possible, Sheppard remembered thinking, to be completely happy in marriage.

"I didn't hear you," Mobius said.

"She said, 'Come on, Sam, it's going to improve." And for a moment, Sheppard couldn't help but smile.

Mobius crossed his arms. "Then what?"

"I woke up."

"Why?"

"I heard Marilyn crying my name."

"Did you know there was someone else in the house?"

"No, I didn't know what was happening. I thought she might be having uterine spasms."

"And?"

"I ran upstairs to our bedroom and someone hit me."

"Did you see him?"

"I'm not sure. I saw a form."

"What do you mean?"

"I couldn't make anything out very clearly. It was dark. Sometimes I remember him differently."

"How?"

"Sometimes he's bushy-haired. Sometimes he was bald like me."

"But either way, somebody knocked you out."

"Yes."

"Then what?"

"I came to, lying on the floor. My police-surgeon badge was right next to my face. It was usually in my wallet, so I didn't understand. Then I saw my wallet under the bed. I sat up."

"And?"

"That's when I saw the blood. There was blood on the door to my right. Droplets of every size all the way down to a fine mist. Then I stood up and saw Marilyn."

"She was on the bed."

"Her face was turned toward me."

"She'd been bludgeoned."

"Beyond recognition," Sheppard said, though in his mind he realized the fallacy of this expression. It was just something you said. The truth was that Marilyn was completely recognizable, that as the years had passed he remembered the exact shade of her hair color more clearly as it flowered out from her face and clung to the blood around her head, the strands clumped thick in places like they'd been too long exposed to the sea, or pasted in thin strands to her cheek as if by sweat. She was entirely recognizable in her expression, which was the troubled and worried one she always wore when she slept, fitful with dreams that she almost always told him about when she awoke, an expression that made him want to pull her to him in the night.

"Then what?"

"I was groggy. I wasn't sure what was happening. But I kneeled on the bed and took her pulse. She was gone."

"And?"

"I went to Chip's room to check on him. He was asleep."

"But you said there was screaming. Marilyn had been beaten savagely."

"He was like me. He could sleep through almost anything."

"Why didn't you call the police?"

"I heard a noise downstairs, so I rushed down. The man was still in our house. I saw him by the patio door."

"You could see him?"

"I could see his form."

"What did it look like?"

"A man's."

"What did *he* look like?"

"He was big, like me. So bushy-haired it was almost standing up."

"Then what?"

"He heard me and bolted. I chased him outside, down the stairs to the beach. I caught up with him finally and tackled him. We fought. I was still groggy and it was dark. I couldn't get a good hit in. It was like trying to punch somebody in a phone booth. He knocked me out again."

"How do you know?"

"Because I woke up lying on the beach. My shirt was gone. My legs were in the water."

"How long were you out?"

"I don't know. It was near dawn."

"You sat up and realized what had happened."

"Yes."

"You remembered that Marilyn was dead."

"I knew that I'd lost her."

"And at that moment, Dr. Sam, tell me: What *exactly* went through your mind?"

Richard Eberling sat in his van at Huntington Park and watched the Sheppard house.

He thought to himself that the smart thing to do would be to get one of those cameras with the superlong lens so he could watch Marilyn all he wanted without her suspecting in the least that she was being watched. Then he could take pictures, pictures of her at her window or sitting down on her patio or on the beach, and then he could have them developed and show her how pretty she was, because when you talked to Marilyn Sheppard you could tell she didn't think she was all that pretty, which made her prettier still. He could show the pictures to her and say: *See, this is you out in the world when no one's watching but me. This is you how I see you, and these are the things I like: I like your thick curly hair and your hazel eyes. I like how you always seem a little sad. I like your thin legs and your small breasts and I especially like how you laugh. It's a nasty laugh. It's the laugh of a girl who knows secrets.*

I want to tell you my secret.

Three days ago, Marilyn had told him he looked like Dr. Sam. He looked at himself in the rearview mirror and saw how she could say that. They had the same thick eyebrows and full lips—even their ears were the same shape—but although they both were going bald, Dr. Sam had a widow's peak that was distinguished and he walked like someone who at any moment could break into a run that was faster than you ever were. And he seemed like a man who never looked in mirrors because he already knew everything about himself that he needed to know. Eberling had seen him leaving the house last Wednesday, pulling up in his van just as Sheppard said something to his wife from the kitchen door. Eberling got his cleaning supplies and equipment and came around the van walking straight toward the doctor, who was leaving now, and he appreciated how Sheppard's double-breasted suit widened at his shoulders and narrowed at his waist, admiring his luxuriant red silk tie and shining black tasseled shoes, thinking: Dressed like that, I'd look just as handsome. That's what I'd look like if I was a doctor. They walked by each other, and Eberling, his hands full with pails and squeegees, said, "Good morning, Dr. Sheppard." Without looking at him, the doctor said, "You too," and walked right past to climb down into his brand-new convertible Jag—he'd gotten rid of the MG—and briefly revved the engine before driving off.

Eberling stopped for a moment and watched him disappear around the corner.

It was bright outside, and when Eberling entered the house, his eyes had to adjust from the glare; and there, in the kitchen, emerging as if from this blackness, was Marilyn, kneeling down before her boy, holding him by the arms as if she were cross. She whirled on Eberling suddenly.

"How could you be so inconsiderate?" she said, then stood up.

"Oh," she said. "No. I'm sorry, Dick." She looked over his shoulder. "I thought you were Sam."

"I'm sorry, Mrs. Sheppard. I should've knocked."

"No, no," she said. "I didn't mean to snap at you." She shook her head and laughed. She was wearing shorts and pressed her boy's head to her naked leg. "Call me Marilyn," she said. "Mrs. Sheppard sounds so *old.*"

In the van now, Eberling rolled down his window. It was getting hot, and when it did you could smell the cleaning solutions in the back, the Fantastic and the Windex and the rags still stained with Pledge, the faint scent of ammonia and oil soap that clung to the mops. He had four houses to clean today. Everybody was having a party for the Fourth and wanted their house to look as pretty as a diamond so their guests would think it was *always* like that; that instead of the little smudge of shit on the toilet seat or the dog hairs all over the couch or the caulk clots of toothpaste in the sink, you *always* saw your reflection in the fixtures and faucets and could eat safely off the floors. Then the envious guests would think how much cleaner and shinier and nicer this house was than their own, and therefore how much better their hosts' lives were—and did anyone thank Dick's Cleaning Service for his good work? Hardly. No one ever thanked him except Marilyn.

In the distance, at the Sheppard house, Eberling saw a figure appear at the bedroom window. He was sure it was her. He got out of the truck and the breeze hit him, hard and cool. From the bushes beneath the house, a pair of boys bolted down the stairs and then up the beach. It seemed to Eberling that Marilyn was looking over here, and he wondered for a moment if she could see him as well. And if she knew it was him, would she raise the window and wave? Would she give him some kind of sign?

Three days ago, after finishing up, he went and knocked on the jamb of the enclosed patio at the back of the house, looking over the lake. It was just after lunchtime and Marilyn sat at the table with her boy, eating brownies and drinking milk. She wore white shorts cut high on the thigh and a white blouse that revealed her tan skin between the buttons, and a glimpse of her white-lace bra.

"I'm all done here, Mrs. Sheppard."

"Thank you, Dick."

He watched her watching Chip eat his brownie and felt a sharp stab of something like hunger. "If you want, you can have a look around before I go," he said.

"No, that's fine," she said. "You always do a good job."

Eberling smiled and when Marilyn smiled back he noticed she had more green than brown in her hazel eyes. Then the boy knocked his glass of milk off the table.

"I'll get that," Eberling said. He pulled a rag from his back pocket and wiped up the milk, staring for a moment at the kid's fat little legs dangling from his chair, at the balsa-wood airplane down there whose wing Eberling pressed his knee against until he heard it snap. When he was done, he went to wring out the cloth in the kitchen sink. Marilyn got the milk bottle out of the refrigerator and a new glass, but before going back out to the patio she asked, "Can I offer you some brownies?"

Eberling raised his eyebrows and pointed to himself.

"I just made them this morning," she said.

"That's nice of you," he said; then he waited.

"Come," she said. "Join us."

"All right."

He washed his hands thoroughly and, not wanting to disturb the neatly folded towels by the sink, rubbed his palms against his pants. When he came out onto the patio, a large glass of milk was waiting for him along with five brownies on a plate, the china as white as the milk and Marilyn's shorts and blouse, her skin sun-dark like the treats and as tantalizing and soft. Who could tire of such a woman?

Marilyn sat with her arms on the table, one folded over the other. She patted the seat next to her. "Sit," she said. "You're probably starving."

"I think I am," Eberling said.

"Help yourself."

At first he tried to eat slowly so as not to make a pig of himself, but Marilyn and the boy sat watching him as if it was the most fascinating sight in the world. Self-conscious under their attention, he began taking larger bites of the brownies to hurry things up, much to the child's delight, wolfing them down one after the other and making animal sounds now as he chewed, Marilyn and her son both laughing now, egging him on. The wet mass of brownies threatened to choke him if he swallowed, rendering him speechless for what felt like ten minutes.

Marilyn laughed so hard she had to put her hand on his arm.

"Oh my," Marilyn said. "You *were* starving."

"You ate a *lot,*" the boy said.

"I guess I did," Eberling said, then wiped his mouth. His fingers were covered with icing, so he let the dog lick them clean under the table.

"There's more," Marilyn said.

"No more, please. But thank you."

The boy asked to be excused and Marilyn said yes, wiping his face before letting him leave. Then she and Eberling briefly looked at each other and turned toward the lake. A breeze was blowing in off the water. They sat quietly, staring out. A boat raced across the chop, and for a time the only sound in the world seemed the *chok, chok, chok* of the hull hitting the small waves, the noise it trailed fading to silence before the craft was out of sight.

"This is a pretty spot," Eberling said.

Marilyn kept her eyes forward. "It is, isn't it?"

He always knew what to say to women, especially when they were sad or lonely. He knew what to say to Marilyn now but was afraid.

"I should probably appreciate it more," she said.

"Would that make it any nicer?"

"No," she said. "But it might make me less of a bother."

Eberling waited for her to look at him, which she did. Then he pressed his finger to the crumbs on the plate until the plate was white again. He was aware of her hands resting on the table and wanted to touch them. "I can't imagine you being a bother," he said.

Marilyn put her palm to her face and stared so directly that he should've been uncomfortable. For a moment, he imagined this was his house and Marilyn his wife and the two of them were talking of a breezy afternoon, their boy leaving them alone, and his fear disappeared.

"You know something?" she said.

"What?"

"You look like my husband."

"Mrs. Houk says that all the time," he said.

"You do," she said. "But a different version."

"How different?"

Her eyes darted back and forth across his face. "Your eyes," she said. "Your lashes. They're softer. Longer."

Eberling waited.

"You have sad eyes," she said.

"I don't feel sad," he said.

"No?"

"I don't think sad things." He smiled broadly just to show her.

"I meant sad like sweet," she said.

It was funny, Eberling thought, how Dr. Sam was in this room now, making her sad, making her say these things, making him stay right where he was for as long as he could so he could remind her of how different he was from Dr. Sam. Which was the key, Eberling thought, to be the same, but different: to be the man her husband was, yet not. Though this wasn't what he wanted. Otherwise, they'd always be conjoined. "You don't look like anyone I know," he said.

Marilyn shook her head and laughed her nasty laugh. "What does *that* mean?" she said.

Eberling waited for her to stop. He'd dreamed of telling her this, had imagined doing it in the very place they were sitting, and now it was happening. "It means that whenever I hear the name Marilyn, I think of you—of Marilyn Sheppard. Anyone else is just borrowing your name."

Silence fell over the room, nailing every one of Eberling's limbs in place. He was sure it gripped Marilyn too.

"That," she said, "may be the nicest thing anyone has ever said to me."

They looked at each other and there was nothing else to do, he thought, except kiss this woman. But he waited too long, and she looked down at her plate.

"Thank you for the brownies," he said, getting up.

"You're welcome," she said.

He turned to leave.

But she touched his arm to stop him. "You know, Dick, the next time you come here, you should bring your swim trunks."

"Sorry?"

"You could swim at our beach after you're finished and have a chance to play."

Eberling looked out at the beach and back at Marilyn. "Really?"

"I'd like that," she said.

"You would?"

"I like to know someone's enjoying our place."

"Well," he said, "I come next Wednesday to clean."

"I'll plan on that then," she said.

"I'll see you," he said.

In the van, watching the Sheppard house, Eberling imagined next Wednesday for about the hundredth time since he and Marilyn had talked. He saw himself change into his swim trunks in Dr. Sam's study and then walk through the house to the patio, out the door, and down the steps to the water. Then he'd wade in, aware of Marilyn watching him from her bedroom window, and swim until his arms ached and all the work smells were washed off him. Then he'd dry himself off down at the beach and be sure to sit and wait for the wind and sun to dry him more so he wouldn't seem too eager. Then he'd make his way back up to the house. Once inside, he'd find the downstairs empty. Then Marilyn would call to him from the bedroom upstairs. And if that happened, he wouldn't fail himself like he had on the patio. He'd be ready. The house would be dark and cool, his hair and trunks damp from swimming but his body dry, and he'd walk up the stairs to where Marilyn was waiting. She'd be in her bed, the one nearest the door that he knew was hers because he sniffed the sheets whenever he stripped it. She'd be lying in them waiting for him. Then he'd take off his swimsuit and lie down next to her and take her in his arms and fit himself against her back, spooning her tightly. Her body would be warm and his cool. They'd listen to the breeze off the water, the leaves rattling the window screens. And that was when he'd tell her his secret.

"You know, Dr. Sam," Mobius said, "there's this funny thing that happens to some men before I kill their wives. Kind of a buyer's remorse, I guess, because occasionally after the money's changed hands and I've got my mark's brakes set to fail, her patio rigged to collapse, or the furnace ready to blow CO_2, every so often the husband will phone me in a panic the night before to call the whole thing off. He'll be apologetic. A little embarrassed. He claims he doesn't care about the lost deposit. Just abort, he says. And I'll agree—it's a substantial sum of money—but when I ask why he doesn't want to go through with it, he says the same thing every time: 'Things,' he says, 'are getting better. Things,' he says, 'have improved.' There's real *optimism* in his voice, practically newlywed glee. Sometimes he'll even say, 'Thank you, Mr. Mobius. If it weren't for you, I don't think my wife and I would've gotten to this point in our relationship. We're happier now than ever. I owe you more than you know.' We hang up, and I smile a little smile to myself, because a week or two later, the same guy calls back and says the exact same thing."

"What's that?"

" 'Kill the bitch.' "

"You're demented."

"And you didn't answer the question."

"You didn't ask me one."

"Can you tell the story of your marriage?"

Because Sheppard was a detective, he often reviewed the history of his relationship with Marilyn, jotting down his thoughts on a series of yellow legal pads, especially during the months he spent in prison before his trial and the ten years afterward until his verdict was overturned. Beginning sequentially, he then examined every last facet of it, uncovering every dark place, in an attempt to prove his own guilt or innocence and his degree of complicity, because at times he saw her death as being inextricably intertwined with their love, the terrible and logical conclusion of their togetherness, the culmination of a pattern of behavior on his part that he'd been conscious of but waited too long to put to a stop. And in this version of their life together, Sheppard considered himself as guilty of killing her as the man who'd bludgeoned her to death.

We orbit, Sheppard wrote, *we repeat.*

This pattern was there from the beginning.

The boy's real name was Sam, but soon after he was born his father called him Chip. It meant "off the old block," of course—like Sam, he could sleep through a tornado—but Marilyn saw it differently. In the mornings, after she woke him, he was so irritable she thought of him as Chip-on-my-shoulder. After spending a whole day together, after obeying as many of his little commands as seemed reasonable and arguing with every one that didn't, each respective disagreement sending him spiraling into a tantrum, she called him Chip-away-at-my-sanity in her mind.

"Chip?" she called from the foot of the stairs. "Are you awake?"

"No," Hoversten said, "he's not." He appeared at the landing, or rather his silhouette. He had a mallet of some kind in his hand, and his appearance startled her. "I just checked on him," Hoversten said. He made his way and moved down the stairs in white shoes, white pants with a white belt, a red cardigan vest over his shirt. The mallet was a putter and he was carrying a bag of golf clubs. "What the hell's that contraption on his face?" He stopped on the small landing above her.

Marilyn crossed her arms. "It's a chin brace," she said.

"What's wrong with his chin?"

"Nothing," Marilyn said. "It just juts out. Sam thinks that if we don't fix it, he'll have problems with his bite."

Hoversten shrugged. "Well, tell Sam that in my professional opinion the kid's going to have more problems with his self-image if he has to wear that thing every night. It makes him look like Frankenstein."

"I'll be sure to pass along the prognosis."

Hoversten snorted. His eyes were ringed black with sleeplessness. The night before, Sam had confessed to Marilyn that there was talk of Hoversten's medical license being revoked and some concern about "mental issues." One of the nurses at Sam's hospital had told her that during a breast exam he'd had the patient remove her gown, pinched both her nipples as if he were about to pull down a blind, and said, "Nothing wrong with these."

He smiled at her emptily.

"Sorry I can't stay and chat, but I'm playing golf with Dr. Stevenson."

"I thought you were working with Sam at the hospital today."

Hoversten's eyes drifted toward the ceiling. "I think I need a little R & R right now. Tell Sam I'll be staying with Stevenson for the rest of the weekend." He leaned his clubs against the railing and labored back upstairs, using the putter as a cane.

"Would you mind stripping the bed before you go?" Marilyn called after him. She dreaded touching his sheets. Upstairs, she heard a couple drawers slam closed, then the bedroom door shut quietly. Hoversten took each step back down slowly, heavily, until they were at eye level. Holding an overnight bag, he shouldered his clubs and looked at her.

"I'll let the help do it," he said, then turned to leave.

"You son of a bitch," she said.

"Careful with the cursing, Marilyn. When you're dead you might end up in hell."

"You're a failure, you know that?"

Hoversten stopped at the door. "Oh, really?"

"A goddamn failure."

He set his clubs down.

"Look at you," she said. "Fired from the hospital. Deserted by your wife. Fat as a pig. And you show up at our door asking for help. Help and shelter. And we give it to you. We feed you and give you comfort, Sam even offers to get you a job, and that's how you talk to *me*?"

"Keep it coming."

"You arrange dates for my husband. Those nurses when we were in California. Then you have the gall to make a pass at me. You're such a failure you try to share it."

Hoversten stood there calmly, his weight resting on the putter. He shook his head slowly, his tongue pressed to his cheek. "Are you done?"

"Yes."

"Good," he said, and pointed the end of the club at her. "Because *you're* the failure. A failure of a *wife.* You want to know why Sam's been with all those women? Because of *you,* Marilyn. Because you *take,* but you never give. Because you need and then you need some more. God, you're a greedy bitch. Sam puts a beautiful roof over *your* head, buys *you* clothes and nice things, and all *you* have to do is feed him and keep his house, take care of the kid, and just *once* a day be a loving wife. But that's too much to ask, isn't it? Oh, you think he didn't tell me? You think he didn't complain? And you blame *me* for the dates? Please. He *wanted* to go on those dates, Marilyn. He wanted a *break.* For all you know he's on one right now."

"Sam's not doing that anymore."

"Really? Well, I'm glad Sam's changed. Have you?"

"Get out."

From the kitchen door, she watched Hoversten back out of the driveway. Pulling into the road, he blew her a kiss and peeled off.

She sat down on the kitchen steps with her hands clasped behind her neck, her hair hanging over her face. She closed her eyes, and in her mind saw Sam—though she urged herself not to—having sex with someone, and then the woman came into focus. She couldn't help it. Because Lester mentioned Dr. Stevenson, she saw Susan Hayes, first sitting and waiting in his car, the red MG Marilyn made him get rid of when they came back from

California this March; then she imagined the two of them fucking in it, Marilyn feeling not jealousy but a terror that had nothing to do with the act or the betrayal, only with him *not* being where he said he'd be *right now.* That's what scared her most. It was irrational to think he was with Susan—she was long gone, back in Los Angeles—but if he wasn't where he said he'd be, then he could be anywhere. And if he could be anywhere, Marilyn thought, then one day he could be nowhere. She could come home to find him gone. What she needed to know, more than anything else, was exactly where he was just this minute.

She went to the phone, called the hospital, and spoke with Patti, Bay View's receptionist. She recognized Marilyn's voice, checked Sam's schedule, and transferred her to surgery. Donna Bailey, the receptionist there, told her she'd seen Sam in the OR about fifteen minutes ago. "Give me a second," she said, "and I'll locate him." In the silence, Marilyn hoped he was about to pick up the phone but was sure he wouldn't.

"Marilyn," Donna said, "I can't locate him, but I know he's around. He's scheduled straight through the afternoon. I'll try to track him down and have him call you. Is everything all right?"

"Yes."

"Are you at home?"

It wasn't easy talking with her because it was Donna who'd clued her in about Sam's last fling, who'd opened the letter that Susan Hayes person had sent him from Los Angeles just a few weeks after their return and in turn passed it on to her: *I was terrible when you were here, Sam. I know I was acting like a child because I wanted more from you, wanted too much too fast, but I'm still waiting, I promise. Don't think you lost me. I'm looking at the watch you gave me right now and thinking about our actually having time together.* Donna knew exactly why she was calling now, and her tone of concern had a touch of complicity in it, as if the two of them shared a secret. Donna made her feel as if she and Sam were a fraud.

"You know," Marilyn said, "it's not that important. We're having the interns' party tomorrow and I just wanted a final head count before I went shopping."

"Are you sure? I'm happy to find where he's got off to."

"Really," Marilyn said, "it's fine."

It *was* fine, she thought when she hung up. He was *there.* She had to believe that's where he was because that was the trick: to suspend her disbelief, to trust her husband's version of his own schedule, *not* to buy into Hoversten's doubt. She'd go through her day confident of where Sam was because that was what he'd told her he was going to do from now on. That was the agreement at which they'd arrived. Meanwhile, there was much to do.

"Chip!" she said at the foot of the stairs. "I want you up now, please!" Not hearing so much as a stir, she went upstairs and opened his door. The mobile of black and white swans was spinning slowly in the breeze above his bed, the room so quiet she could hear their balsa forms clacking lightly against one another on the draft. Chip was asleep, on his back, the brace straps fastened across his chin and forehead. He looked exactly like Sam when he was asleep, though the brace held his mouth open slightly, and she unfastened the buckles and removed the apparatus, the belts leaving red imprints on his face that looked like tribal paint. "Chip," she said, pressing a palm to his arm. "Chip, wake up." He didn't react. She poked him twice in the ribs. "Chip! Hel*lo,* Chip!" It was like he was dead, and now she had to do what she hated doing: she took him by the shoulders and shook him so hard, almost lifting his little body off the bed, that it was as if she were smashing him against a wall. "Chip, *please,* wake up!" The boy whined painfully—she thought he might cry—but was awake now. He opened his eyes, saying nothing, his expression sour. "Let's get you dressed," she said. She sat him up, pulling him by the arms so his head hung back, balancing him, then turning him around so his feet hung over the side of the bed. He stayed hunched there for a moment, his eyes still closed, his chin pressed to his chest, his palms turned up to the ceiling like a marionette whose strings had been cut.

We'll just go about our day, Marilyn thought as she dressed him. We have a lot to do, a lot to keep on our mind, and that's how we'll proceed. She looked at the clock by his bed. It was almost nine forty and she hadn't accomplished a thing, and once Chip had eaten breakfast it was half past ten and Sam still hadn't called. Chances were he was very busy. He'd told her the night before he was booked solid, that he was going to try to squeeze in all his appointments before two, so it was best to leave him alone. She left Chip playing in his room while she straightened up the living room and the kitchen, spot cleaned the guest bathroom, then walked back down to the boathouse to tackle that job but at the sight of it turned around in disgust and thought she'd try the hospital just once more, changing her mind when she picked up the phone. She snuck another cigarette on the patio. By the time she'd packed up Chip into the car to go to the supermarket, it was eleven thirty. Backing out of the driveway, she realized she'd forgotten her list. She went back in the house, found it in the kitchen, looked at the phone, and then dialed it.

"I found him," Donna said. "I gave him the message."

"Thank you," Marilyn said. She'd closed her eyes and was pinching the bridge of her nose. "Is he there now?"

"He stepped out."

She looked at her watch. "For lunch?"

"He didn't say."

They waited, and any relief she felt was immediately obliterated. "Well," she finally said, "as long as he got the message."

"I gave it to him in the flesh."

"Did he say when he'd be back?"

"He just said soon."

Later, as she and Chip drove into town, Marilyn reflected on how little she really knew about her husband's schedule—and, in turn, how little he knew about hers. In fact, as long as she had got everything done that he expected, he didn't give her daily movements a thought. She could go anywhere right now because she was operating under his presumption. She drove down Lake Road, studying the drivers in the oncoming lane. Where were these men and women off to? Did their husbands or wives know? Were they where they were supposed to be or was everyone sneaking around? And what if she did? She had, if anything, greater latitude than Sam, and if she chose to could enjoy even more convenient forms of deception because in the past he'd predicated his deceptions on her absences. When they lived in California and he was in med school, he'd had most of his dalliances during her trips back to Cleveland; once they returned home, he'd done most of his slinking around in the odd hours of emergency calls, at lunch hours, coming back from work. His affairs must have been so rushed, so hurried, because he'd had to fit them in only when he could plausibly claim to have been somewhere else. As for her, she could simply stay at home and do whatever she liked because Sam never gave home a thought. She considered Wednesday for a moment, when she and handsome Dick Eberling sat out on the patio. She could've hustled Chip over to the Aherns, where Nancy could watch him while he played with her kids, and Dick could've had his way with her in complete privacy and then finished cleaning, with Sam paying for the whole experience.

If Sam isn't back at the hospital, she told herself, I'll sleep with Dick Eberling the next chance I get.

The thought made her momentarily heady. She imagined him coming to the house next Wednesday. She'd told him to bring his swim trunks and knew he would, positive he'd do anything she said. She'd have him change in Sam's study and let him go down to the beach and swim. Then she'd go up to the bedroom, take off all her clothes, get into bed, wait until she heard him come back in the house before softly calling him upstairs. He'd come up and be docile with her—gentle, if she told him to—and she could tell him to do anything she wanted and where to touch her, and he'd do it. And from then on, he'd always be there . . .

Not surprisingly, what with all the parties going on this weekend, the supermarket was crowded. Chip wanted to sit in the basket and at first she said no. He was already too big for this and it would make the cart hard to push, but her other choice was to chase him around the store, so she caved and let him climb in. And he was antsy. He grabbed items, knocking things over as they passed by, so she had to stop twice to reprimand him. Afterward, he kicked his feet, rattling the cart's cage. She took his ankles in her hands. "Stop banging your feet, please," she said. So he started banging her hands with his. "Chip, do you want to go sit in the car?"

He looked at her, laughed, and bent double, rubbing his forehead against the back of her hand, which made her let her guard down. "You're not going to put me in the car," he said.

"Oh, how do you know?"

"Because you never do."

"Maybe this will be the first time."

"No it won't."

"How do you know?"

"Because it's hot and I could die."

"Only if I left the windows up."

"You wouldn't leave me even if they were down."

"And why is that?"

"Because a bad man might take me away."

"I think you'd drive a bad man crazy too. I think a bad man would put you right back in the car and run away."

They looked at each other and laughed, and then Marilyn took his chin in her hand.

"Well, you're right, and that's why I need you to sit still."

He thought about this, during which time she enjoyed a few efficient minutes, blacking out line after line on her list, and then Chip said, "Can't I walk with you?"

"You can, but you'll have to walk *with* me. You can't go exploring."

He shook his head sadly, then caught sight of something on the shelves. "Can we get pickles?"

"Yes," she said. "Pickles are on the list." She pulled a large jar down from the shelf.

"I want to hold them," Chip said.

"You can hold them," she told him, "but you can't *drop* them. If you do, we'll have to pay for them, and then there won't be any pickles to eat." She winced, knowing what was coming next.

"Can I eat a pickle now?" he asked.

"No, you can't," she said, "not until we pay for it." She tried to take the jar, but he gripped it tightly and she relented. "Until we pay for it, they're not our pickles."

"But we're *going* to pay for it."

"It doesn't matter."

"But you always do," he said. His eyes were welling up. "Don't they trust you by now?"

"Trust has nothing to do with it, Chip." She tried to take the pickles once more and now he hugged them like a sailor gripping a mast in a storm. "This isn't a restaurant."

"I'm so hungry I *need* a pickle."

"No," she said, pulling down three bags of hot dog buns, "you're going to have to wait."

"I'm starving."

"You're not starving. You're *whining.*" She grabbed ten pounds of ground beef, five packs of hot dogs, three packages of bratwurst, and three whole cut-up chickens. *It's not like it's a fancy meal.*

Chip began to cry. "I'm going to starve. I can't starve, Mom."

"Stop it," she said, squeezing his arm. "Stop this right now."

"Can't I have even half of one?"

"*No.*"

He then tried to open the jar, and if Marilyn hadn't been so furious, it would've been comical—Chip trying with both his hands and all his might to twist off the top, the act looking proportionally like a man trying to unscrew a wine barrel. Just to keep him busy, she was tempted to tell him he could have a pickle if he got the jar open, but then he nearly dropped it, and she yanked it away and placed it in the seat of the cart, which set him howling.

"Chip," she whispered. "Stop this *right now* or so help me you'll spend the rest of the day in your room."

This only upped the volume. Women were passing by and shaking their heads, some sympathetically, some not.

"*Enough.*"

"I . . . want . . . a . . . pick . . . cull," he gasped.

She had stopped at the freezer aisle, wider and brighter and cooler than the others. "Last chance."

He was red-faced with screaming, now mouthing the word in slow motion: *pick-cull.*

"All right, then." She gave the cart a hard push, just like she'd seen the boys do in the parking lot, aiming the carts into the backs of others as if bowling. The sudden speed got Chip's attention. He immediately stopped crying and watched her, wide-eyed, as more and more distance separated them and she became smaller and smaller, Chip looking like a baby bird in a nest of groceries. A woman with her daughter in tow turned to watch the cart whiz by. "I'll have to try that," she said.

Chip sat in shock. "Momma?"

She saluted him and turned the corner.

She could hear him calling as she walked down the aisle, grabbing a tin of coffee and some oatmeal, trying to remember what else was on her list and feeling that odd sense of conflict, enjoying Chip's suffering for all the times he'd made her suffer, relishing his fear like a big sister might, while simultaneously sensing her own blood collecting along her left side, as if he were magnetized and she drawn to comfort him, his terror pulling at her bones. But turning the corner she worried that rushing to his side would make him into his father's double, confirming for him that she was at his disposal, so she hoped he might remember this abandonment, that her momentary disappearance might just once make an impact on his behavior. And then she addressed the child inside her: I could walk away from him. I could walk away from them both, from Chip and your father. But not you, love. Not you.

With a hand resting lightly on her belly, she saw a clerk standing by her cart, an old man with a dead eye, the pupil cream-clouded with glaucoma. He must be new because she didn't recognize him. Chip was standing up in the basket but hadn't found the courage to jump off and come find her. The stranger held him by the shirt, trying to comfort him, but his craggy, ghost-eyed appearance only made Chip more upset. Though his mouth was open, no sound at all came out.

"Is this your boy?" the clerk said.

Marilyn crossed her arms and squinted at her son. "I'm not sure," she said. "What's his name?"

"What's your name?" the clerk asked him.

Chip took a deep breath and said his name, then closed his eyes again and continued throwing his silent scream, tears dribbling down his cheeks.

"Hmm," she said. "That's my son's name, but this doesn't look like my son. At least, I certainly can't tell from his expression." She squinted at Chip, who was reaching out to her with both arms. The clerk held his pants while Marilyn stayed just out of reach. "Maybe I could tell if he stopped crying."

"She says you should stop crying," the clerk said, tugging at Chip's pants. "Let her get a look at you."

He stopped crying so quickly it was like he'd turned off a spigot. He was breathing so hard his little shoulders pumped up and down.

"Can you tell now?" the clerk asked her.

Chip, aghast, stared at her as if his life depended on it.

"He looks like Chip," she said, "but he doesn't act like him. Are you a good boy?"

"Yes," he said.

"Can you sit down in your seat?"

With the help of the clerk, he sat down.

"My son listens to his mother. Do you?"

He nodded.

"Can you stay quiet while you're in the supermarket?"

He nodded even more forcefully, given that he had no voice. His lashes were clumped and dewy with tears.

"Yes," she said to the clerk. "I think that's him."

"All right," he said. He patted Chip's head. "Mind your momma, now." Then he walked off.

At the checkout line, Marilyn thumbed idly through *Screen Annual*'s promotional stills of Grace Kelly and Jimmy Stewart's new Hitchcock film, *Rear Window.* The director was ogling Kelly, pretending to sneak up from behind and choke her. God, Marilyn thought, looking at Stewart, *there* was a perfect man. Wasn't he dating Anita Colby, and hadn't she dated Clark Gable? Good for her. And Grace, Marilyn thought, was *so* beautiful. She remembered seeing her at the Hollywood Tennis Club years ago, and she was even prettier in person. But hadn't she broken up the marriage of her costar, the one from *Dial M for Murder,* was it Ray Milland? And didn't she always have some new lover? Well, she might live like a man, though she seemed none the worse for wear. Maybe it was simpler than she thought. Her own father had walked away from her. After her mother died giving birth to her stillborn brother, he'd sent her off to live with her Uncle Bud and Aunt Mary, claiming terrific grief. But perhaps he simply wanted to be alone. Or he saw in his wife's death the opportunity to start all over. And was that simply a man thing? A capacity they retained once children were in the picture that women rarely could: to walk away. She looked up at Chip. Of course she couldn't leave him. Yet most of the time it had seemed that Sam was simply daring her to walk away, pushing her into leaving. Why, so that the burden of breaking off wasn't on him?

"Hello, Mrs. Sheppard."

"Oh, hello, Timothy."

"Having a party?"

"I'm afraid so."

"It'll be pretty for the fireworks tonight. All weekend, in fact."

"So I hear."

"Hello, Chip," the clerk said.

He looked at Marilyn for permission.

"Say hello," she told him.

"Hello."

"Timothy, what time do you have?"

"It's a quarter past twelve."

"Could you watch Chip while I make a phone call?"

She called the hospital and asked to be put through to Donna, who knew what she wanted the minute Marilyn said hello.

"He canceled his last surgery," she said. "He left about thirty minutes ago."

After saying good-bye, Marilyn stared at the black receiver. She saw Susan Hayes in her mind, sitting in the passenger seat of Sam's car, waiting for him in their garage.

The truth, Marilyn thought, following the bag boy to her car, was that she'd been a fool to think that Sam could change—which was fine, if only because they'd tried. So now that they'd failed, she was going to show her husband that *she* could change. By inviting another man into her bed, or any number of them. She'd make it a sport. Hadn't he once said as much, explaining that it was kind of a sport? She could take the Dick Eberlings and Don Aherns and Spen Houks, all of whom wanted to have their way with her, and play Sam's game, then see how sporty he felt when it was happening to him, when the men who came to him for care had enjoyed his wife's favors, when their *wives* knew, even his nurses and store clerks. After all, hadn't the bedrock of her fidelity enabled him to do all this? Didn't such behavior—as well as his appeal, his unattainability—require that things be one-sided?

Driving down Lake Road, she saw Dick Eberling's van parked in front of the Houks' house and thought, Why not start now? She pulled into their driveway, told Chip to sit quietly for a minute, and knocked on the door.

Esther answered, in a tizzy about getting the place cleaned up.

"I saw Dick Eberling's van outside. I have to change an appointment with him."

"He's upstairs somewhere," Esther said.

Spen, Bay View's mayor, was by profession a butcher, and their house always smelled smoked or charred. It was dark on the second floor, close and warm, quiet and carpeted. Marilyn padded silently toward the bedroom, stopping just outside the door to watch Eberling from the hall. He was sitting on the ledge of the window, leaning back as if he were on a swing, soaping down the outside pane with his brush in figure eight over figure eight until his figure was blurred, until he appeared foam-streaked, and then skimmed it clear in the same motion of his squeegee, so he now appeared as though he'd just surfaced from the sea. He looked so much like her husband it was uncanny, though he was perhaps more handsome. He was leaner, for one thing. He'd stripped down to his undershirt, and she could make out the knots of muscle in his shoulders and stomach through the sopped fabric, could tell from just his hands that he was a strong man. Her husband's hands were large, but they were soft, almost like a dentist's, from all the scrubbing down. But mostly it was Eberling's eyes that made him beautiful. They had the same color eyes, he and Sam, but Eberling's were sad. Something had happened to him, and everything about him bespoke of this terrible event. Whenever he looked at her, it seemed he had something to tell her on the tip of his tongue.

"Dick?"

"Mrs. Houk?"

He pulled himself back inside the house. Stepping into the room, she said, "No, it's Marilyn."

He stared, sitting on the sill and blinking until his eyes adjusted, and then he looked down at the floor. "Hello, Mrs. Sheppard."

Wanting to take his chin in her hand, she said, "I saw your van outside." She was afraid to swallow.

He sat hunched at the window.

"I was thinking about next week," she said, "and was wondering if you might come over to clean on Monday instead." Her heart was racing. This was easier than she'd imagined. She could feel him waiting on everything she said. "Come over in the afternoon. Chip could go next door for a while. He won't bother us."

Eberling, still looking at the floor, was smiling now.

"Like I said, you could bring your swim trunks." She moved closer to him. His skin was like wet copper, so dark he was almost black. "We could play."

He stood there silently, not moving a muscle.

"Would you like that?" she said.

"Yes," he said. "But . . ."

"But what?"

"I wish it were sooner," he said.

She couldn't help it. She was whispering. Except for Sam, she'd never spoken to a man like this. "I wish it were too." She couldn't believe herself. "I wish it were tonight."

Eberling seemed to process what she said, then looked up. She thought he almost looked angry.

"Mrs. Sheppard, will you tell me something?"

"Certainly."

His exhaled loudly, through his nostrils. "You're not lying to me, are you?"

The question made her blink. "Of course not," she said.

"You could like somebody like me?"

"Yes," she said.

"For a long time?"

She shrugged, feeling a flash of doubt. "Why not?"

He looked down again, smiling at the floor.

"Monday, then?" she said.

He nodded.

"I have to go."

She walked down the stairs, thinking, that's all it took to become someone else. When Esther called good-bye, she didn't answer. It was sweet and mysterious what Dick had said. *For a long time.* And it was odd. Even before love started, everyone wanted to make sure it would last.

She turned on the ignition and backed out, the Houks living only two houses down. She was about to shift gears when she saw Sam's car parked in the driveway.

She drove up slowly, pulling in next to his Jaguar, then closed the door gently after she got out. She left the groceries in the car and, Chip in hand, approached the house as carefully as if she'd suspected there was a burglar inside. She entered through the kitchen. "Sam?" she called. There was no answer. She sent Chip off to play and opened the door to the basement, calling out Sam's name again, then closed the door and went upstairs to their bedroom. He wasn't there, but his bed was made. The sight of this made her heart skip a beat.

Through the window, she could hear Sam down by the boathouse.

She paused on the landing above it to regard Sam through the wooden railing. The wind had calmed some, but it was breezy enough that he couldn't hear her approach. Dressed casually, in corduroy pants and a

T-shirt, he was hard at work. He'd paired all the skis, hung the life jackets out to dry, arranged the towlines in neat coils, piled the towels together, and even brought down a garbage can for all the food and beer bottles. He'd resecured the boat to the slip and was hosing off the prow.

Hearing her when she stepped onto the dock, he turned around and, when she was close enough, took her in his free arm and kissed her neck, training the hose on the boat with his other hand. "You've ruined my surprise," he said.

"Which was?"

"That I was going to have this all cleaned up before you got home. Plus the bedroom and even the bathroom. But I guess you beat me to it."

"Not all of it."

"Sorry I left this place in such a state. I'm glad you didn't bother."

"I haven't been down here in days."

"Well." Sam shook his head once and then closed his eyes, as if he could fall asleep standing there.

"What is it?" she said. "What happened?"

"I don't . . ."

"Tell me, love." She put her arms around his waist.

"A boy . . . got hit by a truck. He was only eight. It just backed into him. He had massive internal injuries. He came in conscious but died almost as soon as we got him on the table. The father . . . he really lit into me afterward." He dropped the hose and put his hands on his knees and began to sob, covering his eyes with his hands. "I just don't know why it's bothering me so much."

He was shaking so hard she bent over and made him sit down, then she sat herself and held him. She'd seen him cry like this over patients only twice, and he now was trying so hard to hold back his sobs that he wheezed.

"I'm sorry," he said finally. "I did everything I could to get his heart going, but it was futile. And his father . . . he called me a killer. He said I killed his son. I'm sorry, Marilyn, I'm so sorry. I came home early to clean up. But I was too late."

She told him, gently, to hush, to be quiet, and wrapped her arms around his still trembling shoulders. His body was hot with the effort and remorse. The breeze picked up and she shook too, chilled. Because what she felt, more than love for Sam, was how close she'd come to a perilous slip. But she was safe now. There was no harm. She was back, and Sam was nowhere but *here;* she was grateful for that—for *knowing,* and for this child, and for a great many things, and most of all to have been so blessed by luck.

. . .

"Let me tell you some of the things about your case that baffle me," Mobius said, "the questions I can't get out of my mind. Maybe you can answer them, because every piece of evidence is so ambiguous and contradictory that I find myself wondering sometimes if the Devil himself, or whatever animating spirit of evil traffics in our world, decided to turn your life into a hellish game—a labyrinth where the truth keeps falling down holes as you stumble through the maze."

"I don't believe in the Devil," Sheppard said.

"What do you believe in?"

"Consciousness."

Mobius rolled his eyes. "You called your neighbors—the Houks, Spen and Esther—first thing that morning, around five forty-five. Your first words to him over the phone were, 'My God, Spen, get over here quick, I think they've killed Marilyn.' Why *they,* Doctor?"

"Detective."

"It's such an interesting mistake with the pronoun. Did you really think you'd seen multiple people in the house, or was it just a slip of the tongue? Or were your injuries—the blood in your mouth and on your chipped teeth, the contusions on the right side of your face, above your right eye, and on the back of your neck, not to mention the broken cervical vertebrae there—so severe that you were completely disoriented, that your brain, playing tricks on your short-term memory, had somehow split the first form you claimed to have seen as you ran up the stairs into two? Did the man who first knocked you out become a second, the one you claimed you chased down to the lake, who overpowered and then knocked you out—again!—and conveniently left you there to soak in Lake Erie, your body half in and half out of the water? Was it simply one person—or two entirely different ones? How considerate of your wife's killer—this man who'd beaten her face into a pulp—to leave you in a position where you wouldn't drown. 'My God, Spen . . . I think *they've* killed Marilyn.' I think *he* killed Marilyn. Or, I think *I* killed Marilyn. Isn't *that* what you meant to say?"

"No," Sheppard said.

"Of course not," Mobius continued. "Given the nature and extent of your injuries, it's nearly impossible to believe they were self-inflicted. Someone gave you a good beating, but whoever it was didn't beat you dead. And Marilyn *was* quite the athlete, wasn't she? Terrific water-skier. A lady who could drub you—a college football player and track star—in tennis.

She could've put up quite the fight, after all, or at least caught you with a good enough shot to send you into a blind rage. It's not impossible, is it?"

Sheppard listened impassively.

"And then, of course, there's the question of severity. Your injuries certainly *were* severe if we're to believe your brother's medical report, since Stephen whisked you off to your family's hospital almost immediately, less than an hour after you called Spen, even before any detectives arrived. Meanwhile, Coroner Gerber found no indication of a broken neck in *his* x-rays, did he? Is it possible your good brother was protecting the Sheppard dynasty by pulling the old x-ray switcheroo?"

Sheppard cleaned his pipe and then stared at the floor.

"But I'm getting ahead of myself," Mobius said. "Spen and Esther arrived nearly instantly and found you in your study, soaked and hypothermic, disoriented and naked above the waist. 'Somebody needs to do something for Marilyn,' you said. But you'd taken her pulse already. You knew she was dead."

Sheppard nodded but wouldn't look up.

"What happened to your T-shirt, Doctor? Am I to understand that in your struggle, this form or those forms took your shirt, tore it off, and kept it as a souvenir? As convenient—wouldn't you say?—as your position in the water, since whoever beat Marilyn to death would have been *covered* in blood. Or *you* would have. Or was this the same shirt found several days later on the property adjacent to yours, the one torn from waist to sleeve and with brown stains the authorities didn't bother to type for blood, and thus ignored?"

"I don't know."

"It *is* true," Mobius said, "that you had no open wounds on your body, not even scratches or cuts, defensive wounds on your hands or arms to be expected if it was you who beat Marilyn, though there was some blood on you—the large circular stain on the knee of your pants, from when, you claimed, you knelt on the mattress to check Marilyn's pulse."

"That's right," Sheppard said.

"And that gook on your knee matched Marilyn's blood type—O negative—corroborating your story. If *you* were the killer, how in the world—in a room misted, sprinkled, and splattered with blood, where on the wall running alongside her bed there was a white outline of the killer himself, white because his body had absorbed that spray from her head and face—did you manage to have none on you at all?"

"There was no blood on me because I didn't kill her," Sheppard said.

"Sometimes I'm inclined to believe you. I am because of Marilyn's injuries, especially her broken tooth, her upper incisor snapped at the root, the one detectives found in her bed, yanked out as opposed to smashed in, so most likely her killer cupped his hand over her lips to shut her up and she bit him hard enough that when he pulled his fingers away it took the whole tooth for a ride. She must've bit him down to the bone. *That* must've bled like a *bitch,* wouldn't you agree, Doctor?"

Sheppard shook his head miserably.

"And yet I wonder how," Mobius said, "Stephen was able to arrive at your house within less than fifteen minutes of being called that morning—showered and shaved and dressed in jacket and tie. I believe one of the Cleveland detectives made the same drive at the same hour and it took him twelve minutes. Was *Stephen* an accomplice? Did you call him in a panic in the middle of the night, *after* beating Marilyn to death? Was it the two of you who staged the robbery? Pulled out the drawers in the living room and study but took not one thing of value in the entire house? Knocked your medical bag over but didn't take any of the drugs inside? Left Marilyn's gold watch, flecked with blood, and the loaded shotguns in your study—one of which you could have easily grabbed before chasing her killer down to the beach? Didn't even take your wallet after knocking you out in the bedroom? What burglar is willing to take a life but no loot? That's a zero-sum game, don't you think? Doesn't that give credence to the witnesses who said they saw all the lights on in your house at two a.m. that night? That old couple who happened to be driving by? Or, more conspiratorially, more deviously, more gamely, more metacriminally, did somebody try to make it look like *you* were trying make it look like *you* were covering up a crime? Oh," he said, "*that* would be good."

Sheppard stared at the barred window in Mobius's cell.

"Yet why would you kill your wife after the two of you had happily announced her pregnancy at dinner with your family just a month before? Or did Dr. Bailey—Donna Bailey's husband—*not* tell the truth when he testified that when he congratulated you about the pregnancy on the morning of July third, your response was, 'That's what you get when you forget to use birth control'? Does that maybe answer that?" He took a deep breath.

"Perhaps it's simply the dual nature of marriage, the proximity of violence and love. Marilyn's clothes were laid out on the chair in your bedroom, no? That meant she folded them neatly before putting on her pajamas and going to sleep. She went to sleep peacefully, routinely. If the Aherns saw you asleep on the daybed when they left just past midnight, as they claimed, that would mean you woke up and went upstairs with the *intent* to kill Marilyn. Or *she* woke up and then woke *you* up to start a fight that turned vicious enough for you to snap, bludgeoning her with a weapon that was never recovered. Who bludgeons his wife twenty-seven times *on the head*? How mad do you have to be to do something like *that*?"

"I have no idea."

"Why didn't the dog start barking?"

"Kokie was meek."

"If you *did* kill her, how was it that a man of your strength instead of barely denting her dura couldn't smash through her brain plate? Did the killer lack conviction? Was he a weak man or just meek like the dog?"

Sheppard closed his eyes.

"And what about the green duffel bag found the morning of the murder, in the woods halfway down the stairs to the lake, with your school ring, keys, and watch in it—the watch not only flecked with blood but also stopped at four fifteen and the crystal full of condensation. When asked about the blood, you said it must have gotten there when you took Marilyn's pulse. You also told the detectives, without them asking, that it had gotten wet several days beforehand, when you played golf in the rain. Interesting you'd felt the need to explain *that,* just as it is that Eberling—not even a person of interest at the time—should, when questioned by police, blurt out that his blood was all over the Sheppard house because he'd cut himself removing a window screen the previous week and then went to the basement to wash the wound. There *were* multiple blood spots found in the house, from bedroom to kitchen to patio to basement, on the stair risers too, more than a trail, really, more like something from a meandering headless chicken—moreover, blood that investigators couldn't match to yours or Marilyn's. And yet the police were so sure it was you who did it they neither questioned Eberling further nor typed his blood. Interesting. Just as interesting, unidentified red fibers were found under Marilyn's nails that matched nothing you were wearing. Just as it's interesting who Hoversten should go off to play golf with the day before the murder, Dr. Robert Stevenson, to my mind the only man who'd really *want* to destroy you, since you'd been fucking his fiancée, Susan Hayes, for years—up until that March, in fact. Since *you'd* destroyed that relationship without giving it a second thought—which must've been galling to him, no? And if anybody wanted to hurt Marilyn herself and then came up with the sick idea to make it look like *you* killed her and tried to cover it up, well, you couldn't really count Lester out on something that demented, either. Or could you?"

Sheppard shook his head.

"Here's the hole in your story. Or the hole your story falls through. It comes back to the watch. Are you listening closely?"

Sheppard lit his pipe.

"You claimed that when you first came to consciousness, you saw your wallet lying under the bed, yes?"

"That's right."

"You stood, saw Marilyn, then took her pulse—which was how the blood got on your watch's crystal and wristband, correct?"

"Go on."

"You heard someone in the living room, raced downstairs, saw somebody, pursued him to the lake, struggled, and were once again overcome."

Sheppard said nothing.

"The duffel bag with your watch in it was found halfway up from the lake. Correct?"

"Yes."

"That means that Marilyn's killer left your wallet under the bed and your watch on your wrist after knocking you unconscious the first time. Then he ransacked the house, taking *nothing* of value—not your wife's gold watch or the drugs in your medical bag or the guns—and after his struggle with you on the beach, after knocking you out *again,* this same burglar then removed your ring, watch, and keys and then what? Abandoned this loot on his way *off* the property. Why not take it since he was home free? Why go back in the direction he came? Was *that* the genius of the setup? Did the person framing you anticipate this implausibility? Or did *you* simply run out of time, racing around that dark, quiet, horrifically lonely house with Marilyn dead and your boy asleep in his bed and you all alone, injured and needing to come up with a believable story? You're not much of a storyteller, are you, Doctor?"

"*Enough,*" Sheppard said.

Sometimes, when Sheppard thought back to that night, he couldn't distinguish what was real from what wasn't.

For instance, when he remembered the moment he woke to the sound of Marilyn crying his name, he wasn't sure if he went back to sleep or not. How long, he often wondered, did it take to bludgeon someone twenty-seven times? He thought he might have heard the blows themselves, or that he'd heard two voices, Marilyn's and another person's, though sometimes there were more than that. Or had he heard their grunts, Marilyn's and her attacker's—sounds like lovemaking and that of blunt-force trauma, of an object hitting bone, something heavy enough to dent a body but not shatter it? He couldn't be sure.

He remembered running up the steps and pulling at the banister, and the breeze off the lake, and then, as his momentum carried him forward, seeing the form in their room that became the bushy-haired man he fought later. But in reverie-memories he came through the door and felt the blow—it was like being struck by a wave—before seeing anything. So which was true?

As a doctor, he knew the disorienting effects of the neurological trauma he'd suffered, that it wasn't surprising for his memories to be so jumbled, but in the end this diagnosis wasn't much of a comfort.

Or he remembered looking at Marilyn's punched-in face and shattered mouth and then heard someone downstairs and racing out of the room; at other times it seemed he'd stumbled into Chip's room to check on him and *then* heard someone downstairs. And he would wonder if he'd dreamed about checking on Chip out of guilt because it wouldn't have been the first time he hadn't given the boy a thought.

Yet the memory could unfold in perfect sequence: the dream, Marilyn screaming, the race upstairs, the blow, the coming to consciousness, the sound of the intruder downstairs, the sight of the intruder by the patio, the race down the steps to the beach, the struggle, and then waking up at dawn and seeing his home in the morning light, and knowing that Marilyn lay dead in the bedroom. Or there might only be his dream of cradling his daughter in his hands as Marilyn watched from the water, so quietly, so lovingly, and this made him think about dreams he'd had as a boy—in his most vivid, a giant owl caged in his room burst free when he entered and he had to jam his hands into the sides of its beak to protect himself—and how the dreams were unmoored from time, were a kind of time in and of themselves. Though over the years, the events came to seem unmoored from time too.

The outline of the intruder once he came downstairs by the patio door: he was large, Sheppard's size and build, and his hair seemed to stand straight up, a bushy crew cut. He could tell the blacked-out form had turned to see his own blacked-out form, then run from the house.

Often, Sheppard dreamed what he thought were memories of that night—for instance, racing toward the beach after the intruder, but in the dream he was practically flying, taking four or five steps at a leap like an astronaut on the moon, catching tremendous air with every stride, hitting the figure as hard as a falcon its prey. In one dream he managed to pin the intruder down, gripping the man's neck in his hands, but this clearly hadn't happened because the face and the neck he was strangling were his own. "Do I look like that?" he thought. He couldn't kill *himself,* of course, but he remembered thinking, mid-dream, "My God, this is a dream, and I'm wrestling myself because I killed Marilyn." In any case, his double used the moment of surprise to wrestle him off, throw him back into the water, and once again raise his fist to ready a punch. Then everything went black.

He wondered occasionally if he'd killed his wife in some kind of psychotic episode and blocked it out, though no evidence supported this. In a room as flecked with blood as a Pollock painting, he had some only on his knee and on his watch, on the crystal itself, fogged with water after he lay half-submerged in the lake. True, sleepwalkers were capable of remarkably precise and coordinated actions; his father once told him that his mother had watched as he sleepwalked to the refrigerator, took out a ham, and cut the meat into fine slices. Also true, we occasionally respond physically to mere dreams; once, while he was supposedly locked in battle with his father, Marilyn heard him groan, tried to wake him up, and took an elbow to the nose for her trouble. But he'd searched his soul and could find no blood rage, even in his darkest moments, toward his wife.

Still, there was one thing he remembered with utter certainty.

It was after he woke up on the beach, half-naked and waterlogged, his shirt missing, his pockets filled with sand. He raised himself to look at his house, at their bedroom window, realizing that Marilyn was gone, and what he recalled was his first thought: there had been a time, wretched and seemingly interminable, when he'd wanted this very thing.

As Hoversten drove toward Kent, he couldn't help reviewing his exchange with Marilyn in his mind—except in this version, after Marilyn said, "You're a failure," he didn't repeat all the shit she already knew, since that kept things on a woman's "strictly emotional" level, but instead nodded twice in consideration, pretended for a moment to take it all in, and then, in response, took his putter in both his hands and cracked the goddamn cunt's head wide open with it.

"Or better," he yelled from his open convertible, "I knock out some of your fucking teeth." That would be the ticket: a hard thrust with the sole of the club right above the lip. He imagined her stunned by the blow—there were probably as many nerve endings around your mouth as on a man's dick—before falling back. "And *then* what would be nice," he screamed, looking at himself in the rearview mirror, "what would be delectable, would be to step around your head, put the clubface to your ear, take a nice backswing, and tee the fuck off." The bitch's feet and hands would be twitching, her cheeks and nose rendered as soft as sirloin. Once he'd shattered through her brain plate and bone started knifing through the gray matter, her whole nervous system would run riot in neurological disaster. Maybe he'd pause for a moment to let her speak, though it would sound more like gargling, her words as round as a mute's: *Fease fop, Fester, fease.* How about a cock in the mouth now? That would be like getting a blow job from a woman who'd pulled out her dentures. So how about it, Marilyn? A nice, soft mouth fuck?

When he pulled around a semi, he had to cover his crotch with his hand.

The bad mood stayed with him the whole forty miles to Kent, Hoversten completely unaware of how fast he was driving. He made excellent time, though, and got to Robert's club an hour before their tee time. That too was excellent, because he never warmed up enough and Robert always took his goddamn money. He grabbed a bucket of balls and took some heavy divots on the range, long scalps of flying turf. He hadn't played in a while and his short game was always the first thing to go, so he worked on his pitching for longer than usual. When you hit a pitch, Gary Player says, pretend you're striking a *metch.* Oh, he was feeling it today! It was breezy, but he worked himself up into a good lather. He was actually drawing the ball with some control, especially when he pretended it was Marilyn's temple.

"Some cheater's been practicing," Robert said.

Hoversten hadn't seen Dr. Stevenson come up behind him, but he'd been watching him hit, his arms crossed, a true student of the swing. They said their hellos, and Hoversten could tell, even through the long, dark tunnel of his own mood, that Robert was in a bad place himself. We'll have ourselves a game today, he thought.

On the walk to the first tee, caddies in tow, they agreed to a five-dollar Nassau, rich for a man out of work, Hoversten thought, but he'd been killing the ball on the range, especially his driver—a nice pro flight whose low, boring trajectory climbed and climbed. They flipped, Hoversten called heads, won the honor, and striped his tee shot, stepping out of the box without even watching it land.

"That'll hunt," Stevenson said.

"That's a real nice ball," said his caddy.

Stevenson put his tee in the ground and looked down the fairway. He took a half swing, then addressed his ball. "That will *hunt,*" he repeated.

Hoversten couldn't help watching him set up. It was like a study in perfect form. Stevenson was a tall, handsome man, hyperfit, long-boned, and muscular, and his stance had an athletic geometry, with the inverted triangle of his upper body resting atop the triangle of his spread legs, the triangle formed by his arms hanging relaxed between his shoulders and ending in the triangle of his large hands. It was an Apollonian image, what with his high head of curly hair, and the ball was like one of his arrows—fired down the fairway a good twenty yards past Hoversten's.

"That's a dandy too," said Stevenson's caddie, already getting a head start on the three of them.

Hoversten and Stevenson said next to nothing to each other until the fourth hole, though again Hoversten couldn't help noticing how down the man was. Oh yes, Hoversten thought, Stevenson was in a very bad place, but unfortunately it was helping his game—he'd opened birdie, birdie, par—and there were important matters to attend to, like not losing all the cash in his wallet and where to sleep tonight.

"Someone else has been practicing too," Hoversten said, then spit.

"I can't complain," Stevenson said.

"I need a favor. Do you think I could stay over this evening?"

"I thought you were working with Sheppard this week."

"I am. But I can't be in the same room as his wife."

Stevenson looked at him for a moment, then stepped between the markers and took his beautiful setup. But he backed off, clearing his throat. Number four was a 175-yard par three with water fifty yards short left, a small lake that fronted the green on that side, never in play for Stevenson, who always hit a power fade. Yet for some inexplicable reason he proceeded to pull his shot right into the hazard.

"Well," he snapped, "I can't be in the same goddamn room as *him.*"

He reteed and blocked his next shot so far right he'd nearly have a sixty-foot putt for his fourth, then gave his five-iron such a powerful hammer-throw that it almost reached the lake.

Hoversten stepped up. The flag was tucked left, and on a normal day he'd settle for the middle of the green, away from trouble. Instead, he hit a fade over the water, the ball landing gently ten feet from the pin.

They walked toward the green, putters under their arms, caddies clanging ahead.

"And why is that?" Hoversten asked.

"Why is *what*?"

"Why can't you be in the same room with him?"

"Sheppard? Oh, come on, Les. Don't play dumb."

Hoversten shrugged.

"You're telling me you don't know?" Stevenson said.

"I have no idea what you're talking about."

"*Susan.*"

"Your Susan?"

Stevenson turned to the caddies. "Gentlemen, please meet us up at the next tee."

They nodded with the impassivity borne of watching a million bad shots, then started walking.

Stevenson waited until they were out of earshot.

"As it turns out, she never *was* my Susan," he said. "She was *his* Susan."

Oh, Hoversten thought. "Oh," he said, shaking his head. Oh, Sam. You goddamn *dog*. For a moment he quantified the long line of women Sheppard had bedded, and they were all of them—but Susan Hayes in particular—a breed apart. "For how long?"

"Long before we'd gotten together and the whole time after."

"Even after you were engaged?"

Stevenson nodded.

Hoversten whistled, his only hope to keep from laughing. "Son of a *bitch*," he said.

"You've got that right."

There was nothing else to do upon hearing such news but concentrate on one's putt. Hoversten had a downhill slider for birdie, but Stevenson, after a terrible lag, had a fifteen-footer for a double. Feeling dandy now, he got aggressive and might well have raced his putt off the green, but luckily the ball hit the back of the cup, hopped once in the air, and came to rest less than a foot behind the hole. The momentum is shifting, he thought.

After two-putting, Stevenson walked up to Hoversten and tapped out a pitch mark. It was a lovely, windy day, the gusts quieting the course and making it seem even more private, drowning out all the surrounding noises.

"That's why you broke things off with her."

Stevenson spit in disgust.

"Honestly, Robert, I didn't know. I just thought you weren't ready."

They stared at the caddies up on the next tee box.

"Can I tell you something?" Stevenson said.

Hoversten waited.

"It's not something I'm proud of. But ever since Susan and I broke it off, ever since she told me everything, I swear to God that not a day's gone by, not a single fucking *day*, when I haven't—"

"Don't say it."

When Stevenson looked up, his eyes were bloodshot.

Hoversten couldn't help it. All alone on a golf course and he still looked around to see if anyone was listening, as if what he'd thought had somehow been spoken aloud. It was a desire he had with this beautiful man standing before him—one he felt otherwise only with Sheppard—to please him, to *care* for him somehow. To take him in his arms and kiss his mouth.

"You know," Mobius said, "I can list all your mistresses. From the time you were fourteen, when you started dating Marilyn, right until her death."

"Don't you think that's a little perverse?"

"There was Frances Stevens, first. The summer after you gave Marilyn your fraternity pin, after your senior year of high school, after she'd gone off that fall to Skidmore, here comes chesty Frances darkening the door of your parents' garage where you liked to fool with your Model A. You two have a date, and next thing you know you've offered *her* your fraternity pin, you Indian giver, since you took it back as soon as your father scolded you for your behavior, but of course that was only the beginning of a long history of not telling Marilyn about other commitments. There was Melanie, the wife of that med student you were in school with out in LA. You started up with her right after Chip was born, didn't you? After Marilyn went through that bad postpartum, sliding into that deep pit of depression. She wouldn't even touch you, would she? And you were a man of regular needs. You *liked* your once-a-day tumble. Then there was that little foursome with Lester and those two nurses. And right after that, Margot Wendice, a nursing instructor who that fat pimp introduced you to. You two dated for a year while Marilyn was back in Cleveland with Chip, still recovering. And Julee Lossman, just a couple months before Marilyn died—"

"Nothing happened with her."

"No, your honor, we were just friends, the Lossmans and us. We went boating on Lake Erie one day and decided to stop at that small island near Put-in-Bay, and Julee and I decided to disappear into the woods for a while—over an hour, actually—and yes, we'd slept together several years before. Sure, her husband slapped her face after our little jaunt. But nothing happened while we were gone, your honor, I promise."

Sheppard shrugged.

"And, of course, the lovely Susan Hayes. How long were you two together?"

"We were on and off for three years."

"Right up until March 1954. We do need to talk about her, don't we?"

"Why's that?"

"She was, after all, your motive for killing Marilyn."

Sheppard and Susan Hayes were driving back to Los Angeles from San Diego. They'd attended an acquaintance's wedding, though Sheppard couldn't recall the groom's name. It was nighttime and nearly freezing outside. The convertible Sheppard had borrowed from Dr. Miller—an MG—had a broken heater, and the wiper on the driver's side was shot, so he'd taken the top down for visibility in fog that had rolled in as they drove up Highway 1.

"Can you see?" Susan said.

"Sometimes," he answered over the motor's snorkeling, which limited their conversation and was fine by Sheppard, who had nothing to say. As for whatever Susan said, he didn't want to hear it, though she wouldn't stop.

"You could *switch* it." And when Sheppard indicated his ear, she added, "The *wiper blade.*"

He turned to face her. She was sitting with her arms crossed and her back against the passenger door, mildly furious and half-amazed. Her thin features were paled by the dim dashboard light, sharpened and predatory, revealed in the dark as the old hawk-lady she'd become decades hence. That they were building toward a fight only married people had, like he and Marilyn, was off-putting. Yet it suddenly dawned on him that next to Marilyn, he'd never been involved with another woman for a longer time.

"Then you could put the *top* up," she said.

Where was the woman Susan had been three years ago?

Regardless, it wasn't a bad idea. He was cold himself, though not unpleasantly so, and several minutes later he stopped at an overlook, a gravel promontory bulging over the Pacific. He left the headlights on to see, then checked the blade. It was fastened by two Phillips head screws, so he searched the trunk for tools (only a tire iron) and then stood problem solving by the closed trunk, watching the fog's underbelly slide across the headlights and arriving, after a moment, at other means. He came around and leaned inside, and Susan's look of disgust nearly resembled fear. Reaching behind the wheel, he turned off the ignition and pulled the keys. The car shook to silence with a tremor down the chassis, and all they could hear now was the punt and sigh of the ocean, a ceaseless concussing that, blow after blow, would erode millimeters of coastline until one day this road itself, he thought, would dissolve and slip into the sea.

"What are you doing?" she said. When he didn't answer, she simply faced forward.

He held the key to the light. The flat edge was sharp enough to grip the screw's slot, though the metal seemed too thick—but it did fit, just barely. He removed the first two screws with little difficulty and placed the warped blade on the hood, refusing even to glance at Susan lest she feel any more haughty about her solution. The second blade looked good though its screw was welded with grit, so he used the key and tried prying it loose, but it slipped and dug into his thumb, hacking the skin back, the pain zinging down his arm. Sheppard dropped the ring and, when he heard the passenger door open, roared, "Just stay in the goddamn car!"

She did, at least for a while. He staunched the blood with his fist and then dressed the wound with his handkerchief, clenching the cloth with his teeth and tearing off two thin strips with his good hand. He'd come around the car and leaned against the hood, cliffside, to collect himself, and she joined him from the opposite direction, taking his throbbing thumb in her hands. She tied the bandage together over the knuckle, patted it, and said, "That was a bad idea." They turned to face the ocean, the night moonless, the sky star-splashed through strands of fog, the crash of waves rumbling up the rock into the soles of Sheppard's feet, the sound tracing both the height of this cliff and the vastness beyond. This, in the darkness, set him even more adrift and conferred the vaguest sense of threat—that he was somehow at risk of not surviving this night.

"It's not so cold when we're not moving," Susan said, rubbing her arms with her hands.

He wondered again, Where had she gone? Where had she hidden her? The other Susan, the old Susan, was simpler, braver, and this one had made off with her. She was here just days ago, when Sheppard had arrived in Los Angeles with Marilyn. He and Susan had been corresponding since February, when she left Cleveland to move out here, after she and Dr. Stevenson had officially broken off their engagement. Sheppard had arranged this trip for intensive training and board certification in vascular and neurosurgery—a milestone, to be sure—under Chappie. But in truth it was to see Susan. "While I'm in Los Angeles," he told Marilyn, "you could head up to Big Sur with Jo. You'd like that, wouldn't you?" They were in his bed together and Marilyn stared for a time at the ceiling. "Los Angeles," she finally said. "Doesn't that feel like a lifetime ago?" It had been only four years, but he said, "Yes." The trick, of course, was to make it tempting and unappealing at the same time, to imply that he wanted her there in spite of the many restrictions: a vacation together she'd have to enjoy alone. "We could leave Chip with Richard," he said. "I'll be in surgery round the clock, but you'd be free to roam." She put her arms around his waist while he sat up against his headboard. Usually she started the night in his bed, then went back to hers after he slipped off. Suddenly, she hugged him, hard, and he stared at the top of her head, imagined her scalp was a screen and he could see her brain and know what she was thinking. He kissed her, smelled her hair—a scent so familiar and unique he might as well have tried to describe the odor of blood.

She lifted her head from his shoulder and kissed him on the cheek. "We could bring our racquets and play at the club again."

"We could," he said. "Maybe I could get away one afternoon."

"We never play tennis anymore," she said. "Why is that?"

"We're busy."

"We were busy then."

"We will," he said, smiling, scheming, remembering playing together back when he was a resident at Los Angeles Osteopathic, those gray clay courts at the Hollywood Tennis Club, the pleasure before they'd hit of sweeping them, smoothing away the previous match and dusting the lines to brightness, of watching Marilyn, who had real talent, whose racquet on contact made a sound he simply couldn't generate, a ringing impact that was more report, the angle and pace she used to attack his forehand and backhand acts of supreme control that made his own strokes easier to hit, the whole rally an act of generosity that made him feel like *he* was dictating . . .

But that was long ago. Now—even as he remembered those days—his thoughts turned toward Susan, interpenetrating everything, Susan written over these scenes in invisible ink. Marilyn could come along for all he cared. He'd still manage to see Susan.

Every day of that shortest month became a countdown to March. Once things were set up with Chappie, those two weeks he'd x-ed out on his calendar became a lodestar drawing him on, beckoning him even now as he sat with his wife in bed remembering their early years together, some of the very best times, before he and Susan Hayes had ever met.

It was an event he recalled vividly. It was in Bay View's pathology lab, his brother Richard giving Susan the tour of the hospital, where they'd hired her as a lab technician, their third addition to the staff in a month. He'd just come out of a routine appendectomy, and yet he felt anointed by the procedure's efficiency, with the sense of order restored, the same tidiness and rectitude he felt when he changed his car's oil and slammed the hood shut. He was naked under his scrubs—how he liked to work—and this contributed a kind of bedtime calm and comfort, a distinct libidinal alertness as he strolled the halls pendulant and free. He always felt most manly after scrubbing out.

Sheppard walked into pathology—Susan's back was to him—and when she turned, Richard introduced her. Afterward, he reassembled her features in his mind: the strong, slender hand; the curly auburn hair; the golden brown complexion; the freckling across her cheeks and nose, so distinct it seemed tribal. He had to do all this after their introduction because the initial sight of her had somehow obliterated it.

"I hope you like being busy," he'd told her.

"I do, Dr. Sheppard."

"We start bright and early."

"The bus from Rocky River's always on time."

"No car?" Richard said.

"I thought I got one when I was hired," she joked.

They all laughed. Even Richard was smitten.

"Rocky River?" Sheppard said. "Where?"

"Fifty-nine oh three."

"I'm only a block down."

"We could take the bus together," she said.

"I was thinking I'd drive."

"Careful, Sam," said Richard. "This is a nice girl. She still lives with her parents."

"If Dr. Sheppard wants to drive the bus," she said, "that's fine by me."

She talked like a movie starlet, Sheppard thought in his office later. And she was as pretty as one. She, of course, could be forgiven for the former. He put his feet up on his desk, his hands behind his head, and stared at the ceiling. Usually, he took a quick nap between his morning surgeries and lunch, but now he was wide awake. Before, with other women, he might simply be thankful that life had once again become interesting, but this was different.

You'll see her tomorrow, he told himself.

She was waiting for him in his red MG the very next morning.

Sheppard came into the garage and there she was, sitting in the passenger seat as if she'd been there all night, so confident she didn't even look up.

It stopped him, cold and amazed, for a second, her presence genie-granted even before he'd made the wish. He'd decided on his blue pinstripe suit this morning, and for some reason he stopped and touched his tie, looking down at his chest and smiling to himself; then, collected, he walked over and opened the driver's door. She looked at him, again with a directness that silenced any questions and nullified small talk, a gaze that he found wonderful and unsettling to return. He started the car, backed out of the garage, and drove to the hospital uncharacteristically slowly, though not once during the whole ride did they speak. The car was dying to climb out of third, and when he downshifted before a stop he could feel each of the gear box's grooves. Once the light changed he accelerated gingerly, as if he were driving on ice. In the parking lot, she said, "Thank you, Dr. Sheppard," and then waited; instinctively, he hurried around to open the door for her—something he never did for Marilyn.

He held the hospital door open for her as well, and she walked to the lab without saying as much as good-bye.

If he saw Susan today, whether in the halls or the cafeteria, he knew they wouldn't speak. He was as certain of this as he was that she'd be waiting in his car the next morning.

She was, her hands crossed over her lap. He didn't hesitate this time and again they didn't speak; speak and something might change. It was mid-May, spectacular spring weather, the dogwoods sneezing, cherry trees flowering like cotton candy, the redbuds like newly popped corn, various colors humming like Susan there next to him, Sheppard afraid to look straight at her lest the same magic that had placed her beside him make her disappear. At work it was more of the same. When they had to talk, it was strictly professional and in her realm of basic pathology. He gave specific directives. Coworkers, seeing them interact, might think they despised each other. Often, she didn't even look at him. Gone was the starlet's repartee. He knew they had the same agreement, which was highly unsettling and odd but strangely kept him focused. Knowing she'd be waiting in his car tomorrow let him blot out all distractions. To alter anything—to proceed otherwise—would've been apostasy.

"Who *is* that?" Marilyn said to him the next morning. She'd just come in from the garage, still in her nightgown. Chip, now four years old, was fast asleep.

He took a last sip of coffee. "Susan Hayes. She's a new lab technician."

"What's she doing?"

"What do you mean?"

"She's sitting in your car."

"I'm giving her a ride to work."

"Why?"

"She doesn't have one."

"A ride or a car?"

"Either."

Marilyn crossed her arms. "Is she getting one?"

"I have no idea."

Marilyn shook her head in amazement. "Should we expect her tomorrow then?"

"Why don't you ask her?"

Marilyn waited. There was only one thing to say in response, but for years now she'd been unwilling to.

"I have to go," he said.

He got into his car. Again, Susan didn't acknowledge him. No smile, no hello, not even a nod. Yet Sheppard found himself nodding at her impassively, as you do to someone taking the next seat on a bus or standing by an elevator. He turned his head, placing his hand behind Susan's seat, and backed out of the garage.

"Was that your wife?" Susan said.

Startled, he had to stop at the end of the driveway to answer. "Yes."

"She's pretty."

He said nothing. To answer would be to compare them, and in the strictest sense that wasn't possible. When Susan didn't continue, he drove on.

"She asked why I was in your car," she said a few minutes later. "I told her you were giving me a lift to the hospital."

Once again, Sheppard was driving so slowly that occasionally cars swerved around him.

"She told me you'd be late and that I should go on."

When he turned left or right, his hands came together at the top of the wheel and then slid back, once he'd finished the manuever, to ten o'clock and two.

"I knew you weren't going to be late." She angled the side mirror toward her face and regarded herself. Satisfied, she readjusted it and sat forward. "So I said thanks and stayed right where I was."

She was in control, Sheppard thought. Like Marilyn when they played tennis, Susan was dictating, and if he'd learned anything from that experience it was to realize that any effort on his part to wrest power from her would ruin everything. For two whole weeks she showed up in the garage. It was what he looked most forward to, opening the door and seeing her there, as much a part of the car as the wheels, as surprising as seeing a cat uncurl itself from the front seat and scamper across the grass. He would open the door and look at her. She had a long, lovely neck; arched, haughty eyebrows; a small mouth to which she applied no lipstick, the upper lip on the verge, it always seemed, of a snarl. He walked toward her slowly so he could take in as much of her as possible before he entered that zone of silence, of blindness. Her hair, auburn and curly, was still damp at the neck from her shower; her upper lip freckled near the twin peaks by the philtrum. He took his seat, put the keys in the ignition, started the car, released the brake, pulled the stick to neutral, moved the gear shift from side to side once before dropping it into reverse, this last action allowing him to regard her hands. She had long fingers, thickly veined, the metacarpals as distinctly visible as the delicate fingers that stretched taut the wings of a bat.

"I can't drive you home this evening," he said, cutting the ignition. They were in the hospital parking lot. "I'm on call."

"That's lucky," she said. "I am too."

It was a Wednesday. Twice a month, Sheppard did a twenty-four-hour rotation with a seven-to-seven shift. The weekends tended to be busy, a euphemism for bad, particularly now that spring was in full force, early June now, more boaters out on the lake, more accidents, mostly boys doing stupid things. They'd lost a sixteen-year-old last month who'd slipped off the back of an outboard. Unaware of this, his older brother gunned the motor and shredded his hands, arms, and right leg, severing six fingers as well as the superior mesenteric and internal iliac arteries, the blade dicing the cephalic and basilic veins. He'd lost nearly nine pints of blood by the time they got him on the table; and standing over this mess, the boy's skin milk white from shock, Sheppard froze. The right side looked like it had been mauled by a mythical creature, the blooming gashes revealing veins, tendons, and muscles so grossly mashed that he concluded both limbs would have to be amputated in order to give the kid any chance of survival. But he died within minutes. Afterward, his brother's face was contorted with calamity and his parents agape, absorbing the news with something near awe, their grief so palpable and strong and localized, their arms over each other in a scrum of protection and anguish, it was like the force field between opposing magnets, thin and utterly impenetrable. And it was with such sudden accidents, when death didn't just appear out of nowhere so much as erupt, that Sheppard allowed himself to give thanks for his own safety, for a life free of suffering. For his own brilliant luck.

This night, however, had been so very quiet that Sheppard actually longed for disaster. He was bored. He did rounds he easily could have left to the nurses. He took a detour by pathology, walked as inconspicuously as he could past the door, and through the frosted glass he made out Susan's gray form—like an outline shaded with the flat side of a pencil—just inside the room. He could hear her heels striking the floor, and when they turned toward the door, he hurried off down the hall, went back to his office, and took a nap.

Later, close to five, a man in his midthirties was brought in by the police. He was well dressed, wearing a suit. But he was also disheveled: shirt untucked, tie loose, coat wrinkled, pants muddy at the cuffs, the shoes splattered and flecked with grass. There was a day's worth of stubble on his face and his eyes were glassy, the rims red, but Sheppard smelled no alcohol. "We found him walking down Lake Road," the cop said. "He can't speak coherently." When Sheppard asked the man his name, he looked up, baffled, as if he'd heard only a distant echo. "Put it in *there*," he said. "Please." He held up both palms, then coughed violently, hunching over. A gob of green sputum hit the floor between his feet. Sheppard had the nurse bring him a container and scooped it up with a tongue depressor, then laid the patient on the bed. Happily, the man closed his eyes. Sheppard listened to his lungs, which sounded like a water whistle. The spleen was enlarged, the abdomen hot. When Sheppard touched it, the man winced alert. "How many times do I have to *say* it?" he said, looking around as if he'd just landed on Mars. His blood pressure was low and falling. Sheppard thought for a moment, then ordered IV fluids and drew blood, a procedure the patient regarded bemusedly before dozing off again.

"Have Miss Hayes do a CBC, please, and a urinalysis," he told the nurse. "Tell her to bring me the results as soon as she gets them." Then he went to speak with the police. The man had no wallet, no ID at all, though he was wearing a wedding band. Neither of the officers recognized him.

"Is he on drugs?" one said.

"I don't think so," Sheppard said.

"Is he sick?"

"Very."

Sheppard returned to the room and waited with the patient, whose blood pressure continued to fall. He checked his watch; it had been almost twenty minutes. When Susan entered, he managed to remain calm.

"Is this him?" she said.

"Yes."

She looked at the patient for a second, then handed Sheppard her chart. For a moment, each had a hand on the clipboard.

"His white count's markedly elevated," she said.

"How much?"

"Twenty-two thousand."

"What's his hematocrit?"

"Thirty-five," she said.

The figures were right there on the page, but he wanted to ask. "What about the peripheral smear?"

"I noted vacuoles in some of the white cells."

Sheppard took in her scent.

"He's clearly septic," she said.

"Do you have results on the sputum?"

"He's gram positive."

"Single population?"

"Yes."

"What do they look like?"

"Lancet-shaped."

"Go on."

"I'd say diplococci. But you can review the slide if you'd like."

He let go of the clipboard. She put her hand on her hip and pressed the page to her breast, looking at him as if he were about to correct her.

"Very good," he said.

She smiled.

"Anything else?" he asked.

"I noticed inclusion in the red cells."

Sheppard smiled too. It was the longest conversation they'd ever had. He took a step closer and they stood together at the foot of the patient's bed. He laid there, a young man in a suit, a John Doe, blood pressure falling to fatal levels. His breathing was labored, whistling slightly.

"What would your diagnosis be?" Sheppard asked.

"I'm not a doctor."

"But if you were."

Her faced flushed. He wanted to take it in his hands and kiss her.

"I'd say pneumococcal pneumonia. That would account for the low oxygen levels in his blood. And the disorientation."

"Anything else?"

"Peritonitis. Also septicemia."

"How would you treat it?"

"IV penicillin, immediately. And fluids, of course."

Sheppard took the clipboard off the man's bed and made a note. "Then that, Miss Hayes, is what we'll do."

She waited for a moment, looking at the man and then back at Sheppard.

"That'll be all," he said, and watched her leave.

His brother Stephen arrived early, around a quarter till six. By then Sheppard's patient had stabilized. He brought Stephen up to speed and went back to his office; exhausted, he took off his doctor's coat and put on his suit jacket, then decided to peek his head in pathology before leaving.

But Susan was gone. Tricia was already mulling over some slides in her place.

"Good morning," he said.

"Good morning, Doctor."

He tapped the door once, looking around the lab, and left.

She was waiting for him in his car.

It was surprisingly humid outside, overcast, and it made the whole world bluer, all sound seemingly muffled by the promise of rain, with occasional birdcalls and the peculiar, particular brand of quiet you noticed only at odd hours or during dreams. Sheppard got in and started the car. "Are you hungry?" he asked, though he couldn't look at her. "Yes," she said, sounding as anxious as he felt. It was as if they were running from something. The need for food gave him license, and he pulled out; instead of heading toward Rocky River he went west through Bay Village toward Avon, though in truth he had no idea where he was going. It made him nearly desperate, this wandering. They had to *get* somewhere. It was as if he were in an unknown city, in a dreadful neighborhood, low on gas and lost. Before the township, he saw a brown sign with THORNTON PARK in gold letters above icons for a picnic table, a camper, a boat. He made such a hard right the MG fishtailed slightly, spraying the bushes with gravel. As he weaved down the narrow, winding two-lane road, Susan pressed her hand lightly on the dash. They came around one more curve and there it was: Erie in all its vastness, gray water against gray sky. A landing. A slack tide. Not a boat to be seen. The water looked forbidding, poisoned in its stillness. The wooded parking area with picnic tables was empty. Sheppard pulled in, cut the ignition. There was no sound except the quietest lapping, just beyond the bushes blocking a view of the beach, of the small waves. He faced forward for a long time and saw nothing.

She touched his leg.

He was upon her. If he could, he would feast on her mouth; he couldn't press his to hers any harder. He tore his arm from his coat and took the back of her head in his available hand lest she try even for a moment to break away, then slipped his other arm out of the sleeve. She pressed his shoulders back. His lips were trembling and his teeth began to chatter. She was as still and calm as the lake. "The seats," she said. He reached beneath her, between her legs, pulled at the latch and pushed her seat, hard, as far from the dash as it would go. He reached across her waist, his cheek pressed against her blouse, and lifted the latch by her door so that the bucket seat fell to near horizontal—then he was on her again. And just the feeling of her legs in each of his hands as he kissed her—the slightly moist crook of her knees and the soft, leather-warmed underside of her thighs—might be enough to satisfy him, or the pain of her heels hooked into his calves as she lay beneath him, or simply the sight of her as she crawled up the seat on her elbows so he could slide her panties off the leg he pressed bent to her chest and then down over the knee of the other to dangle at the ankle. Or how she slowed him down, unbuckling his trousers, lifting him up at the hips so she should could push his pants to the floorboard with the sharp toe of her shoe, stretching the boxers away from his cock, so it arched taut and free in the warm morning air. He raised himself up toward her chest, Susan taking hold of him—"Lie back," she said—and never letting go while he slid beneath her, guiding him in while she eased herself down slowly, gently, the containment and spatial restrictions of the car itself, that it wouldn't give either of them full freedom of movement, augmenting the bliss. "God-*damn* it," she said, pressing the heel of her hand to the headrest for balance and gripping the door handle with the other, both of them finally finding the right purchase, Sheppard shifting until he was nearly diagonal, his leg thrown over the stick and his foot smashed against the brake. "Are you ready?" she whispered. He closed his eyes. She moved so fast he was afraid to look, this physical incantation as she thrummed a brand of magic above him, something that might transform him into a pillar of salt if he dared open his eyes, a spell whose effect was to suck away something feathery that he hadn't realized was lining his whole body. When she stopped, he lay there blind. His stomach, for a time, contracted uncontrollably and his extremities tingled so violently he had to tense up to keep from convulsing. And then he felt it: the warm wash spreading over his lap, an issuance that made him instantly erect and almost immediately ejaculate again. He lay still, groaning, and opened his eyes to see her watching him. Her hair was pasted against her forehead, her neck and chest shining. Her large nipples had burst from her white brassiere. She laughed now, wickedly, leaning forward and gathering his collar into her fists while he regrew inside her yet again.

"Did you *feel* that?" she said.

He blinked away his sweat.

"Who are you?" he wanted to ask.

. . .

Where was *that* Susan? he wondered now, staring at nothing over the cliff. And did she wonder herself? For it was a car just like this, Sheppard thought.

Once again and in spite of everything, he came around to the passenger side and opened the door for her, though this time she didn't thank him. He took his seat and started the engine, his thumb throbbing, then pulled out onto the road. He shouldn't be surprised that things between them had changed; like health, no state of being endured. Yet they'd reached what seemed to Sheppard a perfect arrangement: they were the exact answer to each other's needs. Marilyn had cut him off, after all, or at least urged him to leave her alone. He was free, she said, just so long as she didn't know. And so through all of that spring and into the summer of 1951, he and Susan had fucked in that car until they arrived at something they both believed approximated lovemaking, that felt necessary. But it was different, he realized: utterly new, something *more.* Even through the fall they maintained a pure pragmatism to their relationship, an unspoken agreement to make plans at some point in their shift to meet (between visits to patients, say, or in stops at the lab), after which it was a longing for the day to end. She'd be waiting in his car, he'd drive, and then they'd find deserted parking lots at stores closed for the night, alleyways whose blind walls rose from lanes pocked and puddled, the locked-down loading docks bumpered with black rubber, the fences topped with barbed wire, places where buildings hid air conditioners, dumpsters, and downspouts from sight, service entrances marked RING BELL OR DELIVERIES ONLY. And during very late nights, either on call or after emergency surgeries, they parked in the backs of grocery stores buttressed by towering stacks of emptied wooden crates that put him in mind of lobster traps, or in the scores of parks along Erie's shore, paved roads dissolved to gravel and sand, Sheppard cutting the lights after screeching to a halt.

"Can't we ever make love in a real bed?" Susan asked finally.

Sheppard found the request disappointing. After months he'd still never seen her completely naked and secretly didn't want to. Half-exposed, she was more beautiful; like the armless Venus de Milo or the headless Winged Victory of Samothrace, it was what was missing that conferred on her a kind of perfection. It was how she looked when she did what she *did,* and Sheppard would look up from the floor while talking with another doctor—hearing the sound of her heels in the hallway—to see her ankles, her thin calves, her skirt brushing her knees. He'd call her into his office, order her to come around his desk. He'd run a hand up her thigh, beneath her skirt and between her legs. She'd let him squeeze her hard, the heat rising off her, her eyes starting to close like a doll tipped to sleep. But then she resisted.

"Can't we?" she said.

He was becoming reckless.

At the hospital's Halloween party, Sheppard decided to go dressed as a woman. He even shaved his legs, Marilyn laughing at the sight of them, at his black, discarded clippings webbing the drain. "How do you women do this every day?" he said. She did his makeup, giving him lashes long as a movie goddess, lips as red as his MG, cheeks rouged up like a drunk's. He donned a bouffant wig and wore the most alluring dress Marilyn could find in his size. Standing with him in front of the mirror—Marilyn, as Alice in Wonderland, carried a cup labeled DRINK ME—she said, "Thank God Chip's a boy." When he asked why, she declared, "Because you'd make an ugly girl." Sheppard drank two martinis to nerve himself and ordered Marilyn to drive, though she was tight herself. They entered arm in arm—the party was in Bay View's cafeteria—and he picked Susan out immediately. Dressed as a man—like Sheppard's father, in fact—she'd pasted a mustache above her mouth, put on the same round, black-rimmed glasses, and slicked back her hair. She came up to him, reckless too, for Marilyn was standing right there. "Got a pipe, miss?" she asked. "I do," Sheppard said, pulling one from the waistband of his skirt and handing it to her. She put the tooth-dented stem in her mouth and made her black Groucho Marx eyebrows dance, then tapped his chest with the slicked end. "Now," she said, "I'm Dr. Sam!" Marilyn looked at him, baffled and appalled. He shrugged, then watched Susan shoulder her way into the crowd. "I'm Dr. Sam!" she announced, and pinched Donna Bailey's ass. He drank more. He mingled. He knew where Susan was at all times. Marilyn spoke to him; he spoke with others and pretended to listen, not hearing a thing. He spotted Susan dancing with a resident, Stevenson, and approached them. Even in baggy pants and a suit coat whose sleeves she had to roll up, he could make out the shape of her thin, boyish body.

"May I cut in?" he asked.

Stevenson was a tall man, fit and broad-shouldered, and Susan acted vaguely disappointed at Sheppard's appearance. But he didn't care. He'd waited long enough.

"He's all yours, Doctor."

She had a stethoscope around her neck now and she looked up at him, glassy-eyed. "You're a *big* missy," she said.

Sheppard was so hard he thanked God for the pantyhose.

"What're you here for?" she said. "Rectal? *Hernia* exam?"

She went to reach beneath his skirt but he restrained her, catching sight of Marilyn watching them, shocked.

"Ah," she said, "*I* know. It's your heart." She pressed the scope to his chest, slipping the cold disk onto his skin. "Hmmm," she said. "It doesn't seem to be beating." She leaned up to his ear. "I think all the blood's in your dick."

He pressed into her and they danced for three songs, and when he looked up Marilyn was gone.

Later, all the lights were off in the apartment. Sheppard had to hold the banister and press against the wall with his other palm to make it up the stairs. He took a piss and saw his harridan's face weaving in the mirror. Knocking his earrings off the edge of the sink, he stumbled out and found Marilyn in the guest room. She'd wrapped herself in so many blankets they looked like a cocoon.

"You did it," she said. "You actually did it."

"Did what?"

"You're fucking that woman."

He laughed: just the thought of it. "I wouldn't say *I'm* fucking her."

"You decided to take me up on my offer."

"The one to stop fucking you? Or the one to fuck?"

"And I really thought you wouldn't," she said.

"Well, what's a girl to do?" he said, then swayed off to their room.

When he woke in the morning, she was staring at him from her bed. His hangover was like a pall.

"I don't care," she said. "I just don't want to see it."

Sheppard looked at himself. Still dressed as a woman, he had to get himself under control.

"Promise me," she said.

But he wasn't up to it.

Late that fall, he and Marilyn bought a home on Lake Road that had three bedrooms upstairs, a boat landing, and a screened-in porch with a spectacular view. Massive saucer-shaped clouds gathered low over the lake, layered in varying depths of gray, all pregnant with snow. Every body of water, Sheppard thought, was a mystery, as unique each day in appearance as a letter of the Mayan alphabet. Their move had made Marilyn happy. She'd been in a flurry of homemaking; his only responsibilities, she told him, were the boathouse and his study. Something had eased in her; she'd become more compliant. One night, as they talked in their separate beds, he could discern the black outline of her form as she told him she wanted to try. And so, in the afternoons, after warning her, "I'm coming home for lunch," he'd eye the sandwich and glass of milk she'd laid out in the kitchen and hurry upstairs to their bedroom. Marilyn had ordered him to buy two twins, so he wouldn't disturb her on nights when he was called into the hospital, and she lay waiting now in hers, her body still bath-warmed, clean and odorless, her white robe peeled open like the petals of a flower. She stared out the window while he undressed, draping his coat, pants, and shirt over the chair by her bed. When he climbed atop her, she tensed and said, "You're freezing." They kissed. Her mouth, her soft lips and their fit to his, was as familiar as the oddly metallic taste of her nipples, Sheppard so well-versed in the sequence of their lovemaking it was like walking through their living room in the dark. She kept her eyes closed, her expression, as he entered her, always of pain. Only at the very end did he feel anxious, did it seem, her face filling his sight, that she might say something disappointing. But they didn't speak in those brief moments after. She kissed his cheek and gripped his neck in her arms. "That was nice," she finally whispered. He went to the bathroom and rinsed himself off in the sink, proud of his postcoital size, then dressed, ate his sandwich, and drank his milk. Driving back to work, it was as if he'd left an alternative reality, Chip and Marilyn and their lives together something he'd dreamed.

He couldn't help but compare those afternoons to his times with Susan. Honoring her request, he fucked her now in a real bed, in the interns' apartment the hospital had rented, four modestly furnished rooms. Privacy wasn't a problem, as rarely were more than two interns staying there at a time, sometimes none at all, and their schedules were easily checked. He'd been wrong to fear Susan's nakedness, to think this new arrangement would change anything. But this leisure did allow them to slow down and, by eliminating the fear of discovery, made new explorations possible. They would arrive separately, Susan now in her own car, and he would enter the silent apartment and stand in the common room until he heard her breathing behind one of the doors, already undressed, lying in the single bed with the same look of idleness she'd worn during those weeks she'd made him wait, her expression part entitlement, part boredom, and she'd be oddly slow to look at him, even as he stood over her, took her hand, and pulled her up to face him. It sent a twinge of fear and dread through his mind that she might deny him. He touched her body while she indifferently, unresponsively removed his jacket and tie, his shirt and pants, as if to remind him that it was *she* who made these decisions. "What took you so long?" she asked one day. "I had to talk my way out of a speeding ticket," he answered. Smiling now, appeased, she then kissed and climbed him, *engaged,* her legs wrapped round his hips, still climbing until she was onto his shoulders, this girl as thin as she was strong, his hair bunched in her fists while he fed on her little cunt. It amazed Sheppard that a thing so small could provide such delight, could supply what seemed as essential as water. He lifted her off his shoulders, placing her face down on the bed, and when she raised her ass toward him and turned around to look, the tiny spray of freckles across her cheeks and nose reddened, his cock drawn to her as if magnetized, so stiff it was as if it were a beak pressing itself out of his body's shell. It was a feeling, as he clutched her hips, that they were in furious pursuit, chasing something *down.* He turned her over and watched her orgasm slowly bloom. She tilted her head back as if she were rinsing her hair, tears forming at the edges of her closed eyes, the folds of her vagina so radiant and wet, the warmth coiling through her torso and limbs, that when he pressed his cheek and chest to hers he was like a child lying waterlogged on the hot concrete of a pool.

"Whose room is this?" he asked after they'd used the same one several times. He was sitting in a chair by the bed with his pants on, watching Susan open a bottle of men's cologne on the dresser.

She smelled it—wearing only Sheppard's dress shirt—and then pressed a drop with her finger behind each ear. "It's Robert's." She replaced the cap and carefully replaced the bottle. "Dr. Stevenson's."

"He's not a doctor yet."

"He will be."

"Of course he will."

"He loves me, you know."

Sheppard raised an eyebrow.

"I think I love him too," she said.

"I didn't know you were seeing him."

"You don't know anything about me."

He did. They talked. They were talking now. "I think I know everything I need to."

"Did you know that your father's firing me?"

Flabbergasted, he sat forward and crossed his hands. "What do you mean?"

"Well," she said, "*fire* isn't exactly correct. He's relocating me. To a job at Armstrong Labs downtown."

"And why is that?"

"Apparently I'm a distraction."

"To whom?"

"To you, silly."

She went on, but Sheppard, dressing, heard nothing.

Back at the hospital, Sheppard entered his father's office without knocking, though the man didn't look up, just sat there writing reports. He organized everything in stacks whose arrangement only he knew, a brand of encryption that drove his secretary nearly mad, piles forming a buttress along the perimeter of his credenza and desk that made him seem an old king behind walls, forever safe from harm.

"Have a seat," he finally said.

Sheppard wanted to stand—his hands were jammed in his pockets—but he detected an order as his father scribbled away. And no matter how mad he was, he couldn't overcome that, so he took one of the chairs that faced him.

"I know why you're here," his father said, putting his pen down. He was gray-colored, both sideburns and mustache the same slushy mix. Despite his glasses, he'd squint when looking at you, and this made him raise his chin and appear to frown. "You're here to talk about Miss Hayes."

"I am."

"I'll let you talk. But before you say a word," he said, "I want you to think about it. I want you to think if there's really anything to say."

"All right."

"Because if you're here to argue that she stays, I don't see how that's defensible. Not just because this is a hospital but because you're a husband and a father."

"What does that mean?"

"There's been some talk among certain staff members. There's some concern."

"Are you implying I've been negligent in my job?"

His father waited.

"Are you?"

"I'm implying more than that."

"Do you really think I'm that easily distracted?"

His father leaned back in his chair. "Are you having a love affair with this woman, Sam?"

"I wouldn't call it love."

"What would you call it?"

Sheppard considered this. "I'd say we have an understanding."

"What does that mean?"

He shrugged. "That we're very good friends."

"Really?"

"Of a sort, yes."

"Does Marilyn know you're friends?"

"She does."

His father shook his head. "Most people wouldn't believe that. Probably the rest wouldn't understand."

"I don't care what other people think."

"No?"

"No."

His father took the stack of papers before him, knocked them square, put them back down, and folded his hands over them. His glasses glinted in the light. "Then you're on your own."

Sheppard waited for a moment. "What do you mean?"

"I mean I'm terminating our partnership," his father said. "You heard me. I can't work with someone who doesn't care about other people's opinions." Then, when Sheppard began to speak, he swept a hand in front of his own face. "Divorce Marilyn if you wish. Leave Chip. Move back to California. You've talked about it before, and it doesn't matter. You're no longer a member of my hospital. You will *not* bring shame on this family *or* this institution. And I will *not* condone such behavior while you work under this roof. Do you understand? Go elsewhere if that's how you want live. But if you intend to divorce Marilyn, you'll divorce yourself of this place first."

"I don't—"

"Don't what?"

Sheppard waited.

"Don't what? *Want* that? Yes you do. And you don't. You want that, and you want to be here. You want to be part of this family, of your family, and you want to carouse. What you don't want is to own up to everything you *want.* It puzzles me about you, Sam. It always has. It's compulsive."

"Don't diagnose me."

"You're a brilliant doctor and a terrible person."

"Enough!"

"If your marriage is sick, find a way to treat it."

"Don't *you* talk about my marriage!"

He slammed both hands on his father's desk and leaned there facing him until—much as his father always had, dispatching all passion with his implacable rectitude, his resignation, his *discipline*—he finally calmed down.

"All right, Sam," his father said.

Sheppard rubbed his eyes, then sat down and crossed his legs and arms. "I'm sorry," he said.

They sat across from each other and looked out at the water. The lake appeared as wide as an ocean, yet it didn't instill the same awe as the sea.

"You know," his father finally said, "as I've grown older, my ideas about sin have changed. I used to believe that sins were things you did, but I don't think that now."

His father was going to tell him whether he cared or not.

"I think sins are what you ignore," he said.

Sheppard, still shocked at himself, couldn't speak.

"Because we know what we do." His father removed his glasses, cleaning them on the hem of his doctor's coat. "Everything we do is a response to that—to knowing." He held the lenses to the light, then replaced them. "Now make a decision."

"About what?"

"Are you staying or not?"

"I would never leave," Sheppard said, amazed by this unalterable truth.

"Good," his father said. "Now if you'll excuse me, I want to get this done before I go home."

In March, Susan quietly left Bay View for her new job; by May, she and Dr. Stevenson had moved to Minnesota for his residency. Sheppard neither saw nor spoke to her before she left. It was as if there was no need, though out of habit, he'd glance into pathology when he walked by. The world without her wasn't lacking in feeling or satisfaction, merely expectation. At dinner one night, out of nowhere, Marilyn said, "I heard Susan Hayes and Robert Stevenson got engaged." He held his knife and fork crossed over the meatloaf, gazing at the food on his plate. There'd been a great deal of conversation at the table that night, but these were the first words he'd heard. "That's wonderful," he said, then cut.

May and June were infernally busy; it was amazing how quickly time passed once summer had arrived. Only the shape of Chip's body seemed to capture it. When did his face become that of a little man? Sheppard couldn't recall ever spending more than an hour with him. He'd find Chip coloring on the patio, lean down, press a palm to his cheek, and kiss him, but the boy would push him away and call for his mother. Or he'd simply say, "No," and collect his book and crayons and leave—a rebuke that left his father stunned and blinking. There were evenings at work when he wanted to rush home and gather Chip in his arms, but he didn't. And though Sheppard still came home for lunch, he often ate alone in the kitchen. He could hear Marilyn's bath draining upstairs, hear her pad across the hallway, but for some reason he was afraid to see her. One late-August morning, when he came home early and Marilyn had just finished bathing, he led her to their bedroom, stirred by the idea of lovemaking. He took off his clothes and lay down next to her. "My diaphragm isn't in," she said. He went to the medicine cabinet and retrieved it. Their room was warm and filled with light; the wind made waves on the lake that they could hear lapping on the beach. Sitting on the bed, he slathered the rubber cup with the spermicidal meringue. She lay beneath him with her robe peeled open; and after Sheppard slid the diaphragm in and up against the knob of her cervix, he looked at her bared body, at the small dollop of paste stuck to her black hairs (which Marilyn, noticing too, pinched away), and realized something he could no longer hide from himself, that made him look out the window in hopes she wouldn't see it on his face: he felt no desire for her. Sitting here beside her, it was like his cock was dead. And if this was only a season in their marriage that, like this summer, itself would pass, would his loneliness be so overwhelming? Yet if his father was right and we *knew,* then why couldn't he be sure that this was in fact their end, that whatever had been between them was now permanently extinguished? "It's all right," she said, and stroked his arm. "We don't have to today." He lay there next to her and listened to the leaves ticking against the screens and, while she cried, took her head in his hand and pressed her temple to his, holding her like a brother might a sister.

"But Susan came back that summer, didn't she?" Mobius said.

"Yes," Sheppard answered.

"Alone?"

"With her fiancé. With Dr. Stevenson."

"Did you resume your affair?"

"Yes."

"Just picked up where you left off?"

"Not exactly."

"How was it different?"

"We didn't see each other as much."

"Why not?"

"She didn't have as much freedom. And she was more hesitant perhaps."

"Why?"

"This time she had something to lose."

"Didn't you both have something to lose?"

"It's difficult to say."

"Because Marilyn was so tolerant."

"Resigned, more like it."

"Because of your 'agreement.' "

"She knew she couldn't meet certain needs of mine, yes."

"But she never suggested you get a divorce?"

Sheppard shrugged. "Not seriously."

"Did Susan?"

Sheppard didn't answer.

"Did she?"

"Yes."

"Did you ever tell her that you'd contemplated it?"

"Yes. But I also told her about my father. About the attention it would bring the family."

"And what was her reaction to that?"

"She told me she didn't want to see me anymore."

"So she ended things between you?"

"She tried."

"What do you mean?"

"We might go several weeks without speaking, but after a time I'd call and we'd meet again."

"It sounds to me like you were in love."

"You're entitled to your opinion."

"Doc—"

"Detective."

"Listen to yourself."

Sheppard refilled and lit his pipe.

"So much of what you say flies in the face of common sense."

"With regard to what?"

"Your marriage."

Sheppard blew smoke toward the cell.

"What's sensible about any marriage?"

"People can't share each other like that."

"I'm not disagreeing with you."

"People can't endure that kind of unhappiness."

"There I think you're wrong."

"Really? Look at Susan. She broke things off with her fiancé."

"*He* broke it off."

"But isn't that just incidental?"

"I don't see what you mean."

"Isn't that too convenient an explanation?"

"I don't agree with what you're implying."

"Come on now, Doctor."

"Detective."

"State the *facts.* Susan Hayes returns to Cleveland from Minnesota and you immediately resume your affair. A year later, she and her fiancé break off their engagement. True?"

"Yes."

"That February, four months before Marilyn's murder, Susan moves to California, a place you'd always considered living yourself. Tell me, did you see Susan before she left that time?"

"Yes."

"Give her a nice send off? Good-bye and good luck?"

"I did."

"And you made plans, didn't you? To see each other again."

"The following month, yes."

"When you arranged to do surgery training in Los Angeles. But you could've done that anywhere, no?"

"Perhaps."

"Did you give her any gifts before she left?"

"I gave her a suede jacket—"

"Something to keep her warm."

"—and a signet ring."

"And something that promised a future."

"Everything you're implying is wrong."

"You get to California and send your wife three hundred miles north to Big Sur with Jo Chapman the minute you land. You go see Susan immediately, true?"

"Yes."

"And that night you bring her to stay with you at the home of your good friend, Dr. Miller, to a party he's having, no less, with people who know Marilyn."

"If I was planning to kill my wife, why do something so flagrant?"

"I didn't say you were planning to kill her *then.* I'm saying you didn't care anymore. I'm saying you did it *because* it was so flagrant. You wanted Marilyn to find out because then her only option would be to demand a divorce."

"Wrong again."

"If she demanded a divorce, what could your father say?"

"It never entered my mind."

"Where's the Übermensch in you? Where's the spine? You never could stand up to the old man, could you?"

Sheppard chuckled.

"Two days later you and Susan move into a hotel in LA. You train during the day and spend your nights with her. As if *you two* were the ones on the vacation together. As if *you two* were married."

"No matter how it looks from the outside, you're still wrong."

"And that weekend you even take her with you to a wedding. A little dress rehearsal for the future?"

"Susan and I ended things after that. On the drive home."

"Just like that?"

"No. Something happened."

"What?"

"Something terrible."

"Tell me, Dr. Sam. If it was over between you, why didn't you tell the detectives about Susan after Marilyn was murdered? Just days after she was killed, you were asked directly if you'd had an affair with Susan Hayes, *and you lied.* You said you were just friends. You lied then and again at your inquest. If things were over, why bother lying?"

"I lied because it had no relevance. Because it was over."

"Then why did *she* lie? When the Los Angeles DA questioned her, she said you two had never had an affair."

"I had no control over what she said."

"She had everything to lose by lying. But we know why she lied, don't we?"

Sheppard took off his watch and wound it.

"She was thinking about the future, wasn't she?"

"I don't know."

"*She* was your motive. You agreed to break things off in Los Angeles so it wouldn't *look* like it was planned."

"Things ended between us. On that drive."

Mobius shook his head.

"An affair like that takes commitment, Doctor. It doesn't just end one night."

"I'm not talking about commitment," Sheppard said. "I'm talking about love."

That summer, just days after Susan returned to Cleveland, to Bay Village, Dr. Stevenson's ring on her finger, just minutes after she and Sam met at a motel in Avon, just moments after they had sex, Sheppard burst out, "I love you."

And he knew this was untrue, an utterance that was merely a veil over love's absence; like sonar, it was a shouting out to receive an echo back. But saying it and then cursing himself for the loss of control, he partially realized why.

For over a year, he and Marilyn had been almost completely chaste, a year interrupted by nights of drunkenness, late evenings with the Aherns or the Houks, with his brothers' families, Sheppard counting Marilyn's drinks and watching them empty like sand in an hourglass until she took his arm and notified him that the room was spinning. "Take me home," she said. He excused them, helped her into the car, helped her out when they arrived at their house, watched her stand smiling at the sitter, deaf and dumb, red-eyed and heavy-lidded during the report on Chip, Sheppard paying the girl and seeing her out while Marilyn staggered upstairs, biding his time by the refrigerator drinking water with Alka-Seltzer and then standing over her bed while he removed his clothes and pulled hers off as he would a child's while she mumbled a sometimes happy, sometimes angry protest. And finally he fell upon her, kissing her with passion, putting her hand on his cock to which she ministered semiconsciously and burying his face between her legs to taste something of Susan, struggling to conjure her when Marilyn, in a burst of wakefulness, sat on his hips and pumped away, Sheppard pinching his imagination to its limits of vividness until for a second Susan *was* there. And then he lifted Marilyn's hips and moved her whole lower body off his when he came, because the diaphragm wasn't in. He threw the covers over her afterward and crawled into his own bed, so shocked at himself that for the longest time he couldn't sleep.

"Oh, Sam," Susan had said, "I love you too."

Yet they saw each other far less than before. Once a week, perhaps. Sometimes they might not even speak for three. It was partially logistics; Susan lived with Robert now. And it was something else. She'd changed. In her year away, she'd gained weight—fifteen pounds, maybe. It was becoming on her. He could no longer see her ribs; her hips had widened slightly. "The food up there," she said, "it's all meat and cheese." She'd also taken up smoking: Chesterfields, like Marilyn, but Sheppard didn't enjoy watching her as he did his wife. Susan inhaled and exhaled almost immediately, without relish in the act and probably how she'd seen a movie star do it, whereas it remained the most sensual thing Marilyn did—at least when he managed to catch her at it.

"What is it?" Susan asked him. They were lying in a motel bed. (It was

September already.) She was under the covers, the ashtray resting on her belly. Sheppard watched as she stubbed out the remaining half of her cigarette.

"Nothing," he said.

She put the ashtray on the bedside table, then flung off the covers. When she put on her panties and bra, she did it with her back to him. "I think we have to stop this now," she said. She found her skirt, snapped it like a sheet twice, then stepped into it.

"All right."

"I want you to stop calling me," she said. "I want you to promise." And when he didn't speak, she whirled on him. "I said I want you to promise."

"I promise," Sheppard said.

He called her a week later. It gave him an odd sense of delight, her silence on the phone when she answered, the ease with which she broke down. "I'll be at the Perkins motel in an hour," he said. "If you're not there, I understand." He waited in the room, not even bothering to turn on the lights or the radio, lying on the bed with his suit still on, his hands clasped behind his head, making bets as to how long it would take her to arrive. When she knocked softly, he let her in and sat down as she stood beside the bed. Then he pulled her down next to him. She let him kiss her resignedly at first—her cheek, the edges of her lips, her mouth—and soon they returned to the place they always found . . .

Of course, Sheppard thought, she had more to lose this time.

She stood by the mirror, replacing her earrings. When she was done, she rested her fingers on the bureau and looked at him in the reflection. "Sam," she said. "I want you to do a favor for me."

He couldn't help but cross his arms and smile.

"A big, big favor."

"Name it."

"I want you to leave, right now." She was near tears. "Stay far away from me and don't come near me again." She wiped her eyes with her middle fingers: one, two. "There isn't going to be anything more between us. So please, good-bye . . . good luck. No conversation. Just leave."

"Right away?"

"Yes."

"No questions asked?"

"Yes."

"No, I can't do that."

"Why not?"

"I think you know."

"Then say it."

"You tell me."

"I'm in love with Bob."

He jumped up behind her, staring at her in the glass. "How can you be in love with Bob and be here with me?"

"How can you be in love with your wife and be here with me?"

"I guess you love Bob like I love my wife."

But he regretted having said this as he drove back to the hospital—a weak man's line, strictly expedient. Worse, it was a lie. They were slipping more and more often into argument. And he didn't want to talk about his marriage in Susan's presence. His love for Marilyn should be sacrosanct. Yet who, then, was he to speak about love?

He loved Sunday afternoons in the fall when he could work on the boat, fix the stairs to the landing, or paint the fascia boards. He loved these chores because he could get them *done*—unlike the steady stream of things at the hospital, the endless revolving of the sick, the patched, and their return—and then he could drink beer in the afternoon and sit without the remotest chance of interruption, dozing on the daybed to the drone of the Indians or Browns on the radio, as pleasant as falling asleep to the sound of his parents talking during the long family car trips they used to take. In October, the tree leaves leading down to the water were curled up and bone-dry, as husked and brittle as the shells of dead beetles, black leaves falling in tatters against the bright water when gusts bent the branches. The yard was graveled with buckeyes, twigs, and acorns, and the grass had long stopped growing. He was sitting in the rocking chair on the porch, slipping off to sleep, when Marilyn appeared. Wearing her thick school sweater and jeans, she leaned against the screen facing him.

"I saw Susan Hayes today," she said finally.

Sheppard, alert now, took a pull at his beer.

"We saw each other at the market. She said hello to me . . . which made me sick, really. Because why even speak?"

He put the bottle on the floor and crossed his hands over his stomach, rocking back and forth.

"You didn't tell me she was back," Marilyn said.

"Should I have?"

"Do you see her?" she said. "No, don't tell me. I need a cigarette."

She stamped through the living room and into the kitchen, checking the old hiding places behind the bread box, in the silver goblets or the clay pitcher. A glass broke. Then he heard her pulling down medical books in his study, all of which he'd have to pick up later.

Sheppard closed his eyes, then turned toward the door. "They're behind the bowling trophies."

She returned to the porch, a glass ashtray in hand, and took a long drag on her cigarette. It was as if her body was a jar and he could see the relief filling her up.

"Is it like this?" she said.

"Like what?"

She indicated her cigarette. "Is it like smoking? This *need* you have. Because I don't want to smoke. No, that's not right. I don't want to feel so *weak* afterward. I don't want to feel like such a *failure.*" She waited. "Is it like that?"

"Not exactly."

"Why don't you explain it to me?"

He thought for a moment. "Isn't the fact that I have to explain it explanation enough?"

Marilyn shook her head. "No one knows you better than me," she said. "No matter what you do."

"I know that."

"No one would ever give you this kind of . . . room."

He continued to rock.

"Are you going to say anything?" she said.

"Wouldn't that violate our agreement?"

Marilyn's face darkened. She threw the ashtray at his head and it hit the chair beside his left ear and shattered—a sound like a lightbulb bursting. The pebble-spray hissed against his cheek. His fingertips, after he touched his face, were covered in blood.

By the time he looked up from them, she was out the door. He listened to her car start, the tires peel, and sat rocking for a long time.

He tried to feel the coagulation: the heat of new blood inflaming the wound; the rush of white cells and platelets layering beneath the cut like so much brick; the blood already scabbed, hard as dried glue within minutes.

Later, when Kokie came onto the porch, he let her lick his fingers. Finished, she lay with a thud at his feet and sighed.

If life was always like this, he wondered, if it was always this quiet, would he be sitting here now longing for noise?

She would come home, he decided. In the past he might've wondered; he might've worried or he might've hoped. The trick, of course, was to understand that things righted themselves sooner or later. Decisions were forced on you, or else finally made.

Marriage was a long wait.

One evening in late November, Susan called him at home. Marilyn was upstairs bathing Chip, and it was blind luck he answered the phone. "I need to see you," Susan said, sounding terribly upset. When he asked where to pick her up, she told him to come to her parents' apartment. The meaning of this didn't register on him until he was in the car, having told Marilyn there was an emergency at the hospital. It was raining out, a terrible late-fall storm, and so cold it was nearly sleeting, the wind full of leaves that caught in the wiper blades or pressed like starfish against his windshield. When he turned into the lot at the apartment house, Susan appeared in his headlights. She'd been standing outside and was soaked, and when she got in the car it made the interior feel colder. She was sobbing.

He drove, though he didn't need to go far. On a night like this, nobody could see anything out their windows, let alone into his. He parked on a side street. It was as good as private.

"Bob and I, we're not . . ." She wept again. "We're not getting married." She pressed her eyes to her arm and then looked at him. Even crying she looked beautiful. "He said he isn't ready." She started to laugh. "You might see how I found that funny."

Sheppard offered her his hand.

"I want to be married," she said. "But I want to be in love." She took his hand and looked at him imploringly. "Do you want to be in love?"

"I do," Sheppard said.

She pulled him toward her and kissed him. Her face was cold. "I needed to see you," she whispered. "I needed to see you when Bob was gone to see if it changed anything." She kissed him again and he kissed her in return, his desire for her endless and inexplicable. She pressed her hand between his legs. "And it hasn't."

"No," he said.

"Has it changed anything for you?"

"No," he said, thinking to himself: Why would it?

She'd already unbuckled his belt. "So you see," she said, kissing him, "we're always like this, you and I." He lifted himself up and she pushed down his pants. "We could *always* be like this."

"Yes," he said.

"Do you want that?"

"Yes."

"I'm not afraid to have this kind of joy."

Joy? It struck him as the oddest word for her to use because he'd never thought of their time together as being joyous. Theirs was a brand of freedom they created and affirmed, a kind of carnal honesty coupled with an ecstatic lack of restraint and words, words, words. He'd admired her directness, how she'd mow down anything that got in the way of having him. Even now the pleasure she took in pleasing him revealed itself as generosity, just as when hitting a tennis ball with Marilyn she could somehow magically make you play better. But joy? This Sheppard reserved for his wife, no matter what was happening—or not—between them. Joy was *her* province. Joy was the first time he'd kissed her, when he was fourteen, alone in her uncle Bud's den, in the kind of quiet conferred on a place that grown-ups might return to at any minute. It was how Marilyn would wait to lean into him until he pressed the small of her back, her face flushed and lips hot. (Were there women you were born to kiss?) Joy was seeing a movie with her in Hollywood when he was in medical school, on his one precious day away a month. They'd planned to go to the beach but it had started to rain, and joy was sitting with her in the cool theater, feeling her arm and leg pressed against his as if the touch itself was secret. She wore short white shorts from which her bathing suit peaked out; she was tan beneath her white blouse. The movie was *Shadow of a Doubt,* and joy was listening to her explain its meaning as the credits rolled, how the director had portrayed Joseph Cotten's character as a vampire: "Did you notice how he avoided sunlight and slept during the day?" Joy was following the operations of her mind. "You look like Teresa Wright," Sheppard had said. "You do. You're just as beautiful." They sat in the theater together long after the lights went up, the attendants bent cleaning the aisles. It was telling her afterward, "You could never bore me." Joy was delivering Chip himself during his residency. The OB had invited Sheppard to scrub in, and for sixteen hours Marilyn had labored, all her fear of dying giving birth, of following her mother into oblivion, vanishing once her water had broken, the terror she'd tended for months replaced by an athlete's determination to get the baby *out.* This one needed forceps, and Sheppard was shocked at how hard the doctor urged him to pull, the child like a screw stuck in plaster, until the incremental give he could feel down the birth canal. "Give me everything you've got," he told Marilyn. And joy was Chip's sudden rubbery slide from her, which left Sheppard, beholding him, in a state of shock. In his hands, the newborn's arms were free to bend at the elbows, his fingers to wriggle in the air. He howled so loud it seemed the umbilical cord, uncut, was supplying the boy with additional power and disclosing to Sheppard the limitless supply of Marilyn's own. The boy was covered with her blood and amniotic fluid, the latter as yellow as pollen, and Sheppard, holding the baby's ankles between his fingers and cradling his head in his palm, offered him to his wife. "I love you," he said, all of them crying. "I love you so much."

Joy was revealed in its utter absence.

In February, Susan called him at the office to tell him that she was moving to Los Angeles, where she'd secured a job at Good Samaritan. She was going to start her life over.

The day before she left, he took her to lunch at Leytonstone's and brought her two presents: a suede jacket and a bloodstone signet ring.

He told her he'd see her by March.

It was all he thought about until then.

"Some people memorize poems," Mobius said, "others famous speeches. Me, I memorize confessions. And yours, of course."

"I never confessed to Marilyn's murder."

"Would you like to hear it?"

Sheppard shifted in his chair.

"It's from the journal you kept in prison." Mobius cleared his throat. " 'When this tragedy first occurred and for several months thereafter I gave not a thought to love, except Marilyn, and I could never love again like I did M. I'd never consider serious love again. I had feelings of remorse that I had not been more tender to M at times and that I had not taken time to enjoy home a little more.' "

Sheppard thought for a moment. "Can I tell you something I've learned about love?"

"Certainly," Mobius said.

"If you love someone truly, and they love you, there's no such thing as a confession."

Somewhere over the desert, on the flight from Cleveland to Los Angeles, Sheppard noticed Marilyn was crying.

She was facing the window and weeping so silently that he wouldn't even have heard her but for a brief sob, and when he asked what was wrong she said, "Nothing"—an answer she'd given him so many times over the course of their marriage that he again felt like a fool. For a while he tried to ignore her, but her efforts to remain quiet had turned into a whimper and, now frustrated, he ordered her to go to the bathroom. She hurried to the back of the plane, sobbing visibly, and when the stewardess walked by he ordered them both a drink. He stared out the window at the desert below, visible on this cloudless part of the trip. It was staggering, America's size, and this made him wonder at the small structure drifting beneath them, a white speck that was perhaps a house, nearly comical in its remoteness, at the end of a needle scratch of road. Who could live in such a place? The stewardess brought him their drinks. He wasn't sure of the cause of Marilyn's suffering, but he guessed it had to do with going back, to Los Angeles, where their adult lives had begun, the dream-state that flight brought on, and the inescapable reflex this return engendered to unspool the four years since they'd left and then take stock, examining it frame by frame for clues about the present. That strip of negative was *theirs,* but the images, he had learned, were utterly different and the contrast between them could make a person despair.

Marilyn returned to her seat and lifted the martini glass by the stem. It shook in her fingers. "Thank you," she said.

They didn't speak again for the rest of the flight.

Of course, the maddening thing about these episodes was their sudden disappearance; they were as fast moving as a squall. Deplaning onto the tarmac, in sunlight so bright it was painful to behold, Marilyn clutched her hat in the breeze and said, "I can't believe we're back!" She was suddenly so excited and happy that she took Sheppard's arm, which revolted him as surely as if her touch were radioactive and might somehow sicken him. But she didn't notice this, which only further disgusted him. Her mood eclipsed her ability to notice anything other people were feeling; her mood *was* the world. Months ago, he'd promised himself to ponder this feeling long enough to do something about it—to finally leave. It was why he'd come. In the meantime, he helped the skycap find their bags.

And suddenly Jo Chapman, Chappie's wife, was at the terminal, both her arms in the air, hands waving at the wrists. "You two," she said. "*You two!*" She wore a tight white turtleneck, riding pants, and boots; her brown hair was tied off sportingly, her face thinner, a bit haggard around the eyes, the result, Sheppard guessed, of smoking, the stress of being a surgeon's wife, and the burden of relaxing all the time. She hugged him with that equestrian's strength, power he could feel straight from her core, then held him at arm's length to look at him. "Still a handsome dog," she said, then turned to Marilyn. "Emphasis on *dog.*" It made Marilyn laugh. And Sheppard, smiling inwardly, realized that Jo had always held him at arm's length. He was a man, she always had to remind him, and in her book men were almost entirely fools. She and Marilyn would be better off without them. Or perhaps it was that in their lives as a foursome—Jo, Chappie, Marilyn, and Sam—she always felt compelled to stress that loyalty-wise, Marilyn came first.

"Should we drop you off at Dr. Miller's?" she asked him.

"It's in the opposite direction," Sheppard said.

"I don't mind. Do you mind, Marilyn?"

"I do if it doesn't get us on the beach before sunset."

"I'll take a cab," he said. "You girls go on."

Sheppard had the skycap load up the car and kissed Jo good-bye.

"Is Chappie driving you up?" she said.

"Yes," he said. "On Sunday."

Before Jo got in the driver's seat, she said over the roof: "Be sure to tell him to go to hell."

She was always offering this sort of public complaint. Over dinner she'd tell you how many eons it had been since they'd slept together. Its familiarity made Sheppard chuckle, though Jo didn't: she was busy lighting a cigarette and starting the car.

He and Marilyn stood facing each other. She seemed sad again, but he couldn't bring himself to ask why.

Then she put her arms around his neck and hugged him. "I'll be thinking about you up there," she said. She waited for him to speak, and when he didn't, she searched his eyes for a moment and then she kissed him passionately. It was unlike her to be so affectionate in public, and he was so surprised that his resistance was only compounded. She got in the car and, just before they drove off, rolled down the window and smiled, at once knowingly and sadly. "Don't have *too* much fun," she said.

When they pulled out, Sheppard watched the car merge with other traffic until he couldn't see it anymore.

And later, in a cab, on the way to Susan's apartment, he couldn't shake what she'd said. He wasn't sure what she'd meant by it, if it was merely an offhand remark or her condoning what he was about to do, though he had no idea how she could know. She'd said it with that Mona Lisa smile of hers, both the utterance and her expression impossible to decode; and no matter what she meant or how hard he tried to relegate it to the back of his mind, it had the effect of making the world seem unstable. The palm trees outside appeared so spindly they looked as if they might topple over from their own weight, their armadillo bark splintering open to reveal jagged insides, the houses that climbed straight up the hills from Rodeo Drive seeming in danger, at any second it seemed, of shearing off and tumbling down into the road. Sheppard tried to ignore all this, writing off his anxiety as a symptom of travel, time change, and the effects of moving through great altitudes at high speed. Also, he thought, of his desire to see Susan. Anticipation this extreme, he knew, was close to fear, yet the feeling just wouldn't go away. It was as if Marilyn had somehow banished him into a dream, with all its mutable landscapes and attendant confrontations, each figure like a puzzle you had to put together or a riddle to be deciphered, with the consequences of failure carrying the potential to ruin your life.

It unnerved him, and made Susan's apartment building appear even more ominously drab in spite of the blinding sunlight. It was a nondescript three-story complex on North Alfred fashioned of white-painted brick, its courtyard gated off from the street. A fountain stood dead within, the water mottled with algae. On the intercom outside, Susan had written her name next to her roommate's—*Shaw/Hayes*—and the very lines of her letters looked scratched instead of penciled, thin and delicate as a bird's bones. Her voice, when it came over the microphone, was an unrecognizable squawk. "It's Sam," he said, then waited, the street silent and empty. The Santa Monica Mountains were visible in the distance. For a moment, it was as if there was no one else alive in the world.

The buzzer sounded and he let himself in, shaking the gate behind him when it closed to make sure. His heels echoed as loudly in the courtyard as in a tunnel. A motorcycle roared past, the engine's sound ricocheting off the walls, and Sheppard, wincing, put his hands to his ears and turned toward the source but through the bars of the gate saw only the street. Exposed hallways framed the courtyard. The apartment windows had their blinds or curtains drawn. He didn't know what he expected coming here, just that he expected something else.

He'd expected Susan to be home, for one, but it was her roommate, he realized, who'd spoken to him over the intercom and now answered the door. She was wearing a nurse's outfit, though her cap was off. Her top two buttons were undone. "You must be the doctor," she said.

"I am," he answered, though suddenly paranoid that Susan had even mentioned him.

"I'm Janet," she said. She took his hand, held it limply and delicately, and then let her arm fall as lifelessly as the other at her side. She invited Sheppard in and he followed her, her hands banging into her hips like clappers on a bell.

"Susan's not back yet," she said. "Traffic must be bad." Her voice was so flat she seemed to form words using the least effort of lips and mouth. She went to the kitchen off to Sheppard's right. She was making a drink and offered him one, which he declined. She dropped ice cubes into a tall glass, then nearly filled it with scotch and added a splash of soda. "I worked the night shift," she said, raising the glass in a toast. "I'm about to go to bed. Be smarter if I drove to the park and took a walk to wind down, but I never do."

She was chubby-cheeked and shallow-chested, slack-eyed and glum.

Nearly pretty, he thought, though everything from her small torso to her pear-shaped face had conspired to keep her from getting there. Her beautifully manicured nails were painted a cherry red so dark they were almost black. When she noticed him looking at them, she tucked the back of her hand under her elbow.

Sheppard checked the time. It wasn't quite one, but he'd been up since three that morning. "Maybe I will have that drink," he said. "Same as you're having, if that's all right."

Leaning against the counter that separated them as she fixed his cocktail, he surveyed the place. The only thing on the walls was a large mirror in the shape of the sun, the glass surrounded by jagged strips of gold-plated iron. Hanging over an ugly green couch on the far wall, it was heavy enough to kill the person sitting below it if it fell. Susan's room—he recognized her shoes beside the dresser—was more or less an extension of this common area, partitioned off the kitchen and without a door. Her single bed sat between two courtyard windows whose venetian blinds were drawn. Only Janet's room, behind him and to his left, enjoyed the light of three high windows, even that muted by the building next door.

"Cheers," she said.

They touched glasses.

"How long are you visiting?" she said.

"Two weeks."

"Susan said you'd only be here one."

"I'm going up to Big Sur for the second," he said.

"Lucky. I hear it's beautiful."

"It is."

"I'd give anything to go up there."

"You should take a drive one day."

"I mean a place. I'd love to have a place somewhere like that."

"Who wouldn't?"

"I'd just die to have one."

"Maybe you will someday."

"Not unless I marry a doctor." She spun the ice with her finger again and stared at him. "Is it just you going?"

"Excuse me?"

"Next week. Is it just you?"

Sheppard looked at his drink and, half-affronted, considered his answer, but then Janet said, "I hear Susan."

She appeared at the door, having caught it before it flung open, and stood there in the brightness spilling into the apartment's lightless gloom.

For a moment the two faced each other, with Janet leaning against the refrigerator watching, and they didn't know how to react. Sheppard hadn't expected this either, though he realized immediately how much had changed for her—how terrifying this new life was—and yet how little it really had, for here he was as well. They took each other by the hands, speechless, and he was moved to see that she'd refreshed her makeup.

"I'm sorry I'm late," she said. "Work was . . ." She looked over his shoulder at Janet, still watching unabashedly. There was an exchange between them, an allusion to some agreement they'd made that Sheppard could tell, by Susan's expression, Janet had somehow violated.

"I'm going to go lie down," she said. "Nice to meet you, Doctor."

She went to her room and lay down on her bed—the foot of it visible through the doorway—but didn't close the door.

It was all so different, he thought, pointing a thumb toward Janet. Susan shook her head and led him into her dark corner, where, half-hidden, they finally kissed; and Sheppard, forgetting everything for a moment, couldn't keep from touching her. "Not here," she said, then whispered. "Not with *her.*" They kissed again and Susan stopped him once more. "Not now," she said. "Just let me look at you." They lay on the narrow bed, kissing and touching and staring into each other's eyes, though when Susan held him, squeezing his neck so tightly it hurt and explaining how difficult it had all been, the same terrible anxiety seized him anew. Over her shoulder, he stared at Janet's legs, visible through her door, so still they might as well have been amputated.

He sat up on the edge of the bed and whispered, "I can't do this."

Susan sat up too, looking startled. She grabbed his arm. "What do you mean?"

He pointed at Janet's Wicked Witch legs. "Is she staying here?"

Susan seemed puzzled. "This is her apartment."

"I mean this week. Couldn't you have made arrangements?"

"I thought . . . ," she said. "I thought you would."

It hadn't occurred to him. He'd assumed it wouldn't be like this, that they'd have some privacy. He pinched the bridge of his nose: the flight and the drinks were catching up with him.

"I'm going to go," he said.

"Why? Where?"

"To my friend's house. Dr. Miller's. Where I'm staying."

"You're not . . . I thought you were staying at a hotel."

"No."

"But how will we—?"

"We will," he said. "It'll be fine." He put his hand over hers, his mind racing. "I promise." He stood up.

"Please don't leave," she said, grabbing him by the wrist.

"It's just for a few hours," he said, now unnerved that she looked terrified, but he smiled and rubbed her arm. "I'll call you as soon as I get things squared away."

He was at once thwarted and furious. There was something about Susan's panic that he'd never seen before, and in the cab to Michael Miller's he thought about what to do. To suddenly move to a hotel would make Marilyn suspicious and could lead to confrontations he wasn't ready to have, at least not yet. Yet being apart from Susan was already making him ache, transporting him back to the time before they'd ever made love, and then, afterward, to the overwhelming need to *get* somewhere. Neither was this what he'd expected, these obstacles so far from what he'd wanted.

Though on arriving, he forgot these troubles temporarily. Michael had moved to a beautiful house in Beverly Hills, a giant colonial just off Burton Way and within a mile of Coldwater Canyon. He looked hale and tan, his snow-white hair slicked back, the ridge of his long, proud nose burnt as pink as his golf shirt (he was just back from a round at Hillcrest). His wife, Emma, had laid out a lovely late lunch by the pool, which glistened as brilliantly as the day itself. The children appeared, and in four years' time they'd grown into little people: Anne, at ten, bespectacled and bookish, was carrying *Ivanhoe* under her arm; Roger, eight, wanted to know about Otto Graham. "Is he really your friend?" Sheppard nodded. "We race cars together," he said, then produced an autographed poster—it was Marilyn's idea—that sent the boy sprinting to his room to hang it. He gave Anne *Charlie and the Great Glass Elevator.* "I'm going to start reading it right now," she said, and ran off too.

This left the adults alone for lunch, and they talked long after they'd finished eating in the kind of place on the kind of day that made Cleveland seem like Nod.

"Number one," Michael said, "if you moved out here, your golf game would improve. Number two, you'd get a lot richer."

"Are you really thinking about it?" Emma said.

"I think about it all the time," Sheppard answered.

"Oh," Emma said, "I'm so sorry Marilyn couldn't come. And now she's going to miss the big party."

Sheppard looked at Michael, who said, "It's nothing."

"Maybe not for you," she said. "You don't do any of the work."

Michael rolled his eyes. "It's a monthly thing," he said to Sheppard. "Poker game for the junior doctors and their wives."

"You make it sound like the wives are allowed to play," Emma said.

"They could if they took it seriously, but all they do is *talk.*"

"That's because poker is so *boring.*"

Michael sighed, then reached out and squeezed Sheppard's shoulder. "Sam, if there's a mistress you need to go see during this rare stretch of freedom, please don't feel like you have to stand on ceremony."

"Could I bring her tonight?" Sheppard said.

It was a joke, of course, but it would be lovely if the solution was that simple. He decided he needed a swim—a swim and a nap—to clear his mind, and then he and Susan could talk and make another plan. He changed into his trunks and strode out onto the diving board, and after a jackknife he did several vigorous laps. Happily, he'd lost no power over the years. Though even while swimming he was preoccupied by his wife and what she'd said—"Don't have *too* much fun"—and her expression, like she *knew.* Now they were apart again, yet here he was still haunted. So much of their life was a cycle of separations, whether it was his leaving for work in the morning or being called away in the middle of the night; and it was also the women he'd been with in the past, either leaving Marilyn to be with them or using her absences as an excuse to play. He thought of Frances Stevens that summer long ago, after Marilyn had gone off to college his senior year, Sheppard looking up from under the hood of his Model A to see her standing at the garage door watching him, for how long he had no idea but with the same awareness as she walked toward him that Marilyn was *there*—witnessing this very exchange. He remembered the four-way he and Lester had with those nurses back in medical school, when Marilyn returned to Cleveland for a few weeks to see her father. Even today, so many years later, he could recall the heart-stopping beauty of the girl Lester had set him up with. Andrea: raven-haired and ruby-lipped, as black-eyed as a deer. Dinner and drinks as if he wasn't married, and the drinking game afterward, Buzz, the four of them back in Lester's living room, his friend and the other girl waiting for them to make some sort of decision while they all got drunk, until it was up to Sheppard to hand his glass to Lester to give to her as they sat cross-legged on the floor around the little coffee table and tell them, as they both held the cup, "Give it to her, Les." His friend had finally put the drink down, checking back one last time with Sheppard as if for permission, and then he kissed the woman, the two moving lip-locked to the couch, as Sheppard took Andrea's hand and hurried her into the bedroom, pushing her down face-first onto Lester's bed and throwing up her skirt and yanking off her panties, his hand on the back of her neck, the sounds of them all mingling while he rammed away. Yet oddly Marilyn's face had drifted in and out of his mind, her expression vaguely disappointed when the other woman and Les appeared half-naked in the room, falling with them onto the bed and winding around one another, Sheppard raising himself up for a moment as if he were a charmed snake and they, coiled below, were the rest of his body. And Marilyn watching from above with that same look she'd shown him before driving off today. Why now? Sheppard wondered. Why *still*? "Don't have *too* much fun." He didn't *want* fun. That wasn't what he was here for. Though what he was here for wasn't as clear to him as it had been.

He was resting in the deep end of the pool, his arms over the edge and his chin atop his locked hands. He could feel the sunlight on his scalp. There was something about Susan today that had repulsed him. It was unfair to her, but he could no more shake that than what Marilyn had said. The freshened makeup didn't really hide the dark circles under Susan's eyes and she had the off-putting odor of fear and hope on her breath. When she took his arm, trying to stop him from leaving, her nails had dug into his flesh and it had taken every ounce of his control not to yank it from her grip. And even *then* Marilyn was there, when he was finally ready to act. It was like being under perpetual surveillance. Though in truth it wasn't like that at all. It was more as if she were waiting for something from him, but what?

Later that night, well into the poker party, he called Marilyn at Jo's. It was long distance and it was late, nearly eleven, and like everyone he was drunk. Part of him wanted to speak with her while another simply wanted her to know he was here, where he'd said he'd be. He wanted to maintain the illusion in her mind that he'd soon be asleep in his bed, readying himself for the long day to come—when in fact he'd be off to meet Susan. He let the phone ring several times. By the tenth, told himself to hang up and at the same time he thought to wait, so when Jo answered the phone he apologized.

"No," she said, "don't worry. I must've passed out."

"Could I have a quick word with Marilyn?" He heard the clatter of the receiver dropping, a silence, a mumble, and the sound of footfalls.

"Sam?" she said.

"Hello."

"Is something wrong?"

"No."

"You woke us up."

"I know. Go back to sleep."

"What's going on there?"

"It's a party. Just a small gathering."

"Where are you?"

"At Michael's. It's at his house."

She waited.

"I just wanted to hear your voice," he said.

"Here I am," she said. "Here's my voice."

"All right. Tell Jo again I apologize."

She hung up before he did.

He stood staring at the phone, then shook his head.

He called Susan and told her to come over immediately. When she asked him whether he was sure, he said yes. When she asked if the party was dressy or not, he could hear the excitement in her voice. A group of women had gathered nearby, so he described what they were wearing and told her to hurry. He walked to the bar and made himself another martini—the drink, he thought, he'd regret the next day—and then joined the men playing poker in Michael's study. There were eight of them at the card table and so much cigar and pipe smoke that it looked like the felt had caught on fire. Two of them, Joseph Newton and Herbie Hawkins, were old medical-school classmates, their wives friends of Marilyn's, and Sheppard felt a sharp twinge of fear about Susan's arrival.

But later, when she was shown into the den by Emma and she stepped into the circle of light under which the men sat, the sight of her dispelled all his doubts. She was wearing a green dress, a matching green belt and coat, and a string of pearls around her neck. The bloodstone ring Sheppard had given her was on her finger. Out of defensiveness, perhaps, her haughtiness had returned; she was the girl she was three years ago, her original confidence and forthrightness restored. She seemed ablaze as she leaned over and put her arm around Sheppard's shoulder—he'd placed his hand on her hip—and then kissed him, and they kept their hands where they were while she introduced herself to everyone. Her beauty drew all of their focus away from the game and seemed to embolden her further; she ran her nails gently along Sheppard's neck while they played the next hand, then excused herself to get a drink after he folded. All the men watched her until the door closed, and when it did they passed glances between one another and then back at Sheppard, a couple clucking their tongues or half-whistling while another, a man who Sheppard didn't know, softly laughed in derision or appreciation—he was too drunk to be sure.

"Goddamn, Sam," Michael finally said.

Sheppard stared at the cards he'd laid on the table, then leaned back in his chair and laced his fingers across his stomach. He felt the rictus of a smile on his face.

"I don't know," Michael said. "That's just . . . *something*."

Neither Newton nor Hawkins could look up from their cards, though after a long silence, Herb said, "Goddamn's about right."

Sheppard left the study and, passing through the living room where the women were, left a wake of silence behind him. He found Susan out by the pool, smoking a cigarette and staring at the candles that floated on the water. Slipping his arms around her waist, he kissed her neck and smelled her perfume mingling with the honeysuckle and jasmine on the breeze—Cleveland a blessed universe away.

"I shouldn't have come," she said.

"Of course you should've."

She nodded at the house.

"No one in there will talk with me."

"That doesn't matter."

"To you it doesn't."

"To us it shouldn't."

"Why's that?"

"Come with me."

He took her hand and led her into his room through the sliding door right off the pool. And as he closed it, he caught Emma staring at him, her eyes brilliant with fury. This he was able to forget once they were alone, and even his wife and what she'd said. He made love to Susan angrily and passionately, though now it was as if *he* were hovering overhead—that his prowess demanded he be utterly detached, or like one of the men playing cards in the other room, aware of what was happening here in the dark but feeling none of it.

This detachment remained with him once he tried to sleep. He was conscious of Susan there, of her body, yet he couldn't keep far enough away from her, as if merely sleeping in the same bed with another woman was the real sin he'd committed and by maintaining this literal separation he might bolster his claim of innocence should someone burst into the room. Or perhaps it was that he was unaccustomed to sharing the space, since he and Marilyn never did anymore. Either way, his discomfort buoyed him on sleep's surface. When he finally looked at his watch, it was 4:15. Susan lay facing away from him with the covers off her torso, the sheets forming a V at the small of her back, the braids of her spine as discernible in the shadows as the imprint of a fossil. He propped himself up to look at her face. He'd never woken up next to her, he realized, nor did he know her parents' names, her middle name, her birth date—all essential facts and stories. He then was gripped by such a panic he had to lie back and drape his arm over his eyes, forcing himself to breathe slowly and deeply, slowing his heart to the point where he could begin to believe that this night would end. Over an hour later, out the window, the sky finally turned blue, a tracery of light burning along the edges of the hills, for which he thanked God. The two more hours of rest he needed were cooking the backs of his eyes like yolks and he wanted coffee but didn't feel like foraging. So he woke Susan and told her to dress, found the keys Michael had left him to his MG, and drove her back to her apartment through this blue world of empty streets—Los Angeles in the morning feeling more like a desert than at any other time of day.

Instead of stopping somewhere for breakfast, he went straight to the hospital and was greatly relieved to see Chappie, who was all grip, all talk, taking him by the shoulder after they shook hands and squeezing it too in welcome, so hard it made Sheppard smile and go limp. Chappie was short but he felt as strong in the hands as someone twice his size. His energy seemed to run through every fiber of his body: the hairs on his arms and ears bristling with the discharge, his eyebrows lightning bolts. No matter how accomplished Sheppard ever became, around Chapman he always felt he was struggling to keep up, and as they walked toward surgery Chappie talked about the upcoming procedure so far ahead of the explanation in his mind that it came out of his mouth *in media res.* Sheppard, nodding, still felt shaky, but he reacquired focus once they scrubbed in, habit's blessed restoration of clarity, this presurgical routine priming his brain; and once they entered the OR his fatigue and emotionality fell away, replaced by keenness, by calm. It was an open-heart procedure he was observing today, a magnificent, stirring thing to behold, the incision down the sternum and then the circular saw along the chest bone, which before being split looked, with the ribs and clavicle bones branching off of it, like the back of a giant bug. The stainless steel retractor was inserted, its crank turned smoothly, and there in that rectangular window was the heart, blanketed in purple pericardium, this protective tissue incised and these four triangles lifted away like a present's wrapping, their ends clamped to the retractor's rails so that the revealed organ appeared to sit on this splayed canvas as if it were in a hammock. The patient, Chappie explained, suffered from acute aortic valvular incompetence, her condition so critical she required an experimental prosthesis, a caged ball valve with multiple-point fixation rings secured to the ascending aorta. It was an astonishing seven-hour procedure that required a degree of technical precision and reliance on technology Sheppard had never experienced before. *I could live like this out here. In joy, on the vanguard, the tip of the spear.* He was allowed to implant the replacement valve, an obscenely difficult job given the condition of the woman's aortic tissue.

"This one's so compromised," Chappie said, "what we really need to do is swap it out with part of a pulmonary."

"Where do you get that?"

"Donors," he said. "Cadavers. Unfortunately we've had problems with rejections."

When they brought the woman off the pump, Chappie watched her EKG and said, "Let's see if this motor will run."

The woman died on the table.

When he picked Susan up at her apartment, he was too tired to tell her anything about his day. All he wanted was to go to sleep. But Susan was hungry, and he could tell by the outfit she had on that she was ready to be taken out. Chappie had recommended a place in Santa Monica—Ernie's, on Barnard Way—and it was a wonderful call. They sat outside with a view of the pier, the carousel's organ sounding its plaintive notes over the glassed ocean, the distant Ferris wheel appearing to Sheppard like a dilated eye. Still, he struggled to shake himself out of his inner quiet and remoteness, the lingering detachment brought on by the hours of surgery and the night before. Out of discomfort, perhaps, Susan launched into a story about her superior, the woman who ran the pathology lab. And even while Sheppard's attention wandered, it occurred to him that she always established someone at work as her enemy, who from the get-go was determined to limit her potential and make her life impossible—at Bay View this was Tricia—so that when she did finally leave, or was fired, she'd bear no personal responsibility at all.

"Did you hear me?" she said.

"I'm sorry," he said, placing his hand over the back of hers. Though that too was like an act, a pantomime of intimacy. "I'm exhausted." He took her fingers and looked at the bloodstone ring he'd given her, the green flecked lightly with red.

"Sam," she said. "In your letters, you kept mentioning something you wanted to tell me when you came out here."

"I know," he said. All certainty suddenly seemed to have fled.

"Are you going to tell me?"

"I am," he said. "But I've just arrived."

She looked puzzled.

"What I mean," he said, "is that I'd like for us just to *be* for a few days—to be us. Let me get my feet on the ground."

"But you'll tell me?" she said.

"Yes," he said. "Of course."

Dinner lifted his spirits and Marilyn was far, far away. After leaving the restaurant, they drove north along the Pacific Coast Highway toward the Palisades, then east past Will Rogers Park. Occasionally Susan leaned over and kissed him or ran her hand up and down his thigh, and his indifference and remoteness dissolved, and once again it was obvious that they had to get somewhere fast, that his attraction to this woman was an ever-burning thing, and upon returning to Michael's house—it was late now, past ten, and no one met them at the door when he unlocked it—he hurried her to his room. And afterward, as they lay there together, she whispered, "I've dreamed this before."

Then she fell asleep, starting to snore so loudly that it made him sit up. And then he began to think. Another night of sleeplessness would kill him tomorrow. But he was thirsty from too much wine and wandered into the kitchen. Standing at the sink, he downed two glasses of water and was about to turn off the light when Michael appeared. With his hands pressed into the pockets of his robe, he looked at Sheppard grimly and nodded toward the guest room. "Is she in there?"

"Susan? Yes."

Michael raised his shoulders and let them fall. "What are you doing, Sam?"

Sheppard said nothing.

"Let me put it like this: What are you doing *in my house*? There are kids here, for Christ's sake. We're Marilyn's friends on top of that. How could you put us in this position?"

"I don't want you to say anything."

Michael tapped his forehead. "Sam, that's the point."

"Well, I'm sorry then."

"Are you and Marilyn divorcing?"

Sheppard shrugged.

"You should."

"Michael, please—"

"Please nothing. You're behaving pathologically."

"I think we've both had our pathological moments."

Michael stepped closer and whispered, "You're out of line. And you need to have your fucking head examined. I'm serious. You need to see a shrink."

Sheppard, ashamed and furious, couldn't look at him.

"You leave early," Michael said. "Like this morning. Take the car. I don't give a damn. Drive yourself to a hotel and knock yourself out. But do *not* be here when Emma wakes up. Because I swear I don't know what she'll do if you are. Do you understand?"

"Yes," Sheppard said.

Oddly, the confrontation imparted clarity. Why was he waiting? What was wrong with him? He checked them into the Argyle Hotel the next morning.

The move seemed to confirm something for Susan, somehow thrilling her. When he got back from the hospital that evening, she had fresh flowers on the dresser and a martini just poured for him from a shaker. "Welcome home, Doctor," she said, walking toward him with the glass in her hands. And even before he could finish his drink she was on him like the woman she had been three years ago, hungry and inventive and tireless, though afterward, in the semidarkness, she said, "Tell me what you wanted to say. I've been waiting, Sam. I've been waiting patiently."

"Do you mean that I love you?" he said.

"You've said that before," she told him. "But you can say it again if you'd like."

Her insistence put him on the defensive. "Maybe some food will jar my memory," he joked.

While they dressed, she turned quiet and made herself another drink; and when he came up behind her at the mirror and took her by the shoulders, she stiffened. Now it was Sheppard who talked to fill the silence, who tried to turn the conversation to something . . . like his training. He'd always enjoyed talking with her about it. Unlike Marilyn she was knowledgeable—she knew what questions not to ask—but he couldn't coax her from her funk.

Over dessert, while he was describing that afternoon's procedure, she dropped her spoon and it clattered loudly in her dish. "When do you leave?" she asked.

"What do you mean?"

"Here," she said. "Los Angeles. When do you *go*?"

"I leave on Sunday," he said. "You know that."

Her eyes filled with tears. "And when do you come back? Or *do* you?"

"I do," he said.

"When?" she snapped. The couple at the table next to them glanced over. "Say when. Say something *specific.*"

"Keep your voice down."

"Don't treat me like a child."

"Please," he said, "this isn't easy for me." He had traction here; it was true, after all. "Was it easy for you to leave?"

He reached for her hand but she ripped it away and crossed her arms.

"Imagine what it's like for me," he said.

"I've already done my part," she said.

They sat staring in separate directions for a time. He paid the bill and they left without speaking. But when they returned to the room, she said, "I'm sorry. I'll be more patient." She came up behind him at the mirror and laid her entire weight against him. "I promise I will," she said.

Later, they made love, and it began as something tender but turned vicious and abandoned. She fell asleep quickly afterward, and her breath, as she snored lightly, smelled of garlic. It was odd to be awake; he always fell asleep before his wife. He found himself floating through foggy recollections of her busying herself while he drifted off, his awareness in that netherworld of her reading a book next to him, or doing the dishes softly downstairs, of a light being on in the house that should be off by now, or the sound of the porch door rapping closed, which meant she'd slipped out for a cigarette. He thought of her expression again, of what she'd said about *too* much fun. It was a form of mockery, he thought now, a brand of maternal ribbing of a silly boy. He got up, naked, walked to the window and stared at downtown Los Angeles. Its skyline, bunched and piled in the distance, sat protected by all the lit flatness surrounding it. You never felt *in* Los Angeles. It always seemed somewhere *out there* that you were trying to get to, so this view was in fact the perfect view, as if you were a nomad camping for the night in the outlands before making the final push across the peneplain in the morning . . .

He was out the door well before six the next day. He'd done his utmost not to wake Susan and was relieved to be heading to work without having spoken to her. But while driving to the hospital he felt anxious once more. Why was he hesitating? There was Chappie and surgery again and then in the doctors' lounge one of the young surgeons, Bart Elster, who'd completed his residency at Bay View three years ago, introduced himself and asked Sheppard to join him and a group of surgeons for lunch. It soon came up that he was getting married in San Diego on Saturday. Would Dr. Sheppard like to attend the reception?

Back at the hotel that evening, he expected Susan to be excited by the news of a trip down the coast, but instead she lit into him.

"Why would I want to go to a stranger's wedding?" she snapped.

Sheppard, stunned, explained the young man was merely an acquaintance. In fact, he'd know next to no one at the reception. It was more an excuse to leave town.

"Why do we need an excuse?" she said. "Couldn't you just think of something yourself?" She pulled the jigger off the bar shaker to pour him a drink, splashing the countertop when his glass overflowed. "It's like staying at the Millers' all *over* again," she said. And when he told her he didn't understand, she flung his glass against the wall. "Just go yourself if you're so anxious to leave!" Then she collapsed sobbing on the bed.

Sheppard, watching her back shake, wasn't sure whether to flee or stay. When he pressed her shoulder, she yanked it from his grasp.

"Don't touch me!" she said, and sobbed harder.

"All right," he said, but just stood there. When she continued to cry, he picked up his jacket from the chair and put it on.

"Where are you going?" she said.

"To get some dinner."

"You're just going to leave me here?"

"If you can't tell me what's bothering you, yes."

She sat up and turned toward him. Her mascara, streaked down her cheeks, gave her a wild look. "Don't you under*stand*?" she said. "It's a wedding. And I have nothing to *wear*."

The concierge gave him a list of stores that stayed open late. Ransohoff's, he said, was closest. Sheppard, fuming from the fight, felt withdrawn and shaken. He'd never seen this side of her until coming out here. It was desperate, something impulsive and furious. Was this who she really was? Feeling a sudden need to be back in Cleveland, he thought longingly of the lake, of routine, of home. If he left now, there'd be no harm to him. He could escape unscathed.

Yet she took his arm when they entered the store and held his hand with the other. "You can be mad at me," she said. "I know I'm being ridiculous." After he sighed, she whispered in his ear. "Say it."

"You're being ridiculous," he said.

She stopped him and folded her wrists behind his neck. "It's just that I want you to take care of me," she said.

"Is that right?"

"Don't you want to?"

"I do."

"There now," she said, "it's settled"—which magically it seemed to be.

A saleswoman led them to the dressing room, and as the models came out of the changing rooms and paraded before the couch where he and Susan sat, their shoes silenced by the carpeting, the large gray room so quiet they could hear the fabric of the dresses swishing, the light of the two chandeliers reflecting off the mirrors surrounding them so brightly that it was impossible not to appreciate the quality of the clothes. Seeing Susan's thrill at each new dress, he found himself wondering with a kind of scientific curiosity why it had never occurred to him to do this with Marilyn. Why the countless dreams of wooing others, of walking hand in hand with them (or Susan) through exotic cities? Why this sudden generosity? The lovely dinner later. The expensive hotel. His doctor's spending power fully flexed, with not the slightest sense of hesitation in his cheap guts when the saleswoman quoted the prices, yet all the while the scrimping with his wife at every turn.

Susan's favorite was a black dress with a bateau neck that showed off her collarbone and thin shoulders. When she tried it on and came striding into the room—multiplied, as it were, for the mirrors reflecting each other created a contrail of images behind—he was beside himself with desire. Something in her—in her *beauty*—eradicated any previous unpleasantness. She could appear anew, like Venus from the sea. To fail to take her over and over again was akin to neglect, and he reminded himself of the freedom they had now, and, if he chose, could always have.

He called Marilyn that evening.

"God," she said, "there's no place more beautiful than this. It makes living in Cleveland seem foolish."

"You didn't think so when we lived here," he said.

"Yes I did," Marilyn said.

"Oh, come on, you were always going home."

"I was younger. I was stupid. That doesn't mean we have to compound the stupidity. We're being stupid now, Sam. We could be happy here. Think of Chip growing up on the ocean."

"You'd change your mind again. It seems wonderful now that it's temporary."

She was silent for a moment. "Actually, sweetie, if you remember, Chappie gave you the open door. *You* wanted to come home."

"Can we stop talking nonsense?" Sheppard said.

There was static over the line that sounded like the sea. He could feel both their moods tumbling.

"Have you been busy?" she said.

"Yes."

"Has it been good?" she said. "Being here?"

"Yes."

"You should do it again."

"I will."

"I guess I'll see you Sunday," she said.

Hanging up, he believed he could break away.

He kept this in mind as they drove down Highway 1 that Saturday. He and Susan left in the afternoon, close to four.

This route would make the drive longer—a solid two and a half hours to La Jolla—but the weather was spectacular, the afternoon unseasonably warm, the sky wiped as clear as his mind. He was ready to tell her. Tonight. He was leaving tomorrow morning for Big Sur and plans had to be made. True, he could tell her now, but it was too pleasant to interrupt it with talk when you could *be* the engine's submarine gargle and gentle tug of the curves, the dips that left your stomach hanging in the air, the approaching traffic that bobbed silently in and out of view and the brown cliffs, furred with patches of green bush and scrub grass, that climbed up from the road toward tall stands of pine. "Weather like this should last forever," Susan said. He agreed and held her hand.

But by the time they arrived at the yacht club, a front had moved in and the utterly calm ocean reflected the last of the hazed sunlight. Only later would Sheppard consider how long it had been since they'd eaten. The reception had hors d'oeuvres aplenty but even more champagne, glass after glass after glass, and before he'd caught himself he'd moved on to gin. By chance, Susan knew several people in the wedding party from Cleveland, and she left his side almost immediately. Trapped in a long conversation with an ophthalmologist from San Francisco, he excused himself when he noticed rain spotting the windows. He'd left the top of the car down and hurried out to close it and then closed his eyes and breathed deeply as he stood still, listening to the masts of the moored boats clanging and whistling in the breeze. The rain was fitful, more mist than shower, but it had turned colder and this cleared his head enough for him to recognize that he was very drunk.

Coming inside, shocked at how loud and warm the room was, he now hurried to find Susan. He had a burning need to be alone with her, to tell her the things he'd been storing up, to say he was finally sure, but she was nowhere in the banquet hall. Not until he entered the main bar did he see her standing with a young man in the far corner of the room, laughing, her chin tilted up toward him, a drink resting in the fingers of both her hands. The man stood against the wall, calm and arrogant, basking in her undivided attention. He was dark-haired and sharp-featured like she was and he bent to her ear to tell her something about a guest he was pointing to, something that made her laugh and then grasp his wrist in agreement. The transparent bubble of intimacy that enclosed them nearly stopped Sheppard in his tracks, and when she turned and saw him, her eyes flashed. He might not have felt so suddenly jealous and enraged had she not then turned her back on him as if he held no interest whatsoever.

"Hello, Sam."

"Susan."

He looked at the stranger, who in turn looked at him. "I'm Dr. Sheppard."

"Dr. Kessler."

"Mark and I work together at Samaritan," Susan said.

They waited.

"Can I talk with you?" Sheppard said, taking her by the arm and leading her away. "I've been looking for you," he said.

"Well, you found me."

He stopped and studied her. Her eyes kept sinking toward his neck, then bobbed back up.

"Maybe we should go," he said.

"I'm not going anywhere."

"No?"

"Not now, no. I'm having fun."

Sheppard glanced over her shoulder at Kessler. "Maybe you're just drunk."

"Really? Thank you, but excuse me."

She turned to leave and he took her arm again.

"Let me go."

"Let's get some air."

"I don't want *air*, I want to be *away*. From you."

"Is that right?"

"That's right. You're a big, *embarrassing* question mark."

"Susan—"

"Even Mark, he just asked me. He said, 'Who are you *here* with?' And when I told him, he says, 'Are you two involved?' And I couldn't answer really, could I? Because what are we? What do I say? What do I tell people anywhere, let alone at a party?"

"You're being foolish."

"You're right. I'm a fool. I'm your fuckmate of a fool."

He took her by both elbows and raised her whole body toward him, her ear nearly pressed to his lips. "If you ever want to see me again," he whispered, "you'll walk with me out that door right now. Do you understand?"

She chuckled, and he squeezed her in his fists.

"Do you?" he said, and he let her down.

She looked at both her elbows, at the fading red marks where his fingers had gripped them. Then after she checked to see how serious he was, her eyes narrowed and she smiled. "You're a funny boy," she said.

It had been a mistake to take the coast road, Sheppard thought, not just for the weather or the state of the car but because of the added time of the added miles, the winding road's restrictions on his speed, because he and Susan could have gotten back to Los Angeles sooner, which would have meant being safely asleep, and then he could wake up the next morning and be off with Chappie to Big Sur, where Marilyn was now. It was a mistake and also, in these conditions, dangerous. It was one of many mistakes, he thought, his thumb throbbing so badly where he'd cut it earlier he was sure he'd need stitches. And now the same anxiety he'd felt earlier came over him—the irrational, nameless fear that he wouldn't survive this night, not with every single mistake somehow conspiring to bring about his own death, here, with Susan, so his dying would bring only harm. Sickness presented symptoms, diagnosis trailing infection or accident, but mistakes were the results of choices, of sequences that could be traced back to their origins. It was a mistake, Sheppard thought, to have gotten involved with Susan, then to think that the woman he'd known as a mistress could be anything more. No, their beginnings were themselves a set of limits imposed on any possible future. But none of these observations led to anything approaching a solution or remedy.

And with a sudden clarity he understood what his wife's last words had meant. *Don't have* too *much fun.* She knew. She *always* knew. He smiled humbly. From the minute she came out here, and probably long before, she knew that he'd see Susan. She knew and she forgave him from the outset, but that was only part of what she meant. The rest was this: *she was waiting.* If this was to be their end, so be it. If this was just another of his flings, that was fine. She, meanwhile, would wait for him to come around. He might cut her loose; he might embrace her. But she wouldn't end them. She would wait. She loved him, would give them another chance—and that was final.

Lord, Sheppard prayed, get me home.

"Stop the car," Susan said.

"Why?" he said.

"I'm *freezing,*" she said. "I want you to put the top up."

"The cold keeps me alert."

"Stop this car, Sam, or I swear to God I'll jump out."

"Jump out, then. I don't give a damn."

"No, you don't. You never did."

"Not tonight I don't."

"Not ever," she said.

"Not after that little performance."

"Of course. Anything that doesn't conform to your narrow preferences is a performance. Well, this isn't a goddamn performance. It's the real thing."

He held his right hand up to her face and went *blah blah blah* with his fingers.

"You're pathetic," she said. "*Pathetic.* And a coward."

"Go to hell."

"You don't take a stand on anything. Or stand up to anybody."

He turned on the radio.

She switched it off. "You don't stand up to your father. You're just his little boy living out his little vision of your little life."

"Shut your mouth about my family." He was doing eighty-five, the tires humming with the speed.

"So you carry out these little rebellions," she said, "to give yourself the illusion that you're big and free."

He licked his upper lip.

"You don't stand up to your wife. You don't end things with her even while you whisper how you love me. So with three little words you manage to disrespect us both."

"Keep your mouth shut."

"You don't even take a stand right now. 'Not after that little performance.' As if that were the straw that broke the camel's back."

"Will you shut the hell up?"

"God, was I a fool. Robert was a good man. He loved me. At least he knew what love was. What his limits were."

Sheppard was laughing now, so mad he could spit. He touched ninety and wanted to yank the wheel left and send them rocketing over the void, just to see her fear as they hurtled toward the Pacific.

"I always lose with you!" she said. "You're like a curse on my life. You're like a curse on everything."

"I'll be gone tomorrow."

"Who's next for you, I wonder? What lucky lady doesn't know that sometime soon Sam Sheppard's coming to suck her dry."

"You're the last one, believe me. You're a permanant fucking caution."

"I pity your wife!"

He turned and put his finger in her face. "Don't you dare talk about my wife!"

She screamed—at something ahead of them, her eyes widening while she threw both hands against the dash.

And in the split second that he turned back toward the road and punched the brakes, Sheppard saw the form—and brown hair, the exact color of his wife's—right before impact, and what he wanted to scream was "Marilyn!" sure that some horrendous coincidence or demonic convergence had brought her hundreds of miles down from Big Sur to this road at *this* instant, that the body they'd struck was hers. The sound was sickening, the crunching and tearing of flesh and bone synchronized at impact, more detonation than collision, followed by the thud of it under the right rear wheel as they fishtailed. His time spent racing cars saved their lives: instead of correcting, he turned into their spin, the MG rising briefly on its left wheels like a catamaran and then immediately retouching the road, a banshee whine during all three revolutions while they drifted into the other lane and then came to rest, pointed in the same direction they'd been headed.

A good hundred feet beyond the smash, they sat for several seconds in silence.

"What was that?" Susan said. "My God, was that a woman?"

Sheppard put the car in reverse, flooring the accelerator and stopping within view of what looked like a limb. "Stay here," he said, then pulled the emergency brake and got out.

By training, the rush of adrenaline conferred on him a hyperalertness and cool. The brake lights had cast the scene red, and though his mental state was one of crisis assessment he felt palpable relief on seeing that the limb belonged to a dog. He went toward the body—it was a large breed, a standard poodle—and only when he got within a couple of feet could he tell the animal was still alive.

He stood over her. She was lying on her right side, and the gash where the front leg had been sheared away revealed entwined snakes of muscle that were corded and shining in the crimson light.

He kneeled down. Her torso was black with blood, her hind legs broken severely near the paws. Both proximal tibias were compounded at the joints, bent toward the road like a pair of kickstands. Blood leaked from her ears and mouth, yet she still possessed comprehension. At the sight of him, of master and man, she lifted her head up to face his and whimpered, curling the forelimb beneath her in surrender.

"There now, girl," he said. "There, there."

He felt her neck: no collar.

"I'm going to take care of you," he said, then marched back to the car.

"Is it a woman?" Susan asked. "Or a boy?"

He said nothing and opened the trunk. He grabbed the lug wrench and strode away, Susan following him until the leg came into sight and suddenly retching.

Sheppard knelt down before the dog once more.

This, he thought, was the cost, every step in the chain from three years ago when he and Susan had first met leading to *this.* And things could end here if he was strong. This could be the *only* casualty, or else a harbinger of others to come. He must not let that happen.

He touched the dog's cheek, his palm now warm with her blood. She tried to get up again and yelped, then sprawled back and relaxed. "Easy," he said. Her legs curled into her—the contracted muscles at the gash alive—and she stared straight into his eyes. And the love with which she regarded him, imploring and passive and utterly obedient, *that* was what he'd defiled.

He got on one knee, took her scruff gently in his right hand, and beat on her head in blows so fast he roared, raining them down on her skull, until the wrench broke through to the road and gonged, the X splitting in half and ringing in the silence, until he himself was drenched with gore, until no sound came from her and he could hear only his own breath—Sheppard sure, for the first time he could remember, of what was right.

It's a rare thing, Richard Eberling thought, when what you most deeply wish for comes true.

He had four houses to clean today, a schedule to keep, but from home to home Marilyn accompanied him in his mind, and he recalled sitting with her on the patio, his missed chance and then her offer ("You could swim at our house after you're finished and have a chance to play"), and he thought that the harder he worked, the sooner Wednesday would come. Time would otherwise be a torture. He thought about his days in the orphanage and how he'd learned to sleep for fifteen hours if need be. But that was impossible now. Things had to be done. He kept rehearsing how his day with Marilyn would go, and every time he ran through the fantasy that ended with him going up to her bedroom, he told himself: I must be brave. I must believe. I must not hesitate for a moment. I will slide under the cool sheets and then I will tell her my secret.

He wanted to get her a gift. He thought maybe a book would be the ticket, perhaps of poetry, and while at the Newharts' house in Huntington Park he studied their massive library with its windows looking out over the water (and a bitch to dust), pulling down random volumes by authors he didn't know, flipping through the pages hoping chance itself might show him what he needed.

> *Thanks be to Venus, I too deserve the title of master,*
> *Master of Arts, I might say, versed in the precepts of love.*
> *Love, to be sure, is wild and often inclined to resent me;*
> *Still, he is only a boy, tender and easily swayed.*

I'm a boy too, Eberling thought, amazed. Tender and easily swayed. And love had resented him. If he'd become a doctor like Dr. Sam, then it might not have, and he flashed back to how the man had brushed by him when he'd said hello the other day, like he was invisible. Or the high school football game when Dr. Sam rushed out onto the field to tend to a boy who'd torn up his knee, and a pretty girl behind him sighed and said to her friend, "A doctor like that makes me want to be sick"—which made Eberling sick too. He read more but he didn't understand much of it, the following lines full of strange names and deeds—though he could imagine himself reading the poetry aloud to Marilyn. That could be his gift. She would understand it. And later, when Marilyn read it by herself, it would be like *he* was reading to her, like he was still there. She'd hear his voice when she read it. It would be like he was impossibly small while she was a giantess, and he would climb into her ear and whisper. He slid the book into the back pocket of his coveralls.

He made good time through the Newharts'—neglecting the guest room, but it seemed untouched since last week—and he had the Bradfords' house next, where he was sure he'd find something for Marilyn. Mrs. Bradford's mother, Priscilla, lived in the bedroom above the garage. The old coot didn't even know her name anymore but she had a drawer full of jewelry organized in little decorative boxes and grouped by type (rings, earrings, necklaces) and on top of this dresser was a multishelved glass box full of odd knickknacks: a silver fish whose mouth was a locket that opened, a ring with a secret compartment behind the stone, a delicate watch with a black face and gold hour and minute hands. The key to taking anything from here was putting Mrs. Bradford at ease about the old lady. "Mrs. Bradford, did you want me to bring some tea up to your mother?" Or, "Mrs. Bradford, maybe you should come up there with me when I clean, in case your mother gets upset at the sight of a stranger." And she'd touch his shoulder—a horny old girl herself—and say, "Dickie, for all she knows you're the son she never had," then light one of her thin little cigarettes and laugh.

When Eberling went up, Priscilla was sitting in the corner, her chair turned toward the back window that overlooked the lake. At first he made a big to-do, rattling his pail and mops, cleaning the toilet and tub energetically, letting the seat slam, waiting for the screen door to clap shut and to see Mrs. Bradford, whiskey sour in hand, slink down to the beach. And then he went up to Priscilla, standing so close he could see his reflection in her creamy eyes, and studied the jewelry she had on (Mrs. Bradford dressed her every morning) and once he got a fix on the rings and earrings and necklace—the hag tilting her head at him unknowingly and expectantly, like a friendly dog—he sifted through the drawers to match it all as best he could, the pearl earrings, say, or the gold locket, then held each piece up to its closest twin as if Priscilla were a mute model. Then he swapped them out and dropped her jewelry in his murky pail, the old bird helping him, in fact, turning her earrings toward him or even lifting her arm slightly when he took her hand to look at the rings.

Thinking of Marilyn, he mouthed: *I want to tell you my secret.*

Eberling had been cleaning the Bradfords' large house for two years now and had yet to meet Mr. Bradford himself. He knew he was around, though, because sometimes in the room off the master the bed was unmade, and a suit matching those in the closet was laid out across a wing-back chair. Eberling often felt the breast and pants pockets of the suit and found surprising treasure: good cigars wrapped in cellophane, monogrammed golf tees, a silver business-card holder, an engraved money clip. The key, here too, was *never* to take everything opportunity presented you, to abstain from the most obvious valuables, because these easy catches could be traps, trust's pop quizzes and employers' ambushes that he *always* left right where he found them. No, the true gifts were to be discovered beneath dressers and bedside tables, in boxes stuffed in closets marked PICTURES but with that label crossed out and therefore written off as forgotten, hidden in places where their discovery would come only during a move—or by a child or spouse rummaging through them after a loved one's death.

"Dickie?" Mrs. Bradford called. "Come upstairs, Dickie, and take a break."

Oh, she was horny, all right. She'd be waiting for him in bed, both arms outstretched against the high headboard, resting her high mound of silver hair against it too, a set of wings carved into the wood that seemed to spread from her shoulders, her drink always perfectly refreshed, the glass frosted and a cherry trapped beneath the ice like a red iris in a brown eye, her cigarette burning out in the never-to-be-filched gold tray on the bedside table. Mrs. Bradford liked to undress ahead of him for efficiency and waited now atop the sheet, which he'd dutifully wash afterward. He moved upstairs glancing at the pictures hung on the walls with their happy-family poses, with mother, father, son, and daughter alike staring just off to the right and smiling, of course. But every marriage in every house Eberling had ever cleaned had its own brand of dirt, unique as scent, as ingrained as a lifetime's cooking. Thinking this is how he would move up the stairs at Marilyn's next week, he could already smell the cigarette smoke and taste the ash and sugar in Mrs. Bradford's mouth, on her long, cold tongue, the remnants of cherry in her teeth, a touch of lipstick smeared on an incisor like dried blood, his secret already bubbling up, his mind returning to his foster home, the Eberling farm, where after moving between five different families he finally grew up, where his foster mother, Christine, would crawl into his bed if he cried out from a dream and hold him until he slipped off to sleep, who in the middle of the night pulled his boy's body on top of her as if in a trance, like the dream you sometimes have that the person beside you is someone else, who pressed his pajama bottoms down with her foot, his underwear clawed between her toes, her nails scratching his thin legs, and pulled her nightgown up, still trapped, Eberling was sure, in her lovely dream, telling him "slow, slow, slow," and who afterward took his face by the ears—Eberling fearful of her strength—and pushed it between her legs as if the head itself were separate from him, holding it there, lifting it up and down, adjusting the pitch and angle of his outstretched tongue that she sometimes pinched between her thumb and index finger, who then wiped his mouth with her hand afterward, still asleep it seemed, and whispered in his ear that he was "precious and lovely," though she never said his name, that he could "do anything he wanted," which he thought meant with his life, that he "shouldn't be afraid," that he was her "special thing."

Then: "And put your jammies on now."

He slept.

In the mornings she was always up before him, making him breakfast. "Dickie, come down and eat."

It was Christine's fault, he thought to himself now. It was the reason he was *nothing*, was no Dr. Sam, but he could be. All wasn't lost. You could still be surprised by life. Marilyn had proved this to him. He would tell her all this next week and she wouldn't be afraid. Which was the key: finding one who wasn't afraid, who believed in him. He was sure it was her. He could talk with her, could tell her his secret, and she could tell him hers. For everybody had one, didn't they?

There was time after finishing at the Bradfords' for lunch, so he drove back to Huntington Park, parking where he had that morning, the Sheppard house vacant so far as he could tell from here, and he suddenly felt anxious, full of doubt. He'd removed his prizes from his coveralls, from the pail, resting them on the dash to dry out, and though shiny and glinting they seemed paltry to him. Cheap. Marilyn would look at these things and not know what to say. They'd scare her. *He* would. The person in your mind, Eberling thought, isn't the person in the world. He must realize this. He'd made that mistake many times before, with boys in the home who told on him when he touched their penises in the bathroom stalls. The girls he tried to kiss who ran screaming to the nurses. Why would Marilyn have anything to do with him in the first place? Downgrade from Dr. Sam? Sleep with the guy from Dick's Cleaning Service? She had everything to lose, her boy and all that money, the nice house with that view, and all that unhappiness she hinted at was trumped by the previous three. He'd been a fool. He wouldn't even bring his swim trunks on Wednesday, just arrive and go about his business. Maybe not even come. Tell her he'd completely forgotten. Maybe quit working for her altogether.

It made him mad that she'd suggested any such thing in the first place.

He started his van.

I don't care if I ever see you again, he thought.

He was a little late to the Houks', not that Ethel cared. Now Mrs. Houk, there was a nice lady. Somebody who never deserved anything bad happening to her. Same for Mr. Houk, not only the mayor but also the town's best butcher, and if he was there when Eberling finished up he sometimes gave him a New York strip as a gratuity, pressing down on the cold, moist paper it was wrapped in. "Rub it in olive oil," Houk said, "sprinkle salt and pepper liberally, then four minutes high flame, no more, each side. But the secret, the most important thing, is to let it rest. Understand? Let the meat sit for half the time it's cooked so all the juices spread." Houk shook his finger at Eberling, then smacked him once on the cheek, like a father might have.

Eberling was only doing Mrs. Houk's windows today, though that was plenty to do before racing to the Humphries', and then he was finished.

I don't care if I never see you again, he thought, leaning out the Houks' second-story window, then he heard someone say his name. He thought it was Mrs. Houk and answered, and he pulled himself in to sit on the sill, waiting for his eyes to adjust, and then Marilyn emerged from that black pool.

"Hello, Mrs. Sheppard."

She seemed a little winded, maybe from the stairs, but was smiling at him brightly, just the way she had a few days ago, and the sight of her was so overwhelming it confirmed for him that we're afraid of what we want. He couldn't look at her for fear he might laugh or cower, might give himself away, so he stared at the floor. She was talking very quietly. Eberling knew how sound carried in every house as if each were a fine instrument. Mrs. Houk couldn't hear them now, but Marilyn was making sure.

"I was thinking about next week," she said, "and I was wondering if you could come over on Monday instead."

He could hear her swallow nervously. It was impossible that she was here, it was a dream, and he was so completely unseated he couldn't speak.

"Come over in the afternoon," she said. "Chip could go next door for a while. He won't bother us."

Eberling, still looking at the floor, was smiling too.

"Like I said, you could bring your swim trunks." She moved closer to him. "We could play."

He sat there silently, not moving a muscle.

"Would you like that?" she said.

"Yes," he said. "But . . ."

"But what?"

What was that he hadn't imagined this. It was all so much stranger, so much more wonderful, that he told her now what he'd thought all day. "I wish it were sooner," he said. Now that it was out, he braced himself for impact. This was the penultimate step before telling her anything he wanted from here on out, and he trembled.

"I wish it were sooner too," she said, lowering her head and speaking even more softly. "I wish it were tonight."

He exhaled loudly, through his nostrils, and looked up, feeling suddenly angry. If this was Mrs. Bradford, none of this would mean a thing to him. But this was different entirely. This was love. "Mrs. Sheppard, will you tell me something?"

"Certainly."

"You're not lying to me, are you?"

"Of course not," she said.

"You could like somebody like me?"

"Yes," she said.

"For a long time?"

She laughed her nasty laugh, a laugh that had confidence in it, conviction. "Why not?"

He looked down again, smiling at the floor. Dr. Sam wasn't here now, he thought. It was finally just the two of them.

"Monday, then?" she said.

He nodded.

"I have to go."

And she left.

For the rest of his time at the Houks' and later at the Humphries' he went through the motions stunned. Occasionally he'd catch a glimpse of his reflection doubly reflected, like when he cleaned the mirrors in the Humphries' bathroom and could see both his back and his profile, as if he'd come upon a stranger, and he took stock of himself. He was strong-armed, wiry, tanned from mornings and afternoons hanging out of windows. He had ideas. He'd do great things! He'd look back on this as the very beginning. He'd *always* remember it because this was the day he was surprised. When he realized that what he'd thought was impossible and unattainable had in fact been possible and attainable all along. Therefore what was beyond his grasp? What couldn't he do?

I wish it were tonight.

He was so filled with anticipation it was almost like madness.

He went home, showered, made dinner. Ate. He drank and turned on the Indians game. The White Sox were up in the third. He drank more. He lay down in bed, tried to sleep, pulled the pillow over his head. He had another drink and decided to reorganize all the jewelry he'd taken over the last two years, rings with rings, necklaces with necklaces, and so on. He looked at his watch. Barely an hour had passed.

I wish it were tonight.

He couldn't take it any longer.

There were fireworks tonight over the lake, the pre-Fourth show a preview of tomorrow night's big bash. He got in his car and drove back into Bay View. So many cars were jammed into Huntington Park that he had to find a space several hundred yards away. He walked toward the lake among the crowds, the families, between fathers with children on their shoulders, then climbed down to the beach and walked toward the Sheppard house, the beach full too. It was cool, windy, and as darkness descended, the first offshore salvo rose slowly, a single missile let fly, then another, the rhythm at first almost like boys playing catch, Eberling moving between people invisibly, all eyes on the water. He made his way up from the beach on the

Houks' stairs, cutting through their yard at the landing and now stood below the Sheppard house. They had company. Among the voices, he heard Marilyn say, "Oh."

Watching their porch, he could see the faces of Dr. Sam and Chip, of the Sheppards' guests—it looked like the Aherns and their two children—of Marilyn, all of them strobed by the detonations, turning white and black and red, a double image of them floating in his vision when he closed his eyes, a negative on which he now focused. Her mouth was open. The image was white.

I wish it were tonight.

The show was building toward its climax, salvo to salvos, drumbeat to full-on rolls, and he walked directly beneath the Sheppard house and tested the crawl-space door, and once the finale was bursting, once the hundreds of upturned faces from beach to park looked like the flicker of a million dead, as black as mountains on a stormy night, Eberling removed the screwdriver from his pocket and pried the door open and stepped inside.

He'd brought his long Eveready flashlight, and after deciding on a hiding place, should one be needed, he spent his time looking through the Sheppards' things: old waterskis and toolboxes, outboard replacement parts, boys' bats, stacked board games. A heavy bag hung indented in the middle of the room. When the fireworks stopped he turned out the light and sat listening in the dark. It reminded him of childhood because he could hear only grownups' voices, and after he was sure he'd slipped off to sleep he heard a door open and a light flick on, then feet creaked downstairs.

It was Dr. Sam and his boy, who was carrying the small balsa-wood airplane, broken at the wing. The doctor looked tired. He was wearing corduroy pants and a blazer, a white T-shirt underneath, and while he helped glue the wing he rested his face in one hand, yawning and talking to the boy more impatiently than he probably realized, a tone that stung Eberling for breaking the plane in the first place. They fastened a clothespin to the wing and left it resting on the worktable, then turned off the light and clomped back upstairs.

He sat in the dark, feeling like a kid who'd just triumphed at hide-and-seek, and listened to the sounds of the radio above him, the Indians game buzzing through the speaker, the announcer sounding like a taxi dispatcher with his patchy rhythms of call, then breaking out into terrific shouts, as if witnessing the start of a race or a sudden disaster, and when Eberling woke up again the house was completely silent.

I wish it were tonight.

Or was he dreaming? He came up into the kitchen, flashlight in hand, and wandered into Dr. Sam's study. He couldn't help himself. He sat down in the large leather chair, which was like sitting in the arms of something strong and alive that cradled him perfectly, and then he saw the trophies across from him in the darkness. They were the doctor's, he guessed, the plaques impossible to read but the figureheads posed midthrow or dive. He'd never won a trophy in his life and, unsure what seized him, pulled several down and broke the little gold men in half.

He came out of the study and up the small landing that led down into the living room or up into the bedrooms. He could feel a breeze off the water, and that's when he noticed himself, reflected in the mirror over the mantel, a black figure standing bent, callow, and scared. The sight had frozen his blood, and his heart, stopped for a beat, was now racing. He looked down and at his feet saw Dr. Sam, lost in the deepest sleep on the daybed—and Eberling froze once again. He came quietly down the stairs and bent down before him, Eberling's neck stuck forward like a lizard or a bird. They looked so much alike, like brothers, Eberling balder and darker skinned and slightly hunched whereas Sheppard lay long and tall. One good blast across the temple with the flashlight and he'd be out for good. Eberling might even tell Marilyn this. He's down, he'd tell her; I took care of him. He won't bother us. I'm sorry I woke you, but I couldn't wait.

He looked up the stairs. He'd promised himself to trust his instincts, that when the moment finally presented itself he wouldn't hesitate. It's sooner, he'd whisper to Marilyn, covering her mouth so she couldn't scream. It's tonight.

He straightened up and started up the landing, but then he heard a noise and froze for the third time. It was footsteps. He stepped into the living room.

Through the windows looking out onto Lake Road, he saw a shadow at the kitchen door, and then, just before he hurried back to the basement, he heard a key sliding tooth by tooth into the lock.

"Is that your theory?" Mobius asked.

Sheppard looked at him impassively.

"Is that all you have to add?"

Sheppard shifted in his chair and then cleared his throat.

"Because you've already fucked up, you know that?" When Sheppard remained silent, Mobius said. "*I* know."

. . .

Eberling stood over the both of them—Dr. Sam and Marilyn—in the bedroom, breathing so heavily at the sight, so horrified, that his heart was like a flag being ripped apart by a gale. But for that it was so quiet, so much quieter now. His cut wrist was bleeding heavily and he stood in the doorway with the flashlight slick in his hand, Eberling too afraid to turn it on. Marilyn to his left in the blackness, in her bed, pulled down to the middle of the mattress. Her pajama top was bunched near her neck, her legs hung beneath the crossbar. Her face was mashed—he could make that out now—and looked almost melted, inexpressive and glistening blackly, the black blood encircling her head like a queen's ruff. Yet Eberling wanted to touch her. He couldn't help it. Her torso was like a thing apart, unsullied from the neck down and pubis up, her breasts and belly as white as alabaster. It was the only part that was still *her,* and he wanted to love it; but this only made her seem more remote than ever; and he felt himself begin to cry. Sheppard lay between his legs, his head by Marilyn's feet. He looked perfect and unblemished in his white T-shirt.

It was all so still that it was like he wasn't here, like it was a dream, and Eberling couldn't move, even to turn away, and let only his eyes wander. So much blood was sprayed on the white walls and right up onto the ceiling that the room looked like the negative of a star-filled sky. He *had* to *go.* But it was like he was standing on the most fragile glass, or ice on the instant of liquefying. One wrong move and everything would be irrevocably changed.

Contemplating inching backward, he felt his balance falter and almost fell. The room was like something painted all around him, his very presence something that might leave a smear, and he was nearly sobbing now. Arms out, he took a timid backward step. And then, at his feet, Sheppard groaned.

He ran down the stairs, falling at the first bound and sliding down to the landing on his ass and one palm—he still carried the flashlight in the other—and leaping right into the living room, then rolling his ankle so badly it sounded like a bundle of sticks snapping. He lay clutching it for a second, fetal, and was up again, back down on his knees, and up once more. He hopped at first, moaning when he put weight on the foot, and made it out to the porch, sure he heard Dr. Sam behind. Once into the yard, he turned and saw Sheppard standing inside—or at least a black form in a white shirt.

Down the steps toward the beach with the doctor pounding behind, at the boathouse he almost jumped the rail and thumped down the steps onto the sand. His back cracked when Sheppard hit him, a crunch that shot right up to his neck—and the doctor was now on top of him, swinging at his face like a drunk, his arms as unwieldy and soft-limbed as if he were asleep, his grip weak. Eberling kicked at his midsection, lifting his whole body up, and pulled at the collar of his T-shirt so hard that it tore away, Sheppard flying over his body and then landing in the water behind him.

They faced each other on their knees, Sheppard's hands at his sides. He looked disoriented, drugged.

Eberling hammered his jaw with the flashlight—a massive blow that landed the doctor face-first in the water, and Eberling mounted his back, took his neck in his arm, and twisted the chin toward him violently. "Why did *you* get to have her?" He shook him. "Why *you*?"

But the doctor couldn't hear anything now.

Eberling let him drop into the water again and stared for a moment at his bare white back. He took the T-shirt floating like a jellyfish and used it to staunch his own wound. Then he turned, gimping along the wave break toward Huntington Park, broke right, up the hill into the woods, and once he was webbed deep in a thicket, once he thought twice of being found with such evidence, he threw the shirt away and blindly climbed out.

Mobius shook his head.

"No closure," Mobius said. "No real ending."

They didn't speak for a long time.

"Unless," Mobius said, "you're lying." He limped to the cell door, wrapped his hands around the bars, and pressed his rottweiler's mouth to the gap. "I'll give you one more chance. Did you kill your wife?"

"No."

"I don't believe you."

"It doesn't matter."

Mobius let go and sat down. "On the other hand," he said, "it's perfect in a way."

Sheppard had gone white with rage. "Perfect?"

"No one really knows what happened to her," Mobius said. "Maybe not even you. Isn't that remarkable? Sometime between twelve thirty and four fifteen that morning, Marilyn was sucked into a wormhole—whether we believe you or not."

Sheppard picked a chip of pipe stem from his tongue.

"Only she knows," Mobius said. "And all we can know of her now is what we imagine."

Sheppard lit his pipe, blew a stream of sweet-smelling smoke.

"That's true for us all," he said.

Once Sheppard stopped crying, purging thoughts of the dead boy from his mind, he and Marilyn got up from where they'd sat and went down to the boathouse hand in hand, and already his spirits had lifted, even more so when Marilyn told him what she was making for dinner, that everything would be fine for the party tomorrow—she'd taken care of everything—and then Marilyn kissed him, let him slide his hands under her blouse and lift her up, wrapping her legs around him so he could feed on her breasts, making no excuses and not stopping him. He could feel her added weight from the child inside her, more of her all over, and it was all so different, something had changed in her some time ago, a resistance not just to him and what he wanted but to her own awareness of what she needed; it had all somehow completely broken down. She let herself down and undid his trousers, slipping out of her own shorts and panties as well, climbing his body again as if he were a tree, taking him inside her, her hazel eyes tearing up slightly and her face flushed. She let him kiss her and she kissed him back, and though he needed and wanted her now what he wanted most was to kiss her; he would have been content with that, for he'd discovered that this kiss was the same one they'd shared from the beginning, since they were children, really, their current embrace seemingly eternal, existing before and after them, as if at this moment they were themselves a buried, undiscovered sculpture of a kiss, that was, he thought, a kind of mystery, something whose particular brand of bliss—no science could explain it—bound their lives together still, and it was through this kiss they were trying to reach down deeply into each other through this netherworld, inhabiting it and feeling for something they were sure was *there,* as if they were at once two mutes lost in a cave and the cave itself.

Later, as they walked up the steep steps from the beach to the patio, Sheppard said, "The house is awfully quiet." Marilyn, holding his hand and leaning on his arm, said, "You don't suppose Chip managed to kill himself, do you?" Truth be told, she was a little worried. And when they got upstairs and saw Chip, she gasped.

He was napping on the daybed.

Sheppard checked the time, then massaged his temples with his hand. "God," he said. "He'll never sleep tonight."

"I'd better wake him," she said, though she was afraid to start the whole process. She looked at her husband and he at her and their exchange of glances was nearly telepathic.

"Or not," she said, and then they walked quietly and quickly together upstairs.

Such afternoons, he thought later as they lay in his bed, Chip still deeply asleep, Marilyn's bed white and pristine next to them, such afternoons when the breeze blows off the water and leaves a taste of the lake in your mouth, when the tree limbs rattling against the screens becomes the world's only sound, when the body rises from sleep and is perfectly warm or cool, made Sheppard believe in God. And not the god whose son entered history, not a god of specific instructions and protocols who rewarded good behavior eternally with afterlife or punished conversely for the opposite, which no doctor who'd seen as much senseless trauma as Sheppard had could ever rightly believe, but rather a god of *this* moment, an even more generous god who conferred on those who fought through all the obstacles of love, and held on through all of its cycles, this perfect silence, this tranquility, this bliss. He held Marilyn to him. He touched her hair. He kissed the top of her head. Never in their lives together, not even when they were children, had they made love as they had these last few weeks. Sheppard, trying not to wake her, sat up gently and stared out the window at the lake, where a sailboat bounced like a toy triangle on the cast-iron and white chop. He realized now when it had started. Not just the lovemaking, but his and Marilyn's recycling, this new era, the *change.* It had started in Big Sur, after the long, three-hour drive north from Los Angeles, when Chappie told him how his and Jo's life together was falling apart, Jo onto his affairs now, the mistress he kept in Santa Monica, Susan Hayes on Sheppard's mind the whole time, whose sex for so long had seemed so important to him but was now somehow diminished, who'd panicked at the sight of the dying dog, bending over to vomit in the road. There was something so weak in her, he thought, as well as something explosive that made him even more so. Something that didn't know the things Marilyn knew, or had always known, about herself and about the world: something so un-Marilyn. What a strange turn of events. For so many years he'd seen Marilyn in terms of lack, had compared her to other women and found her wanting, but as he drove Susan to a gas station to clean herself up after being sick he compared her—and all the women he'd been with—to Marilyn, and they all fell short. He found a Shell station a few miles down the road and Susan got out of the car, taking her purse with her, and that, too, bothered Sheppard. Why take her purse? What could possibly be in it that she needed? He watched her walk toward the restroom, her heels clicking smartly even in the gravel, like a woman newly arrived to the party, about to make an entrance, and he realized immediately that it was her makeup she needed. She still believed, even now, despite the puke covering her mouth and chin and the sleeve of her coat, that she needed to look pretty, to pull herself together—whereas Marilyn wouldn't care. After several minutes she emerged from the bathroom and took her seat. They didn't speak. Their fight had permanently shattered something between them, shattered or exposed it, something that somehow called attention to the fact that this was an arrangement, their time together a last fling, a brief vacation that was almost over: futureless. They were so close to the end that even basic consideration was no longer necessary.

Don't have too *much fun.*

He wanted to get home to his wife.

"My purse," Susan said when they arrived at the hotel. They hadn't spoken the whole last hour of the drive.

"What about it?"

"I left my purse in that bathroom back there."

Back there might as well have been Mars.

"My watch," she said. "It was in my purse. My mother gave me that watch. And now it's gone."

He waited.

"If you hadn't hit that stupid dog, none of this would've happened."

Sheppard could not help it. He looked at her for a long time, then he laughed. He changed out of his horrid clothes, showered, and then made his bed on the couch.

In the morning, before dropping her off at her apartment, he took her out to breakfast. She'd asked him to, and he was hungry himself, and this would be his last chance to grab a bite before driving to Big Sur. They ate in silence. What else was there to say? By chance, there was a jewelry store across the street, and he walked her there after paying the check and told her to pick out any watch she wanted. Without hesitating she choose a Lady Elgin, tapped on the glass with her fingernail, the exercise joyless, a quid pro quo he regretted immediately, her final little *Fuck you,* and he promised himself to expense the gift, to treat it all as a write-off and be done with it. In front of her apartment she said she'd write him, Sheppard knowing full well she wouldn't, or that if she did it would simply be to tell him what they both knew: they'd never see each other again.

"So that's it," she said.

She looked awful. Though she'd showered this morning, her makeup was caked on like an extra face. He saw her as an old woman and was disgusted. What a mistake I could have made, he thought. "I have to go," he said.

It was during the drive with Chappie, while listening to him describe how he'd completely detonated his own life and was entertaining moving to Cleveland and coming to work at Bay View (home, Sheppard thought), that he reviewed those last hours with Susan Hayes and realized the only woman he'd ever truly cared about was Marilyn. For a time, yes, others had seemed terrifically important, but that importance was bound entirely to his love for his wife and a reflection of how they'd managed to lose each other. It suddenly seemed so obvious. And all he wished for now was that Chappie could make the drive go faster so he could tell Marilyn all this sooner, so between then and now he didn't lose her again somehow. And when they did arrive at Chappie's ranch, he stepped into the living room where the girls were sitting by the fire, the mood already wounded the moment Jo and Chappie looked at each other, it being clear, by how the girls were seated on the couch, knee to knee and face to face, Marilyn's right hand almost touching Jo's left, that emergency plans had been made, exit strategies discussed—for Jo, and possibly for Marilyn herself. Women together make plans, he thought. Men and women together unmake them. No, Sheppard thought, he wouldn't have it. It couldn't be allowed. He'd come to a realization. He went straight to his wife. "I have something to tell you," he told her, as if Jo weren't even there. He took his wife's hand.

"Can it wait?" she said.

"It can't," he said.

He took her other hand and helped her up and led her out of the room, wanting to put his arm around her (though she only let him take her elbow), leaving Jo and Chappie to their own decisions, guiding Marilyn through the stables, where he finally let her go, and to the fence that ran along the edge of the Chapmans' property and overlooked the ocean. Then he told her what he'd realized: that the two of them had somehow fallen so far apart, and had been for so long now, that it seemed their resting state, that this was the source of their unhappiness and that this awareness of the growing gulf between them was not only what kept them from crossing it but also, oddly, from falling even further away.

"We only orbit each other now."

"Be careful who you call 'we.' "

"I want you," Sheppard said. "I just want to feel your want too."

Marilyn shook her head. She'd leaned her chin on the fence. "You make it sound like it's me."

"No," he said, "it's us. I'm not good at this, but I've thought about it. I think that if we can feel each other then it's going to improve."

He wasn't sure if she understood, but he knew she was listening. If he could feel her want, he went on, if he could prove to her that he'd always be there to feel it, then they'd be complete. She'd be as close to everything to him as another person ever could be. At this point, he didn't care how she took this or what she decided to do. So much had happened between them, he admitted, perhaps unforgivable things, but to apologize now would oversimplify the matter. They'd gone thousands of miles past things like fault. He just wanted her to know that he believed this to be the answer. It was, he said, their diagnosis.

"And it's going to improve," he said.

Marilyn said nothing. All she did was take his arm.

It began there, Sheppard thought, at that very moment, everything that had changed between them, and then it continued that night. He rose from a deep sleep, unsure of where he was, to discover Marilyn naked with her head between his legs (unsure initially, in fact, that it was even her), his cock in her mouth and his balls in her hand, squeezing them firmly, easing off, and pressing the heel of her hand into the bulb of his penis, spreading his scrotum taut, a generous pressure she exerted against his pelvic bone, her lips tracing out the heart shape of his glans, bottom up and top down, with a rhythm to the whole loving exercise she'd never imparted to it before, which she varied and changed and would herself decide when to finish—for when Sheppard sat up and tried to kiss her she pushed his chest down with her free hand, kneading and descending and rising on him again, as if his orgasm must be gathered from the bottom of his body's well. He fell back and closed his eyes; it was pitch-dark in the room, but he could hear the sea and imagined lying on the sand, with Marilyn a goddess risen from the water to pleasure him as she was now, because the knowledge she demonstrated, her care and expertise, was so completely strange and divine. She stopped and then kissed her way from his stomach to neck, never letting him go until he was inside, pressing her hands to his shoulders as if he were a pinioned bird, and when he finally did come he felt the synchronous sea-wash inside her that then dissolved in a long, quiet dark between them like foam.

In their bedroom now, in Cleveland, as Sheppard remembered, the wind of the lake blowing through the trees whose limbs rattled the screens, Marilyn touched his back and said, "What are you thinking about?"

"I was thinking about Big Sur," he said, and smiled.

She smiled back and took his hand.

"Feel," she said, placing his palm on her stomach, and together they felt the small fillips.

"Boy," he said.

"Girl."

That was where it started, Sheppard believed; and that night he was sure was when this child had been conceived. He believed in science, not omens, yet the thought of this child's conception occurring in such a state of joy also bestowed on him a sense of calm about the success of the pregnancy, both the fetus's and Marilyn's health. "It's almost six," he said, standing up.

Marilyn grabbed her watch in disbelief. "Oh, God," she said. "When are we due at the Aherns'?"

"Quarter to seven."

"How the hell am I going to get dinner ready?"

He shrugged and said, "I'll help." And she gave him a look, standing up herself and pulling on her underwear, her shorts, buttoning her bra, her blouse. "I don't need that kind of help."

Of course it would be disingenuous to pretend they'd simply sailed on after that moment, he thought as he woke Chip. Too much had happened. There was too much history. Weeks later, after they'd returned from California, sure now that they were in the clear, he'd come home to find Marilyn in the kitchen, smoking and staring out the window onto Lake Road. She didn't turn when he greeted her, and when he asked where Chip was, she explained she'd sent him off to her father's house for the evening. On the table before her was the expense report, the amounts circled in red—for the hotel room, the repairs to Michael's car, the watch—all these pages forwarded from the hospital by Donna, along with a personal letter from Susan that said, he imagined, that everything was over.

"Go ahead," Marilyn said. "I'm waiting."

He sighed, then recounted everything that had happened with her in California clinically and dispassionately—how he'd felt about it: "That was before."

"Before what?"

"Before Big Sur," he said. "Before now."

She stubbed out her cigarette, watching its last smoke rise, its odor fade, an odd combination of anger and humility pervading the room. "You think," she said, her voice both choked and furious, "in straight lines." She lit up again, then wrapped one arm around her waist and propped her elbow against her hand. "Like there's a beginning and an end."

"I don't know what you mean," he said.

"*This.*" She picked up the papers on the table and shook them. "This is the same thing all over again. We just go round and round."

"No," he insisted. "That was before."

Marilyn took a long drag on her cigarette. "I'm going to my father's," she said.

He was in no position to argue. There was, he believed, a beginning and an end. The walls had tumbled down. They were off the loop, but only if she believed.

She stayed at her father's for a week. They didn't speak for three full days. After that, she called him once in the morning, once at the hospital every afternoon, and once at night. They didn't say much to each other, virtually nothing at all. She just wanted to know where he was, she said. He kept the house as clean as he could manage, but when she returned a week later with their boy, her first words were, "What a wreck." And later, after sending Chip upstairs, she said, "Prove it."

"Prove what?"

"That it's going to improve."

It required nothing miraculous of him. He simply had to be there, for Marilyn and for his son. There, as in inhabiting his life at home. There, as in treating *now* first. On a practical level it was the simplest thing: He took the boy off his wife's hands when he returned from work. When she asked him for something—a favor, a last-second errand, or help with a household chore—he gave it. When she came to bed they talked. But spiritually and psychologically it was entirely different and required what couldn't be faked: he was there. Whereas before he'd seen his wife and son as a kind of encroachment on his life, their needs as something that halved and rehalved the distance between him and what he wanted, and he'd therefore at every turn resisted every little thing asked of him, now he did the opposite. And he could feel the small joy it added to everything, and which in turn added accrued interest. It was so simple, really. He was just *there,* which was not only what Marilyn wanted but also what he discovered he did too, and which had the effect of spreading his joy to her, that same joy enfolding their lives as if under a giant set of wings. It was Marilyn who had, a month later and unprompted by Sheppard, announced at dinner with his parents and his brothers and their wives that she was pregnant. It was still a little early, the beginning of June, before she was even through her first trimester, but she wanted to tell them when they were all together. And while her pregnancy with Chip had been fraught with anxiety, haunted by her mother and brother's death, and came afterward to symbolize their marriage's turn for the worse, the beginning of his sustained absence, her own loss of freedom, and the end of their sex, now she seemed eager to embrace this new child. And at the dinner table, while her sisters-in-law gathered round to congratulate her, Sheppard was stabbed with regret and pained for Chip, fearful his son might have inherited some of these doubts he and Marilyn had conjured up, their collective angst passing from their souls to him via the womb.

I have to be a better father, he thought, walking with Chip over to the Aherns' house. I've failed him in so many ways. Was it possible that the boy had registered his absence all along? Was a child's sense of love and its lack that refined? Were the things Chip took so long to learn, like tie his shoes or cut his food, his attempt to call out to him, confirming with each little assisted task that his father was there? He and Chip looked a great deal alike and both could sleep through an artillery barrage, yet the similarities ended with that. In fact, the boy had the worst of both of them. He lacked Sheppard's athleticism and the confidence that came with it, but had Marilyn's emotionalism and sulkiness, her moods, in spades. He was so utterly remote, Sheppard concluded, that it must have been caused by what had transpired. You could be saved, he thought, but never fully. He and Marilyn had been saved, but for Chip there'd been a cost.

He came up behind the boy and lifted him into his arms. "Your father loves you very much," he whispered.

But Chip squirmed loose without looking at him and ran ahead.

Bless Don Ahern. The man could make a drink. A martini was simple enough, but his just tasted different, and far better. They stood on the back lawn watching the boats gather for the fireworks show, families starting to congregate on the beach. Ahern's son and daughter had included Chip in a game of Keep Away and Nancy was walking toward Marilyn, meeting her midway between their houses, a whiskey sour for her in hand. "I'll bet you've had a day," Nancy said.

"A day and a half," Marilyn answered—and gave Sheppard a look.

"I'll tell you what," Ahern muttered. "That lady of yours still has the figure of a girl."

They watched their wives take each other by the arm and clink glasses, Marilyn catching Sheppard's eye once more. Was it possible, he wondered, that he could still be aroused? He felt so physically spent right now that no matter what reserves he tried to tap he knew this was going to be a short night. Yet he felt like taking her now, all over again, excusing themselves for the evening, to sound the depths of this joy.

"Work any miracles today, Doc? Save any lives?"

"Actually," Sheppard said, "I lost a boy."

He ran through the story again, finally able to talk about it without seeing it all in his mind. It had become a story, encapsulated, having a beginning, middle, and end, and in the version he told Don, the father became a bit player, not the central figure who'd forced Sheppard to flee the hospital in a near panic because earlier he'd felt guilty as charged. He *was* a killer, not of the boy, but the murderer of his and Marilyn's days together. And even worse, he still needed these angels to come into his life and wake him up to facets of his character at once pathetic and sad, chiefly his own rapacious nature. If that boy hadn't died and his father hadn't berated him, Sheppard might have forgotten his sorry actions, might yet be unappreciative of Marilyn, might still be that unknown to himself. My first instinct will never be to put other people before me, he thought.

"Well," Don said, "I'm sure you did everything you could."

"Yes," he said. "I'm sure of that."

Then Marilyn approached. "The hospital just called," she said. "A boy broke his leg. They want you to come down and have a look."

In the x-ray room, Sheppard examined the break the boy had sustained, a clean fracture taken off a brother's shoulder to his thigh playing in a friendly scrimmage that with a cast, gravity, and musculature would set and finally seal as strong as it was before. Eight weeks and the boy would be fine, he figured, and when he sat at Hunter's bedside while the attending made the cast, he said something it seemed he repeated all the time at his job: "You'll be like new." It was another one of those automatic expressions whose overuse hid its built-in, deep-seated hope, along with the human questions it always begged. Was there progress? Did we actually become better people? His wife had accused him of thinking in straight lines, when in fact nothing was further from the truth. For so many years he'd thought of their lives as a toiling of cycles, and that had been his own self-serving justification, his rationale for license. There was no improvement, only reprieve, and neither of them could really change, so he must gorge himself on every opportunity life presented him. But did he still believe that, even now? If so, did that mean he was destined to slip again? Would this moment of joy be eclipsed by the next phase of sadness? Or could you finally grow beyond certain forms of evil and sin? This place where he and Marilyn now found themselves, wasn't it somehow possible to make it endure? So he someday could tell his unborn son or the daughter Marilyn thought they were having: *I changed. We changed. We became happy, and from that point on, child, everything was different.* If only, he thought. Please let me be able to say that and then pass along genuine hope, instead of the hopeless advice to simply wait, to just hang on.

I want to *arrive,* he decided, pulling out of the hospital. I want to be finished. I want to be done with the person I was.

Back at home, Marilyn and Nancy were frantic and he could hear the kids screaming in the background. Don, exasperated, told them to keep it down. "I'm trying to listen to the game!"

Marilyn came out of the kitchen. "We're really running behind with dinner," she said.

Sheppard checked his watch: quarter to nine. "What can I do?" he said.

Nancy touched her fingers to her chest in amazement. "Is he offering his assistance?"

"I think so," Marilyn said.

"Are you feverish, Sam?" Nancy rubbed her hands in her apron, then felt his forehead. "Is something wrong?"

"I'm fine."

"All right," she said, and nodded. "You can take the kids off my husband's hardworking hands before he kills them."

"I can do that."

Seizing this chance to be with his boy, Sheppard hustled them all to the basement and turned on the light in the back, where he'd set up the heavy bag. "How about we learn how to throw a punch?" he said. Todd, the Aherns' oldest, was crazy for the idea, but Jennifer and Chip seemed a little scared.

"Don't you want to do this, son?"

"I don't know if I'll like it," he said, twining his arms together shyly and stretching the tangle toward the bag.

"Well, let's give it a try."

He felt it was important to first set down some rules: never to punch each other once they learned how, and never to punch other children unless, of course, they'd been hit first. Then he threw a couple jabs and right crosses, then some solid body shots, emphasizing the proper form, the importance of always keeping your hands up, your feet planted—"The ground's where you get your strength," he said—the kids agog at how far the bag moved when he hit it, the three of them blinking with each blow as if the force of impact blew puffs of air into their eyes. His exertion seemed to get them all riled up, even more than they were before upstairs, and sooner than he'd expected, Chip was whaling away on the bag while Todd held it steady, laughing when he stopped to shake out his hands. When

Sheppard bent toward him to tell him how well he was doing, Chip ran up and gave his leg a bear hug. The top of Chip's head was sopping wet, and he rubbed it gently while his son looked up at him.

"Dinner in five," Marilyn called.

He told the children to clean up. Sheppard was sweating himself and went upstairs to wash his hands. The breeze off the lake was stronger and cooler now, and he felt chilled. Trembling, his teeth chattering, he grabbed his corduroy jacket off the back of his bedroom door, then went downstairs. Nancy and Marilyn were at the last stages of setting the patio table, Don already in his chair, the cottage ham and green beans and rye bread set out, the blueberry pie baking in the oven, the aroma annihilating all other thoughts in Sheppard's mind, the children served already and seated in the kitchen, far enough from earshot for adult conversation but close enough to be heard if need be. Neither Marilyn nor the Aherns had heard him come downstairs, and Don, who installed ventilation systems for hospitals across the state, was in the middle of a story about Hoversten. Sheppard stood by the television for a moment and listened.

"He'd be a liability and a half if Sam took him on. You know how he lost his last job, don't you? At Grand View Hospital?"

"No," Marilyn said. "Sam wouldn't say."

"I want to hear this," Nancy said.

"He got frozen out by every single female member of the hospital staff."

"Frozen out? As in what?"

"As in ignored. Rendered invisible. Literally annulled. I mean, from secretaries to orderlies to the nurses themselves. He'd groped so many of them, said so many lewd things, that after several senior women complained to the administration and were rebuffed, one day they just stopped working with him. One of the chief surgeons told me it was the damnedest thing he'd ever seen. He figured they must've had a meeting the night before, because the next day literally every woman on the staff agreed to pretend Hoversten didn't exist. It was *that* coordinated. He walks in the hospital, asks for his surgery schedule, and the secretary walks away from her desk like he's a ghost she can't see. Hoversten figures she's either crazy or playing a joke, so he gets his rotation himself and scrubs in but can't get a single nurse to help him with his gloves or gown. When he calls out, it's like they're all deaf. They won't even glance in his direction. He walks into the theater for a routine tonsillectomy and nobody's there but him and the patient. Of course, the chief of staff is furious once he gets wind of what's going on—and that's within minutes, because Hoversten's standing in surgery screaming his lungs out. So he pulls the head nurse aside and orders her back to work, at which point she lays down her ultimatum: It's us or him. Either Hoversten goes or the whole hospital shuts down. So the chief, who's had to put up with his goosing nurses and ogling patients for months, sits him down in his office, explains the situation, and tells him to pack his things."

Marilyn covered her mouth.

Nancy clapped her hands and laughed. "Who says there's no justice?"

They all went quiet as soon as Sheppard entered.

"At ease," he said. "I'm not mad. Quite honestly, it's news to me." He turned to Marilyn. "Where *is* Les, by the way?"

"He went golfing," Marilyn said. "In Kent."

"Who with?"

She hesitated. "Dr. Stevenson."

Nancy looked at her.

Don, a little late, rubbed his hands together and said, "*Yum,*" then began to serve himself.

"Is he going to join us?" Sheppard said.

"I think he's gone for the rest of the weekend," Marilyn said.

He couldn't stand the silence but was too tired to be frustrated—at Hoversten's negligence or everyone's discomfort. "So," he said, "more pie for me then."

That too was before, he thought. And *before* was as much the people you surrounded yourself with as a state of mind. Perhaps Don was more right than he knew, and Hoversten was a liability not just for the hospital but also Sheppard's own new life. Why honor the years they'd known each other, given everything that had happened? Why keep him near? Like everything else he wanted *out* of his life, why not just let the man pass—though at the mention of Dr. Stevenson, he couldn't help but recall an episode they'd had several months before Stevenson had broken off his engagement to Susan Hayes. They were scrubbing in, alone together, Sheppard making small talk about the Indians game the night before, aware with each word of his little secret, the memory of sex with Susan that very morning fresh on his mind.

"Dr. Sheppard," Stevenson interrupted, "may I say something?"

"Of course."

"While I'm working under you, you can count on me to give you my complete dedication as a resident. I'll follow any orders or procedures you ask of me to the letter. I'll learn *everything* you have to teach me. But beyond that," he said, now facing him directly, "I don't want to hear a goddamn word out of your mouth."

Sheppard turned to look at him, taking in his furious expression, his raised finger between them, then glanced away because he was smiling. He couldn't help it. He was on the verge of laughter. Something about the man's melodrama seemed so rehearsed, his righteous anger having no more impact than a whiffed punch. He felt oddly embarrassed for the both of them. Above the sink, in the reflection in the window looking into the surgical theater, he saw Stevenson turn away from him and scrub brutally at his hands, and then he saw his own smiling reflection, but his smile reminded him of a drunk's, with an enormous gap between his expression and what was in his brain. A drunk would smile as easily at an insult as a word of praise. Was that what suddenly disgusted him so much? (His revulsion was suddenly so sharp he wanted to run out of the room.) Was it that he had no response to Stevenson's demand except to smile? Or that his first reaction to something so serious, which involved other people's hearts, was the most damning? You care about nothing, he had thought.

Even now, sitting on the patio, the memory made him wince.

The kids came out during dessert, only seconds before the first fireworks started, as if they each had their own built-in clock set to announce the celebration. Chip sat on his mother's lap but Sheppard signaled him over, took him between his knees, and explained how the explosives worked and how the lovely shapes were formed. The shell on top of each rocket was stuffed with black powder and explosive stars, each one a light you see in the sky, the bursting charge down the middle timed to go off after the rocket reached a certain altitude, thus igniting the powder and throwing the stars away from it with uniform force and in prearranged patterns—flowers or concentric circles—and those bursting half a second later in brilliant color. "Those are chain reactions you're seeing." And whether or not Chip understood, he looked on attentively and, when the show reached its crescendo, the explosions rattling the silverware on the table, he clutched Sheppard's legs, his little fists bunching the corduroy.

"I always get depressed when it ends," Nancy said.

Don gathered up their kids to take them next door and put them to bed while Nancy and Marilyn cleared the dishes. Before leaving, he turned on the radio; the Indians were up by one in the middle of the seventh. Sheppard stayed seated on the patio, watching the crowds peter out below, smelling the smoke and powder that wafted off the water. Did battlefields smell like this at nightfall?

He slept.

When he woke, Chip was tugging at his arm. He looked at his watch. It was half past ten.

The boy was in his pajamas, with a balsa-wood airplane, a glider, in his hands. "Dad, will you please help me fix this?"

Sheppard looked at it. The wing was broken on the left side, split but not shorn away. The boy almost never came to him for help. "It's past your bedtime," he said, rubbing his hair, "but since you asked like an adult, yes. Let's go see what we can do."

By now Marilyn and Nancy were seated in front of the television, talking lazily, Nancy lying on the couch. Don sat by the radio, the top of his head pressed against the wall and his eyes fixed on the ceiling, staring so intently while he listened it was as if there was a screen there.

"Do you mind if I smoke?" Nancy said.

"No," Marilyn said. "There's an ashtray on the patio."

She got up. As Sheppard passed by Marilyn's chair she reached out to him, taking his forearm in her fingers and gliding her nails down his wrist and across his palm.

"We're going to fix his airplane," Sheppard said.

"Before you do that," she said, "will you lock the patio door?" But Nancy was already locking it, the ashtray in her other hand.

In the basement, Sheppard turned on the light, led the boy over to his workshop, got his Elmer's glue, and explained to Chip how to spread it lightly across the bottom of the wing, struggling to keep his patience as the boy squirted the white liquid onto the tabletop. "You have to squeeze it carefully," Sheppard said. He found a bunch of clothespins in a bucket by his tools and handed him two of them. "Now," he said, "how can you clip these on so the wing holds its original shape?" He watched, so exhausted he thought he might fall asleep right here, as the boy pinched the wing between the clothespins and looked to him for confirmation, thinking again that something was wrong with him. There was a fissure in his character that made him manifestly uncertain of everything. When he fixed the clothespins on each side of the wing, pinching it back into shape, Sheppard was sure that the plane was permanently crippled.

"Do you think it will fly again?"

"We'll see," Sheppard said, turning the plane upside down with the broken wing atop a tin can, the weight of the body helping to restore its aerodynamic line.

Chip's shrug was a perfect imitation of his mother. "At least we tried," he said.

Upstairs, Sheppard handed him off to Marilyn, who took him to his room, and then he sat down in her chair and crossed his arms.

"Are you cold?" Nancy asked.

"A little," he said. On the television screen, a man in a suit was standing next to the Planters Peanuts character, talking to the mascot as if he weren't dressed in an absurd costume, his only replies coming in hand signals and dance moves. "What are we watching?" Sheppard said.

"A brief word from our sponsor," Nancy said.

"Is there anything else?"

"There's a movie coming on in a second."

Feeling Nancy's eyes on the back of his head, he turned around and saw her lying on their sofa smoking a cigarette, the top two buttons of her blouse undone.

"I'm sorry about the boy," she said.

"I am too," he said.

"Do you dream about it—about things that happen to you during the day?"

"Sometimes," he said.

He'd always found Nancy attractive. She seemed to realize this, acted like she felt the same way about him, and always spoke very intimately whenever they were alone. This, however, made their conversations weirdly stilted.

She nodded at him weightily, utterly stumped.

There was a time when he'd looked for sex everywhere, trying to sniff out discontent or interest in every woman he met, as if every interaction was like a door to a new opportunity, another possible reality, every conversation not about the thing itself but something else. Now everything had shifted back.

Marilyn came downstairs. "I think he's going to sleep," she whispered, then sat in his lap and buried her face in his neck, putting her lips to his ear. "He's going to sleep," she said, and the words themselves made him shiver in pleasure.

Behind them, Don clapped once and winced in guilt at the noise he'd made. "Sorry," he said. "The Indians won," and then he looked at Sheppard and Marilyn and then at his wife, who said, "I need some affection too."

He cleared his throat and moved over to the sofa, where she laid her head across his lap. "How's that?" he said, and patted her shoulder.

Nancy looked at Marilyn and shook her head.

"Well, it's something," she said.

The movie was called *Strange Holiday* and from what Sheppard could gather—with Marilyn nuzzling his cheek and neck—it was about a man who goes off on a fishing trip in the deep woods and returns to find the country taken over by fascists. He could've poked a hundred holes in the premise but instead he pressed his face into Marilyn's hair.

"Do you know what I was thinking about?" she whispered.

"Tell me."

She slid her hand down between her legs and his and squeezed. "I was thinking about Sandusky."

"That was nice," he said.

"Sandusky was *very* nice," she said.

He thought for a moment of the cottage they'd rented there just two weekends ago, having sex morning and night. Marilyn was rubbing him now as surreptitiously as possible and he wanted to laugh, feeling as aroused as he'd been earlier when watching her take that drink from Nancy between their houses. He'd driven in an amateur car race that weekend, his penis sore between his legs, thrumming with every lap, and every time he roared by the grandstand he'd been able to pick Marilyn out among the hundreds of people, as if hers was the only face not in motion, her features strangely distinct.

"Are you sleeping?" she said.

"Let me get up," he said.

"Stay."

"I'll be back." Then he got up and went to the daybed and lay down.

He slept.

He sat up. Everyone was watching the movie, and Marilyn turned to him as if somehow signaled by his waking. She waved him over as he rubbed his eyes. "Come watch," she said.

He looked at the screen: a man seated behind bars was repeating the same phrase over and over.

"Come on, Sam," she said. She tilted her head and smiled. "It's going to improve."

He chuckled at the allusion and then lay down again and looked at her, his arms crossed over his chest like in a Mexican standoff, and he smiled back. She shrugged and turned around. He stared at the back of her head for a moment, at her hair through the bars of the rocker, at her blouse with its little wing designs, at the athletic curve of her legs, one crossed over the other, at the moccasins on her feet. She'd let one half slip off and was tapping it against her heel.

It is possible, he thought, to be completely happy in marriage—though you must be willing to hold on when your ship was lost at sea and there was no guarantee of rescue. They had both held on, at times by means unbeknownst to the other that might not look to an outsider like holding on at all. It is possible to be completely happy. And just as surely that happiness could pass. It was a fact. As it was that when the new came, it seemed like it would last forever, endure as a permanent blessing, carrying with it the promise that it could be tended, like a flame. Tend this, he thought. Let it last.

Pleased, he slipped off to sleep.

Marilyn woke.

She was still in the rocking chair when Don gently shook her shoulder and she looked up at him, startled. Except for the kitchen, nearly all the lights were out in the house, and Marilyn could hear Nancy putting up the last of the plates. "Don't do any more," she said, standing up and squinting in the brightness.

"I'm done," Nancy said, and smiled, folding up the dish towel.

"What time is it?"

"Twelve thirty," Don whispered.

They walked quietly through the kitchen and said good-bye and Marilyn was about to close the door but stopped for a moment to listen to the wind whipping the trees, then turned out the light, locked the door, and through the window watched the Aherns walking across the lawn under the trees, Nancy's arms crossed.

Poor woman, she thought. Earlier, in the lull after dessert, the two of them talking quietly by the sink, she'd said, "He doesn't touch me, and that's fine. I can take that. We're busy. Him especially. But he *avoids* me. He's avoiding me now. We get a moment together and he says, 'The *game*, Nancy, I've been waiting to listen to it,' as if this was the only game ever played. Watch, and you'll see how he keeps a space between us, like we're brother and sister chasing each other around a table." She wiped her eyes. "How did you change things with Sam?"

Marilyn didn't know. It wasn't anything *she* did. What she believed was that she'd just waited, that Sam had somehow been waiting too, until and at the same time they were both tired of waiting.

There was no other way to put it.

"It's nothing that would help you," Marilyn said. "Please, don't take that wrong. It's just . . . you have be willing to hold your breath longer than you think you can," she said.

She was sitting on the daybed with Sam now, stroking his hair. He was sprawled there in the shape of an S, facing her, his corduroy jacket on, hugging himself, his mouth open. He looked like Chip, like a boy. There was just room enough to lie alongside him and she did, listening to him breathing . . .

She woke. She was cold. She thought to wake Sam but it would take the same effort as it did Chip, and he slept down here all the time. She walked up the stairs to their room and took off her clothes in the dark, folding them neatly and setting them on the chair, putting on her pajamas and then getting under the cold sheets. She was tired of sleeping alone. She didn't care anymore if Sam woke her up. She'd asked him to push the mattresses together last week, or buy them a new bed. "I want to feel you next to me at night," she'd said. She'd remind him tomorrow.

Waiting for sleep to come, she couldn't help it: she thought about Dick Eberling, first about his body revealed in that window as he cleaned it, the plaited armadillo shell of muscles along his stomach, his dark skin browned. She bit her lower lip gently, remembering how he'd looked at the floor and asked if she could like someone like him and then, "For a long time?" It made her sad. Everyone should be lucky enough to be loved for a long time. To know what that was like—to be loved and to change, to be privileged to suffer it, to remain. To know, as she did, that there was only one person she could ever love. To know it incontrovertibly. To *accept* it, with all of the attendant limits. Once you did, it was the closest thing there was to safety.

To her delight, she heard footsteps slowly rising up the stairs and entering the room. She turned around and saw his approaching form.

"Sam?" she said.

"So," Mobius said.

"So," Sheppard said.

"Quid pro quo."

Sheppard reached under his chair and held up the manuscript.

"Is this the only copy?"

"No. But it is the original."

Sheppard slid it through the bars. Mobius hefted the pages.

"You have until tomorrow morning to read it," Sheppard said.

"All right."

"Then you'll tell me everything I need to know about Alice Pepin."

"Everything you need to know is right here."

"No, it's not," Sheppard said. "There's no ending."

"There will be," Mobius said.

Sheppard folded up his chair and carried it with him to the guard, who buzzed him out. "He's a suicide risk," Sheppard said. "Check his cell every ten minutes. And get a doctor over here immediately. Have his bandages removed and the gauze confiscated. I don't want him to have anything he can hurt himself with. Get two other guards and strip-search him. And recheck his cell. Strip his bed. Not even a blanket for the night. The only thing he can have in there is the book he's reading."

"Yessir."

Despite those orders, Sheppard thought about Mobius all day. He called downstairs to the guard repeatedly and even returned to the cellblock twice. On both occasions he entered to the sound of Mobius laughing, then stood before the bars as he sat there with tears in his eyes, pointing to the page.

"This is killing me," he said.

Seeing him calmed Sheppard down. Mobius's gauze dressing had been replaced with plastic bandages, the guard had checked the cell three times to make sure, and when Sheppard called later that evening, Mobius had just finished dinner without incident. Over the phone, Sheppard could hear him cackling in the background.

Sheppard went to bed. He slept fitfully at first, then slipped into a deep sleep and dreamed, and when he woke he remembered the whole thing completely.

He was back on the beach, chasing down his wife's killer. But the killer was Mobius, and his wife Alice Pepin. He finally tackled the little man, but he was remarkably strong and as slippery as a fish. When Sheppard tried to punch him, he whiffed, and when he tried to grapple and pin him, Mobius reversed the hold and threw him to the sand. And once again he was overwhelmed, Mobius above him now, his knees pressed to his chest, his fist raised to his ear for the final blow. And before Sheppard woke, before Mobius's punch fell and blackness came on, he suffered that same sense of terrible defeat, of having not been able to save his wife or overcome her killer, of somehow being an accomplice in the crime.

The phone.

He turned on the light by his nightstand, rubbed his eyes, looked at his watch. It was 4:15.

"Sir," the guard said. "It's Mobius."

"What happened?"

"He's dead."

"Dead?" Sheppard sat up. "How?"

"Asphyxiation."

"I don't understand."

"He choked to death, sir."

"On what?"

"I can't say a hundred percent. The paramedics are finishing up now. But it looks like he blocked his windpipe swallowing pages from that novel."

But the middle, David wrote, is long and hard.

He meant his book and he meant his marriage. At some point his book had become his marriage, or consumed his marriage. Or else his marriage had consumed his book. Did real writers suffer such problems? He certainly didn't consider himself one. Real writers kept the boundaries between art and life clear, didn't they? Knew dreams from days. They had to. Otherwise, how could they discern the arc of a story or recognize their themes? Ride narrative logic like a wave, from swell to shore. His book had become something entirely different. It wasn't a story anymore. It was him. It was Alice. It was them.

His book had become an act of cannibalism.

In the five years since her miscarriages, he and Alice had lived the same routine with minor deviations, and he hadn't made a lick of progress on his book. He hadn't written himself into a corner: he'd written himself into a round. His book and his marriage had become a long wait for something to happen.

So he welcomed this recent turn of events. True, he hadn't needed her to be hospitalized for them to come about, but now Alice was going to change her life! He wasn't sure what that meant, exactly, but chances were it was something *new*.

In the meantime, however, she remained remote, quick to temper and slow to warm; they hadn't made love in months. Sometimes, when he came home, he caught her on the phone, which quietly she hung up. "Who was that?" he'd asked. "No one," she'd say. And they left it at that. Her laptop was off-limits. Her cell phone bill was, of late, nowhere to be found. Her bank and credit card statements were gone. She was going off the grid. She often worked late. She went to suspicious meetings about which she told him nothing, wearing full-on makeup and her nicest clothes. "What's all this?" he'd asked. "What's what?" she'd say. He regarded her for a moment. How much weight had she lost? Twenty pounds? Thirty? None at all? He couldn't say she looked good, just less. But less, in Alice's case, was still more. Was she having an affair?

"I'm going to the gym," Alice told him one day.

He watched from the peephole until she was on the elevator, then rushed down the eight flights of stairs. He followed her east, toward Third Avenue, where she signaled for a taxi and landed one immediately. But when David tried to hail one, there were none to be found.

They never have these problems in movies, he thought, giving up.

He called a car service the next day and instructed the driver to wait on Third. But leaving the building she turned left toward Lexington, their one-way street headed east, and by the time the car made it around the block, Alice was gone.

He called two car services the next day, had one car waiting on Third, the other on Lex, canceling the latter once she headed east.

"Follow that cab," he told the driver.

"Seriously?" the man said.

"Just do your fucking job, all right?"

Characters in movies never have to park either, and if they do, there's always a space. If they're in a rush, they never have to start a PC. There were never delays. In the plots, no time was ever wasted, and why was that?

She got out at the Y.

Why, for that matter, did every Y smell the same? That particular brand of human humidity, of armpit and sweat sock mixed with a healthy dash of pool chlorine. Every time he'd been here, the same retarded man in his caricature's costume (thick-rimmed drugstore specs, YMCA logo on his T-shirt, too-short shorts, high tops with black socks pulled up knee high) was vacuuming the premises. Were those the only clothes he owned? Was vacuuming all he had to do? "You missed a spot," David told him, and pointed, and the man thanked him and obediently pushed his machine toward the phantom dirt. David cut through the men's locker room, a place, he thought, only Dante could have dreamed up. It wasn't that it was rank or befouled. In fact, it was quite clean and well-lit, the freshly laundered towels as warm as baked bread. By the sinks, combs stood submerged in canisters of Clubman cologne. But there were monsters here, of the human kind, men built of circles and blocks attached to each other who all seemed compelled to walk around naked, blissfully unaware, apparently, of their own deformities, as unselfconscious as children. Dripping with sweat from the steam room or sauna, their skin as red as cooked lobsters, they approached other men as casually as if they'd bumped into each other on the street. "Leland," one said, "how the hell are you doing?" and the other replied, "Slim, how the hell have you been?" *I'm not looking at your penis,* David imagined was the subtitle followed by, *I'm not looking at your penis either.* But *he* looked. It was strictly an underworld fascination, exactly what Virgil was on to when he offered the tour: such a broad selection, such a wide range of shapes and sizes, you couldn't *help* but look. Elephant penises, horse cocks, dog dicks, Jewish men's shlongs, and donkey dongs. Penises with one nut descended, with one nut, with no nuts at all. Micros on giants, macros on midgets, and vice versa. Black men's penises, the heads as pink as a dog's tongue, in sizes confirming and debunking every stereotype; Oriental penises confirming and debunking same. Circumcised penises, the foreskin pulled as tight as a facelift, so little give as they hung flaccid that it looked like they'd hurt getting hard. Even pierced penises—Prince Alberts, they were called—with the hoop poked into the shaft and out the urethra like an ox's nose ring. It was a panopticon of penises, a field of phalluses, and in the presence of so much dick all David could think of was how no laws seemed to govern the universe—no guaranteed gifts for the good or punishments for the bad, no fairness in what the Lord giveth or taketh away, except for the undeniable fact of corporeality, and thus one's own death.

He spotted Alice in the weight room. She was on her back, balanced atop an enormous ball, her feet planted on the ground, another ball held in her hands above her substantial chest. Her face flushed, she moved the smaller ball back and forth across her torso while her trainer counted out reps.

He decided to tail her the next evening. He had an excuse to leave home before she did, Jack Stoney's annual birthday bash. David had asked Alice to come but she declined.

"Let me guess," he said. "You have a meeting."

Her eyes flashed. It was the anger he didn't understand. No, it was how long she could *stay* angry that baffled him.

She got out at the Unitarian Universalist church on 76th and Central Park West, where a group of men and women stood smoking outside.

He waited several minutes before entering, but it was easy enough to find her. He heard her voice down a long hallway lined with rooms full of support groups, AA meetings and Al-Anon and NA. Co-Dependents and Debtors Anonymous. He peeked in the door. Everyone inside was fat, men who had to sit off to the side of foldout chairs, women whose shoulders and bellies were so enormous that it seemed the purses they held in their laps measured the closest their hands could come to touching. She was telling a story—he couldn't see her, but every word she spoke was clear, Alice interrupted now and again by calls of support, by yeas and amens.

"You know what I mean," Alice said. "You know what it's like to know your commute in terms of pit stops. The Hudson News stand for a magazine and a Butterfinger. And a Hershey's. And a Charleston Chew. Almond

Joy's got nuts. Mounds don't. The one that's just a short walk—so at least you're exercising—from your track. The McDonald's on Exit 13, Sprain Brook Parkway, run by hardworking Mexicans, the morning crew that keeps the grease so fresh you never have that bitter taste to the hash browns or fries—and that odd alchemy when mixed with Diet Coke. You know what I mean. You know the hot dog guy on Forty-third and Lex for a quickie before you get home. How would you like it? With everything, of course. The delicate pop when you bite the casing, the bun perfectly moist from the steam, perfectly soft. Thank you, sir, I'd like another. His stand's right across the street from the Sbarro. Fact: you upload the glucose from potatoes faster than straight sugar, my friends. How do you spell relief? K-N-I-S-H.

"You know what I mean when I say I dream crazy concoctions, that such inventions promise the same bliss as great sex. Forget Subway, my friends. *I* am the sandwich artist. Slice a Krispy Kreme in half, add a thick layer of jelly, spread the other slice evenly with whipped cream cheese. And you're not going to believe this, but trust me: Add bacon. Add bacon to anything! Peanut butter—I can't eat it but I can dream—and banana between the halves of a sliced New York pretzel. Prosciutto and fried eggplant between two slices of Sicilian. Cut away any crust. Give me tenderloin *only.*

"You know what it's like to eat the things other people neglect. The chipped chunks of fried batter from KFC, the white knuckle of ligament at the end of the drumstick; the rind stuck to the last remnants of a round of brie, the pieces at the bottom of any bag of chips poured into bowl of guacamole like it was cereal, the plastic string hung with niblets of meat that circles your bologna. You know what I mean when I say that Oscar Mayer has a way with B-O-L-O-G-N-A.

"You know shame. You know the laughs that make you fart, so you also know the double fear of laughter. You know the slip and slide of a permanently dirty ass. You know underwear as wide as a kite. Bra sizes lettered like cattle brands, with names like dude ranches: the Double F and the Triple E. You know the urban legend about the morbidly obese woman admitted to the hospital, so fat they found a rotting tuna fish sandwich under the fold of her tit. You know what it's like to check those folds to find strips of pink, inflamed, sunless flesh caulked with that gunk down the trench, the same yellow, hardened accretion you find behind babies' ears. You know the sting of a hot rag when you scrub it away. You wonder: What if I just let it grow?

"But permit me a list: You know what it's like to look up from your plate and see people looking at you. To get into a car ass first. To dread going to the movies on opening night. To have permanently forsaken wearing boots. To resent shoelaces, loathe stairs. To know that if you were accosted, you couldn't run. To see a report on obesity on CNN, the teaser when they show people from ass to neck and think, 'Oh my God, that midsection's me!' To see everyone look down when you board a plane. To see the humped space between seats on a bus and think it's for the crack of your ass. To weigh more than your husband. To be woken by your own snoring. To think you look like a pig when you're wearing the mask of your sleep apnea machine.

"You know what it's like to feel trapped in your own body. To feel as if you're a cripple. An addict when it comes to food. To say, 'Today, I'm going to get this under control.' You know when the pain of hunger is so bad those first few hours that you want to cry. You know the relief of breakdown and gorging. You know the guilt afterward. You know the fear of thinking you may continue to grow and grow, like Alice in that house in Wonderland. You could become like one of those poor people too big to leave a room, in need of a winch when the ambulance arrives, in need of firemen with sledgehammers to widen the jamb. You know the forgetting afterward—the surrender.

"But here's the hope," Alice said. "You know what it's like to *change*. Look at yourselves. Look at me! We've changed. We've changed radically! We got from there to here somehow, though how we did is no longer important. Just look at us. Look at each other right now! Turn to your neighbor! We ourselves are examples of the possibility of transformation. We are arguments against despair. Don't tell *me* people can't change! I, my friend, have changed something awful. And so of course I can change again, but not back.

"Here's the challenge, my hungry caterpillars: To think of your own skin as a chrysalis. To hatch the chick in this adipose shell. You, me, all of us, we can't get back to what we once were. Those people are gone. Which means underneath all of this is someone new! There's a matryoshka doll in this matryoshka!

"But how do we get to her? That's easy: It's the same as the first rule of writing. We start with what we know. Let me tell you about the children I lost," Alice said. "That way I can explain to you not just why I eat, the void I've been trying to fill, but also what's been eating *me* . . ."

But David left. He didn't want to hear that. He was done with that story. He was done.

He took himself to the party. It was one long beeline, cab to office to

Georgine, who saw him the minute he got there. She looked like she was waiting for him, and she was. He walked right up to her. "Remember what you said about being direct?"

"Yes," she answered.

"Show me where you live."

By the time he got home, it was well past Alice's bedtime. He'd turned off his cell phone at Georgine's, but now, when he powered on, he saw that his wife hadn't called once. Not a shred of curiosity about when he'd be coming home. Her indifference killed both his anxiety and his regret. He considered taking a shower, washing Georgine's dusty evidence off Mr. Penis, but what was the point? His wife was fast asleep.

The moment David got under the covers, Alice ran her hand down his stomach. "Make love to me," she said.

Terrified, he grabbed her wrist and held it.

Naked, she pressed her breasts against his back, the nipples hard as marble, and ran the end of her tongue from his scapula to his neck. "Come on, David," she moaned. "It's been *forever.*" She pinned his arm behind him with both of hers, like a police hold, then arched her crotch agilely to where she clasped him, sliding herself up and down the banister of his thumb. "Squeeze me," she whispered. "Hold me as hard as you can."

What was with the licking and squeezing? This was new. And the dirty talk? New too. David, fresh off his own transgression, became paranoid again. *Was* she having an affair? Had she learned all this somewhere else? Was she trying out new moves in their bed?

He flipped over as commanded and, in spite of his suspicions, was tremendously aroused, growing an erection so fast he could feel Georgine's sex flaking off him like brick shedding mortar in an earthquake.

"Kiss me," she said. He went to kiss her. But instead of lips he found her tongue, extended toward him in the dark. He stuck out his own and touched hers with it, the two fighting for position and rolling round each other like a pair of seals. They Frenched like this for so long that David could feel their spit getting cold. All brand-new, he thought.

He stopped.

"Come on," she said. "Kiss me."

"I *am* kissing you." He went to kiss her again but there was that tongue, stuck out from her mouth like a kid catching raindrops. "What's with all this?" he said.

"What's with what?"

"This?" He opened his mouth and went, "Ahhhhhh," like she was his doctor.

She laughed. "Come on," she insisted. "Kiss me."

"Kiss regular," he said.

"Kiss unregular," she said.

He could see the whites of her eyes staring at him in the dark.

"All right," she said, then got out of bed, put on her robe, and went to the kitchen.

"What did I do?" he called. He could hear her filling the kettle with water.

"Nothing," she said exhaustedly.

For weeks it was like he didn't exist, and now that he did again, he'd done something wrong.

The tea kettle whistled.

He threw the covers off himself and went into the kitchen, where she was sitting at the table, her hands wrapped around a cup of green tea, waiting for him.

"We need to talk," she said.

It took all his wind. He put his hands on the table and, like an elderly man, pressed his weight against the top while he eased himself down.

Alice tucked her hair behind her ear. Her eyes welled up and she cleared her throat. "There's something I need to tell you," she said, wiping a tear with her palm. "I've been so torn up about this for so long that I've kept away for our own protection. But I can't go on like this any longer. I can't keep it to myself anymore."

David's heart was pounding.

"We're in a rut," she said.

So utterly relieved for a moment, he asked her to repeat what she'd just said.

"A rut," she said. "But that's not the right word. It's worse. Crisis might be closer, but that suggests we have a choice to make, and I can't figure out what the choice is between."

She took a sip of her tea, concentrating, her focus drifting inward. She looked fitter than ever. She had a nice color in her cheeks; tone, if you could call it that, in her thick shoulders and arms.

"Stuck might be it too, but I don't know if there's a converse. If we get unstuck, I don't know if we're better off. Bored might be a little closer, but I *know* there's something we could do."

She reached out to touch his cheek.

"Can't you *feel* it?" she said. "Where we *are*? It's like limbo but without being dead. It's like everything's the opposite of the way it should be. Now that we know each other better than ever, we don't know each other at all. Now that we've grown closer to each other than to anyone else, we've grown farther apart. I can't really describe it. But if we stay like this for much longer, I think I'd rather die."

"Don't say *that,*" David said.

"Am I really alone here?"

"No."

"So the question I've been trying to answer," she said, "is what to do about it."

"I've been asking myself the same thing."

"Do you have any ideas?"

He thought of Georgine. "You first."

"Do you ever think maybe we should live our life from here on out like an experiment?" she said. "Treat our marriage like the moon shot, like space exploration? The final frontier! I know I'm being vague, but think about it. Why do we live here, for instance, and not somewhere else? Why not dedicate our lives to living in every one of the United States? To eradicating world hunger? Raising free-range chickens in the French countryside? How about we become marine biologists and study the Great Barrier Reef? I don't even know what it is. It's because I've been so busy with *me.* I'm so busy with me I'm dumb. I want to unlearn me. How about we hike the Appalachian Trail?"

"You're not serious."

"I'm serious," she said, "though those are still the wrong examples. But what are we *afraid* of, David? What's holding us back?"

"From what?"

"From whatever we're not *feeling.* From whatever we're not *doing.*"

"What aren't we feeling or doing?"

"More."

"I feel like I feel plenty. I feel like I *don't* want to feel any more."

She nodded. "I understand what you're saying, but you're talking about the last few months. You're still not understanding me."

"What are you talking about?"

"What if we thought of our marriage as an experiment in the achievement of mutual bliss?" she said. "What if we vowed, I don't know, to fuck every day—like some kooky Guinness stunt but with no interest in breaking any records? I don't mean just hump. I mean dedicate a certain period of time every day to giving each other some novel form of pleasure."

"Are you saying our sex is bad?"

"I'm saying we need the *new,* David. We need New Zealand or Newfoundland. A new state of affairs. A new *world.* What?" she said. "What is it?"

David had covered his eyes.

"I agree," he said, shaking his head.

"But what?"

But *why,* after he'd been fucked cross-eyed by another woman, did Alice want to reinvent fucking? Why, after desperate weeks of *not* addressing their problems, did she so desperately want to address them now? Wouldn't it have helped their situation just a little if they'd talked about this, say, yesterday?

Alice took his wrists and uncovered his eyes. "Look," she said, "what if we wrote down everything in our lives we felt restricted by and vowed to help each other become unrestricted."

"You mean sexually?"

"Sexually, spiritually. Physically, spatially. Sure, sexually for starters."

"Are you saying you want to sleep with other people?"

"Are *you*?" Alice took his hands in hers again and squeezed them. They were warm from her tea and his were cold. "Do you want to take a lover, David? In a way, that's what I'm getting at. Take a lover and tell me all about it. Or don't. But you get what you want because I free you to get it. I'll help you get it and then you help me."

"I don't want a lover," he said. It was a lie, though as it applied to what Alice was saying, it was true.

"You must want something," she said.

It was a desire that had haunted him ever since he'd started his book, but instead of saying what it was, he said, "What do *you* want?"

"Oh." Still holding his hands, she leaned her head back and closed her eyes. "I want . . . to be a cannibal in Papua New Guinea and learn how to shrink a head. I want to ride a camel in the desert and see a mirage and then find water there. I want to join a cult and be deprogrammed and then I want to become a deprogrammer. I want to feel what it feels like to spend an unlimited amount of cash until I don't have a dime to my name. I want to be shipwrecked on a desert island for years and build huts with elevators like the Swiss Family Robinson." Pulling at his hands, she lowered her head and faced him. "I want," she said, "to make you *impossibly* happy."

David could barely keep his head up, he was so distraught. "I don't know what to say."

"Say 'yes.' Say 'When can we start?' "

"When can we start?" he said sadly.

"Right now," she said, and smacked the table. "Could you walk away from Spellbound?"

"Sure."

"Do you have to live in New York?"

"No."

"Tell me, when are you going to finish your book?"

He narrowed his eyes at her. "What are you talking about?"

"Your book. That you've been working on."

"How the hell do you know about that?"

"Well, I saw some pages on your desk one day, but I only read a few words. It's none of my business."

"No, it's not."

"Have you finished?"

"No."

"Can I ask why?"

"I don't know how it ends."

"Trash it," she said. "Burn it. Throw it away."

"No," David said. He dropped her hands.

"Then go off somewhere. Just finish it. If I knew you were doing that, if I knew you had the end in sight, maybe I'd know what I was waiting for."

"I don't need to go away to finish it."

"But you do need to *finish*, right? *We* do. This is what I mean. If it holds you back, if it keeps us apart, if it weighs you down—like my weight does me—then go. Or let it go. Then I can go too."

"I don't know what you're talking about," he said.

"Don't say you don't, because you're smarter than that."

"Don't patronize me."

"I mean, you're the smartest man I know."

"You act like we can both just change. You act like all you have to do is snap"— he snapped his fingers—"and it's done. Like your whole life is something you can throw off. But it isn't. We *can't.*"

"Yes we can."

"You haven't been able to."

"I know," Alice said. "But I was afraid. I'm not afraid anymore."

"Why not?"

"Because," she said, "there's nothing after us."

It was true. Without children, their marriage was only about each other. It had never occurred to him before, but now that she'd said it, he realized it was something he'd been afraid to admit.

"I'm not sad about that anymore," she said. "I'm not even mad. In fact, now I think it's what makes us special. Singular. You're the *only* way I see the world. You're it. I know it sounds romantic, but that's how much I love you. I can't imagine you gone."

"But you're the one who's been gone!"

"I know," she said, nodding. "That's why I know. So, I propose an experiment: us. *We'll* be the experiment, but not in the classic sense. We'll be purpose *without* procedure. The procedure's the part we'll make up."

"What does *that* mean?"

"That we forge ahead."

"Toward what?"

"Something new," she said. "Some*where* new. Tomorrow. Let's just go."

"Like where?"

"You pick."

"I'll leave this one to you."

"All right. I, for one, have always wanted to see the Great Barrier Reef."

"Oh," he said, "Australia."

"The land down under."

"Or should we call it Oz?"

"*Please,*" she said. "This is our chance."

He stood up, leaned against the stove, and stuffed his hands under his arms. This was silly, he thought. It was unreality. The reality was that he'd slept with another woman tonight and wanted to sleep with her again. Oh, to have light little Georgine spinning on him like a top! What would Alice say if he told her that? How exciting would their experiment be if he told her he'd already started one? Didn't that prove there *could* be no experiment?

"We can do anything," Alice said. "We love each other."

"Anything?"

"Anything we want."

"Well, right now I want to go to sleep." He felt so terribly disengaged and tired with their life together that he could barely bring himself to walk down the hall.

"I know you don't believe me," she said, "so I'm going to show you."

"Yes," David said, "you do that."

The next morning he woke in the middle of the bed, stretched across it diagonally, and for a blessed moment he thought his conversation with his wife was something he'd dreamed. He sat up, then recalled Georgine bucking above him and wondered if that was a dream too. But it wasn't. Sunlight flooded the bedroom, though not brightly enough to annihilate his regrets. It was windy outside, brilliant and clear, too beautiful a day to feel so terrible.

He called his wife's name but the only reply was the refrigerator's motor shuddering to life. He looked at the clock. It was almost eight thirty. He could smell acrid, bottom-of-carafe coffee, so he went to the kitchen and made a new pot. He thought about Georgine and felt no small degree of shame, then wondered how he might handle what had happened between them: best to end things immediately, have a talk over lunch, say, and be done with it. Though another part of him was wondering what he should wear today and what her reaction would be when she saw him, because he was so excited to see her he couldn't wait to get in to work. And another part of him was so mortified that he thought about calling in sick for the rest of the week or going somewhere new like Alice had suggested, remote, out of cell phone or e-mail range, like the Congo.

Alice's note was propped against the coffeemaker.

David,

I'm leaving for a while. I was going to tell you about this last night, but after our talk I didn't feel like you'd understand and might try to stop me. There's a chance I may not return and that terrifies me. If things work out that way, I promise you'll get an explanation.

Please think about what I said—or don't. But no matter what, I want you to live as if I was gone for good—as if I'd died and you were allowed to start your life over again. Or start a life without me now.

Understand this is all part of the experiment.

Please don't try to find me. No one knows where I've gone. When I came back from the hospital a few months ago, I told you I was going to change my life, and this is the first step.

Remember: purpose without procedure.

I love you,
Alice

Reading her note a second time, David was surprised at his lack of emotion—perhaps because he didn't believe a word of it. *There's a chance I may not return and that terrifies me.* Please, he thought. This was yet another go-around of some kind and Alice would be back—maybe by tonight. He imagined her showing up at their door—a search through her closet revealing she hadn't even taken a suitcase—with her head hung low, embarrassed or perhaps even angry with him over her newest failure. "Don't say it," she'd say, and he wouldn't, and she'd go back to the bedroom and begin the period of waiting for both of them to forget what had happened—or hadn't.

He decided not to give the matter any more thought. Meanwhile, he concluded, he had to end things with Georgine as quickly as possible, so in the shower, he rehearsed what he was going to tell her, and how, and where, and he took extra time shaving and grooming and tried on three different shirts before heading into the office. Walking to the subway, he called Alice's cell phone. A recording explained that the number wasn't in service, and this news annoyed him. It was just like her previous diets. He could see himself calling their cell phone company when she returned by week's end, paying a reconnection fee, maybe even having to buy another phone. On the platform, he stood near the yellow line as the train came barreling down the tracks. Against the cars' reflection, he could clearly make out the frown on his face before the train gradually halted before him. It would be the same thing as her teaching, he thought. When she'd left Trinity midyear, it made getting another job nearly impossible—thus Hawthorne Cedar Knolls School for the emotionally disturbed. But that wasn't his problem anymore.

No, if Alice can take a holiday from me, David thought, running his hand up Georgine's leg as she stood behind his desk, then I can take a holiday from her. The office door was open and he and Georgine pretended to work while he touched her, feeling his way past her panties, the both of them gone quiet, Georgine radiating heat and her eyes half-closing.

"When," she whispered, "can we get out of here?"

Later, on the rear balcony of Georgine's Greenwich Village apartment, drinking orange juice out of the carton, David felt like a convict who'd made it safely across the border. Why even give Alice a thought? Why not take her up on her offer and live as if she were gone for good? He could hear Georgine humming pitch-perfectly in the bathroom while she dressed to the sound of a piano playing across the courtyard. From his perch, he watched the songwriter in the apartment to his left play a few chords on his piano and then make notes with a pencil he kept behind his ear, the old man in the apartment with him—a cowriter, perhaps—nodding approvingly while he wound the clock on his mantel. David nodded as well. The music, he thought, was like a soaring love song about freedom! He himself felt free and young again, and a keen sense of surprise about everything at the moment—this view, for example, and his newfound sex partner, in fact his whole life! He felt capable of remarkable, undreamed-of things, the bones of his new wings—humerus, ulna, radius, and manus—springing from his back and spreading wide in the bright sun. Was this the new world Alice was talking about? The new state of affairs? Or had his body and mind been transformed only because she was gone?

Alice didn't come home that night. Or the next night, or the following—nights that soon turned into a week and then into two. Initially, David was untroubled by his wife's absence, though out of habit he called out her name whenever he came home. There was a novelty to his solitude, plus the apartment was all his. He could order in and not take the garbage out. He could eat anything he wanted and catch any movie on a whim. And conversely, her desertion made him feel her presence acutely. It was like a tug-of-war between perfectly matched opponents, a stalemate that wouldn't end until one side grew exhausted and let go—and he wasn't about to do that. *He* was going to ride this out. *He* was going to hold on. *He* was going to be here when she came back. And she *was* coming back.

Two weeks turned into a month—October now—which turned into two. To pass the time, he kept himself occupied with Georgine, but it was strange. As time wore on, he needed to pretend that Alice might show up any second for their trysts to remain hot. If the phone rang in his office while Georgine was blowing him, he had to convince himself it was Alice calling from the front desk. If his cell phone rang while he and Georgine were in a hotel, he made her answer it while he was inside her. "He's right be*hind* me," she said, and handed him the phone. If they were walking on the street together and he saw a woman who resembled Alice, he took Georgine's hand and picked up the pace, just to get close enough to be sure.

One night—four months now, maybe five; it was January and he counted backward—he even convinced Georgine to come home with him. His wife, he said, not untruthfully, wouldn't be back until very late. It was a risk, he admitted, standing at the door, but he wanted them to have sex in his own bed. He'd never felt hornier in his life. When they entered, he called out Alice's name.

"Jesus," Georgine said, "is she here?"

"I don't know," he told her, practically laughing. Unsure they were alone, he showed Georgine inside quietly, careful to leave the front door ajar. To set the mood, he turned on the stereo, raising the volume loud enough to be unable to hear Alice come in unannounced. In spite of Georgine's protests, he left the bedroom door wide open as they undressed. Then, in knots so complicated they'd be impossible to undo quickly, he tied her wrists to the bedposts with two of the ties Alice had given him for past birthdays. Ties, he thought as he dropped his pants, when the fuck do I wear ties?

"You're positive she won't show up?" Georgine said. She was honestly scared.

"No," he told her, scared himself. "I'm really not." And he made love to Georgine angrily and passionately, right in plain sight, as if Alice had been there to see.

Where *had* Alice gone?

True, he thought, as five months became six and seven and winter became spring, he'd been unfaithful and had to call things off with Georgine immediately. True, he and Alice were in some kind of rut, or crisis, or limbo, or unnameable terrible place. But this stunt she'd pulled wasn't funny anymore! They never had spent such a long stretch apart, and although he didn't miss his wife *at all* and was still very, *very* glad she'd decided to take this break or hiatus, the thing that was driving him crazy about her little experi-vacation, or her disappearance of self-discovery, was that he had no idea what to do with all of this goddamn time!

Of course, it was the perfect opportunity to get some writing done, he realized, and by the beginning of May, the ninth month, he finally took his manuscript out of the box and read the pages leading up to where he'd gotten stuck. He looked them over again and again until he came to the same dead end. Being in the middle of a novel was like being trapped inside a tangled ball of yarn. It was different than designing a game. A game's players could enjoy infinite variations of action, but the lines of code, albeit vast, were limited. You were building a kind of wind-up toy that you too could see go. Once you'd written yourself into the middle of a novel, however, it seemed it could grow and grow around you. He stared at the page and waited and then stared some more. It was so peaceful now, so perfect with the house quiet and the world calm, but with Alice absent, his concentration was shot, his imagination dead. It was as if the book suddenly lost all importance and had no reason to come into existence. He sat at their kitchen table and looked at one page for so long that the page disappeared, and his thoughts turned back to their last conversation and his wife's idea of living as if they were an experiment—as purpose without procedure. He didn't know what she meant, exactly, but he did know that the process of writing fiction was purpose without procedure. You felt some sort of resolution or ending luring you forward but had no idea really how to actually arrive at it, though you had to get there nonetheless. Life, when you came right down to it, was like that too. Oh, the psychologists and philosophers, the politicians and priests, posited paths for you, but how often did people, in spite of all this advice, really feel sure of their way? Didn't think someone else knew something that they didn't? Was on to something better than you were? Was on the right road while you raced into oblivion? Was this what Alice was doing? Was this what she was trying to show him? That with the slightest effort they could get off the path they were on, singly or together? Had they together somehow been hiding from each other this truth? Was this a chance to figure out a correction from here on out? Was her disappearance less a desertion and more of a gift?

Maybe give her idea a try, he thought, then asked himself what he felt restricted by.

His book. Unfinished, his book consumed his life.

He wanted to finish it but didn't know how to. He hadn't a clue as to how it ended. Throw it away, Alice had said; trash it. But then the fact that the book had been abandoned incomplete would gnaw at him forever. Even Alice should have known that. David remembered what she'd told him at the doctor's after her third miscarriage—that she'd most likely never be able to carry a child to term. "Nothing sticks to my insides," she'd said to the doctor, and wept. But the worst part, she told David later, wasn't that they'd never be able to have children. No, it was that she constantly thought about the children she hadn't been able to have. "I think about those little peanuts all the time," she said.

He had to finish the book and be done with it. Be done with it, and a whole new world would open before him: the world without his book.

He had to finish it but didn't know how to. He didn't know what happened next. And the only way of knowing this was to have it happen.

Perplexed, he got up from his chair and went to the cupboard and got down a can of peanuts from his secret stash of forbidden foods. He poured out a handful and ate them and then wiped the salt from his empty hand on his pants. He looked at the chipper Planters Peanuts man tipping his top hat hello and thought about how one bite could kill Alice dead.

Of course! David thought.

But now he had to find her!

No denying it, his wife was a smart woman, but he didn't think she could disappear without a trace. Yet, after a search through her desk and the discovery of her laptop (hard drive erased), it seemed she'd done just that.

Convinced there must be a clue in the apartment, he began to turn the place over. Not sure what he was looking for, he started in her closet. From the top shelves he brought down all the boxes of her old clothes and rifled through them, occasionally taking breaks to sniff the fabric that still smelled of Alice, remembering her wearing a particular outfit, the countless mornings before she left for work when she modeled one, after she'd stamped her foot to get his attention, so that he could take in her whole frame, and said, "How does this look?" as if she needed him to see her in order for her to see herself. He searched through her piles of sweaters and T-shirts and multitiered shelves of shoes, Alice preferring pumps to heels, David thinking of her feet, fat long before she was, not a bone visible in them, and her ankles fat too. "I have my father's feet," she used to say woefully. "If we have girls, I hope they get yours." He mulled over old photos of her family and of Alice as a child, two-by-three-inch prints, the dates printed in the border, their color washed out with time, the pixilation pitiful compared to cameras today, a focus that seemed Seurat-soft, the focus of dreams, of memory, David realizing, sadly, how few stories of her childhood he knew or, even more sadly, how few happy stories of her childhood she had. In one, age five, perhaps, in polo shirt and jeans, her chestnut hair so short she looked like a little boy, she was by the lake with her golden retriever, famous in her mind and special in her heart for saving her whenever she climbed the picket fence in her backyard, Princess leaping over it to trot after her, take her wrist in her own soft mouth, and lead her back home, and who, because she barked so much (not allowed inside the house), was one day sent away, as Alice would be later, by her father. David found old photos of Alice and himself that he'd forgotten, and he could see in their expressions that they'd once been happy; and in their appearance then, the difference in their age now was visible in the smoothness of their skin, in the size of faces, waistlines, the lack of double chins, as if marriage itself were a fattening before the slaughter. He found file folders of letters they'd written to each other, a form of communication as dead as the dinosaur, as film in cameras, David tickled by their banality, by Alice's girly-girl print, an innocence in the very morphology of the letters themselves: the harmless roundness of her little *b*'s and *d*'s, a sweetness in the disproportionate contours of her *a*'s and *g*'s. *O*'s like those wouldn't hurt anyone, he reflected, and *z*'s like Alice's aimed to please. She was a good woman, a loving wife, and he needed to track her down to find out what happened next, so he kept tearing through the place. He took down tins she'd marked XMAS, the strings of lights tangled no matter how carefully she'd spooled them the year before, the cords that came out of storage as coiled as snakes in a den. And boxes marked DECORATIONS, with at least one ornament in each mysteriously shattered, no matter how delicately it had been put away; even untouched things could break. He dumped out her personal files from file cabinets: job applications and professional correspondence and old papers she'd written in college that he read now with interest, page after page revealing the shape of her mind but leaving no tracks to wherever she was now. He looked through legal pads stuffed between phone books in their kitchen cabinets, tried to decode notes she'd scrawled between messages left for him, numbers without names circled between age-old shopping lists and doodles and to-dos. He looked through her lesson plans but found no secret plans, pulled down books from her bookshelves and checked the margins of novels for notes that might provide hints, finding only observations too cryptic to decode or too general—*Yes!* she wrote, or *True!*—to be considered leads but that spurred him on to read the underlined passages themselves. *A man is born into this world with only a tiny spark of goodness in him. The spark is God, it is the soul; the rest is ugliness and evil, a shell.* Yes! David thought. True!

Until, at his wit's end with so many dead ends, he began to tear the apartment down. He pulled the drawers from the bedside tables, kicked the furniture to kindling, then searched through the contents he'd poured into a pile: kite tails of condoms and spent tubes of K-Y jelly and berets and spools of thread and sewing needles (*sewing needles?*) and safety pins and pennies black with age or lichen green. In her bedroom dresser, in the very back of her top drawer, he discovered a cache of conditioners and creams from hotels, her favorite things to filch, a collection of combs, a brush webbed with her hair, dead pens, even love letters he was touched she'd saved in an envelope he'd once addressed to *ALICE.* (He read those as well.) He pulled out those drawers too, checked their bottoms and backs, then stacked them up, and with the dresser lightened now, within his strength to lift, he pulled it from the wall and heard something fall to the floor, the small jewelry box Alice thought she'd lost years ago, the diamond earrings he'd bought her (and replaced) still there, pinned in that limbo between furniture and wall. "Found it, Alice," he said aloud. He looked under the bed and pulled the things they'd stacked there out from a moonscape of congealed dust beneath the place they slept: a mirror and a poster of Hitchcock's *Rear Window.* Then all that was left to search was the bed itself. He removed the comforter and sheets to reveal the naked challah braids of the mattress's skin. With a butcher knife from the kitchen and a power he didn't realize he had, he hacked a gaping wound in its center, burying his arm up to the shoulder in the hole like a farmer helping a large animal give birth, feeling around its spring-and-foam guts for something he *knew* was here—but nothing was. That left only the box spring beneath. He went to the toolbox for a saw, prepared to dismantle the thing piece by piece if necessary; and it was only after he'd lifted the disemboweled mattress and timbered it across the tornado-struck room that David stopped cold—for there, lying dead center, as if the box spring were a giant picture frame, he finally found what he didn't realize he'd been looking for:

Her journal.

It was bound and black, the pages unlined, with a colored print on the cover of Botticelli's Venus rising from the waves. He opened it to the first page, careful to check the date, and the only entry began a few days after Alice returned from the hospital:

FINISH

Oh, he needed to *find* her! He needed to find out what happened next. But he couldn't find her on his own. He needed a professional.

Google "private investigator" and the hits came replete with as many pop-ups as porn sites, with joke names that made it hard to take these services seriously: Check Mate, Check-A-Mate and Investi-Mate; Cheater Beaters, Vowbusters, and Spouse-a-Louse. Just the number of hits alone, 7,494,000, was mind-boggling: a whole city's or separate state's worth of private eyes: Pvteyes, hidemseekm, and Sherlock; RUsure and Bsure.com, Divorce.net. He narrowed his search to New York, whittling the number of hits down to a million four, and baffled still how to choose between so many options, he clicked on the site whose name he liked the most:

DialM.com
Missing Person Specialist
Lost/Found
Click Here to Enter

He clicked, and once he entered the site, saw the only information on the page was a telephone number. After a few minutes of staring at the screen, he dialed—it was a pager—and punched in his number, then hung up.

Almost instantly, a man called back. "Can I help you?"

"I'm calling about my wife," David said.

"Ah," he said. "What did the bitch do?"

"She left me."

"For another man?"

"I'm . . . I'm not sure. I don't think so."

"But you want to know so."

"Yes," he said. "I want to find her."

Silence—for so long, in fact, that he thought they'd been disconnected. "Are you there?"

"I've gotta say," the man said, "you don't sound particularly upset."

"What are you talking about?"

"You don't sound like someone who's been betrayed."

"I don't know if I have been."

"If you're calling me, you don't know anything."

"What am I supposed to sound like?"

"Angry. You're angry, aren't you?"

"Extremely."

"You feel deserted, don't you?"

"Absolutely."

"Like you're capable of anything?"

"If she were here right now I'd wring her—"

"Don't say it," the man said. "Let's meet right away."

They agreed on a Greek-run diner nearby. Anxious to get out of his wrecked apartment, David left immediately, walking the few blocks as quickly as he could. The restaurant was nearly empty but he took a booth in the rear anyway, as far from the few patrons as possible, his back to the giant mural of the Acropolis. The waiter came over to take his order, and it was comforting how little Greek waiters had changed over the years. Still with the buttons of their white shirts unbuttoned and their mats of chest hair exposed, still with the gold chains—never less than one or more than three—from which dangled symbols that looked vaguely Hebrew, but, most of all, still with the complete indifference with which they took your order, that socialite's over-your-shoulder look while you spoke, and then the dismissive rip from their dupe pad whether you'd asked for the right side of the menu or just a cup of tea. The waiter left, revealing another person standing behind him.

"Are you David?" the man said.

For a moment, David thought he'd been addressed by a boy. He stood light-switch high, his belt well below the tabletop, pictures of lobsters embroidered into his tie. Of indeterminate age—he could be thirty or fifty—he had black hair long in the back and bangs that half hid his eyes, black eyes that glinted brightly, like the pictures you see of the deepest deep-sea fish. Though diminutive he was still physically imposing, top-heavy, long-armed, and large-headed too, like a boxer or a pit bull, his mouth so big that a bite from it could kill you. He was carrying a large briefcase that he put down on the floor next to the booth, and when he reached out his hand, David, so taken with his appearance, couldn't help but smile.

"I'm Mr. Mobius," he said.

They shook—and in a flash, David was pinned to the booth, his arm wrenched into a karate hold, his wrist bent back to breaking.

"Don't move," Mobius whispered. With his free hand, he patted David down, felt around his stomach and sides, behind his back and between his legs so close to his cock it made his penis tingle. With one of his feet he felt up David's shins and calves, watching his eyes closely. Then he pulled David's wallet from his breast pocket and flipped it open to his license, looking back and forth between picture and face as carefully as a golfer lines up a putt. "All right," he said. "You're clean."

He let go of David's hand.

"May I?" he said, indicating the table.

"Sure," David said, shaking out his wrist.

The man placed his briefcase on the vinyl cushion, scooting down the booth with a side-to-side gait to hop up on the bag like a midget on a phone book. "Sorry to treat you so roughly," he said, "but as you've learned, you can't trust anybody these days."

"No," he said. "I guess you can't."

When the waiter reappeared, Mobius ordered linguine with clam sauce and a glass of white wine.

"Now," he said. "Tell me *your* side of the story."

Afterward, after David ordered some wine himself and told his story from the beginning to now, Mobius asked, "What do you want me to do?"

"I want you to find her."

"When did you say she split?"

"Last September."

"Nine months. That's a pretty cold trail."

"Are you saying you can't do it?"

"I'm saying it could take time. It could cost you."

"Money's not an issue."

"I understand," Mobius said. "But do you mind if I ask you something?"

"All right."

"Why *do* you want to find her?"

For a moment, David was baffled. "So I can . . . find out."

"Find *what* out?"

"Where she is."

Mobius looked back and forth for a moment. "I understand that. But it's the motivation I don't get. I mean, given what you've described to me. She didn't take your money. She didn't betray you. You're . . . free."

"What are you saying?"

"Why not just let her go?"

David was stunned. "I . . . I can't just let her go."

"Why not?"

David shook his head.

"Don't get me wrong. I appreciate the business, but I've had tens of customers who'd just . . ."

"What?"

"Well, they'd just love to be where you are right now." Mobius twirled the pasta on his fork using his spoon, then opened his rottweiler's mouth and ate the whole tennis ball of spaghetti in one bite.

"I want to find her," David said, "to find out what happens next."

"Next?"

"Alice and I, we're not . . . finished."

Mobius squinted.

"You'll probably think this is strange," David said.

"I one hundred percent doubt it."

"Let's just say I'm writing a book."

Mobius leaned back, pressing his tongue into his cheek and nodding slowly. "I see. Is it autobiographical?"

"Sort of."

"What's it about?"

"It's about a man who may or may not have killed his wife."

Mobius smiled. "Uh-huh."

"But I'm stuck."

"Of course."

"I don't *know* what happens next."

"You need an *editor.*"

"It's more like a plot."

Mobius pointed his finger at David and chuckled. "Oh, that's good."

"Is it?"

"You want to *find* her," Mobius said, "because you want to get to the *end.*"

David was amazed. "Exactly."

"So if I find her, should I . . ."

David waited.

". . . finish?"

"What?"

Now it was Mobius who paused. "The *book,*" he said finally.

"Oh," David said. "I *see.*" His mind drifting, he shook his head sadly. "Sometimes I think I don't want to know how it ends."

"It's usually better that way," Mobius said.

David looked at him. He'd never seen eyes so black, a mouth so big. This had been a mistake. This wasn't the solution. But it was new, and new was good.

"But just out of curiosity," he said, "how much . . . ?"

With his index finger, Mobius wrote a figure in the air: an eight and five zeroes. He shrugged. "Give or take."

"I *see,*" David said. "And how do I . . . ?"

"Over time. With my other clients, I've found it's best for them to set a little aside every day. No lump-sum withdrawals showing up in your bank statements. No paper trail. I tell them to treat our arrangement as a 401(k). As a *retirement* account."

David dreamed powerfully for a moment.

"Again, I'm just curious," he said. "How would you . . . ?

"Oh, I don't know," Mobius said, smiling like an actor talking humbly about past performances. "I never know how it'll play out. I need to learn about the mark first, her schedule, her habits. That's where the artistry comes in, the discipline. Readiness is *all.* But personally I'm partial to convenient acts of God."

The two men stared at each other.

"I'm probably not interested," David said.

"I understand. It's not a fine art."

"What isn't?"

"Finishing," Mobius said.

David watched him polish off the rest of his pasta. Once he was done, Mobius drank the remainder of his wine in one gulp, touched the edges of his mouth with his napkin, balled it up, and threw it on his plate, where it bloomed with the remaining sauce. Then he pushed the check toward David.

"I enjoyed our talk," he said. "I'll be in touch." He hopped off his briefcase, snatched it up, and turned to go.

"Wait," David said. "Did you and I just agree to something?"

"No," Mobius said. "We haven't agreed to a thing."

. . .

Later, walking home in a daze, David felt like he'd been mugged—like something so unexpected and violent had happened that the experience had passed through him before he'd had the chance to react. Though now he felt a cold shiver run through his body, an effect, he decided, not only of being so close to someone so evil but also believing in their evil—enough, that is, to throw open the doors of his marriage. And as he went over their conversation again, he was suddenly terribly and awfully ashamed, both for what he'd told Mobius and what he hadn't said.

First he'd omitted his own affair. And it wasn't that the affair itself was important—which wasn't to say that it wasn't—but rather that in response to whatever Alice was struggling with, whatever had caused her to withdraw from him, he had chosen the arms of another woman instead of relying on his own fortitude, as if he'd somehow deserved more comfort than Alice herself had been able to give, or not. Which was part of marriage, after all, part of the vows: enduring those times. And this sense of entitlement seemed to him an even greater sin than infidelity.

He'd omitted that on some deep level he wished she'd remained fat, because part of him—a small, black, and ugly little part—knew that it made her grateful for as little or as much as he found it convenient to give. And once he'd recognized this, he'd in turn always feared that she would then somehow recognize her own beauty. And so long as she didn't, no one else could recognize it either. And so long as no one ever did, including Alice herself, then she'd never have the confidence to leave him. He'd always be the center of her world—the only person she'd think loved her and thus all she'd ever know of love. She would stay forever. And realizing this, David's wish seemed to him akin to some horrible, voracious appetite.

Finally and most awfully he'd omitted that in dark moments he thought Alice had gained the weight because of him, because of something heavy in his character that had infected her; didn't the experts talk about obesity as a disease? And at these times he felt the best, most generous and altruistic thing he could do for her was to leave, to end them, since in some sense he didn't understand it was their marriage that was making her sick. But he never did. And that he could see this truth without acting on it made him hate himself and love Alice all the more for caring for him at all.

He ran down the street, breaking into a full sprint. He wanted to put as much distance between him and Mobius as he could, but also to feel his heart beat, to drive himself until he was so winded he'd have to stop. He whipped past people, pumping his arms, a whistling in his ears. He wanted to run home but was out of shape and only managed to cover a couple of blocks. He clutched a parking meter while he sucked air. His legs burned; his chest felt splashed by acid. How long had it been since he'd exerted himself like this? He felt as if his skin were a too-thick suit he was eternally condemned to wear. He wanted to be free of it, to be light, to rip his body off like a shirt.

And he wanted Alice back, not to show her that he was worthy but to confess that he knew nothing of her at all. Or more accurately, to admit how little, really, he knew even after all this time. It was enough to bring a person to his knees in humility. It was the beginning but also the end: the necessary conclusion of Alice's experiment.

"Please," he said, leaning against the meter. "Come back to me."

In the lobby, he noticed their mailbox was full.

When he opened it, he saw a large manila envelope, 8½ x 11, addressed to him in Alice's hand. It had been postmarked only yesterday and was sent from New York City. In spite of his excitement, David opened it carefully. Several things fell out: a set of plane tickets and then a small envelope, his name written in her hand as well. The note was less than a page long, and he read it through quickly.

He didn't understand.

He looked at the plane tickets, reread the note from Alice, then dropped all the other mail so he could hold the page in both of his hands. He sank to the floor and read the letter again, his expression going sour with tears. "No," he whispered. "No, no, no." He read Alice's letter once more—in his mind hearing her voice reading the words aloud—and when he'd finished, he screamed like he'd run earlier. He screamed all the air from his lungs. Then, when he got his breath back, he screamed some more.

David spent the next three days in bed.

He called Cady and told him he was taking an indefinite sabbatical but would sell him his shares in Spellbound if he wished, and after hanging up he ripped the cord from the wall with a single pull.

For three days, he lay in his bed in their destroyed apartment. He drew the blinds and had only the vaguest sense of night and day. He left his bed only to piss and shit and drink water from the tap, then crawled back under the covers and went to sleep or lay awake for hours with all the lights off, dreaming in either state. He ignored the pain of hunger long enough until he felt a pleasant, cleansing emptiness that seemed to engender even more powerful dreaming—and there were times he imagined he might never eat again. He often woke with a start, unsure of where he was, and when he remembered he began to sob again, repeating this cycle until he felt nothing, until he was as empty of grief as he was of sustenance. He could feel his stomach shrinking with each day. It was like the opposite of pregnancy, and he wondered at one point if his stomach might pucker so much with hunger that he might not be able to eat again. Then he slept some more.

On the third day he woke up, got out of bed, and opened the shades. He didn't know what day it was but he knew what he had to do. He'd thought that if he found Alice he'd know what happened next; and now that he knew, he understood that there was some work to accomplish before he got to the end.

He was weakened from his fast and walked gingerly to the bathroom and bathed like a man returned from an exile in the desert for months. He drank water from the shower head. He shaved and washed his hair, and after staring at his razor for a minute or more he decided to shave all the hair from his body, which took a very long time. Once out of the shower, he brushed his teeth and then went to the kitchen for a pair of scissors and cut off his thick locks of hair. And then, back in front of the mirror, he lathered his scalp and shaved that as well.

He put on jeans—slightly loose at the waist—and a T-shirt and set to work cleaning the apartment. Chaos is a far faster spirit than order, and it took him triple the time to restore their home. He put Alice's clothes back into the boxes and sealed them, but before putting them back in the closet he reorganized the closet itself, refolding her sweaters and blouses and correctly matching her shoes. He put her papers back in the file cabinet but before returning them he culled every unnecessary page and bill and piece of useless correspondence until the files themselves shrank to half the width they'd been before. He gathered all of the detritus from their bedside tables, separating the dead pens from those that could still write and throwing out the others, separating out the pennies and nickels and quarters and dimes each into their own bottles. He threw out old phone books. He tore scribbled pages from legal pads until he arrived at sheets blank but for the indentations of what had been written on them before. In short, he purged their apartment of their lives' clutter, and it felt roomier, shipshape, arranged. He even crammed the stuffing back into the mattress and sewed the torn gash closed. And before he put the mattress back on the box spring, he returned Alice's journal to where he'd found it, knowing he'd sleep better with it there.

He had a look at himself in the mirror. He looked like a newborn. His shaved skin felt unbelievably soft.

Then he sat down at the table with his manuscript and began to write. Immediately he got beyond the place where he'd been blocked and into whole new territories, with a speed of which he'd only dreamed. He wrote for so long that his eyes and fingers hurt, so automatically it was as if another voice spoke through him, and when exhausted after many hours of this he rested his bald head on the table.

Days passed. Weeks. He fell into a routine. He woke up and put on the coffee and showered while it was brewing. He was always sure to have everything on the dining table arranged the night before—manuscript, pens, notepad, laptop. He ate something light before starting, maybe an egg or some fruit or toast with cheese, then wrote for several hours, three or four, usually, the freshest of the day, though he could go as long as five—the iteration a blink, a devolution or evolution to an animal's sense of time, which is to say he had no sense of it at all. He was given to reading aloud, to shouting his words without inflection to feel the pressure and hear the meter of his sentences. Or he spoke sometimes *as* he wrote, quietly. He ate again, standing at the kitchen counter more often than not. He went for a walk in the park afterward but didn't see a thing. He made a new pot of coffee, though he wasn't beyond reheating what was left in the carafe. The second session could be wonderful, a gift. Mental exhaustion could free him up, bring him closer to dreaming, or it could be a complete wash, setting the hair he didn't have aflame. By the end of the day he was ready for a run. He changed, went to the park again, ran round the cinder track and back. Blood speeding through his veins, flooding his brain, could be hallucinogenic, triggering an associative storm. He made notes as soon as he returned, then did push-ups and sit-ups. He bought himself a pull-up bar, adding an extra rep or two a day. He grew stronger, thinner, leaner, his carb face disappearing, though in the mirror it wasn't him he saw. Alice was right: the skin could be a chrysalis; underneath was someone new. He showered, changed, poured himself some wine, drinking while he made dinner, though it was an act of will to cook for one. Having given everything to the day, he was now spent, utterly, on night's shore, in bliss shelled in by regret. And the next day he started over.

Once, in the hallway, he stopped before his favorite Escher, *Encounter*, the picture in which the little men—one black, the other white—come around from the background, from a conjoined, two-dimensional tessellation, to meet as separate entities in the foreground above the surface of the plane. He saw his reflection in the glass, and when he focused on it the picture disappeared; and then it returned to view.

It was all becoming clearer now.

. . .

Weeks passed this way, his solitude uninterrupted, summer having arrived, June now, and then one night, after working all day with such concentration he'd forgotten to eat, he raised his head to the sound of keys at the door. Surprisingly, he neither started nor got up from his chair. The door swung closed, and he heard the sound of shoes on the hardwood.

"Hello?" the voice said.

It was Alice.

Pepin sat there until she found him. But for the light shining from above the table, all the lights were off in the apartment.

She stepped into the beam the fixture cast. She stopped when she got close. "What happened to you?" she said.

He couldn't speak at the sight of her. It had been over nine months since she'd disappeared. She looked radiant, tan. She'd colored her hair ash-blond, or the sun had. She'd lost, he guessed, over a hundred pounds.

"I changed," he finally said.

"Clearly."

"You changed too."

She held her arms out, then let them fall.

"You had that surgery," he said.

"Yes," she said, pulling up her blouse. There was a long pink scar, the pink of seashell, across her stomach.

"Will you stay here?" he said.

"For a while. Until you're finished."

"I understand," he said. "I'd like that."

She came over to him and put her arm around his neck, her palm on his bald scalp. She looked over his shoulder at the pages he was working on, then flipped through all those he'd written thus far. "You're almost done," she said.

"Almost to the end."

"Are you coming to bed soon?"

"Yes."

She kissed his forehead. "Good."

This close to her, he could smell her scent of the sea.

And then one day, David wrote, Alice began to lose weight.

He'd seen her drop pounds before, but perhaps because of her failed attempts in the past, her progress seemed more remarkable this time; or perhaps because they'd been apart for nine months it all seemed new, but never had he witnessed the kind of transformation she was undergoing now. Every morning there seemed less of her, a thinness visible in the cheekbones, a concavity in the belly, and a deflation of ass that Alice herself remarked on in the mirror with the indifference of a magician who knew the secret to her trick.

She talked to his reflection as he lay there in bed. "You look surprised," she said.

"I am," he said.

"I am too." She turned her body to face him but kept her face to the mirror, looking at her back.

He stared at the crescent scar across her belly. "You're doing beautifully," he said.

"There's still a ways to go."

It was true. Although her weight loss bordered on the frantic and he was afraid to blink lest he miss some new aspect of this werewolf-to-wife transformation, there were aftershocks and wreckage, places on her body so stretched out—her triceps hanging from her arms like the edges of spun pizza dough, a roll around her waist like a sweater's ends bunched belly to back—that no amount of exercise could tone, smooth, or retract. Only surgery could fix this. They'd have to flense her like the blubber from a whale.

"My skin," she said wonderingly, "is like a space suit that's too big." She couldn't leave the mirror, turning from side to side as if her nakedness were a new dress. "And yet it's the oddest thing," she said. "I feel like I'm not dieting anymore. If the doctors could just remove all my skin, they'd find me. Do you get it?"

"I do," he said.

"It didn't used to be like that."

Suddenly he found himself very emotional.

She was still Alice, this Alice-not-Alice. Her smile was the same, her little tics were yet in full effect, but there was a corresponding secretly won confidence that came somehow with her lightness, her nine-month odyssey, and made her seem miraculous, a mystery—not to be solved, mind you, just loved. He could wait to hear all the details.

She turned to look at him now, tucked her hair behind her ears, and came toward him on the bed, crawling on all fours to where she could kiss him, which she did. "I'll weigh myself and then I want you to take a picture of me. And then you write."

The emotions Pepin had kept quelled rose to the surface. "I don't want to write," he said.

Alice took his chin in her hand, raised his eyes to hers, and ran her free palm over his scalp. His head was several thousand periods of stubble. "Finish," she said. "You're almost done."

She went to the bathroom to weigh herself, her hair covering her face as she stared at the scale's readout—"One eighty-eight," she said. Then she put on a dress, tied a ponytail, and went to the kitchen, with Pepin in tow. She stood by the refrigerator, smiling as he snapped the shot, Pepin shaking out the square of film the Polaroid camera tongued from its housing, the slow emergence of the image from white to yellow to the mood-ring shades of blues and greens so much more satisfying than anything digital or instantaneous, until finally, as if in reward for the wait, there was this new Alice, whom the two of them admired together, her face awash with the flash. Rolling a piece of tape into a loop, she stuck it on the back, which she stuck in turn in the upper left half of the refrigerator's door.

"I'll be back," she said; then she left for the day.

Alone again, David wrote with the same quiet, bullet-train speed he'd been composing with since he'd arrived at the novel's apex, a summit crossed in blackest night. He didn't know how much he had left, exactly, though he had a clear sense of the movements required, of the book's final shape. En route to the conclusion it split into a series of penultimates, all of them viable, only one of them definitive, circling back finally to the beginning, just as the book's form demanded. As for the end itself, all he knew for sure was that he was getting there quickly.

She was waiting with Chinese for dinner after he returned from his run. Eating with Alice now was something that required an adjustment. Her portions were positively Lilliputian, measured out in thimblefuls. Course to course, he had to eat fast in order to keep up. In contrast to his bowl of wonton soup (with two dumplings) she poured herself a ramekin (with half a dumpling) that she might as well have drunk like a shot. On his plate he piled lo mein, lemon chicken, beef with broccoli, and white rice—she was back and he was hungry again, so why not?—whereas on a saucer she fit a miniature version of the same. To call hers dinner would be a misnomer, since with her new, peanut-sized stomach she daily ate nine of these minimeals. Yet like Alice herself, with each day the portions seemed to shrink in size. Meanwhile, Pepin gorged.

"The more I disappear, the less I eat. Maybe soon I won't eat at all."

"Don't say that."

"You shower," she said, "while I clean up."

"Then?"

"*Then* we go to bed."

Admittedly, the prospect frightened him. He stood in the shower, arms crossed, waiting. It had been so long since he and Alice had made love that he was afraid he wouldn't know how; or, worse, that she'd feel no desire for him, which fear reminded him of the months following her miscarriages when even an attempt to hold her in the night made her moan in pain and his only choice was to withdraw every extremity—stomach to cock, head to toe to soul—until he was contracted in a carapace of solitude, his heart hulled in and indefinitely encased, when he didn't have to imagine touching her at all. He was also afraid that when she tried to kiss him he might recoil.

Once he was out of the shower, a towel around his neck and another hooked at his waist, she took him by the hand, pulled him toward the bed, and sat down. When he gave a slight tug against her weight, like a fish's sampling of bait, she stood up, took one end of the towel around his neck, and slid it off. The little hairs sprouting all over his chest were like the bristles on a fly. She pulled away the towel at his waist. He stood limp, relaxed, though when she leaned closer he tensed to be tickled, to fall fetal, thinking he might burst into tears. He closed his eyes so tightly that the muscles felt taut in his cheeks. He heard Alice step out of her dress, her bra unsnap, her panties hiss down her thighs, and then she kissed him. He had to consciously relax his lips and mouth, to suppress the powerful urge to snap-jaw her tongue.

She, in turn, persisted gently, feeding quietly and calmly, like a cat lapping water from a bowl. "Kiss me," she whispered.

They kissed, and it was like a watching a sand castle washed over by a wave: merlons of the parapets melted to crenels, turrets toppled and gun slits collapsed, the ramparts sliding into the sea.

"Alice, I missed you so."

They lay together later, staring up at the ceiling and holding hands.

"How did you get to the end?" she said.

He wrote about the beginning.

They met in a film class, Marriage and Hitchcock.

It was all purely chance. His master's in computer science required that David take a couple of liberal arts classes—he'd put it off—and in his last semester this was one of only three courses with openings; another was called Feminism and Schizophrenia in the Fifties, and the other, a seminar in the works of Italo Calvino, meant nothing to him, though the graduate student at the registration desk raved about the author and jotted down a list of his books. Somehow, David had never seen a single Hitchcock film. He was fluent in the famous images from specials and tributes on TV and montages on the Academy Awards—the woman being attacked in the phone booth by seagulls in *The Birds*, Jimmy Stewart lowering the telephoto lens from his eye in *Rear Window*, Janet Leigh getting stabbed to death in the shower in *Psycho*—but knew none of the stories. He'd missed a whole era, and suddenly it felt like a terrible gap. Given the course requirements, it also seemed like a breeze: one term paper and regular attendance for screenings and discussions. Watching movies and talking about them, he thought, wasn't education, just recreation. Yet these films would change how he saw everything, just as seeing Alice for the first time would change his life.

The class was held in a large amphitheater divided into three blocks of seating by four flights of stairs, and he, preferring the back rows, chose the farthest seat right in the middle. Attended by undergraduates, mostly, the class was nearly two-thirds full, many ambling in several minutes late, and the professor was late as well. David pulled the Calvino book he was reading, *Invisible Cities*, from his bag. Engrossed by its simple complexity, and the notion that it would make an unbelievable video game, he was considering whether to transfer to the other class when he saw Alice walking down the steps to his left.

He couldn't move. Even from this distance, it was her hair that arrested him. Growing down to the small of her back, it had a particular equine luster and silkiness that caught light at the crown and made him understand immediately the pleasure of grooming horses and why girls sat before mirrors meditatively brushing their hair at bedtime. He wished he could've been her father and had years of such a delicious sight. She was tall and big-boned, so full-chested and softball-player solid that she made the coeds surrounding her seem like mere girls. Carrying a spiral notebook with a pen quivered in the loops—her light load suggesting an economy, a practicality, he liked immediately—she took each step exaggeratedly, plunking her feet down as if she were amusing herself. He also couldn't help noticing she was alone. She cleared the hair from her eyes and tucked it behind her ear, then turned to him. That nothing indicated she'd registered his presence, though he was obviously staring, made her seem an even cooler customer. There was cream in the hazel of her eyes, a near-gray that made them appear almost wolfish.

This could be the worst class he'd ever take, he thought, but he wouldn't miss a single session. She took a seat three rows back from the front, one section to his left. She pulled her pen from the spiral ring and began chewing its end languidly, like a dog its beloved toy. David, meanwhile, had shifted to a pointer's stiffness himself, on high alert, gripping the edge of his flip-down desk.

The professor—Dr. Otto—came rushing in. He was rangy and soft-spoken, his voice so low that David almost moved closer. Otto had a shock of white hair and a discreet pooch of a stomach that, despite his height and his long Giacometti stride, made him seem delicate. His square glasses rested on a large, pendulous nose. He seemed harried, flustered by his own lateness, but stopped dead for a second, pulled the projector's remote from his pants, held it up, and said, "Ah," then pointed his other index finger in the air.

"Little-known fact about the films of Alfred Hitchcock," he said, and everyone went silent, the type-A kids holding their pens poised above their notebooks. "There's a chicken in every one of them." Several students looked at one another, perplexed. A knowing cluster of grad students to David's left guffawed. "Yes," he said, "a chicken. This was my discovery, and I'm not yet famous for it, but I will be once my book is complete." His soft laugh was almost like a pant. "This I call the Chicken Theory of Cinema. In French, *Le Poulet Subtil.* There is in every movie—not just the work of Hitchcock but every movie ever made—either a literal chicken or what I've come to call the Subtle Chicken. Now, I know what your next question is going to be: What's the Subtle Chicken? Well, I'll tell you. It may be a figurative chicken. Or a psychological condition. It might even be an egg. I noticed a close-up of an egg frying in *Moonstruck* this weekend. Aha, I thought, Subtle Chicken. Not to mention that the characters in the film are all afraid of love or death." He pointed the remote at the projector and partly dimmed the lights. "Of course, your next question is why? Why, Dr. Otto, is there a chicken in every movie? Well, I'm afraid I can't tell you that. Why should I give you the punch line of my life's work?" He dimmed the lights further. "Of course one problem with my theory is that while it covers the entire history of cinema, I've yet to see every movie ever made. And they make new ones *all the time.* I'll never finish!" He laughed again, a wet laugh, Grover-ish, mixed liberally with saliva. The class laughed too as he wiped his mouth, but David could barely bring himself to breathe. "Let's start, shall we? Oh, wait," Otto said, "I have to take roll."

He called her name, finally: Alice Reese.

Then he killed the lights. But before it was dark, Alice turned in her chair, pen still in her mouth and notebook not yet open, and looked up at David. If she was waiting for him to smile, he couldn't; he was too shocked even to blink.

Otto aimed the remote at the projector and turned toward the screen. There was an image of Hitchcock himself, standing with a movie clapboard that read *Psycho.* "To my mind," he said, "Alfred Hitchcock is the William Shakespeare of modern cinema. The comparison is apt on numerous levels, the least of which being that both are British artists. Really, it's the sheer breadth of Hitch's work, the variety of his menagerie, the range of his characters, his pathos, his comfort in genres from tragedy to comedy, slasher to satire, action film to farce, along with his relentless revolution of these forms, his playfulness with spectatorship, for instance, with the audience's expectations—not to mention his output, his magnificent output! Nearly sixty films, spanning silents to talkies, black-and-white to Technicolor, even one or two in 3-D. And that doesn't even touch on his work in television."

A montage of images with no sound followed, clips from his films in black and white and then glorious color.

"Speaking of silents"— he laughed at his joke—"Hitch always said he was trying to achieve what he called *pure cinema.* He was trying to tell stories that were possible only in the medium of film. Because of his training as both a draftsman and silent filmmaker, he was wary of dialogue—not sound, mind you, he was wildly inventive with the use of sound. But it was the image, the image as a way of telling, that he was most interested in, and he left *nothing* to chance with the images he used. From the time he directed his first picture—*Number 13,* which was never completed—he storyboarded every shot before filming. Think about that level of intentionality. *Every shot!* He used to say that making a film was actually the most boring part of the process, because in his mind he'd already made it." Otto turned toward the screen, then back to the class. "He also said he didn't like actors, that they were cattle." Another sloppy laugh, a wipe of the mouth. "He owned cattle too. Cattle and oil fields. Hitch used them as tax shelters when he got really rich. I'm not making this up." He looked back at the screen, back at the class. "Where was I?"

"Pure cinema," someone said.

"Thank you." He paused the montage on a black-and-white image: a taxi, filmed from behind, that had been swerving down a London street, and through two rear porthole windows the heads of the driver and passenger were visible.

"Take this shot here, from the *The Lodger.* Hitch's English period, released 1927. A suspicious man moves into a rooming house. Pretty girl lives there with her family. Boyfriend's a detective. Lodger might or might not be the serial killer who's been murdering women all over London. He's just killed again, so the city's on high alert. And to show that everyone's on the lookout, Hitch has this cab driving down a London street . . ."

Otto hit play. The car swerved back and forth, the passengers leaning accordingly.

"Note that the two heads in the windows look like a pair of eyes looking back and forth, back and forth."

They did, though Otto rewound and let the class consider the image again. "Of course my favorite example of pure cinema comes from a silent where the hero's on a sea voyage. He gets drunk one night during a terrible storm, the boat pitching and rocking, and Hitch cuts to the deck, to passengers getting slammed left to right, right to left. And when his drunken hero appears, what happens? He walks the deck in a completely straight line."

The class laughed.

"Let's see. This is introduction day. What else do you need to know? I've taught this class so many times I don't prepare anymore. Isn't that sad?" Otto stuck a finger in the air. "Ah. Hitch was also a big-time practical joker. Loved to play jokes on his actors and his crew, could be a sadistic *bahstahd.* My favorite: he makes a bet with one of his cameramen that the man can't spend the night alone on the soundstage, that he'd be too scared to make it till morning. Cameraman takes the bait. Hitch says, 'All right, but to make sure you don't leave, I'm going to handcuff you to this scaffolding here.' The cameraman plays along. 'But because I'm a good chap,' Hitch says, 'I'll give you a flask of whiskey so you can calm your nerves when the spirits of darkness appear.' The cameraman says he won't need any because he doesn't believe in ghosts. 'You will,' Hitch says, then locks him up, and the crew leaves for the evening. When they come back the next morning, the man's shivering and sobbing and covered in his own feces—Hitch having added a laxative to the bourbon. 'The spirits scared him shitless!' he proclaims."

A ripple ran through the class as students looked at one another. Alice again turned toward David. He could feel his mouth hanging open like an idiot's.

"Of course, if Hitch had been making a movie of his little practical joke," Otto said, "he'd have injected it with suspense. That was his favorite weapon. The Master of Suspense, people called him. No director until Hitch and even afterward, except maybe De Palma, played with the audience so sadistically. Can someone define suspense for me?"

Students looked around once more, and a girl to David's right raised her hand. "It's when you're waiting for something to happen," she said. "Waiting anxiously."

"You the character or you the viewer?"

"The viewer."

"And why are you anxious?" Otto asked.

"Because," she said, "the thing that's going to happen is . . . bad."

"Okay, but to whom?"

"The character."

"Agreed. But why are *you* anxious?"

"Because . . ." she said. "Because you can't do anything about it."

"Why can't the actors?"

"Well . . ." She thought for a moment. "Because they don't know."

"*Exactly,*" Otto said. "They don't know, but you do. And that's how Hitch created suspense. It was simple, he said: the audience must be informed. They've got to know something the characters don't. If he were to have filmed that practical joke we'd have seen Hitch filling the flask with bourbon, pouring in the Ex-Lax, shaking it up. He would've shot it in close-up as he walked toward his victim, flask looming in the foreground. He'd have shown himself cuffing the poor bastard to the scaffolding and then pulled back as the cameraman took a long swig. 'Bottoms up,' Hitch would say. Then he'd pull away even farther to a high shot, showing the fellow was teeny-weeny now that the medicine was down his gullet. And he would've filmed the rest of the night from the victim's point of view, always stretching for a bucket just out of reach, the one Hitch had placed there just to be gratuitously cruel . . . No music, of course, just the natural sounds." Otto put the back of his hand to his mouth and made some wet raspberries.

Disgusted laughter. Howls.

"How could he have filmed it in the dark?" David called out.

"Excuse me?"

David raised his hand. The professor cupped his ear toward him, and Alice turned around.

"I said, how could he have filmed it in the dark?"

"Excellent question! What's your name?"

"David." He glanced over at Alice.

"Hitch would've overlooked that little detail. He used to say he wanted to tell a completely unbelievable story with inescapable logic."

Otto ran another black-and-white montage: bridges spanning marshlands of what looked like New Jersey dissolving to Joseph Cotten lying on his back in a darkened room. And: more bridges—London Bridge this time, in color—and then a dead woman floating facedown and naked on the Thames, a tie around her neck. The Golden Gate Bridge: Jimmy Stewart beneath it, carrying a drowned woman in his arms.

"A couple of important biographical notes," Otto said. "First, and this is probably the most famous Hitchcock anecdote there is: When he was a boy, his father, a grocer, told him to come along, then turned him over to the police for no reason whatsoever and had him locked up in jail for a while. 'This is what we do to bad boys,' his father said, leaving him there—not for long but long enough. I don't go in much for psychological interpretations, but Hitch's being a Catholic added to this little trauma, and he not only developed an extreme fear of police in particular and a hatred of authority in general but also, you can imagine, an exacerbated sense of original sin, convinced that punishment for something you thought or did was just around the corner. Because we're all criminals anyway, aren't we? You aren't yet, of course, because you're young and unmarried, whereas I've been married for years and regularly dream of murder!"

More chuckles. More images. Cary Grant taken at gunpoint by two men in the Plaza Hotel. Next, him running through Grand Central Station. With Eva Marie Saint now, on Mount Rushmore, sliding down Lincoln's nose. A man hanging from the torch of the Statue of Liberty; another guy grabs him, a sleeve tears, he falls. A man—a mere speck seen from above—fleeing the United Nations.

"Speaking of marriage," Otto said, "in 1921 Hitch meets Alma Reville, a young woman doing continuity—a film editor, in essence, though I love that old term, continuity. They start working on films together, date briefly, and he proposes. On a boat, no less. Romantic, you're thinking, but he does so during a storm. While Alma's seasick belowdecks. I'm not making this up. Wanted to ask while her resistance was low, he explained. Apparently after he asked her to spend her life with him, she puked. Ladies and gentlemen, if you ask someone to marry you and the person pukes, that's a sign."

He laughed and wiped his mouth.

"Needless to say, it wasn't what you'd call a happy relationship. They were great working partners. She tightly controlled people's access to him, including producers, friends, the public in general. Hitch was as shy as he was a showman. She kept him well fed—she was a great cook, evidently—and comfortable and productive. But they were more like brother and sister, and this lack of intimacy was cemented during Alma's pregnancy. Hitch became disgusted with her transformation into, shall we say, a large woman. Not that he should've complained, being large himself—and more on that later—but after the birth of their daughter, Patricia, who became an actress herself and is wonderful in *Strangers on a Train,* he supposedly never had sexual concourse with his wife again. Now, you're young, all of you, you're not married, so you can't imagine this sort of thing, but Hitch, in response to this life of celibacy, developed very intense fixations on his stars, more often than not on beautiful blondes. If you're brunette in a picture of his, you're going *down.* But idealization and the dangers of perfection became major themes, and more on that later too. But what a list of women they were: Madeleine Carroll, Ingrid Bergman, Janet Leigh, Eva Marie Saint, Kim Novak, Tippi Hedren, to name just several. Who can blame him for falling in love? And most of all with Grace Kelly—a real nympho apparently. Go ahead, report me to the administration. I'm too old to be fired or become PC. Anyway, before she bedded a man she'd disappear into her bathroom and then emerge completely naked, so perhaps there's hope for me yet . . .

"I'm forgetting something. Let's see. Oh, *food.* Hitch and food. He struggled mightily with his weight his whole life. Fluctuated wildly. Would lose a hundred pounds just like that and gain it right back. Topped well over three hundred at his heaviest. Hunger, for him, was a form of suspense, the most elemental form, I think, next to dangling from a high place. He said he could never have an oven without a window because if he cooked a soufflé and had to wait until the timer went off to see if it had fallen, the suspense would kill him. And it was a replacement—food was, I think—for his lack of sex. He had to fill up that void, as we all try to, right? I fill mine with love. I fall in love once a year. Drives my wife crazy. Now . . ."

Onscreen, women were being stabbed in showers, choked in chairs, strangled on trains, murdered in the reflection of eyeglasses; they were thrown off church towers, attacked by seagulls, by lovers, or by strangers in the privacy of their apartments, Grace Kelly by a man emerging from behind a curtain while she talked on the phone.

"We need to go over some film terminology," Otto said. "Take a sheet from each of the stacks I'm passing around. The second is the syllabus. But before we get into film grammar, I want to give you one important term plus some visual motifs to bear in mind. If nothing else, write these down even if you drop this class, because once you're aware of them Hitch's work will open up like a flower.

"So, the MacGuffin. Stated simply, this is what gets the story rolling but then fades in importance after it's introduced. Take *The 39 Steps.* The hero, Hannay, meets a woman at a local London music hall who claims to be a spy hunted by assassins. They're after her, she says, because she's discovered a plot to steal British military secrets and something called, of course, the 39 Steps. She's murdered that night in Hannay's apartment, so he's got to prove his innocence while racing all over Scotland and London trying to figure out the secret, which naturally has nothing to do with what the movie's about. What it's about is the hero and heroine's struggles to trust each other. Which is the beauty of the MacGuffin, because once you learn what it is you can immediately get busy ignoring it.

"Next, stairs. Stairs are always significant in Hitchcock's films. A character's decision to make an ascent reflects a central moral choice, a commitment, a willingness to endanger himself or herself for someone beloved, a literal and figurative striving for a higher ground. And mirrors. He uses them to suggest doubleness, and this symbol becomes even more fraught when his work turns darker during his later films, so mirrors in *Notorious* mean something very different from mirrors in *Vertigo* or *Frenzy.*

"And mothers. Mothers are absolutely central to his work. There's the loving but oblivious mother in *Shadow of a Doubt,* then the terrible mothers of *Notorious* and *Psycho* and all the men who are still boys and love their mothers too much. See *North by Northwest* or *The Birds.* A man who loves his mother too much is someone who can never love his wife enough.

"Birds, obviously. For Hitch, birds are symbols of female sexuality. We'll see them above Miss Torso's apartment in *Rear Window,* the predatory bird—a horrific stuffed owl—looming behind Norman Bates in *Psycho.* His first victim's name? Marion *Crane.* We'll see them flying over the water as Jimmy Stewart and Kim Novak stroll before the Palace of Fine Arts in *Vertigo*—where, by the way, we'll also witness her death—her fall from San Juan Bautista's tower, and I'll argue she's an angel who, deprived of Scottie's ethereal, idealizing love, gets her wings clipped and no longer can fly. We'll see *The Birds,* of course.

"Then there's idleness. Pay close attention to characters who find themselves idle, by circumstance or otherwise. Hannay at the beginning of *The 39 Steps.* Young Charlie in *Shadow of a Doubt.* Bruno in *Strangers on a Train.* Jimmy Stewart in both *Rear Window* and *Vertigo.* Ingrid Bergman at the beginning of *Notorious.* The murder committed out of psychological idleness in *Rope* or Tippi Hedren's idleness in *The Birds.* Bates in *Psycho,* notoriously. Stillness, for Hitch, seems directly related to the expression of an inner compulsion, and its expression, projecting something buried deep within ourselves onto the world, is both the most violent thing these characters can do and also their best chance of escaping the lives in which they find themselves stuck.

"Finally, blondes. I've mentioned Hitch's leading ladies briefly, but keep in mind the conflict between the idealized, perfect blonde and the imperfect, ever-rejected brunette. When we idealize, we fail to recognize that we're seeing only our own desires, the perfected *image* rather than the infinite and wonderful imperfections of the beloved. And then there's the license we subsequently take, or don't, which is where the *morality* of Hitchcock lies.

"We'll look at all these themes with a focus on marriage. Do Hitch's movies argue that we evolve so as to become worthy of the beloved? It's been said that the primary function of all movies is the making of a couple. Well, once that couple's made, are they ready for what comes after? Are we viewers? Can this process—the viewing and the going under and the overcoming of these characters, these avatars—be a way out? Can marriage save your life, or is it just the beginning of a long double homicide? Hitch, I believe, knew that on some deep level he'd lost sight of his wife, that Alma, dedicated to him until they died, had always been forsaken by him. Rendered invisible. Do Hitch's movies shake us out of this complacency? Help us see each other anew? We'll see . . ."

That afternoon, David hacked into the school's network to get Alice's schedule. She was a senior, a math and education major, and she also was enrolled in a feminist-theory class that started the next day, which he signed up for with a few keystrokes.

That class focused primarily on female identity, examining images of women in the media in the Fifties, particularly "the suburban housewife and the urban professional," as Dr. Constance Petersen (a flat-out gorgeous woman, David thought) explained. "Consider, if you will, the burgeoning numbers of both," she intoned, "and the countervailing sociological and psychological forces at work, what with nearly nineteen million professional women entering the workforce in a decade when June Cleaver was being celebrated as the ideal woman and the doyenne of that bastion of happiness and safety: the suburban home." The students laughed knowingly, all of them women except for David, of course, him laughing out of peer pressure and not a little bit of fear, whereas theirs was smug and sprinkled with a dash of anger. "And we'll focus as well on the male media establishment's subsequent attempts," the professor continued, "to assimilate or, as the case may be, *subjugate* this Janus-faced Venus by using acceptable but often demeaning tropes and sexualized images, an endeavor that was and *remains* fraught with violence—a gang rape, if you will, perpetrated by the mad men of Madison Avenue. One which then led to a condition I like to call 'protofeminist schizophrenia.' " *This* she described as a form of mental illness specific to women, the modern manifestations of which were legion: bulimia, anorexia, obesity, and infertility, not to mention the enormous uptick in managed depression—"Prozac and Lithium," she said, "were the new One-A-Day for ladies, professional or not, for the subjugated stay-at-homes or the bitches in power suits"—as well as the spike from 1950 to the present in female suicides, brought on by failed attempts to juggle these competing, perhaps mutually exclusive roles.

The class would begin with a study of the famous Dr. Sam Sheppard murder case and its media coverage, particularly the work of Dorothy Kilgallen, a syndicated columnist whose byline was pulled from several major papers after she wrote that the prosecution had failed to prove Sheppard's guilt, or, in fact, anything at all. "The uppity lady had to be silenced, shut up," Dr. Petersen said, which brought her to Hitchcock. " 'Shut up' is something Jimmy Stewart tells Grace Kelly repeatedly when she expresses her opinions in *Rear Window.* Kelly, who's portrayed as an accomplished professional, a buyer for major department stores, and a sexually aggressive woman, who unlike her literally and symbolically crippled lover, who's inferred to be impotent, is *not*—I repeat *not*—trapped in love fantasies but wants love *in reality.* And unlike her emotionally sadistic boyfriend, she's able to move *through* the world as opposed to simply observing it voyeuristically and controlling it virtually. It's a visionary work about women and their struggles as women qua women and as women qua professionals. The movie, for those of you who haven't seen it, is about a photographer who's stuck in his apartment for eight weeks after his leg is broken on an assignment. To pass the time, he watches the tenants in the apartment complexes across from him. He feels his freedom's being threatened by his girlfriend, Kelly, who wants to marry him. And so he projects his fantasies of killing her on to a jewelry salesman who might *actually* have killed his invalid wife. Remarkably, *Rear Window* came out only a month after the Sheppard murder. It was in theaters during the trial. And so the feminine public, the silenced *she*, was treated to a twofold horror show, during the day to the first true media circus of the century over the brutal murder of a suburban trophy wife—young, athletic, and beautiful—by her successful doctor husband. The case captivated the nation, directed endless class outrage at Sheppard, and led to a guilty conviction that sent him to jail for ten years until the Supreme Court threw out the verdict. Yet what was the message to women? *That you can be killed for doing the very things expected of you.* Meanwhile, at night, moviegoers relished Jimmy Stewart's sadistic fantasies about women, even sublimating that character's own impotent revenge fantasies against the sexually aggressive and professionally powerful Grace Kelly. *Rear Window* was, incidentally, the second-highest grossing film of 1954, right behind *White Christmas.*"

The female students again laughed knowingly, David lagging just behind. "It is this intersection"—Dr. Petersen made an X with her arms—"ladies . . . and gentle*man*," she added, nodding at David, at which point only Alice turned around and smiled, "between the aesthetic and social spheres that will be our point of departure. For it is *here*," she concluded, "that the real and imagined roles of women are not only fully figured but also clash *tragically.*"

David didn't understand a word she was saying. But the class was small, and Alice sat three seats ahead of him to his right. He sat in the back, as in Otto's class, and watched.

And he couldn't help but watch—not just Alice, of course, but the movies. On Tuesday afternoons Otto showed each film for the first time, encouraging the class to simply get the plot straight. He showed the movie again in the evening, attendance mandatory, for note-taking. Thursday's class was strictly discussion, and David became as obsessed with Hitchcock's work as he did with the mysteries and ambiguities surrounding the Sheppard murder.

As for Alice and him, it took David a month to work up the courage to talk to her. By that point they'd watched *The 39 Steps, Sabotage, Young and Innocent,* and *Shadow of a Doubt.* By *Notorious* they were sitting next to each other; during every movie they watched after that, they were holding hands. And once the two of them got together, they watched these movies (and more) all over again and spent their nights analyzing images, speculating about what became of these characters after the screen faded to black, arguing about feminism and sexism after having sex, and whether or not Dr. Sam did it or Marilyn's killer was someone else. So when David looked back, this time in their lives was itself a montage, images from these films and the Sheppard murder crosscut with his memories of Alice and of falling in love, and he often thought of Hitchcock's work and the Sheppard crime as being a part of their DNA—a braided filament that augured their fate.

"I remember all that," she said. "We were happy then."

They were still lying in bed together holding hands, and he could see her smiling in the darkness. "So you remember being happy?" Pepin asked.

"I do."

"Do you think we'll be happy from now on?"

"I don't know. I want us to be."

"I want to wake up tomorrow and feel this blessed."

He woke, and he did: he felt as happy. *They* did. And for the next month it seemed as if they'd arrived somewhere new.

Then they were robbed.

By the time Pepin finished writing, it was nighttime.

It had been an awful day—with Alice and on the page—and he went to make himself a drink, but before reaching into the freezer for the vodka he stared at their refrigerator door, at the Polaroids of her and her weekly progress, her diminishing size, though to Pepin now they seemed pixels in a single giant portrait, a floating death's head with black spaces between each fissure, this larger picture not of Alice's face but rather her fragile psyche about to fly apart. What had happened? How did things change so fast? It was as if they'd fallen into a bottomless hole.

He went into the living room to sit on the couch. He hadn't showered, though he'd eaten all through the day. Except for his study, the apartment was completely dark. Clouds hung gray-bellied and low over the city, illuminated by the light beaming from the jagged towers. When he heard Alice's keys at the door, he closed his eyes for a moment and listened to her footfalls enter, stop, and then approach. He looked and she was standing by the window, her fitness now shaming him—she must've gone to the gym after their fight—the sight of her doubled by the reflection in the glass, doubled but still smaller by half in her black spandex tights and Under Armour top, svelte as a superhero after a transformation as radical as his own; he'd gained major weight since she'd returned, was heavier now than ever, had let himself go, his black hair furred out, his beard scraggly, frizzed, wild, and unkempt. But hers was an exterior change only. Her mind was the same—worse, in fact, than ever—and the nights were somehow darker because of it, Pepin dreading her return (tonight as much as every other day) and what mood she might bring with her, the whole apartment doubly darkened with it now. She was in a bad place. He was officially worried about her.

She'd been like this since they were robbed four weeks ago. They'd come home that Sunday afternoon, back from the park, from a walk after breakfast, happy—weren't they happy then?—only to find the door ajar; and when they slowly pushed it open the very air inside seemed supercharged, heavy with disarray, even before they saw the chaos itself. In the living room, Pepin pressed Alice behind him, shooing her back, hissing, "Call the police," for here he saw the books pulled down from the shelves, some scattered and others stacked or lying mysteriously open. In the kitchen, the drawers were pulled out, utensils dumped, cabinets raided, glassware broken. Down the long hallway, the paintings and prints were torn down, their frames shattered; in the bedroom, the books were tumbled as well, the closets rifled, the dresser and bedside tables overturned. Only then did they truly feel the violation, even though nothing appeared to have been taken. Nothing, of course, but their sense of security; nothing, he thought, and Pepin didn't tell Alice this, until he noticed his computer was on, his password somehow cracked, and the end of his novel had been cut, stolen, the external hard drive as well. And in the bathroom, after he heard Alice moan in disgust, he entered to find the medicine cabinet open, her pill bottles lying in the sink and on the floor, and the rim of the toilet dotted with a viscous substance—as yellow by now as wood glue—and floating in the bowl, drifting into formlessness like cloud writing, where the spunk of the intruder made a ghostly, jagged M. Impossible, Pepin thought.

"What've you been doing?" she now asked.

"Nothing," he said.

She crossed her arms and looked at her feet, then turned suddenly as if she heard something and sighed. "The strangest thing happened to me today," she said.

The air was so bad between them Pepin couldn't tell if she even wanted him to ask, so he took a pull at his drink.

"I think," she said, "that someone tried to kill me."

It took him a second for it to register.

"What did you say?"

She lowered her voice. "You heard me."

"I know," he said, "but what do you *mean*?"

That sounded like the beginning of a fight. They'd arrived at a state of communication where every last utterance did. You tried to hold on, to last it out, but he felt a seaman's certainty about this storm.

"You're going to say I'm imagining it," she said.

He let the back of his head slump against the couch.

"I was *there* this morning," she said.

The narcissism of depression, Pepin thought. He'd have to tease the most basic of basics out of her. "*Where?*"

"That accident."

"Which one?"

"The *crane.*"

He lifted his head. "On Ninety-first?"

"Yes."

He sat forward.

"On my run this morning," she said, "I was jogging toward it—I mean the building they were working on—and looked up as I got close. And I swear it was only a second before I got under it that I heard these two pops, like charges going off, and I thought I saw puffs of smoke on the tower itself. And suddenly the crane's tipping, falling toward me, but I wasn't sure, like when you look up at a skyscraper and because of the clouds there's that illusion that the building's collapsing. It was so slow at first, then people started screaming and I ran down the block as fast as I could. And when it hit, the impact blew me off my feet." She shivered. "It barely missed me," she said.

It was an amazing, once-in-a-lifetime eyewitness near miss. At work he'd been watching the live feed on his computer all day. Bizarrely, he'd even thought of calling Alice to make sure she was all right. He didn't, though. That would mean they'd have to talk. "But it doesn't mean someone tried to kill you," he said.

"That wasn't the only thing that happened," she said glumly.

Then she told him about the train, the subway ride to Grand Central during her commute. Two boys were rough-housing on the edge of the platform, and when the train came barreling into the station there was an accidental push. Alice spun round, doing a crazy backstroke over the void. "I just barely caught my balance," she said.

"But that doesn't mean those kids were trying to kill you," Pepin said, his heart racing. He was terrified, furious. He wanted to laugh and cry.

"It wasn't the kids. There was . . ." She looked down, her hands trembling as she wiped her eyes. "There was this man too. This little man. He pushed them. I couldn't tell if he was trying to break them up or push them toward me. And then, after I got my balance, he was gone."

He stared at her, speechless.

"You don't believe me."

"I didn't say anything."

"It's the man who broke into our house," she said. "I know it."

"No," he said, though not to her.

"I see him everywhere. Out of the corner of my eye. In my dreams. He's like the little doll in that Karen Black movie."

"*Trilogy of Terror,*" Pepin said, amazed. He'd just been thinking of it.

"Yes."

"But you're—"

"I know," she snapped, nodding, angry now. "I'm just *imagining* it."

"*No,*" he said.

"No, fine, *all right*! You don't want to hear it. You don't want to hear anything I have to say."

She stormed into their bedroom as, out the window, the low clouds pulsed with white flutters of electricity. Pepin grabbed his cell phone and raced downstairs.

"You son of a bitch," he said. He was on the street, pacing.

"What did *I* do?" Mobius said.

"Enough. Off. Game over, okay?" Pepin said. "Abort, do you understand?"

"Abort *what*?"

"I'm not going to say."

"Abort what, *exactly*?"

"Why did you take the end of my book?"

"It's my book now."

"Oh no it's not."

"Oh yes it is."

"Fuck you."

"The first ending's too sappy. The second's too neat. Me, I prefer to end with a *bang.*"

"What do I need to do to fucking end this?"

"Keep away from me," Mobius said, and he hung up.

Pepin threw his phone down so hard that it disintegrated on the sidewalk.

It began to rain, so instantaneously and heavily it was like a Charlie Brown cloudburst that didn't seem to start until it was directly over Pepin's head. He stood staring at his feet, seeing nothing, listening to the wind tearing through the trees, to his own labored breathing, to the downpour hissing along the curb.

"David?"

He looked up. It was Georgine.

She was as soaked as he was, unprepared for the rain in her jeans and sweatshirt. She'd emerged from the gated entryway of a nearby brownstone as if she'd been hiding in the shadows beneath the steps leading up to the front door.

"What are you doing here?" Pepin said.

"I needed to see you. I was going to call but then you . . . just appeared."

She smiled, and he couldn't look at her. She came to him and lifted his face, his wet beard, up to hers and searched his eyes, and involuntarily he felt himself lean against her palm in relief. He hadn't realized that he'd missed her so much, so consumed had he been by Alice's return, the relief of their reunion, and her subsequent spiral. He'd been so sure things would be different. Georgine's blond hair was in ringlets from the rain, curly and heavy with water. He thought: our children would have terrible hair. Then he thought: what are you thinking?

"I've been worried about you," she said.

He nodded.

"You haven't been yourself."

He shook his head.

"I know we agreed not to talk at work, but I can't stand seeing you like this. And I can't stand not talking to you."

"Yes."

"So tell me what it is. Tell me you're okay."

She kissed him, and the taste of her wet lips was salvation. He rested his forehead against hers and looked at her, at her mouth and eyes, flooded suddenly by memories of their pleasure together, how it was of another order from what he knew with Alice, neither greater nor lesser but wonderfully different. She was strong in ways Alice was not. In spite of this recognition, he was terrified of expressing his own feelings about anything, and possibly of showing any woman any signs of weakness. He couldn't say whether or not this had been a function of his marriage, a deformation of his character because he didn't believe Alice was capable of handling it, or if he'd sought out someone as needy as she was because it protected him from ever needing such comfort. In any case, Georgine's offer was as tremendous as it was frightening, and it seemed to bring him to a fundamental choice. It occurred to Pepin that you could be married to any number of people, that you were simply trading on what you were willing to give and take, on whatever good came with the bad. And it was also a sad truth that you might not be equipped for certain kinds of ease or happiness. Why, because that might set you free? Because nothing, then, was determined? That everything was wide open? Was that the source of the fear?

"I'm not okay," he said, "no."

"Then let's get out of the rain. Let's go get something warm to drink."

"I can't."

"Yes you can."

"I need to get back upstairs."

"David, you can talk to me without it having to mean something."

"That's not true."

"It is."

"I need you to promise not to do this again."

"I can't do that."

"You're wasting your time."

"It's mine to waste."

He thought of Schrödinger's cat. In another universe, he and Georgine went to a diner, warmed up and dried off, and he left with her for good. But in *this* one he couldn't be sure that the lure of such an escape wasn't a function of everything else that was going wrong. "I have to go," he said.

He walked past the doorman into his building and saw himself in the bank of monitors, coming straight toward the screens and then going away. He left a puddle beneath him in the elevator. The apartment was dark. He looked at his watch. Just past nine. Alice would be asleep. Down the hallway, their bedroom was flickering, the television light much like the storm outside, the worst of which had passed, the thunder spent. In the bathroom, he took off his wet clothes and then saw himself, not in the mirror but reflected in the bedroom window, standing in the lit rectangle of the door: how fat he'd become, how flabby and out of shape. He was disgusted. It was like he'd failed his own soul. He turned off the light and, naked, entered their bedroom, where Alice was asleep under the covers except for her arm. She was still holding the remote. When he took it from her hand and turned off the television, she opened her eyes uncomprehendingly for a moment—why was it that silence could wake a person?—and then went back to sleep. He stood looking at her in the darkness, feeling like a criminal who'd stumbled onto a new opportunity for crime. If he were to leave her now, when she was in this vulnerable a state, he was sure it would kill her. But at the same time, their alienation from each other was so complete he felt he could disappear and it wouldn't matter, and these competing fears were the horror of this place where they'd arrived.

There had to be an exit.

. . .

Hastroll sat bolt upright, awaking from a dream.

"I know how he did it!"

"*Wha?*" Hannah said, startled. They'd slid their beds together into what Hastroll called "a poor man's king." If they drifted too close to the middle, the gap between the two mattresses widened slightly and threatened to suck them down, so they kept to their own sides—which was fine with him. Hannah, deep into her second trimester, gave off body heat like an oven, *was* an oven, and it was baking their loaf of love.

He called Sheppard, who took care of the search warrant.

They arrived at Pepin's apartment the next morning.

"Who is it?" a woman said from behind the door.

The detectives, recognizing her voice, looked at one another astonished.

"It's the police," Hastroll said.

"Don't let them in!" Pepin said, farther away.

"Open the door," Hastroll said. When there was no response, he kicked it in.

Georgine Darcy stood there wearing a robe and holding a cup of coffee, which she dropped when she saw their drawn pistols.

"Where is he?" Hastroll said.

Her eyes glanced toward the bedroom.

Hastroll ran, with Sheppard right behind, but it was too late. When they came into the bedroom, Pepin, also in a robe, emerged from the bathroom, his hair buzzed to the scalp. He was thinner, leaner, more muscular, gone from chubby to cut. The toilet was gargling at the end of its flush.

Hastroll raised his gun. "Step away from the door," he said.

Inside, the medicine cabinet was still open. Along the top row were all of Alice's medications, Wellbutrin and Prozac among others, the bottles empty, the caps off.

"You son of a bitch," Hastroll said when he stepped back into the room, holding up an empty bottle. "They were a placebo. *That's* why Mobius broke in, wasn't it? That's all he took—her pills. She wasn't taking anything, was she? You poisoned her by omission, you sick fuck. You brought her right to the edge."

"Me," Pepin said, "or him?"

Georgine appeared at the door, leaned against the jamb, and crossed her arms. "What's he talking about?" she said.

Pepin looked at Georgine, then at Hastroll.

"How'd you push her over?" Hastroll said. "How'd you get her to do it?"

"I don't know what you're talking about," Pepin said.

Hastroll pulled back the hammer. "Are you sure?"

"Come on now, Detective. Are you going to shoot me? This isn't a game."

"Maybe it *is*. Maybe it's bang, you're dead."

"There are real bullets in that gun," Pepin said.

Sheppard put his hand gently on Hastroll's arm. "Ease it down," he said.

Hastroll held the gun on Pepin. The only sound in the room was his breath.

"He's guilty," Sheppard said. "But there's nothing to bring him in on anymore."

Here's how David wished the book had ended:

She lost the weight. There were plastic surgeries to nip and tuck her stretched skin; there were complications, especially related to her gastric bypass, including acute vitamin deficiencies; and there was a dangerous period when her doctors feared she'd have to permanently absorb nutrients intravenously. But she and David came through this time awake to each other, transformed without realizing it, and now here was Alice, 133 pounds, the before having shifted to the ineluctable after, restored to him a different person and yet the same, and without a second's hesitation—once they were certain that her weight was stable for good—they decided to adopt.

On the recommendation of a friend, they went through the Catholic Charities and all the exhaustive prescreening processes, background checks, and preadoption classes. They were warned the wait could last for years. It was an arrogant notion, David thought, or a brand of Social Darwinian measure taking, really, but in class that first night, as he looked around and the other couples broke off into small activity groups and got to talking, he felt confident that when a kid became available they'd get the first shot at him. Or her. Or both. Bring 'em twins. *Triplets.* They were ready. The organization was firmly committed to open adoption, where the birth mother wasn't anonymous but rather maintained a degree of contact throughout the process, starting right after delivery. He and Alice were fine with that too, along with all the other conditions.

Later, he could describe the initial lack of connection he felt to Grace (a name they chose together) when he first held her at the hospital, how in that moment he felt a kind of vertigo, as if her fragility demanded that he drop her just as the ledge whispered that he should jump; how he was scared of her, truth be told; and how it was otherwise no different from holding the daughter of an acquaintance, which he feared Grace herself could tell. But within weeks he could also describe the change that had somehow occurred, as all change secretly comes over us, and the feelings—often after he'd fed her and laid her swaddled lengthwise in his lap so she could face him, the baby then just a wrapped face—of love the likes of which he'd never known, love so inexhaustible and vulnerable that it was better and worse, in many respects, than the love he felt for Alice. Worse because he knew he could survive his wife's death but not this child's, and so he occasionally would snap at Alice for being careless, though that was the last thing she'd ever be with Grace. Better because of the patience it conferred during those first sleepless months of feeding and rocking and sleeping-rocking when the baby's bray would come at the precise second he needed to collapse; because of the magnanimity it imparted, a generosity, a level of energy. The relief and the beauty, the joy of purely giving. He was always *game.* Always there. Present to the child, to anything she needed, and, by dint of this, to his wife. What he felt, more intensely than at any other time in his life, was a fusion between the two of them, a commonality of purpose, no questions asked. On many instances they didn't even have to speak. "Yes," he'd say, taking Grace from her arms, already knowing.

Knowing. Finally he'd arrived, he felt, at his own core, at something nourishing that was contained within the shell of his own being. He finally knew who he was. He was a father. They were a family. Nothing could shake this knowledge.

At the moment, David was sitting on the living room floor with Grace. It was late morning, brilliant outside, and Alice walked over to the window and stared out. On the rug David had spread Grace's little mat, which she loved. It had an illustration of a meadow with a stream running through it, pastures, and a picket fence too. There was a mirror in which she'd study her face, and on soft little structures velcroed to the mat, cows and sheep and chickens and horses would stare back out. Grace would look at herself in the mirror, then at the menagerie, and raise her arms and legs with her toes pointing toward the ceiling and her fingers spread out like a puppeteer's, a position that made her look as if she were skydiving. She giggled happily, which made him laugh.

"What have you two been doing?" Alice said.

He looked up at her happily. "Nothing," he said. "Nothing at all."

Pepin woke, lying diagonally across their bed, and noticed when he sat up that he was naked. Alice had gone to work already, and the realization of this and the lateness—it was almost eight o'clock—made him dizzy with fear. He sat up in bed, though his belly gave him pause and the flab between his thighs and breasts made it an exercise unto itself. This reminded him of Alice at her heaviest, when he'd wake just as she was stirring and feel her enormity behind him, her radiant heat, as if he'd gone to sleep with a bear, her outline exceeding his, and how her getting out of bed required a move similar to his sit-up now. She'd prop herself on her left elbow and throw one leg across the other and shoot her right arm out like a punch, both limbs flung over the bed's edge. There was a moment of equilibrium when she looked like a martial artist frozen midkick, then a slight rock back followed by a push off with her left arm; and like a ship righting herself, she did too. She had to rest for a second, her palms on the mattress, her feet on the floor, her back to him. "One day I won't make it," she said. "I'll just lie there stuck." Her words were snorkeled by her sleep apnea mask, the tube bisecting her scalp and running through her hair like a long braid, the plastic opaque and the color of a shrimp's shell, and when she turned to look at him he realized how much the mask's filters looked like the nostrils of a hog; and he thought of their flight to Hawaii, when all the oxygen masks sprung from the ceiling and the passengers, securing them in the rumble and pitch, looked around wildly at one another. A plane of pigs, Pepin had thought. A passel of swine. Who knew you looked like this before you died?

This last thought now sent him scrambling to his computer. Mobius had said to keep away from him, and that was just the thing to do: take Alice and go *far* away, somewhere the little freak couldn't follow them to, somewhere safe where she could get right, where *they* could, even if that meant halfway around the world. He had a conversation in his mind akin to the one he and Alice had before she'd disappeared, about the Great Barrier Reef, and it was a sign of his own narrow curiosities that he had no idea where in Australia this wonder might be. So he Googled away. It was in Queensland, off the continent's northeast coast, and it was, he read in Wikipedia, the world's biggest single structure made by living organisms, billions of tiny coral polyps, and it supported a wide diversity of life. A place teeming with life, Pepin thought, that could support *them!* That's what *he* wanted: to be a part of life's team! He was on Expedia in a flash, two tickets purchased for tonight out of JFK to Brisbane, a red-eye through LAX. The world had been made virtual, and if you had the means it was like a video game. You could pick anywhere on the globe, click a mouse, hit a few buttons, and you'd be there within hours.

He dressed, grabbed their passports, and left.

It was an against-the-flow commute up to the school where Alice taught, and he drove like a madman up the West Side Highway, the Henry Hudson, and then the Saw Mill, though once in Hawthorne and on the campus itself he drove slowly, organizing his thoughts, his story, his pitch. It was a state-run school for disturbed and abused teens, its buildings fashioned of cinder block, the green and gray halls washed out with fluorescent light. Why had his wife been drawn to this place? Because these children needed endless mothering? Or because like her they were fundamentally stuck?

Ahead, in the parking lot, several school buses were loading up. He saw Alice ferrying kids inside, taking roll as the boys and girls stepped on board, but when she caught sight of him she froze, unsure what to make of his presence, and in this moment of stillness he considered her transformation utterly remarkable. She was so thin now—skinnier even than when they'd first met—and her cheeks so prominent it made her lips seem larger, fuller, her hair, still beautiful, framing her face. He would take this picture and add it to the dated Polaroids on their refrigerator door. Something about this new beauty, coupled with her depression, scared him as much as it warmed him. Like sickness, beauty could destabilize the beholder. Just two nights ago, after a fight in which he'd begged her to see her doctor immediately, he stood by her in the bathroom and handed her a glass of water. "I want to see you take these," he said, holding up her medications. "Now open your mouth," he'd said after she swallowed. "They're not helping," she said, crying. "They *will*," he said, holding her until she freed herself and pushed past him to their bed. She cried there afterward for, by his watch, a remarkable two hours and thirty-eight minutes. Depression, with its endless reserves, was as voracious as her greatest appetites, and it tricked him every time into thinking he could love it out of her.

"What are you doing here?" she said.

"I need to talk with you."

"I'm busy."

"It's important."

"It has to be quick."

Her eyes were red, already liquid, as if his very presence had lit a fuse in her. He could feel them both tensing for the blast. Finally, she handed her clipboard to another teacher and led him inside the building to her classroom.

"I want you to relax for a second," he said. "Just hear me out. Last year you talked about us leaving. Walking away. Purpose without procedure. So I'm game now. I bought us tickets. You and me, tonight. Australia. We just go."

Her arms were crossed. She looked up at him. "What are you talking about?"

"I'm talking about not even packing. I'm talking about going, right now, you and me, no questions asked."

"You're crazy," she said, and turned to walk out.

He grabbed her arm, more angrily than he meant to. "No," he said. "I'm not."

She looked at his hand. "You're hurting me."

"You don't get to just let loose and not let me say something. I get to speak too."

"Then speak."

"Come with me. Right now."

She waited until he let go. "You're always late," she said. "You know that?"

"Maybe I—"

"These things, these ideas, they come from *me*"—she stabbed her chest—"and never from *you*"—she stabbed his—"so when you finally come around, it makes me feel like you're doing it out of pity."

"That was probably right before but not anymore. This is *me* now."

"And this is me saying no. I'm not just leaving with you, dropping everything to discover after a few weeks in the Outback or wherever that you don't want to be there. I'm not going through *that* again." She was crying now, trembling.

"Please," he said. She looked up at him and seemed to soften for a moment. He gently took her arms. "You have to trust me here. We *have* to go."

She shook her head. "The kids are waiting for me."

She went out to the bus and he grabbed his hair in his fist and followed her without speaking and got into his car. Furious, he saw a cell phone sitting on the passenger seat. And then it rang.

"What are you doing?" Mobius said.

"Trying to keep her away from you."

"You'll get hurt."

"We'll see."

"You know what you don't realize?" Mobius said. "There are two moves you can make here, continue straight or swerve, and they both lead to the same thing. No matter what you do. In game theory it's called Hawk-Dove. Also known as Chicken."

"What about what Alice does?"

"I have an ace up my sleeve there."

"What's that?"

"The end."

"Goddamn you," Pepin said, "I don't *want* the end."

"Yes you do, but you won't *do* it. That's why I am." He hung up.

Pepin screamed at the phone and shook it, then got out of the car and looked around as if he expected Mobius to be nearby, as if their phones were connected by string, he wasn't sure why. Alice's bus, followed by another, pulled out of the parking lot. The last remaining bus had almost finished boarding.

"Where're you guys headed?" Pepin asked a student.

"The Museum of Natural History," the kid said.

Alone now, Pepin wrote:

There are two of us, of course, David and Pepin, interlocked and separate and one and the same. I'm writing my better self and he's writing his worse and vice versa and so on until the end. A *good* reader—a good *detective*—knows this by now. If you don't, look in the mirror. That's you and not you, after all, because the person in your mind *isn't* the person in the world. And if you don't know this already, you will.

On the West Side Highway, Alice's bus three cars ahead, Pepin caught sight in his driver's side mirror of a black Ford F-150 pickup, something you never saw in Manhattan, so absurdly large and impossible to parallel park, its hemi roaring like a lion. In the cab, Mobius looked like a child steering the wheel of a giant yacht.

Pepin, in the center lane, let him pull alongside, slowly drifting back into his blindspot, then hit Send on the cell.

"What is it?"

"You said there were two moves I could make."

"That's right," Mobius said. "Straight or swerve."

"What do you think I'll do?"

"You? You'll always swerve."

"Bingo."

Pepin yanked his car left, driving the nose into the Ford's rear wheel and spinning it perpendicular to his hood, pile-driving the truck down the road as white smoke swirled around them, Mobius's arms stuck straight out as he fought the steering wheel, his shoulder pressed to his window, Pepin flooring the accelerator. Horns, behind and wailing past, stretched like strands of gum as the current of traffic flowed closely around their collision. There was a *pop*, as hollow and deadened as a spinnaker gone taut with wind, and the truck was shot airborne and flew over Pepin's hood to become a cloud of smoke and destruction in his mirror, hailing glass as it rolled. He hooted, cursing happily, slapping the dash, and turned to look, the weaving traffic sealing off the wreck's rising smoke, then cut his eyes forward and saw a car crossing into his lane. He swerved, felt the car fishtail and, overcorrecting, went spinning slowly, inexorably, his palms beating the steering wheel. He was briefly facing the traffic, the cars as vivid and fixed as the faces you blur by in a subway station, and then they flashed past, supersonic, as he slid diagonally into a guard rail—a collision so jarring that his neck and back cracked. He'd come to rest, alive. Through his shattered windshield he saw Alice's bus shrinking into the distance, the kids' faces plastered to the rear windows—and Mobius's truck, miraculously righted, spectacularly damaged but operable, roaring by in pursuit.

He restarted the car. It drove, but just barely, the driveline or axle or something dragging along the road beneath him, the left wheel well so punched in that it restricted his turning. He hobbled to the exit at 96th Street and spotted a parking lot across Riverside.

"What the fuck happened here?" the attendant said.

Pepin dug a hundred-dollar bill from his wallet and slapped it into the man's palm. "Park it somewhere safe."

Then he ran.

It was hard, David felt, to remember much of anything from Dr. Otto's class—the discussions, that is, and lectures, so many hours now lost. What he did remember, however, were first moments, first viewings, how priceless it was to be in the presence of works so great—so entertaining and romantic, so new he could never see what was coming—that life up to that point had suddenly seemed lacking. The movies made him feel utterly alive. There was the scene in the wine cellar in *Notorious* when Cary Grant unwittingly pushes a wine bottle toward the edge of a shelf, and if the bottle shattered it might be his and Ingrid Bergman's undoing, a moment so suspenseful he and Alice took each other's hands instinctively; and when it did fall, Alice screamed. He remembered Grace Kelly leaning in to kiss Jimmy Stewart in *Rear Window*, her shadow blanketing his face—without question, Pepin thought, the most beautiful woman that ever was. Or Tippi Hedren sitting in a schoolyard smoking, following a lone crow flying across a cloudless sky and landing on the monkey bars, revealing that the whole playground was packed with thousands of the black birds.

He could go on. But there was one night in particular. He was riding his bike home from the evening viewing, his mind lambent with images, associations, connections. He couldn't recall now what film he'd just seen, only that he'd stopped his bike on the dark road, warmed by and alive with the love and genius in the art, so grateful for it that he wanted to wait there and feel it course through him. This is what life is, he thought, a giving to the void. The artist made—he gave—and I received, and my life, *this* life, would be nothing without somehow giving something back.

He knew this as certainly as he knew he wanted to spend the rest of his life with Alice.

Out of the cab, Pepin paused—befuddled, defeated, and horrified by what he saw. There were school buses *everywhere.*

They were parked along Central Park West, all along 81st Street and in the U-shaped driveway by the Center for Earth and Space. And there were schoolchildren everywhere too, of course, thousands, it seemed, milling at the museum's entrances, a legion entering or exiting. My God, he thought, I'll never find my wife. He wasn't even sure of the best place to enter himself, so he ran up the wide steps on the Central Park West side toward the metal doors between the towering columns. TRUTH, it read on the Romanesque façade. KNOWLEDGE. VISION. In the distance, he could make out the cupola on the corner of 77th Street, its globed spire colored an undersea green, the tower gargoyled by giant eagles.

In the rotunda, under the vaulted ceiling and the high windows flooded with white light, was the skeleton of a barosaurus, her bones as brown as the wood of ancient galleons, reared up on her hind legs to defend her offspring behind her from an allosaurus. Pepin knew his dinosaurs; Spellbound's DinAgon I and II had been massive hits worldwide. The ambient noise here befit some great event: heels echoing off the marble floors, multiplied and ramified, as loud as horse hooves; spoken sentences that carried so clearly—"The Blue Whale's one floor down," a guide said—it was as if they'd been whispered to you alone; and the reverberant talk transformed by the ricocheted acoustics off the octagonal patterns on the ceiling and walls, the hall turning it all to babble.

In a Hitchcock movie, Pepin thought, I'd be waiting in a line to buy a ticket while my wife appeared behind me. He kept an eye out for her while he shuffled toward the ticket counter and after what seemed an eternity purchased his, grabbing a floor plan and scanning it to get his bearings, clueless as to how to track Alice down until he heard her voice as close to his ear as if they were playing a game of telephone.

"Anthony," she said, "put a lid on it, *please.*"

Miraculously, she crossed the hall right in front of him, herding her class as they exited the Butterfly Conservatory exhibit at the other end of the rotunda, her kids a ragtag rainbow crew of Hispanics, blacks, whites, Asians, Indians, the girls dressed for a day trip, the boys in baggy pants and T-shirts splashed with words borderline profane, their hats screwed on wrong with the brims off to one side—one species, to be sure, and sharing the same sad traits of violent family histories and brains stormy with dysfunction.

Shadow her, he thought. Keep her in sight. Intercept predator, if he appeared. And then, when the time came, tell her whatever you need to in order to escape.

The class handed their tickets to the guard and entered the Hall of Asian Mammals, Pepin a safe distance behind. It was quieter here and their pace slowed down, the kids breaking out of their tight formation and mingling in front of the exhibits, fogging the glass and busting wisecracks before moving on. His own attention was divided; he'd have to keep an eye out for Mobius too, though now that he had Alice in sight a calm came over him, the lower ceiling seeming to contain and protect them, the smaller hall narrowing and limiting sightlines. It was pleasant, actually, to tail her; a fantasy, rarely acted upon: to see his wife in her world, in her element, to watch her students—ranging in age, he guessed, from twelve to fourteen—responding to her. What a mother she would have been. A Hispanic boy in all black—pants, shirt, basketball shoes—but for the white gothic *A* stitched above the brim of his black baseball cap came up to her and asked a question. She bent toward him and put her hand on his arm, recognizing that the very act of asking was for him a show of vulnerability, out of character, and therefore in need of reinforcement; and as she answered him his face went open and alert, warmed by the gentle beam of her attention. Pepin walked closer, trying to overhear, so touched by the exchange that he was tempted to take her in his arms. But it was risky enough getting this close to her, so he stayed in her blind spot as he had with Mobius.

They turned right now, moving into the Hall of Asian Peoples. Koto music was playing over the speakers, and while it never sounded harmonic or rhythmic to him, the effect was doubly calming and made him hungry for sushi. He'd eaten nothing before he ran out this morning and lately was always hungry, eating more often, the hunger pains more and more acute, his obesity like a disease. It had to be. Reflected in the display case in front of him, his hair was shocked out like straw, his beard widened his face, the waist of his pants cupped down below his belly like a wide smile. He'd do something about it when he and Alice went away. They would feel good together again, about themselves and each other.

He shifted focus. A golden Buddha sat in the exhibit before him, his eyes closed in meditation, his hands laid gently over each other, his palms up and resting on his crossed legs, his head nimbused with cobras. The plaque read:

> Buddhism assumes that human beings are caught up in an endless cycle of lives, and that one's form in the next life depends on behavior in this life. The way out of this cycle is to understand how it functions and to live life correctly, with passion and with reason.

But he never understood the function until it was too late and was thereby always living incorrectly, so what would his next form be if he were to die now? Certainly something lower than human—a fearful creature, not predator but prey. Chubby, hairy. Mating a problem. A panda, Pepin thought. Yet the truth of the plaque's description arrested him—*an endless cycle of lives*—and the promise of a way out, the Escher Exit, lifted his spirits.

I will not swerve, he thought.

He lost the group and panicked, so he trotted, then ran, turning a corner and nearly colliding with several stragglers from the class, hugging the walls behind the Semai hunter exhibit in front of which they'd gathered, Pepin shuffling to hide in plain sight behind Alice herself, close enough to reach out and touch her, to smell her, almost. The hunter, nearly naked but for a woven-cane bandanna and a noble-savage knapsack, had a blowgun as long as a pole vaulter's pole aimed out of his mouth.

"Check out that swimsuit he's wearing." It was the same boy who'd asked her the question before.

"That's a loincloth, Anthony," Alice said.

"That's a loin*curtain*, is what that is."

Everyone laughed, even Alice.

"*Ta-dah*! It's my dick!"

"Boys," she said, "no cursing, please."

The aboriginal people of Malaya, the plaque read, were admired for their commitment to nonviolence.

> Semai people have lived in long pole houses sheltering several families . . . Today separate houses are common. It is the rule that people who live together must get along well; there must be a bond of mutual liking and respect.

Malaya was somewhere off the tip of Thailand, Pepin thought. So after diving for days along the Great Barrier Reef, he and Alice could head due north out of Brisbane, take a hard left over Indonesia, and cross over Malaysia to land in Kuala Lumpur, then settle for a while with the Semai. Think of all the weight he'd lose blowpiping. It'd be hard to get fat on just rice, let alone on food you had to hunt with a weapon like that. Think of how little there would be to worry about. Live in a pole house together. Tend the rice paddies. Renew their bonds of mutual liking and respect. Those would be their rules.

He thought he saw Mobius's black form reflected in the glass, but when he turned around no one was there.

"Downstairs," Alice said at the landing. "Stick together, please."

"It says dinosaurs is up," Anthony said, holding up the floor plan.

"The dinosaurs *are* up, Anthony, but first we're going to see the hominids."

"The fuck's a *homo*nid?"

His friends doubled over in laughter.

"*You are,* Anthony."

The class busted out in high fives and exclamations, the girls covering their mouths at the dis.

"And *I'm* a hominid. We're *all* hominids. But if you curse once more," she said, waiting for the class to pass by, "you're going to go sit in the bus with the hominid driver." She put a hand on Anthony's shoulder. "You understand?"

The boy waited for the rest of the class to descend out of earshot. "I'm sorry," he said.

"Apology accepted," she said.

Downstairs and past a huge canoe, a giant dugout at least fifty feet long, hung from the ceiling to better display the artwork on its underbelly, the bird designs a kind of paleocomic book in reds and blacks, and the images running from its prow reminding Pepin of the fanged mouths and squinting shark eyes by the props of P-51 Mustangs. He then followed along into the Hall of Human Origins, its entrance also the exit, and his sightlines into the Hall of Meteorites were good, so anyone appearing there would stand out brilliantly, though Mobius was nowhere to be seen.

Alice called the class to gather before an exhibit of skulls of various shapes and sizes, the dotted lines interconnecting them and then branching off to terminus, extinction, and while the boys and girls huddled, Pepin read:

OUR FAMILY TREE

Humans are the only remaining descendants of a once varied family of primates called *Hominidae* . . . Most of these species became extinct, and only one—modern humans, *Homo sapiens*—ultimately survived and flourished.

"Have a look at this," Alice said to the class. "Do you understand what these are? They're our cousins—"

"Not mine, they ain't."

"Eu*gene,*" she said, and shot him a look. "They're *versions* of us—*Homo sapiens*—that came before we did but didn't survive. See? They're grouped by region, but follow the lines to where they end. Look at the different sizes and shapes of their skulls compared to ours. What does that tell you?"

"We coulda had some small-ass heads," Eugene said.

Anthony smacked the boy's cap forward. "Listen to Mrs. Pepin, *fool.*"

"*Boys,*" Alice said. "Now, seriously, what does this chart tell you?"

Everyone stood looking, and then Anthony raised his hand. "That we're lucky," he said.

"Really? That's interesting. What do you mean?"

Anthony looked at Eugene threateningly before he spoke. "Well, look at all those Homo . . . whatevers that didn't make it. It doesn't say why, does it?"

Alice looked. "No."

"And we don't know why, right?"

"I don't think so."

"See, we're just lucky to be here."

"And what does *that* tell you?"

"We gotta make the most of it!"

Alice smiled. "I agree."

"Can I ask something else?"

"Sure."

"How you pronounce that one?" Anthony pointed at the skull shaped like a hammer's head.

"*Homo heidelbergensis*. Why?"

" 'Cause she looks just like Eugene's mom."

Like a firework, the class burst from the middle, the boys and girls covering their mouths as they ran laughing from the center. Alice shook her head at Anthony, who stood facing her. "You'll never change," she said.

It was time to eat.

Alice led the kids down to the lunchrooms on the lower level. Pepin couldn't help stopping in the food court to buy a chicken and Swiss wrap, which he snarfed down, looking over his shoulder all the while, like a hunter being hunted. Alice was sitting at a table off to the side, away from students and the other teachers, her eyes glazed; she appeared saddened, even decimated, the woman he knew emerging now that no young people were engaging her immediate attention and yanking her out of her own mind. She seemed in despair, and this was the best time to tell her, he thought, his best opportunity for success. Let her know he was here and why he had to take her away. He was about to walk toward her when he saw Mobius standing at the end of the hall.

Rather than run, he turned when Pepin approached and walked down the hallway leading to the 81st Street subway station, then ducked left into the men's bathroom. There was a yellow folding sign in front of the door, with a figure whose feet were sliding out from underneath him and CAUTION painted in red.

The tiled room, smelling of ancient urine, was empty but for the two of them.

"You're making this unnecessarily difficult," Mobius said.

"That's the idea."

Like Alice's student, he was dressed all in black, though his form-fitting clothes were made for athletics, with the same Under Armour logo at his neck as Alice's top the night before: U locked with inverted U.

"But you can't stop it," he said. "The end's already determined. I'm just following the beginning's vector—the arrow's arc. And *you* dreamed that part, remember? You called *me.*"

Pepin looked around for a weapon. There was a trash can in the corner, silver, shaped like a bullet. Throwing that at Mobius would be very troglodyte. "So what happens now?" he said.

"We fight, I knock you out, you come to. You realize some things that make this really tragic. There's a little more after that, but I don't want to spoil it."

Pepin stepped forward, took a swing, and whiffed. He'd never hit anyone in his life and still hadn't. Mobius's black eyes glinted but didn't blink.

Pepin swung again, losing his balance and falling forward with the miss, sliding on the floor.

Mobius had him by the neck in a flash, straddling his back and pushing his face against the white-tiled wall. "Go to sleep," he said.

He felt a blow.

Pepin woke.

The back of his neck was sore, his forehead too, and he wasn't sure how much time had passed. But he was up, if unsteadily, on his feet and out the door into the lunchroom, but Alice and the class had already left. Panicked again, he ran upstairs, through the Grand Gallery and the New York State Environment and the Hall of North American Forests and into the Hall of Ocean Life, its entrance guarded by three sharks.

The blue whale took his remaining breath away, gigantic, hanging there impossibly as if it were floating in the sea. And in this sea-blue room, feeling as submerged beneath the ceiling's domed blue glass as if he'd just walked onto the deck of the *Nautilus* itself, he saw Alice and her students wandering along the jeweled dioramas in the hall's recessed level, and then his pants pocket vibrated. It was a cell phone—another plant—and now it rang.

He saw Mobius watching him from across the walkway.

"Remember the beginning?"

"What are you talking about?"

"Of your book," Mobius said. " 'There was Alice, underneath the wreckage. Either she was killed instantly or Pepin was there, right by her side, inserted just before the fatal moment. He held her hand, they exchanged last words, and he eased her into death.' "

"No!" Pepin said, running down the steps with the phone to his ear. "Please!"

Mobius held up something small and black in his other hand. "Boom," he said.

Above the whale were twin puffs of smoke and a simultaneous discharge—two bursts as loud as M-80s—that drew all eyes to the ceiling. Alice was somehow the only person standing underneath, she too looking toward the sound, so she didn't see Pepin running up to tackle her.

The blackness was followed by a dead silence, then moans and screams and cries. A snowstorm of fiberglass and polyurethane dust clouded the room blindingly, seeming to fall and rise at the same time. Alice wasn't beneath him, and he could barely see his own hand, though within moments there was a slight clearing, a settling. People stood up, children too, mummy-white and caked in this billowing plaster, wandering in circles at first and coughing, some with the wherewithal to help whoever was lying beside them, others frozen on their knees, stunned by disaster, their hands on their thighs as they knelt upright like plaster sculptures of samurai. The whale was shattered all around them, its shards white with the dust, like pieces of a hatched dinosaur egg.

Alice was nowhere in sight. It was as if she'd been sucked down a wormhole. There was, between his knees, just her imprint: a snow angel he ran his hands through until he could see only the black floor.

HERE'S HOW IT (ACTUALLY) ENDED:

Dear David,

If you're reading this letter, I'm dead.

There was a great deal of concern about my undergoing gastric bypass surgery due to potential complications related to my thrombophilia. The truth is that I was strongly advised against it. But I couldn't stand the way I was any longer.

I'd planned to take a long trip afterward. Use the tickets if you wish. Find a new beginning. A new world.

What do you say when you come to The End? You can say a lot or a little. I could say that I love you (and I do), that I would do anything for you (and I have), and that I believe you'd do the same for me.

I asked that you not receive notification for nine months afterward. It was long enough to make my absence real. It's long enough for a child to be conceived and come into the world. It's long enough, in other words, for radical change. So here's the thing I want you to answer:

During the time I was gone, what did you do?

After David finished writing the book, he wept.

Because no matter how she died, he thought, in fact or in his imagination, there was an inescapable feeling of complicity. Art was no exorcism, at least not for the artist, and these other things he knew to be true: there were no detectives, no contract killer, nothing at all. Only nothing. And then, because his wishes had been fulfilled, there came a much darker realization: he'd never shake this guilt, would always be stuck in this place. So the

David who left this chair now to walk the world from here on out, the one who carried on as if this were *past,* could only be half-real. An avatar.

HERE'S HOW DAVID'S *BOOK* ENDED:

Pepin returned to his apartment, sick with defeat, with the waiting at the perimeter of the museum and then the endless walking and the futile inquiries with the authorities until finally his only recourse was to flee home.

When he arrived at his building, he saw himself reflected in the front door, his body white from head to toe, caked with dust. But the doorman was gone, the security monitors were off, and the elevator was stuck, apparently, on his floor. On the stairwell's windowpane, EXIT was painted in red.

As you often do in dreams, he climbed like a moonwalker, in airy bounds, leaping from landing to landing, taking ten steps at a time. In fact, he was just running.

He stood at their door, which was slightly ajar, and went through into the kitchen, where she was at the table, showered, in clean clothes, with a plate of nuts in front of her. On the blue cylindrical container, Mr. Peanut tipped his top hat and smiled. She'd cried herself into a kind of exhaustion, her face cramped at the cheeks, mashed at the brow, her eyes red, her cheeks as bathed and streaked as a tearful infant's. Manuscript pages were strewn everywhere, though she held only one in her hand.

He stopped right where he was.

"Is this how you end it?" she said. "Is this what you want?"

"Where did you get those?"

She bunched the page in her fist. "They were sitting here on the table." Then she threw it at him.

"That's impossible."

"You must really hate me," she said, "to have dreamt this up."

Pepin picked up the page she'd thrown and read it.

"I didn't write this," he whispered.

She suddenly went wide-eyed, as if she'd seen something in the back of her mind or behind his back.

Pepin heard footfalls and turned around. Nothing there, but then the door slammed with a bang.

"You kill my joy," she said softly, then took two handfuls off the plate and shoved them into her mouth.

For a second he couldn't believe his eyes because the physiological impact of the allergen knocked her right over backward, still seated in her chair. "Don't!" he screamed and was at once on top of her, pulling her hands from her face. And already the transformation was occurring, the swelling like a werewolf reversion, her lips inflating and curling away from her teeth, her fingers and cheeks fattening, hives rising everywhere, a pink distention rashing along her neck, chest, and hands.

"Call nine one one," she gasped.

A mixture of nut and saliva had collected in the corners of her mouth, and she was gagging while he screamed her name. Then he ran to the bedroom and pulled open her bedside drawers, the EpiPens missing in both and in the medicine cabinet and her purse as well, its contents now spilled out across their bed. She'd thought it through. She *knew.*

He ran back and kneeled before her, pausing at the sight, his hands held up in terror. She was squeezing her neck as if she were choking herself, her face gone purple as violets, gone blue.

There was nothing to be done but he did it. Her esophagus had swollen shut. He rammed two fingers into her mouth, pressing them past her swollen tongue as far as he could into her puckered throat, trying to clear her airway. If someone had walked in, it would've looked like he was killing her, stuffing her mouth with his hand. But instead he was doing something he'd never been able to, something that should've been done long before this, something else he'd dreamed of. He pressed into her with all the strength he had, her hair bunched in his other fist for leverage. Would this be the last thing she remembered? Would it be their last embrace? He reached as far as he could, which wasn't far enough, trying to touch her where she'd touched him, trying desperately to reach back to a time when they were happy, when they didn't know then what they knew now—all the way to her heart.

Acknowledgments

First and foremost, I'd like to express my gratitude to Gary Fisketjon, friend and editor, whose extraordinary work on this book was integral to its realization. Several books on the Sam Sheppard case provided essential background information: Jack P. DeSario and William Mason's *Dr. Sam Sheppard on Trial,* Cynthia L. Cooper and Sam Reese Sheppard's *Mockery of Justice,* and Paul Holmes's *The Sheppard Murder Case.* James Neff's *The Wrong Man* deserves particular praise for its compassion, scope, and utterly convincing presentation of evidence old and new, and so I must express my tremendous gratitude to its author. My endless appreciation is extended to my agents, Susanna Lea and Mark Kessler, for their tireless advocacy. To several readers: Kalen McNamara, whose keen insights and numerous discussions were a boon, as well as the comments and suggestions of Phoebe Carver, George Cassidy, Diana Fisketjon, Emily Milder, and Frank Tota. Thanks to Nick Paumgarten for pep talks. Thanks to my brother, Eban, for help with Hastroll's menu, among many other things. For their time and expertise, I am grateful to Drs. Dan Canale, Donna Crowe, and Tiffany Hines. Special thanks to Ann Teaff and the Harpeth Hall School for the year as writer-in-residence to complete the first draft. Thanks also to Richard Dillard for introducing me to the work of Hitchcock, and, by circumstance, to my wife. Starting never would have been possible without the faith and encouragement of my parents. As for finishing, all the love and support required for that came from Beth.

ABOUT THE AUTHOR

Adam Ross lives with his wife and their two daughters in Nashville, Tennessee.

A NOTE ON THE TYPE

This book was set in Minion, a typeface designed by Robert Slimbach specifically for the Macintosh personal computer, and released in 1990.

Composed by North Market Street Graphics, Lancaster, Pennsylvania
Printed and bound by Berryville Graphics, Berryville, Virginia
Book design by Robert C. Olsson